I0678790

Pendulum Shift

Pendulum Heroes, Volume 2

James Beamon

Published by Nadi Cat Press, 2019.

Pendulum Shift
*Copyright © **2019 James Beamon***
All rights reserved.

No parts of this publication may be reproduced, stored in a retrieval system, or transmitted in anyform or by any means, electronic, mechanical, photocopying, recording, or otherwise, without the prior written permission of the copyright owner.

This is a work of fiction. Any similarity between the characters and situations within its pages and places or persons, living or dead, is unintentional and co-incidental.

Cover art by Micaela Dawn

Nadi Cat Press

Published by Nadi Cat Press 2019
Leesburg, VA United States
ISBN: 978-1-7323862-2-8
This book is available digitally at most online retailers

To Jen,

Who showed me how to rise renewed from my own ashes.

Thank you, little phoenix.

CHAPTER 1
Fallout

Rew Majora walked briskly through the Hierophane, in no mood to attend visitors. These visitors didn't include Rich, and even delegations bringing gifts or good news wouldn't be able dispel her anxiety. Besides, Rew knew this delegation from the Temple of Houses brought neither gifts nor good news.

She nodded at students and robed passersby as she made her way to the audience hall, doing her best to fight the knot in her stomach that turned whenever she thought of Rich. The last time she had heard from him it was in a painfully short scry. He had reported Jason felt the death creature was a day or two away before the scry suddenly died. That was over a week ago.

Now Rew was left with crushing silence somewhere in the Eural Mountains and a mess to clean up in the audience hall. She set her mind to diplomacy as she arrived at the grand doors to the hall.

Inside the chamber, the giant oblong table was already packed. Mages of every robe—red, orange, purple, blue, black, white, green and brown—provided a colorful swath of representation on one side while aians of every house filled the other. Rew forced a smile as she greeted the contingent from the Temple of Houses. Ananna was here personally, which spelled high amounts of pomp for the aians and a sense of dread for Rew.

"Lady of the Third House and esteemed members of the Temple of Houses, welcome," Rew said. She took her seat next to Brigitte, the acting head of security with Druze in the wind.

"I would say I was well met, but I am not often subjected to waiting," Ananna said coolly, the spider tendrils of her hair furling in agitation. "Being Immortal does not simply mean having more time to waste."

Yes, it does, thought Rew. She knew firsthand. Rew wasn't as old as the Queen of Spiders, but after three and a half centuries of living, Rew had probably spent a collective lifetime being bored.

"Your pardon, Lady Ananna," Rew said with a curt nod and smile. "While Brigitte here handles most official functions, I wanted to attend you personally."

Ananna returned Rew's nod and smile. Her eight locks of hair unfurled in a sign of relaxation. However, the atmosphere in the room remained as cold as the granite table hosting the dozen aians and as many mages.

"Well, I am thankful of your presence, Hierophant Majora," Ananna said, the mandibles around her mouth clicking together. "I am here to discuss a matter of serious gravity. The Temple of Houses demands Seat Esotera surrender the mage Razzleblad and his companions Cephrin and Zhufira into our custody."

"On what grounds do you demand anything of us?"

"Razzleblad defaced our most sacred temple, aided by Zhufira and an unknown accomplice. He must stand accountable for his act."

"There is no such robe by that name," Brigitte said.

Rew held her hand up to silence Brigitte. "Lady of the Third House," she said, "as you can see, his name is not a familiar one within the walls of the Hierophane. Why do you think we harbor him?"

"Razzleblad, his companions, they all rode into Nasreddin on the hovering chariots that are strict issue of the Hierophane," Ananna said. "We still have those chariots in our destrier stables. Returning them to you is a given, as that is what a civilized state does. A civilized state returns what is rightfully someone else's charge, without question or resistance."

"Thank you, Ananna," Rew said. "I am glad you brought the hava-chaises to our attention. If you had said nothing about them, we would never have known where to look, as it is also a civilized state that does not go looking for their charges in the wrong places."

Ananna's spider locks curled tight around her face. "Leave us," she said as she stared at Rew.

Instantly, the aians around her got up and left. The mages made no move. Rew nodded to Brigitte and the black-robed woman led the mages out. The granite table seemed monstrous with only Ananna and Rew sitting at it.

Ananna's eight locks furled and unfurled around her head. "When was the last time I saw you, Majora?"

Rew returned Ananna's cold stare. "Ten years ago, I believe, at an aiannasran peace conference."

"Do you know Targhos, the once Elevated of Demir, fell from his lofty perch of highest flyer of the house all the way down to the Fane's dungeons?"

"I had not heard," Rew said, keeping her composure.

"Yes, Targhos went against the decree of the Temple. Once he found himself in the dungeon, with his wings being plucked, he had the most interesting things to say about Razzleblad's brown robed accomplice."

Ananna had learned Rew was there that night, helping Rich free Jason. Targhos had guessed the Hierophant's identity under the brown robe before flying them to safety. It was a secret he had promised to keep.

"I'm sure Targhos would say a lot of things to avoid torture," Rew said.

"Still, in the physical absence of Razzleblad and the guilty parties, Targhos' word is all we have," Ananna said. "That, coupled with the Hierophane chariots, seems like incontrovertible proof that the mages planned and authorized the destruction of the Temple of Houses."

Ananna's words were nothing short of a declaration of war. Spoken publicly, her claims would compel the Eleven Houses to march in force against the Hierophane.

"Razzleblad is not here," Rew said. It was the only thing she could say.

"Child, if I thought he was here, I would have already brought the full might of the Eleven Houses down on your towers," Ananna said with a scoff. "But you were the one who tasked Razzleblad and his ilk, to kill some death creature, I believe. I don't care if that creature was Onus himself, Razzleblad's crimes demand his surrender. You sent him to task. You find him and deliver him to the Temple of Houses."

"Your longevity may command respect among your people," Rew said, shaking her head, "but I am too far enduring in this world to have you address me as a child. I take neither threats nor orders from anyone."

"Do not confuse yourself for a goddess, Majora. I have lived for millennia. What are your years to that?"

"My years are long enough to teach me that you do not saunter into someone else's home to make demands," Rew answered.

Ananna regarded Rew silently for a moment, her eyes dancing as was aian nature. "Well, you may live long enough still to pardon this intrusion," Ananna said. "Serious actions call for serious reactions. Defiling the Temple of Houses is the greatest offense to aiankind your young eyes have witnessed. The temple's reaction is to remove from existence either the person or place responsible for this heinous act."

Ananna rose from the table. "You have a choice, Majora, and a week's time to make it. Good day."

The Queen of Spiders strode from the room, swallowing the aian delegation waiting outside the door into the wake of her stride. Brigitte dismissed the colorful band of mages and came into the audience chamber.

"Hierophant?" Brigitte asked. Normally, she looked ever ready to fight, with the black robes of a destruction mage draping her body and belted like a military uniform, her red hair blazing like fire. Brigitte didn't seem fierce now. Concern rimmed her green eyes.

"When was the last you heard from Druze?" Rew asked. She didn't wait for Brigitte's answer as she rose briskly from the table and made her way to her library.

"A fortnight," Brigitte said, keeping pace with Rew as she answered.

They walked through the gardens. A dozen conversations filled the air as students milled about discussing spells and casting strategies. Birds chirped as they lighted upon trees and shrubs. Even the Aphelion Tower, though broken and stilted now, seemed to gleam peacefully in the early autumn sun.

The Temple of Houses threatened to destroy this tranquility with open war.

"I want to know the moment Druze contacts you, no matter the hour," Rew said.

"Yes, Hierophant."

"Withdraw all personnel in the Nasreddin Mage Delegation Tower, effective immediately."

"As you instruct."

Rew continued through the breezeway into the library study with Brigitte in tow. She walked past her desk and chair, passing library shelves as she gave more directives.

"Contact our delegates in the Southern Kingdoms, from Kirda at our border to the Land of Nod and everyone in between. I want audiences scheduled with the kings, every king, via mirror before the day's end."

Kirda would be able to make the Hierophane within a week's march. Ships from Samegrelo and Colkhis could also make landfall within that time.

"Hierophant?" Brigitte asked.

"Notify all quest-robes in the field," Rew said. "They have five days to complete any ongoing assignment and report back to the tower via portal on the close of the fifth day."

"Hierophant?"

"Inform all instructors that advanced spellcraft classes are suspended temporarily. They will teach nothing but battlemage tactics. All students must be thoroughly competent."

"Hierophant!"

Brigitte's voice was more of a shout this time, bringing Rew back into the library. Rew realized she must have been pacing about, ignoring Brigitte as preparations and plans consumed her. She looked at the black robe. Brigitte was looking back with a face full of question and concern.

"What is all this in regards to?" Brigitte asked.

"We plan for war," Rew said.

"With who?" Brigitte asked. "The Third House?"

"No, my dear. With all the houses."

"But Hierophant," Brigitte said, "we can't fight the whole host of the Holy Aian Empire."

"We can," Rew said, finally taking a seat at her desk. "This region is a free collective of city states solely because of the Hierophane. We are the only reason the aian empire does not stretch beyond Nasreddin. The Eleven Houses need to learn this lesson again."

Rew paused for a moment. She looked at Brigitte.

"You have your tasks," Rew said. "Go about them."

"At once, Hierophant," Brigitte said with a nod before leaving.

Rew was left alone. She rifled through the desk, sorting papers and parchments. The time for planning a war would come after she was thoroughly organized, not before.

Trade requests got mixed in with quest-mage requests. She piled those onto the classroom administration paperwork. New spell approval forms got shuffled in. Finally, she crumpled the lot of it and threw it off the desk.

Rew talked confidently, but the Hierophane had never been tested to this degree. When she was a little girl, the aians had claimed rights under the Onesource to settlement beyond Nasreddin. But back then only six houses made the claim, and Rew had watched Druze, leading Seat Esotera as Hierophant, soundly thrash those houses.

Her eyes fell to her disheveled desk. "Where are you, father?" she asked.

His disappearance wasn't uncommon; there was no keeping track of him. But this time his absence was felt. Her father's insight may help her better prepare. Even if his proposed actions echoed her own, hearing them would help calm her fears.

Rew should have seen this coming. Of all things possible, Rich had carved out a piece of the Temple of Houses. She should have known they weren't going to take "sorry, we can't help you" as an answer.

Still, Rich had made for one exciting rescue. He had even sealed that night's adventure with a kiss.

But now Rich was gone, disappeared into the wilds, with the High Fane demanding his head. Even if he was present, Rew wouldn't have sacrificed him to that lot.

The Hierophane was no one's puppet to perform or offer tribute. The Megrym Hegemony had learned this along with humans seeking kingship in the region and six Fane houses. Now the entire Holy Aian Empire would learn this as well. The Temple of Houses could not demand anything of Seat Esotera. Whether or not Rew cared for the person they demanded was irrelevant.

But Rew did care. And not knowing what had become of Rich was killing her in small doses. She looked out the window, to a bright, sunny morning that was laden with promises. Maybe today.

"Where are you, Rich?" she asked.

CHAPTER 2
Soft Try

Melvin looked at Rich. Rich's body was marble, stuck in a kneeling pose as if he was in prayer. The look on the statue's face was serene, a stark contrast to how Melvin felt.

"You sure it's alright, leaving him up here?" Melvin asked.

Nothing else decorated the flat, open space of this roof except for Rich. He was out of place here, much more so than in the storeroom below.

"Better here than in the store," Ruki Provos said. "If we leave him there, Uncle will try to sell him after we've gone."

Ruki brushed at some dust on his white linen shirt. Melvin would have never guessed him for someone with a taste for the finer things. When he had first met Ruki, the man looked dusty and dragged around.

Road Ruki was different than City Ruki. City Ruki stayed in white bright enough to hurt Mike's megrym eyes to look at directly. He was also generous, providing rooms above the store for the gang.

He had even given Melvin a matte black leather outfit. Ruki called it more enchanting. Melvin called it just in time for fall. It had definitely stopped being steel bikini weather. And it went well with the blue cloak the Hierophane had given him.

Melvin took one more look around. Suusteren was a mammoth city, with buildings both grand and small rimming the crescent shape of the harbor. The sea brought a cool, saltwater breeze and the streets were already abuzz with morning activity.

Today was a good day to get Rich back.

Ruki took Melvin's hand. "Everyone's waiting," he said.

He led the way back down the treacherously narrow stairs. Mike, Runt and Jason were hanging out in the hallway.

"You didn't drop him, break a hand or nothing, right?" Jason asked. He held up his own arm and the brown robe fell down to expose the bone hand. "Cause it's not like he can get one of these any more. It's a limited edition."

"He's fine, no thanks to you," Melvin said. Ruki and Melvin got volunteered to haul Rich up there because Jason and Runt's bodies were a bit too big to navigate the stairs. Mike could have gone, but Mike, being Mike, threatened to drop Rich if he had to carry him.

Speaking of the megrym, Melvin's brother was dog staring Ruki's hand. "Hey, fool," Mike said, his eyes going up from the held hands to Ruki's eyes. "What I tell you about my brother?"

Ruki smiled innocently. "Purely for safety concerns," he said. "There's no hand rail, you see, and I would be sorely remiss if she fell and hurt herself."

Melvin soundly deposited at the base of the stairs, Ruki slid his hand smoothly from Melvin's. "There you are, pretty brother," he told Melvin, his eyes dancing as he talked.

"Now, if we could," Ruki said looking around at the gang, "Suusteren awaits."

Ruki Provos led the way down a bigger, hand-rail equipped stairway to the back of his Uncle's store. They passed all manners of things: birdbaths, curios, furniture, silver jewelry, jade trinkets, hexes, clothing, and all of it being sold under the bright red signage of Provos Trading Company which stretched across the wall.

They passed Ruki's uncle Tavis at the counter, where he was at work preparing for the start of another business day. He was a wiry, crotchety old man, whose face was a cross between Ebenezer Scrooge and the Quaker Oats man. Tavis Provos looked at his nephew with a raised gray and bushy eyebrow.

"Off to sell this lot of vagrants to Varollan slavers, I hope," he said.

"How many times do I have to go over this, Uncle?" Ruki asked. "They're free security for the next caravan run. They're going to save you a smuggler's fortune."

"Please!" Tavis spat. "If there is a next run. You brought back that pitiful wreck of a caravan. I could be outside in the dead of winter at night with no shirt and that thing would still tremble more than me."

"Bah," Ruki said, waving away his uncle's concerns. He didn't slow on his way to the door.

"Bah, yourself," Tavis said. His voice rose to follow the party out of the shop. "That's why I'm giving your cousin Ander the business... at least he doesn't wreck caravans!"

On the street, Ruki grimaced. "It's like the old man is trying to juice the joy out of me so he can bottle it up for paying customers," he said.

Ruki led the way through wide avenues. They passed beautiful buildings of red and brown brick. Hand carved wooden signs announced the businesses within. The streets themselves were cobbled, and fine sand from the coast had worked its way into the cracks. Melvin liked cities, being a city boy himself, and he thought Suusteren was the nicest place he'd seen so far.

He didn't even mind when the streets got a little more narrow, the signs less hand carved and more crudely painted and tacked on like an afterthought. Every town needed a seedy side. Besides, unlike back in the suburbs, he could kick serious ass now.

Still, he wanted something to look forward to, and more of this part of Suusteren wasn't it. He fell back to Jason, who was walking with the hood up on his brown robe. Every race lived and traded in this city and Jason had to be on guard against the aian hive mind inherent in the House of Yol. Still, he carried his severed arm in a modified quiver behind his back, absolutely refusing to go anywhere without it. The exposed gray hand peeked out of the quiver, waving a clumsy hi as it bounced on his back.

"Tell me again," Melvin said, "why you think this will work."

"Simple," Jason began. "It goes back to the mechanics of Rich's spell. The spell action was to turn Druze to stone. The cost for that instant hard case was Rich getting his own flavor of protective coating. So Rich in stone is wholly cost driven, not target driven. That's why we're going to see the witch."

Jason had a maddening way of being general when it came to explaining spell logic. It was like he assumed everyone had spent countless nights poring over lore or game notes and stats. Melvin hadn't been a guy for awhile now, but even when he had been, he hadn't been that guy.

"So you think the witch can cast a better spell than the quest-mage we found?" Melvin asked, venturing to guess at Jason's logic.

"It's not the power of the spell," Jason said, "it's the nature of the spell. That quest-mage took one look and said it couldn't be undone because of how he crafts spells. Mages are taught there is a cost, you must pay it," he said, pointing his bone finger into his palm as he spoke. He realized his exposure and brought his hand down quickly.

"But witches," Jason said, "they're all about diverting the cost. Screw a friend, screw a stranger, pay for it later, anything to avoid that actual cost. Since they know how to avoid the cost, reason has it a witch will know how to worm out of this cost on Rich."

Jason devised the plan after the quest-mage had his moment of epic failure. A natural trickster, Jason loved to bend rules, and this was a pretzel class bend. But the logic was sound. This could really work.

"You're kinda awesome," Melvin told his best friend.

"Wait until I figure out how to make it rain 1-ups," Jason replied.

JASON COULDN'T SEE much of Suusteren from behind his hood, but from what little he saw, rent must be dirt cheap on this side of town.

Ruki led them single file down an alley. Crowded on all sides by tall buildings, the morning sun didn't stand a chance of peeking in to bake the piss puddles. They passed the backdoors of various restaurants and bars, if chicken-scratch scrawled names like "The Half-Roasted Pig" and "Drunk and Happy" were any indication of the businesses they housed.

The party started walking through one of these backdoors. Jason checked the name, a place that went by "Second Chances".

Jason hoped the name was a good sign for Rich, but as far as the bar went, there was no truth in advertising. The fetid smell of stale, spilled beer hung like a shroud. Nut shells, ragged paper flyers, and maybe a few teeth littered the floor along with other unrecognizable detritus. The gaslights burned green, advertising the bar's sole patron. He slept, drooling on his table while he clutched a near empty mug like he had been there all night.

Ruki went over to the frizzy haired, ebony-skinned girl behind the bar. She was spit shining a glass, using real spit.

"Are you Calais?" Ruki asked.

"I am," the girl said, hosting a serious look on an otherwise pretty face. "What'll you have?"

"My friends and I, we're looking for a special drink," Ruki said, leaning towards her, "we all want Happy Endings."

Mike looked up at Ruki, shock on his face. "Word?"

Now Calais leaned over to Ruki. "You know what's in a Happy Ending?" she asked.

"I know what's in it if he don't," Mike said.

Ruki ignored Mike, keeping his eyes on Calais. "Only the right bartender would know," he answered. "Some say it's magical."

Calais nodded. She looked past Ruki, to the guy passed out at the table. "Hey Javon!" she shouted. "What's your verdict of this lot?"

Javon raised his head and regarded them a moment with bloodshot eyes. He raised his thumb into the air and let his head drop back down to the table.

"All right, Javon says you're good," Calais said. She put her towel down and offered her hand to Ruki. "Looks like you've hired yourself a witch."

They stepped into her office, which happened to be a table in the corner. "So what's the job?" Calais asked as everyone took a chair around the table.

Jason was expecting old evil crone witch rather than beautiful girl witch. Calais had flawless skin, full red lips and large brown eyes that made her appear both innocent and clever. Maybe it was stolen beauty, the evil magic version of plastic surgery.

"You any good at witchcraft, other than the work that goes into making your skin wrinkle free, that is?" Jason asked.

"I'm good," Calais said with a bored look. "I keep enough customers to not have to waste time trying to impress any new ones."

Jason looked around at the empty bar. "Must be heinous, all the rush rush."

"Don't be fooled, friend," Calais said. "This bar, Javon, it's all to throw off the witch hunters. The smartest among us know that flaunting power and wealth is the surest way to get a hot brand driven through your heart."

Jason nodded. She had a point. From what he remembered from the lore, witches here get the full on Inquisition treatment.

"So you want a Happy Ending or what?" Calais asked.

"Huh?"

"Some witchcraft, leading to a positive, enjoyable outcome to your current dilemma," Calais said. "I don't have all day."

Mike shook his head like he had just gotten some tragic news. "Man, our Happy Endings back home are way more happier than that," he said.

Per Ruki's instructions, Mike led the way back to the shop, followed by Calais and everyone else behind her. Ruki pulled up next to Jason.

"Can't trust a witch," Ruki said. "They get some of your hair or a swath of your clothing and next thing you know you've got some incurable disease while some formerly rich idiot is miraculously healed and happily destitute. Witches make a fortune off the backs of the unsuspecting. I want her in front where I can see her."

"So why'd you put Mike in the lead?" Jason asked.

"Megryms are immune to witchcraft," Ruki said. "...Probably."

He pointed to Melvin, who was walking in front of them, looking around at all the buildings with enraptured eyes. "Tell me," he said. "What kind of things does she like?"

"Dude," Jason said, "you know underneath the leather cat suit that's a guy, right?"

"I'd love to be in a position to judge that for myself," Ruki said grinning. "That's why I'm asking you," he said. "Help me out, here."

"She likes girly things," Jason said. "Flowers, dainty little nightgowns, stuffed animals and stuff. And pink. She loves pink."

"Really?" Ruki asked with a hint of surprise. "And I was going to venture out with a more tactical gift, like some gauntlets or a new sheath for her sword."

You'll be the new sheath for her sword if you get her something pink, Jason thought with a grin.

Mike led the way into the Provos Trading Company, where Tavis Provos was glaring at everyone as they walked in. He shot Ruki a murderous look.

"I thought I told you to sell these people," he said.

"Bah!" Ruki replied sourly, waving him off.

Rich wasn't upstairs where they had left him. He was in the showroom, with a wooden price sign hanging around his neck. A couple stood around him, marveling at his craftsmanship.

"I believe this is one of Shim Douffrant's earlier pieces," the man said to the woman. "Notice the mage, a symbol of might, kneels in a moment of vulnerability."

"He is fully exposed, the mage, yet serene about this helplessness," the woman said. "Powerful."

"Truly powerful," echoed the man.

"And not for sale," Ruki said, tearing the price tag off of Rich.

From the front of the store, Tavis' voice sounded like a vengeful banshee.

"What do you mean not for sale?! I'll be tarred if you bring merchandise into my store and not sell it!!"

"It's a display loaner!" Ruki yelled to the front. He turned around and forced a smile at the would-be customers. "I'm sorry, dear patrons."

Ruki enlisted Runt and together the two of them hauled Rich up the stairs into the second floor hallway. Rich now safe from prospective buyers, Ruki patted the statue on the head and looked at Calais.

"Here's your job," he said.

"He lose a mage duel?" she asked looking Rich up and down.

"More like the cost of winning," Jason said. "You should see the other guy."

Calais took out red and blue sticks of chalk. She drew blue symbols on the wall, red symbols on the floor and drew lines of both colors that intersected around and flowed through the symbols.

The witch stepped back into one of the symbols on the floor and began speaking words that didn't sound pronounceable. An unnatural chill descended into the hallway, making Jason's neck hair stand on end.

Calais knelt, her fingers splayed out to encompass a mass of drawn circles in front of her.

The natural sunlight filtering in through the windows seemed to flicker. Jason looked in amazement at Rich.

The all white marble statue was gone. Rich had salt colored hair, gray robes, and a pink, flesh-colored face.

Calais was losing color, her mahogany skin turning white along with her hair and clothes.

Then the moment was gone. Rich was back to being a statue. The air was warm. Calais knelt in front of the statue, breathing in ragged gasps.

"Try it again," Jason said. "You almost had it."

"I can't," Calais said, shaking her head. "Whatever spell this mage cast, its cost is too exacting."

She pointed to the symbols around her. "These glyphs, they transfer his cost to other hosts," she said. "So many hosts that the individual burden would have been miniscule, unnoticeable. His cost ignored those hosts."

"So what you're saying is that we need a competent witch," Jason said. "Somebody whose spells actually work."

"Idiot," Calais said, picking herself up from the floor. "His cost is one complete whole, indivisible. I can't cut it any smaller, no witch can. I can transfer his cost, but it would go directly to me. All of it."

She looked at the statue of Rich.

"The only way you're going to free him is if you find something hungry enough and strong enough to stomach the cost in full," she said. She turned to Ruki Provos and tossed him the brown bag of coins he had given her at the bar.

"Either that or find a witch who longs for death."

CHAPTER 3
Resurrection

Burru peered out from the hatch of the family's secret underground den. He scanned the burned and ruined buildings of Olukent. Only a handful of the nasran invaders were out and about this morning. It was time to put the Master's wishes into effect.

He crawled out of the hole as noiselessly as possible, dragging Master Izal's body with him. Burru draped the master's body across his shoulders and set out toward the cave.

The nasrans were routine, predictable. Burru had watched their patterns for a week as he tried to nurse Master Izal back to health. Just as planned, Burro slipped through the abandoned guardhouse—a complete ruin since the nasrans invaded—and into the darkness of the cave without notice.

Burru saw that the invaders had done him a service by keeping torches lit along the cavern. Before he died, Master Izal had given instructions and directions on how to navigate the cave. Burru would be in the presence of the Death Null in mere minutes.

He took out his club as he made his way. The Death Null was waiting for the master, and Burru had prepared too carefully to let some dirty nasran steal Master Izal's grace. Burru reflected on the master's last words.

"Lay me before the Death Null, child," Master Izal had said to him, his voice a grave whisper. "When it sees what has befallen its most vigilant servant, it will deliver its grace."

The master was two days dead now. If anyone deserved grace, it was the master and not that arrogant aian man who had pulled destruction down upon them with his bone hand.

The cavern in which the Death Null resided was easy to find thanks to Master Izal's instructions. And fortune was with Burru, the nasrans were absent from his path, likely lying sleep or drunk or rolling about in their own filth.

Master Izal said the Death Null would be hard to see. It would be a magnificent creature, glowing black yet framed in white. But when he looked throughout the cave, everything was laid bare by the nasran's torches.

There was no creature in this cavern, magnificent or otherwise. Only a statue occupied the room near the center. The statue reached out to something invisible, horror etched on the man's face.

Burru swallowed his despair. He took faith in the master's teachings. The Death Null's full nature was a mystery. It tested its servants, to see if they were worthy before it blessed them.

He took Master Izal over to the statue and lied the body down in front of the statue's outstretched hand. Burru spoke to the statue.

"Please, Death Null, see your servant in need of your grace. Make him whole. Grant him life."

There was no response. The statue remained as lifeless as the body of the master.

Burru closed his eyes tightly. He spoke the words and willed the Death Null's grace to descend with all his being.

"Master Izal is your most deserving servant," Burru said. "Grant him your grace."

Burru opened his eyes to nothing. The statue seemed to look at him like it was aghast that Burru came there at all.

The days hiding, scrounging food, waiting patiently... it all came for naught. The Death Null was fickle, its grace unobtainable. Burru growled his frustration and rage. With a shout, he beat the statue against the side of the head with his club.

Burru's last strike broke the statue. The head tumbled off the shoulders and fell on the ground.

As the head hit the ground, Master Izal sat up with a gasp.

"Master!" Burru exclaimed rushing over to his restored master. The newly risen man looked at his own hands and Burru's face as if he was seeing it all for the first time.

"Who are you?" Master Izal asked.

"Why, Burru, your most loyal and loving servant. When the others fled, I stayed at your side. I delivered you to the Death Null's grace."

Master Izal looked around. "Where is the Death Null?"

"It is no longer here, Master. It left this statue for you, which returned you to grace after I broke it," Burru said, pointing to the broken statue in front of them.

Master Izal looked up at the headless statue. Then he discovered the head on the ground. He looked back at Burru.

"You did this?" Master Izal asked.

Burru nodded. Tears brimmed in his eyes. He would never doubt the Death Null's power and mercy ever again.

DRUZE DIDN'T KNOW WHETHER to thank the buffoon or kill him. After all, this haggard man Burru had freed him from the boy's stone spell. But it was apparent that he had broken Druze's body to do it.

Speaking of bodies, in whom did Druze reside now? He looked down at himself. Judging from the dull pallor of the skin and the grievous, blood-stained wounds along the body, this person was dead.

Burru had called him Master Izal, who he had brought to the cave to receive the Death Null's grace. What Burru got was Druze's unfettered consciousness. Apparently, the ability to inhabit a soulless body was an unforeseen result of the creature's death nullification power.

Druze smiled. He had gotten more than he bargained for when he stole from that monster.

Burru looked at Druze, wiping tears from his eyes. "We should not linger here, master," he said.

"Wait," Druze said. "I need a moment."

Druze closed his eyes and spoke his scry spell as a whisper.

"Druze!" a woman's voice said behind him. "Majora's been worried sick about..."

Brigitte's voice trailed off as Druze stood and turned around to face her.

"You're not Druze," she said, taking a step back. "How did you impersonate his scry request?"

"It's me, Amaya," Druze said, speaking her name from long ago and a world away. Only a handful of people knew it.

"Druze..." she said, her hand covering her mouth as she stared. "What happened?"

He looked behind Brigitte, at the Hierophane security offices. Next to Brigitte's small desk was a wall mirror, where she routinely checked her robe's every detail to ensure her professional, ever immaculate appearance.

"Things have gone... awry," Druze said as he looked upon himself. The face he wore now was not a pleasant one. Izal was ugly, his face caked with white powder that ran in streaks of dirt and sweat. Druze spoke to Brigitte through Izal's cracked, split lips.

"The ones that did this to me are still at large," he said. "They also killed Samedi."

Brigitte's face twisted into anger. Her and Samedi were friends before the pendulum, and lovers of a sort if Druze knew anything about the two.

"Where are they?" Brigitte asked, her words drenched in cold anger.

"If you'll permit me," Druze said, holding up three fingers. "I can show you much better than I can tell you."

She nodded.

Her permission granted Druze access to enhance the scry's sharing of minds into a transfer of thought. Druze closed the gap between them and the line between the cave and Hierophane advanced as well. He placed his three fingers as near to her head as he could.

He showed her all the events leading up to the present. The appearance of the pendulum rejects, their quest, the megrym's treachery in the Hierophane courtyard, Rich's spell of stone. Druze showed her Samedi's demise in the Sprawl as he had witnessed it via Samedi's ring. He also showed Brigitte the ornate clasp on the blue cloak given to the warrior girl.

"The clasp will tell you where they are," Druze said, stepping back from the transfer. He spoke the clasp attunement spell for her.

Brigitte nodded. "The next time we scry, you will see a parade of corpses before me. I will summon La Croix and Kriminel."

Druze smiled. "I would expect nothing less. Inform your old friends from the pendulum. Send them. But not you, I need you at the Hierophane."

"You expect me to sit on my hands while Samedi's killers roam about the countryside?"

"I expect you to be my right hand, as you have always been," Druze said. "Your eyes and ears in the Hierophane are the only ones I can trust now."

He thought of Rew sneaking into the Temple of Houses to help these rejects that put him in a stone prison. She was too close to the boy gray robe. His daughter was no longer reliable.

Besides, La Croix and Kriminel could handle themselves well enough without Brigitte. The pair were efficient killers. Hell, a respectable number of kills came from back and forth bouts of each one eliminating the potential love interests of the other in fits of jealousy. They were even better on assignment.

"You should know," Brigitte said, "the Hierophane prepares for war against the eleven houses."

"Did Majora tell you why?"

"No. She just said we have a week to make ready."

Druze could guess the reason. The aians did not take kindly to the partial destruction of the Temple of Houses. They would want the mage responsible. And Majora was not the type to surrender him.

"All the more reason I need you in the Hierophane," Druze said. "Watch Majora. Report all her actions to me."

Druze held up a finger so Brigitte would wait a patient moment. He looked inward, seeking the word of magic that summed up who he was now. He found it. *Intikam.* He told her the word, his new scry signature.

When a mage's desires, goals, and drives changed enough, their old scry signature was no longer in tune with that mage. His motivations had changed several times over the centuries. Rich's attempted murder and releasing of the Death Null had changed them most recently. Now Brigitte was the only one who would be able to scry with him.

"What will you do?" Brigitte asked.

"I'm going to save all of us," Druze replied. "Keep our dialogues to yourself."

Druze killed the scry. Burru was sitting in front of him patiently, dutifully. Druze put a hand on the man's shoulder.

"Let us leave this place, Burru."

"At once, Master," Burru said with a nod. "Where do you wish to go?"

Druze spoke the attunement spell for the warrior girl's clasp. Its presence whispered back.

"Along the coast of the Middle Sea, I think," Druze said as he rose with Burru's help. He smiled at his new servant.

"Suusteren. Yes, I wish to go to Suusteren."

CHAPTER 4
Bramblefen

Mike was done being an art collector. Having to scrub the witch's graffiti off the walls and floors sealed it. The pigeons could have Mel's friend.

"Third time's the barber," Mike said as he dipped his brush into the pail. "Time to cut our losses on your boy and pop smoke on Neverland."

"What?" Mel said looking away from the section of wall he was working. "We can't leave Rich here like this."

"Yeah, we can. Savvy's hexes didn't work. Quest-mage didn't work. Witch didn't work," Mike said, counting the failures off with his little purple fingers. "I say we haul his ass back through the pendulum and let David Copperfield give it a try."

Mel looked at Mike, his warrior girl face showing that expression girls make when they're tired of jokes.

"You can't be serious," Mel said.

"I ain't," Mike said. "Nobody's gonna cart Mr. Handle-With-Care here halfway across the country. I say we sell him for gas money."

Mel looked at Mike like he had said something offensive, but, shit, it was a long way to the Hierophane. He wasn't about to walk.

"Mike, just chill," Mel said. "It'll come to us. I'm sure the answer's just around the corner."

Jason stopped scrubbing and looked up like the light bulb suddenly went off.

"You know," he said. "The answer really may be around the corner, literally."

Mike and Mel both simply looked at him. Jason was one of those dumb know-it-all kids who expected people to know what he was thinking and fill in the blanks. He got on Mike's nerves.

When no response came from the audience, Jason spilled it.

"We go a few hours south to Bramblefen. And sic the bokoru on Rich."

That got Runt's attention. "A dangerous move, Jason Cephrin," the big man said, not bothering to look at the kid as he scrubbed his portion of wall.

"Yeah, but if anything can eat this cost, it's them," Jason said.

"Okay, what the hell are bokoru?" Mel asked.

Jason sighed. "You know! Bramblefen! We've played a campaign against bokoru. They're like these vamps that eat people's life force."

A hint of recognition flashed across Mel's face. "Are they those things that all look like nosferatus with the elongated head and ears and sharp, rat teeth? Slink around like their legs are fused together?"

"Yep," Jason said.

"I hate those things," Mel said.

"You do well to hate them," Runt said. "And avoid them."

"But we can't avoid them," Jason said with excitement. "Don't you see? They've got a serious appetite for magic. They can stomach the cost."

Mel nodded. "Sounds like a plan."

"No it don't," Mike said, tossing his brush into the pail.

"C'mon, Mike," Mel said.

"C'mon nothing," Mike said. "If Runt don't like it, I don't like it. You know what sounds like a plan? Half off sale on lawn ornaments."

That's when Ruki Provos popped up the stairs. He had left them to scrub out the evidence of illegal witchcraft while he went to "check on the caravan." Lazy bastard.

"Ah! Better than how we found it," Ruki said, smiling as he looked at the clean walls and floor. "And good news, the caravan's back to full steam."

"Great," Melvin said. "Cause we're going to Bramblefen."

"The hell you say," Mike said.

"Mike, we have to try."

"Shit, we have tried, three times," Mike said, holding up his fingers to illustrate. "Bramblefen starts with a 'B', but that don't sound like Bermuda to me. And right now his idea sounds about as good as yours when you said, 'hey bro, play this game with us, it'll be fun.'"

"Well, Bramblefen isn't exactly the place to go picking flowers and having picnics," Ruki Provos said. "Why would you want to go there?"

"Jason's got a great idea on how to free Rich," Melvin said. Then he put his hand on Ruki's shoulder and looked at him with those warrior girl pretty brown eyes.

"You will take us, won't you Ruki?"

"Uh, yes," Ruki said, a sloppy grin painted all over his face. "Of course."

Melvin smiled. He looked at Runt.

"Runt, will you come?"

"I will," Runt said with a nod. "There is hope in Jason Cephrin's plan. Reason enough to try."

Melvin looked at Mike and stuck his tongue out. He was turning into a goddamn she-devil.

Mike was stuck between not wanting to go at all and not wanting to send his brother off to deal with life sucking vampires without him. So instead of heading toward the Hierophane and back to a world that made sense, Mike had to endure another yellow brick road trip.

They loaded Rich up on the newly refurbished caravan. Tavis Provos had a lot to say about that.

"Bring that back! Nary a one of you is a customer. You can't just cart merchandise out of my store!"

"Bah!" Ruki yelled, batting his hand at the old man.

The caravan started with a trembling lurch. Then they were off, following the southern road. Mike watched as the city melted into a smudge behind them.

It was an uneventful ride. They spent the first hour passing acre upon acre of farms. Pomegranate, pear, and fig trees stood in countless rows like soldiers at attention. Pumpkins weighed heavy on the vine, waiting for the harvest.

The farms passed by and the countryside opened up to the wilds. Stuff grew out here like the farms, just without any order or reason to it all. Trees and bushes and overgrown grass mingled with vines bearing strange fruit, thorny weeds and clumps of vividly colored wildflowers.

There was also a graveyard. A dude with lank, gray hair was in the middle of it, digging graves for two people if the pine boxes were any indication of his workload. That reminded Mike.

"We might wanna see what he charges," he said nodding his head toward the old gravedigger. "He may give deals if we pre-purchase."

The gravedigger looked at the passing caravan like it was full of trespassing criminals.

"No need to be pessimistic," Jason said. "This is a train full of badasses, except for Melvin that is. The Ass Whip Express. We'll be in and out before you know it."

"Hey," Mel said, looking indignant. "I don't appreciate you counting me out. I'm pretty badass."

"Huh?" Jason said, craning his neck to hear. "I didn't hear a word after pretty. Yes, Melvin, you are very pretty. You turn heads."

"Seriously," Mel said. "I can hold my own."

Jason stood up. The caravan knocked him back and forth but he swung with it. He reached his hands out to Mel and sang the words, "Who's that lady?"

Mike was surprised at Jason. It was an old Isley Brothers song. Apparently, the kid had a little soul in him.

Mel wasn't amused. His face darkened like a storm cloud.

"Funny," he said with a flat tone.

"Who's that lady?" Jason sang again.

Mike couldn't help himself. "Lovely lady," he sang. He had a megrym voice that could hit high octaves like Ernie Isley now.

That started a full on concert for Mel's benefit. Jason backed up Mike, who took Ernie's parts with gusto. They leaned in together and held their hands out to Mel as they sang "look yeah, but don't touch!"

"No no no," Mike crooned, pulling his hand away as if getting to close to Mel had burned it.

Runt clapped his hands as Mike and Jason simulated the breakdown. Jason strummed the air guitar while Mike hit the drums.

When they finished, Runt yelled "Again," with a laugh.

Mel, trapped in a moving caravan, was captive to the encore serenade. He sat there, grimacing and glowering. It was the most fun Mike had all week.

Besides, if they were going to play with deadly creatures, the least Mel could be was angry about it. His anger meant less back watching for Mike.

They were still laughing at Mel's expense when Ruki Provos stopped the caravan. Ahead of them were thick mounds of reeds, bulrushes, and thorny plants separated by watery inlets. Small trees also popped up along the landscape, limiting visibility.

"All right," Ruki said. "See you all soon."

"You're not coming with us?" Mel asked.

Ruki Provos looked down at himself. "This is Colkhisian linen," he said. "And that's Bramblefen," he finished looking out into the swamp.

Mike figured there was no convincing Ruki to join them. Besides, just as well let him watch the caravan with the rest of them tramping out in the middle of the vampire marshes. You never know when you may have to cut out of a place with the quickness.

Mike jumped off the caravan. "Two biggest guys are on statue detail," he said. He took the pair of gleaming silver lightning gloves hanging from his belt and thrust his hands into them.

He led the way through Bramblefen, doing his best to avoid the soggy, waterlogged areas. Runt and Jason followed, the statue bouncing between them. Mel brought up the rear.

They made their way into the swamp until it was hard to see ten feet in front of them. The bramble bushes tore at their skin and clothes. Weird sounds rose from the foliage... Mike wasn't so sure the noises all came from animals.

"This clearing's as good a place as any," Jason said. He and Runt set the statue down.

"Now we'd better back up a ways," Jason said. "If the bokoru have fresh meat I'd doubt they'd want to take the time to tenderize Rich."

They retreated as far back as possible and hid in some reeds. That allowed them about fifty feet of distance from Rich. Any farther and he'd be lost in the brush.

Mike wished waiting was more glamorous, but it wasn't. It was sitting in one spot, eyes constantly ahead at a scene that didn't change. The wait reminded him of Army deployment, where days ran together into sludge.

"This is boring," Jason said.

"Shut up!" Mike said harsh and sharp. "Your talking disturbs the wildlife and they all go quiet. If these bokoru live here, then a silent patch of swamp's like the sound of an ice cream truck to them. Don't move. Don't talk. Don't get us killed."

The mood now set for the suck, everyone dug in to wait. In about twenty minutes, the swamp around them returned to the strange noises that were normal for this place. Nothing came for Rich though, not even a bird looking to take a dump.

There were a lot of things to think about when there was nothing to do but think. Mike mostly thought of Savvy. She was working to unite all the nasran clans to strike against the Hierophane. Mike hoped she was doing well with that, but he knew it would be an uphill battle for her, being a woman. Hell, even her own clan didn't stand behind her until the Hierophane had turned Maltep into a pile of hot rubble.

After about another hour, Mike was ready to question Jason's world knowledge. It was the middle of the day... if these things were nocturnal then they'd be camping out here forever.

The foliage shook in the clearing beside Rich. Just as Mel described them, three dudes wearing tattered rags slunk out toward the statue, all of them looking like nosferatu.

The bokoru lovingly caressed the statue with their gnarled, sharp-nailed hands. Two of them sniffed the marble while the third licked Rich's head.

They all opened their mouths impossibly wide, big enough to swallow a megrym whole. Their eyes and mouths glowed blue. Blue light came out of their mouths and fell on the statue like a tractor beam.

One of the bokoru started to turn all white, just like Calais had. But it kept on feeding along with the other two.

Mike held up his closed fist. Rich was still marble. Interrupting them now wouldn't help him. The bokoru had to eat his cost first.

They'd have to move fast. If only one was visibly taking the cost, what were the other two eating? Mike didn't know how much time it took to eat a person's entire life force, but looking at the size of their mouths and the trac-tor beams, he couldn't imagine this process taking long.

The one bokoru who was turning white stopped eating. His tractor beam and eye light died. It just hung there, nothing but a statue.

Rich was back to flesh. He collapsed on the ground. The two remaining bokoru descended over him, their tractor beams still on full blast.

"Now!" Mike cried, charging from the brush.

As he ran, an arrow flew into one of the feasting bokoru. The arrow tore through the bokoru like it was made of stitched cotton. It flinched from being torn, but the arrow didn't kill it, only stopped it from feeding. Another arrow ripped the remaining bokoru from its feeding frenzy.

Both monsters shuddered for a fraction of a moment. Then the same blue light the bokoru used to feed began to pull the jagged gashes left by Jason's arrows closed. They were healing themselves.

The team closed the gap and the bokoru sprang at them. Mike clubbed one, and it felt like hitting an empty sack. The body gave token resistance. There was nothing underneath the tattered rags it wore to crunch or crack.

Melvin sliced through the other. The blade opened it to where Mike could see Bramblefen straight through. As soon as the blade finished its cut, the blue light was pulling the bokoru back together.

The bokoru Mike clubbed rolled off the club and was now face to face with Mike. The smell of decay and sulfur hung on the bokoru. It bared its teeth, showing Mike the pointed rat daggers in the front.

Mike when to club it again. But its eyes flashed blue and Mike was rooted in place. He stared at the warm, welcoming light.

The bokoru's mouth opened impossibly wide. The light that came from it beckoned to Mike. It told him there was nothing to fear in its embrace.

Runt's Z-blade cut into the bokoru, ending Mike's trance. The big man stepped in front of Mike and started cutting huge swaths into the bokoru using both ends of his bladed weapon.

Mike felt heavy, tired. A sense of regret hung over him, a feeling of great, utter loss.

He fought the feeling. These bokoru were nasty devils. Not only did they keep you all hypnotized and docile while they fed, but if they ever had to stop feeding they made it feel like you missed out on something great.

Right now Melvin and Runt kept these two bokoru occupied. They were too busy stitching themselves up from the constant blade cuts. But their tractor pull stitch work was almost as fast.

Mike reached down and shook Rich.

Rich groaned. The kid was alive.

"I know, you feel like you missed a free trip to Vegas," Mike said. "But you gotta shake it. Get up!"

Mike hauled Rich up. The kid rose on shaky legs.

"Cover us while we fall back!" Mike yelled. He pulled at Rich, who followed like he had been roused from a deep sleep. Mike turned to see where Jason was so he could bring Rich to him.

Jason was where they'd left him at the bulrushes. Only now there was a bokoru with him. Jason stood still, tranced out while the bokoru's eyes and open mouth glowed.

Mike took out his diskbow. A sharp twang punctuated the air as Mike fired. The disk shot out in a spinning blur, hit the bokoru directly in the face, erupted out the other side and kept going.

Jason fell to one knee. That was the weakness from the bokoru feeding. Jason stared at the ground, shaking his head in sorrow. That was the sense of loss working.

The bokoru was mending the hole in his face. Mike didn't have time to wind the diskbow for another shot. He definitely couldn't make it back to him. Melvin and Runt were too busy swiping at their own self-mending nosferatus.

"Fight it, you asshole!" Mike yelled to Jason. "It's trying to snack on you."

Jason shook his head again, all sorry for himself.

The bokoru was fully mended. It leaned over Jason. Its eyes began to glow.

Jason picked himself up and lunged at the bokoru with a yell. His bone fingers stabbed into the bokoru. He pulled up and raked four gashes through it.

"Keep slashing it," Mike said to Jason. The four parts of the bokoru were quickly coming back together.

Mike kept pulling Rich towards Jason and the bokoru he perpetually slashed at with his bone hand. All they'd have to do was fall back to the caravan, slashing these bokoru down until Ruki could speed out of here.

Their stamina would hold. They would be all right.

Mike got to Jason and his jaw dropped. Out in the fen he saw at least a dozen more bokoru.

They were slinking their way towards them fast, eager to get at the hot meal their bodies offered.

CHAPTER 5
A Pendulum Breaking

Rich was so disoriented he originally thought it all was some kind of weird, cost-derived nightmare.

First, he was out of stone and on swampy ground feeling good. Really good. Then he felt sad and lonely and tired all in the same stretch. Strong, small hands hauled him up, and Mike was telling him to get over it and move.

Rich tried, but his legs were weak. He wobbled where Mike pulled him, looking down and trying his best not to slip in the wet grasses. When he finally managed to look up, he found himself in the middle of a war zone.

Mel, Runt, Jason, they were all tied up fighting monsters. Bunches more nasties were slinking their way towards the five of them.

Mike let Rich go and smacked his gloved hands together. Electricity arced in the space between his hands, which he shot out at the nasties. The lightning hit four of them and they burned up like dry parchment paper.

That left nine of these things. They were closing the gap fast.

Out of nowhere, four people appeared in the marsh midway between Rich's party and the advancing monsters. These four didn't portal or fly or even crawl out of the ground to get here. They just were.

And they were a mixed crowd. One was a brownish-green megrym, wearing a leather apron and tool belt over dark pants and white cotton shirt. Two were aian, a male from the eagle house Demir and a female from the feline house Nadi. The last looked like a mage. He wore gray robes.

"Hollowers," Mike said as he looked at the new foursome.

"What the hell are Hollowers?" Rich asked.

"They're pendulum heroes," Mel said, sparing a look back at the newly arrived entourage between sword slashes at a monster.

"All these bokoru gathering must have triggered the Rift Pendulum," Jason said as he raked his bone fingers at a monster. "It pulled down some gamers running a campaign to do some clean up for real. They'll save us!"

"Or nuke the whole swamp into a crater," Mike said grimacing.

Of the nine monsters slinking across the field, seven advanced on the four new arrivals and two came at Rich and Mike.

Those pendulum heroes had better hurry up with the heroics.

They didn't. Instead, they collapsed into fear and confusion as the nasties descended on them. The nasties grabbed them and dragged them away from the fight while they cried and yelled for help.

What the hell was going on?

There was no time to think about it. The two monsters crawled up to Mike and Rich. Their eyes took on an enchanting blue glow.

Runt stepped in and cut both of the new additions across the face. His Z-blade was disassembled into twin axes, which he used to rip the monsters apart like they were old t-shirts.

Mike stepped over to the monster Runt had been working before the additions. It was repairing itself, blue light pulling its torn edges back together. Mike tried to club it but these things seemed hollow, insubstantial.

Recognition finally flashed in Rich's mind. Jason had called them bokoru. This was Bramblefen. He used to love playing here, going Razzleblad on these life force suckers.

Bokoru were easy kills... for a mage.

Rich spoke a creation spell. He opened his hands as he spoke so he could channel the coming creation into them.

"*Ateshi yaratmam lahzum!*" he yelled the final words of the spell and fire blazed to life in his hands.

He threw the fire at two of the bokoru. They both burned like old paper.

Rich wasn't done. He bent some of the fire consuming the bokoru back into his hands and tossed it at two more. While the two new bokoru burned he bent their fire back to his hands once more and launched both handfuls at the last standing bokoru, who burned up instantly.

All the bokoru burned away like gasoline rags.

"Told ya, we'd save you," Jason said, panting in labored gasps.

"Thanks," Rich said with a smile.

Mel ran into Rich and wrapped her arms around his neck. The sigh that came from the warrior girl was full of relief.

"Welcome back, Rich," she breathed.

"It's great to be back," Rich said.

Before he was turned to stone, it had been increasingly hard for Rich to think of Mel as a guy. Now, it was impossible with her pressing her body against him so tightly. So he didn't. His hands found her waist and squeezed back.

"Let's save the reunion party for later," Jason said, looking out at the empty fen. "Those poor excuses for pendulum heroes bought us some time, but when they disappear those bokoru are going to come looking for something a little more nutritious."

"You dumbass," Mike said, looking up at Jason. "Do you have any idea why those folks acted like that?"

"Duh... they're newbies. A bunch of wet nubs that thought they were too hot for the starter zones," Jason said with a shrug.

"You haven't seen Hollowers in action," Mike said. "Me and Runt have... and they don't act like that. You don't get it, do you?"

"Get what?"

"Replace Bramblefen for weagr infested woods and swap their characters out for ours. What do you have?"

Jason looked up, his aian eyes dancing as he paused to consider Mike's words. Shock ran across his features. "They're rejects!" he said.

"What?" Rich asked. "You mean, like us?"

"Four folks appear out of thin air into a highly dangerous environment and are instantly overwhelmed, confused and in total disarray by their predicament," Jason said. "That was us in Kazawood."

"Only this time, we watched it from the other end," Mike said.

Mel brought her sword up and took a step towards the fen. "We have to rescue them," she said.

"Shit," Mike swore.

Mel turned and looked at her brother. "We can't leave them to the bokoru, Mike," she said.

"Nah, I agree with you," Mike said. "It's still some bullshit though. Let's go."

Four of them ran through the fen, water splashing as they rushed across the marshland. Rich tried to run but his legs were still shaky. Runt Half-weagr had Rich hop on his back and the big man still kept easy pace with Mel, Jason and Mike despite the extra weight.

The trail of muddy footprints was easy enough to follow. They led to the heavily wooded area of Bramblefen. Giant willow trees looked as if they had been undisturbed for centuries, their branches and leaves hanging down like a veil. Some of the giant trees had fallen, and Rich could see their interiors were completely hollowed out. Caked, dried mud bridged the space between fallen trees, tying several trees together into a bigger structure.

The footprints led inside one of the hollowed trunks.

"Aight, watch your backs in Casa Nosferatu," Mike said as he cranked his diskbow taut.

He led the way, his eyes glowing in the low light of the hollow. The putrid smell of rotting plants made the air stuffy and thick. It was quiet in the hollows, even the squish of their boots on the dead reeds sounded muted. None of the bokoru jumped out at them from the shadows.

They turned the corner and Rich saw why. The bokoru were too greedy to concern themselves with other things when there was food available. They were all eating.

There were five bokoru. Three of them hunched over the prone body of the winged aian, mouths opened as wide as caverns as they sucked out his life force. One bokoru each pulled life from the megrym and the cat girl aian, both of whom knelt in peaceful acceptance. The mage was nowhere to be seen.

Suddenly, the mouth lights of the three feeding on the winged aian flickered and stuttered, reminiscent of what happened with a straw when there's little left in the cup. Then their mouth lights died and they all turned towards the cat and warrior.

No one had to spell it out. They were too late for the eagle man.

"Light me up," Jason said to Rich as he knocked an arrow.

Rich put fire on the arrow and an instant later Jason sent the flaming missile through the two snacking on the megrym and cat girl. The fiery hole expanded in both bokoru, eating away at them.

The three remaining bokoru turned to face their new threat.

"*Ateshim gael!*" Rich shouted and the fire still burning on the arrow leapt towards his outstretched hands.

The fire's path took it through the back of one bokoru, who burned instantly. Soon as the fire hit his palms, Rich tossed the fireballs at the last two bokoru.

Mel, Jason and Rich rushed over to two survivors. Both of them had their hands on the ground, sorrow etched on their faces.

"C'mon," Jason said as he lifted the cat girl up. "We have to get out of here."

She looked at the apron clad megrym Mel was helping up, then at the eagle man whose pulse Mike checked.

"What about Trevor?" she asked.

Mike looked up at her and shook his head.

"Where's the other guy?" Mike asked.

"I don't know," the cat girl said, looking near tears.

"Stop feeling sorry for yourself and explain," Mike said. "Where'd they drag his ass to?"

"Clemson escaped," the brownish-green megrym said. "He freaked out before we got pulled in here, roasted the two dragging him and ran off."

"He just left us here," the cat girl said. "With these things!"

"Aight," Mike said. "Everything else can wait til we're out of here. Follow close."

Mike got them out of the bokoru den without any surprises. Once outside, him and Runt canvassed the area and located a solitary set of footprints. The party followed them about a quarter mile until they disappeared into one of the watery inlets and never resurfaced.

"He either drowned, swam, or waded to hell knows where," Mike said. "There's no finding him now."

"We have to find him," Rich said. "He's a gray robe."

"I don't care if he's a candy robe," Mike replied. "You're our only weapon against these things, which limits our search capabilities. Look around you," he said, letting the huge expanse of Bramblefen in all directions do the talking for him.

Rich nodded. Since they couldn't split up, they could be out here forever searching for footprints that could just as well disappear again. Time to cut their losses.

Mike turned around and started walking. Rich, Mel and the new megrym followed. Jason escorted the cat girl. Runt brought up the rear.

The megrym's name was Vincent. The aian cat girl was Gina. They used to date, but apparently even a breakup couldn't come between a solid game group. Trevor had only played a handful of times. And as far as Clemson went, he had been their resident veteran.

"Do you remember anything specific happening to Clemson right before he burned his way out?" Rich asked Vincent.

"I don't know," Vincent said. "We were all looking at the disgusting den they were dragging us to. I think one of those creatures licked his face. Then he just went nuts."

"Nuts?"

"Yeah, eyes got big, started speaking stuff that they probably don't offer on Rosetta Stone, set fire to the things holding him with his bare hands and ran off still speaking gibberish like he was trying to have a conversation with the horizon." Vincent shrugged. "You know, nuts."

Great. There was a newbie with insane amounts of power out there with a character trigger, if Rich had to guess, of either fear or disgust. This new gray robe had no one to explain the cost and was lost out in a world full of a million opportunities to trip into character.

Rich dry swallowed. This was not the most ideal way to return from his stone prison.

CHAPTER 6
The Grave Robber

Druze spoke the destruction spell and around him the ground sank along the intricate lines he had carved out. This worked better than burning the lines into the soil. He looked around, double checking his handiwork.

Burru looked toward the town of Olukent in the distance. A small band of nasrans were running toward them, their backward knees moving quickly like a flock of cranes who had spotted a couple of fat frogs. They were getting bigger by the second. Burru turned to Druze, panic on his face.

"Master, whatever this is, we have to stop. We have to flee!"

"Patience," Druze said still looking over his tether. If done correctly, the wind channel he was creating would make the journey to Suusteren a matter of hours instead of weeks. If done wrong, the wind would cut them apart like razors or not work at all. Too bad all his portal roots had been destroyed with his old body. It would take a century to amass that many portals again.

The tether lines were sound. And since he had destroyed the ground along the lines, the only way the nasrans could break the tunnel was by filling in the whole of the pattern. That would take hours, more than enough time to suit his purpose.

Druze spoke a couple of creation spells and attuned himself and Burru to the wind channel. The spell was specific to the signature on the ground. Now the nasrans wouldn't be able to follow, no matter how fast their backward legs were.

Three arrows landed on the ground next to Druze and Burru. Druze was fairly sure by their garb that these warriors were remnants of Maltep. Seeing how the Hierophane razed and ruined Maltep, these nasrans were likely not fans of Master Izal's black and white dotted robe or the spells.

"Jump on my back, Burru," he commanded.

Burru took a fraction of a second to look at the nasran archers nocking more arrows before scrambling to place his arms around Druze's neck.

"*Aer ruzgar alabilsamiz, ruzgar ekip firtina bichelim!*" Druze spoke.

The attunement spell came alive and Druze launched into a run. The world blurred around them as his feet ran at impossible speeds.

Druze ran within the wind channel for an hour or so. There was little to fear from the outside world while he ran inside the channel. Him and Burru could pass through solid objects as if they weren't there.

Then his ankle snapped.

His steps faltered as the pain rushed. The blur of the tunnel collapsed as he staggered and fell into a patch of grass. Burru's hands still clung tightly to his robe.

"Get off me, oaf," Druze said. Burru didn't listen.

Druze craned his neck and saw why. Burru was dead.

He pried the dead man's hands off his robe. Apparently, a nasran archer had put an arrow in Burru's back before the tunnel opened.

"Ah, Burru," Druze said. "The best servants don't die."

Speaking of death, Izal's dead body was still breaking down. One foot lay like a useless chunk of meat, separated from the bones of the leg at the ankle. The pain, which should've been unbearable, was little more than a wan and muted throb.

Magic was hard on a living body, but it seemed spells were even harder to endure for an animated corpse. Druze closed his eyes and sighed, trying to consider his options.

That's when Druze felt him. Burru, or at least his dead body, emanated an inviting presence. The closest thing Druze could equate the feeling to was getting to a fire when he was cold or seeing a glass of water when thirsty.

He went to the presence. When he opened his eyes, he was looking at Izal's dead body from Burru's point of view.

Druze smiled with Burru's lips. Now Izal's corpse was emanating its presence. Druze rose and walked away from Izal's body. He was a little ways past throwing distance when the presence died. He walked back until he could feel Izal's body again and willed himself to it.

Burru's lifeless body collapsed in a heap as Druze sat up in Izal's body. Interesting. He transferred his consciousness back into Burru. As long as there was a corpse nearby, Druze had options. The best option at the moment was to stay in Burru, the most recent corpse with the two working ankles. He spoke his attunement spell again and the wind channel opened as he set off in a run.

Another two and a half hours and Druze was looking at the expansive city of Suusteren from the outskirts of a nearby farm. He spoke the attunement spell for the warrior girl's clasp. She was no longer in Suusteren, but not far south, along the southern road.

He opened the wind channel again and within twenty seconds of running his ankle snapped. This time he staggered and caught himself by crouching as the blur died around him. It looked like he was in the middle of a fig tree orchard. The girl's clasp still chimed south.

No corpses around, Druze started to hobble his way. Muted as the pain was, it still flashed in uncomfortable jolts as he stepped down with the battered ankle.

It was slow going, but eventually Druze cleared the farms. He was in a cemetery of all places. In the middle of the field, an old man, a gravedigger, had just finished filling in one plot and was about to lower a coffin into the second.

Druze felt corpses emanating all around him. Some were strong, like the one in the box and in the freshly made grave. Others were barely there. He ventured to guess the less decayed the corpse, the better the presence.

The gravedigger saw Druze with his ruined ankle. He let go of the coffin and came towards the crippled man.

"You need help, friend?" he asked.

"Yes," Druze answered. "I need your mobility."

Druze grabbed the gravedigger's throat with both hands and squeezed. The gravedigger tried to break Druze's grip and claw his face, but Druze ignored the gravedigger's raking nails and squeezed harder. Whatever pain this man could inflict would be fleeting.

Soon, the gravedigger's presence joined the ranks of the other corpses in the cemetery, his strongest of them all. Druze jumped into the gravedigger.

After pushing Burru's lifeless body off of him, Druze dragged his dead servant to the open grave and tossed him in.

Burru lay like a newborn in the grave. Entire back soaked with blood, foot twisted, face torn with bloody gashes... Druze had ridden him hard.

He spoke the attunement spell again and felt for the clasp's presence. It was still further south, but it was moving back this way. And quickly. Druze smiled.

What better place for an ambush?

DRUZE WAS STANDING in the middle of the road when the caravan pulled up, resting one arm on the handle of the gravedigger's shovel. The caravan trembled as it came to a shuddering stop in front of him.

"Oy!" the goggled driver said, waving his hand as if to shoo Druze from the road. "Clear the way!"

Even behind the blue tinted lenses, Druze recognized Ruki Provos. Samedi's failure to kill even this sniveling merchant made his blood boil.

Druze saw that nearly everyone he wanted dead was on the caravan, a neat little package waiting to be murdered. The warrior girl and the bone armed aian, the weagr sized man and the foul mouthed megrym, even two strangers who Druze was pleased to kill by association looked back at him from the caravan. Everyone except that nasran hag.

Then he saw Rich, alive and well.

"Boy mage!" Druze yelled, pointing a finger at the fake robe. "Your continued ability to breathe is annoying. I see you are free of stone!"

Rich looked at him with a questioning expression as if he was trying to recognize Druze's borrowed face.

"This is unfortunate kink in my plan," Druze told him. "I was going to grind your statue up and force the dust down your friends' mouths until their gullets closed up and they choked to death."

"What the hell is your ailment, gravedigger?" Ruki Provos asked.

Druze swung the shovel to point straight up and pressed his hand into the shovelhead.

"*Demear fuze!*" he cried, and the shovel's metal head flew off the wooden handle with a snap. Still pointing skyward, the shovelhead moved with the speed of an arrow. The flat of it smashed with a "clong" into Ruki's face. The merchant crumpled.

The whole caravan sprang up in alarm. The megrym Mike was the fastest to react, popping over the front of the caravan and pointing his disk shooter, the same one he had used to kill Samedi.

Druze didn't have his black robes. But he didn't need them. He spoke an altering spell and the wooden shovel shaft lashed out at Mike.

The wood knocked the disk shooter out of the megrym's grasp. Druze bent the wood around Mike's hand and yanked the foul-mouthed cretin out of the caravan.

Druze knelt over Mike. He held the megrym down with one hand. The other hand he raised.

"*Puskurtu olan el,*" Druze spoke and his raised hand glowed red, turned hot like molten lava. He pressed his hand into the megrym's face.

Hearing the twee scream, smelling his megrym flesh burn, hearing it sizzle under his hand... this was satisfying.

A violent push knocked Druze off Mike, forcing his lava hand off with a harsh peel of burnt flesh. Druze turned to see Rich's sleeves bending back to their original place around the fake robe's arms.

"Bent sleeves? Is this all the challenge you can muster?!" Druze asked with a laugh.

The warrior girl was charging at him, her face furious.

How cute. He let her advance.

Her sword entered Druze's host body. He grimaced with pain as it pushed clean through to the other side. Just what he wanted.

He locked his arms around the elbow of her sword hand. He turned his grimace into a grin as he pushed until he heard her elbow break with a hard snap. Her scream was piercing.

Druze grabbed the warrior girl by her face, so pretty as her features contorted in agony. He no longer had his burning hand spell. But he had something better. He had her sword, which he pulled out of himself and raised to cut her down.

Something made his head jerk sideways, bringing with it an annoying explosion of pain. Another jerking explosion happened a moment later. This time he could taste the metal of the arrow the aian boy shot into his head.

The aian boy couldn't stop him. And the fake robe's bent sleeves weren't going to break Druze's grip on either the sword or the girl this time.

No one could stop him. The sword came down.

Druze felt a painful rip at his shoulder. His raised arm flew away from him, taking the sword with it.

The big man Runt had his axe staff swinging. The first swing had come up, severing his sword arm.

The second swing came down, cutting a leg off at the knee.

Druze fell, taking the girl with him in his grasp. Her face was still in his hand.

He began to speak the spell again for burning hand.

Runt cut his remaining hand off. The girl rolled away. That was annoying.

He pointed the bloody stump wrist at the enraged weagr of a man.

"*Kan patlama!*" Druze cried. The blood gushed out as a flood into Runt's face. As Runt stepped back to clear his vision, Druze bent the bone in his arm stump. The bone stretched painfully and Druze scratched the base of an altering spell in the blood on Runt's chest.

Druze spoke the words that sealed the spell. Now the blood on the giant would behave like naphtha pitch, what Samedi had lovingly called napalm.

"*Ateshlemen!*"

The explosion was magnificent. Druze and the warrior girl both received a generous helping of the fiery blast as it knocked them back and away. More importantly, Runt got the lion's share as it blew him away from Druze to crash into the front of the caravan.

Druze, singed and smoking, looked up from the ground with the hopes of seeing a giant charred carcass. Runt was unconscious, smoking and battered, but not dead. The man was thick skinned, weagr skinned.

Runt should have still been in flames, but the boy mage ruined that. He pulled the fire from Runt's body and had it dancing in his hands. Rich launched the fire balls at Druze.

As the gravedigger's body roasted under the fireballs, Druze's consciousness jumped into the corpse in the unburied coffin at the edge of the graveyard.

He pushed open the coffin lid and rose before them. This dead man had a broken neck, causing an unnatural sideways, downward bend to his head. Druze glared upwards, eyes locked on the boy mage.

"Your problem will not simply burn away, child," Druze said. He smirked with satisfaction as he surveyed the damage he had wrought.

The brown megrym stranger was trying to rouse Runt. The warrior girl was using her one good arm to help her brother who still clutched his face. The aian cat woman was trying to shake Ruki Provos awake. Rich and his archer friend Jason looked at Druze's new body in stupefied shock.

"He's no gravedigger," Jason said, horror on his face. "He's more of a Graverobber."

"Rest assured," Druze crooned. "None of you are coming back from this."

Druze pulled the fire still roasting the gravedigger's body to his new host. This corpse was not only robeless, but sleeveless as well. Druze didn't have the patience to craft additional fire buffers in his spell, so when the flames came he offered his new body's exposed arms to the fire.

He fought through the initial jolt of pain as the fire consumed his arms raw. He whipped his arms back and a long trail of flame followed. Then he whipped his hands forward.

Two lashes of fire arced in the air. Their paths would cross at the fake robe's neck, taking his head off and burning the stump.

Druze saw Rich's horrified eyes as the flame lashes came toward him. His lips were a blur, moving faster than Druze's legs in the wind channel. That's when Druze realized Rich was consumed with life-threatening fear.

He should have aimed for the aian boy.

Storm winds erupted from the fake robe's hand. Powerful enough to ruin cities, the wind blew out the fire whips and kept coming at Druze, cutting like razors against his host's skin.

The wind should have picked him up and carried him for miles. Druze looked down. Rich had cast another spell and bent the coffin wood he was standing in to wrap around his host's feet like weighted clamps.

Druze tried to yell a movement spell, but his words were drowned out by the roar of the wind. It ripped and blasted his host, carrying away cut slivers of him until nothing was left.

Druze's consciousness jumped into another corpse and he saw nothing but darkness. This was the one the gravedigger had just put into the ground.

The fake robe had gone gray in his fear and destroyed a solid host before Druze really got going. No matter, there were plenty more.

Working with dirt was magic Druze had always found distasteful. Nevertheless, he spoke an intricate earth spell. He pushed out near the end of it.

The coffin lid and all the earth on top of it exploded up and out. Druze saw clear blue sky as the dirt rained back down to earth.

Leaping out of the grave, Druze turned to get his bearings back on the caravan.

He saw it, speeding off. Everyone was back inside of it, looking at the graveyard and the dirt explosion he had caused. The cat girl was driving that caravan at what looked to be as fast as it could go.

This body was limited to natural speeds, not attuned to the wind channel he had opened earlier. In fact, this body belonged to a woman who had gotten buried in a flower dress.

Trying to run them down for a street fight without replacement bodies on hand wasn't prudent. Besides, many of them were injured. There was only one place close by to seek treatment.

The caravan disappeared from view. No matter. Druze brushed the dirt from the shoulders of his yellow sundress. He took a step towards the road to Suusteren, whistling casually as he made his way towards the city.

CHAPTER 7
Battle Costs

For all the power Rich supposedly wielded, he felt powerless now. All he could do was watch as the people closest to him, friends that had risked their lives to save him, suffered in agony.

The caravan jostled and bounced everyone around violently as it sped down the road to Suusteren. Every shake of the wagon made Mel cry out in pain as she nursed her broken arm. Mike had passed out again, clutching his face in his little purple hands. Runt lay sprawled across the wagon's floor, his face contorting in pain with every hard bump.

Rich couldn't even cast his heal spell, the one Jason taught him in Kazawood. Jason stopped him cold.

"You're a powerful mage," Jason said. "With substandard heals. I don't want to risk a cleric having to work around your magic. And I definitely don't want that cleric to have to go layering spells."

So Rich sat there, unsure, unable, incapable. Powerless.

"There are... water clerics," Ruki Provos got out. "In Suusteren."

He was conscious now, which was good, but looking at him only made Rich feel worse. Ruki talked through swollen, busted lips. His once pristine white sleeve was crimson stained as he held it up to his broken nose. The goggles sat undamaged on his forehead, but the skin around his eyes was puffy, swollen and leaking blood from small cuts where the shovelhead had mashed the goggles relentlessly into his face.

Gina drove the caravan like a functioning drunk driver, her gray cat ears lying back on short brown hair.

"Just tell me how to get there," she said, looking away from the road for a second to address Ruki.

Ruki nodded. Unable to look at him for very long, Rich checked their progress. Farms obscured visibility on either side of the road, where lines of orchard trees rushed past. Ahead of them, the fuzzy outline of the city was coming into view.

Vincent wasn't distracted with driving like Gina was. He kept his eyes pried on the road behind them, as if the woman who exploded out of the ground was going to chase them down like a T-1000 Terminator.

"That guy in the road... he possessed the dude with the broken neck and the buried lady, didn't he?" Vincent asked.

"Looks like it," Jason said. "I don't know why or how. The only thing I'm sure of is that this... Graverobber... was a friend of Druze and he's pissed at us."

The Graverobber had called Rich 'boy mage'. "What if it was Druze?" Rich asked.

Jason shook his head. "Druze is dead, nothing but a hollow statue."

Rich held his hands out. "This morning I was a statue, now look at me. Why wouldn't something similar work for Druze?"

"Because it wouldn't," Jason said with another contemplative head shake. "You know how impossible it is to remove a spell from a target. Hell, we had a bitch of a time getting it off of you and you weren't even the target... your stone prison was only cost based. No way the spell's broken."

"I don't know," Rich said, "the guy seemed like he knew me."

"Like I said, a friend of Druze," Jason said. "Why assume that devious bastard was keeping quiet about us? I mean, he gave you a mini portal viewing ring. How do we know he didn't put a party line on us for all his friends and minions to watch?"

Jason's words didn't dispel the notion that somehow Druze had escaped his prison. Rich shook his head, but no words came from his lips to join his argument. It was just a gut feeling. Jason, never one to leave a disagreement without proving his point, kept talking.

"Remember Olukent? There was a legion of zombies roaming those caves, not to mention all the bodies Mike's team was making outside the cave. If Druze could body jump, why didn't he do it back in Olukent after you turned him to stone? It's not him."

Jason looked at his best friend. Mel was quiet aside from the occasional yelp as the wagon jostled the broken arm. Lost in worry, Mel's free hand rubbed Mike's back as he lied on his side with his hands covering his face. Jason swore and shook his head with a grimace.

"We gotta figure the Graverobber can't take over living people," he said, "otherwise he could jump into any one of us and make us systematically kill each other off." He shook his head and looked behind the caravan. "You know, we passed him this morning on our way to Bramblefen. You should've seen the look he gave us when we passed. At first I thought he just hated his job and hated us for not having his job, but now I'm sure he was setting up that ambush."

Jason looked at Rich. "He didn't expect you to get free of stone. And he definitely doesn't like it. It's obvious he knows what you did to Druze and wants revenge."

Rich nodded. Jason had a knack for making good sense. Five hundred years is a long time to develop a lot of friendships, and Rich could only imagine what kind of friends Druze had. He cast a glance down the road behind them. Somewhere beyond the thick clouds of dust kicked up by the caravan was someone angry and powerful and murderous. That someone was undoubtedly headed their way.

Gina slowed down from breakneck speeds as she pulled into the city. Still, she went fast enough to cause surprised looks from pedestrian passersby as Ruki pointed at one upcoming turn after another. Rich wasn't sure how she had learned how to manage the strange gears and levers in the driver seat.

Apparently, Jason was at a loss as well. "How does she know how to drive this thing?" he asked Vincent.

"She's a forklift driver," he replied, taking his eyes away from the city of Suusteren to look at Gina depressing a lever as she took another left. "This wagon's probably not that far a stretch from that. Plus she used to race for pinks."

Gina turned down a wide cobbled avenue. Beautifully neat brown brick buildings lined both sides for blocks, following a gentle downhill descent until the city ended at the beach. The crystal blue of the sea stretched to the horizon.

They took this street all the way down. At the beach, Ruki pointed to a building that looked like a megalithic clamshell, halfway open, facing the sea. Built on the edge of the beach where sands met water, seawater submerged some of the shell and lapped against the sides.

Gina steered them there, forcing aian and human beachgoers to rush out of their path. Ruki waved to a man and woman wearing turquoise blue robes who stood outside the shell.

"Oy! Need some aid here," he said as the caravan pulled up.

The two blue robes took a look inside the caravan and called inside the clam. Several turquoise robed attendants streamed out. They carried Runt and Mike and helped Mel inside the clam. Ruki waved away the guy trying to help him and walked inside.

Rich and everyone else who wasn't hurt had to wait in the clam's reception area. Having a beautiful view of the sea while he sat in a room of pebbled floors and driftwood furniture did little to calm Rich. The soothing sound of the water features annoyed him.

He looked at Gina and Vincent. They sat opposite of him and Jason. Vincent's diminutive hands rubbed Gina's back as she looked out at the sea. The clam's enclosed shape cut out any glimpse of Suusteren, giving the impression of the water being the only thing out there.

"How are you guys holding up?" Rich asked. He didn't have to imagine this was a lot to take in. He had been there.

Gina stopped looking at the endless expanse of water to face Rich. Her aian eyes danced in disbelief.

"This is all batshit crazy."

"Without a doubt," Rich said with a nod.

Gina leaned back in her seat, closed her eyes and let out a deep sigh. She didn't move; Rich guessed this was as good a place as any to crash. You kinda needed to... jetlag was nothing compared to getting reality snatched out from under you like a magician's tablecloth.

The way Gina leaned back made her chest pop out with prominence. When girls could custom craft their bosom they never skimped on volume. Rich noticed a red stain on her shirt. Blood. The blood stain grew, spreading slowly across the whole of her chest.

Vincent noticed too. "Gina?" he asked as he shook her gently.

Suddenly, Gina bolted up in her seat, her eyes more catlike than they were aian or human. Her cat ears lay down in a sign of hostility. She bared her teeth, showing huge fangs.

Gina turned on Vincent, sinking her fangs into his neck. Vincent could only look at Rich, eyes wide in shock and horror, as Gina bit through his neck.

As Vincent slumped and his eyes glazed over, Gina turned and snarled at Rich. Her eyes were demonic, her mouth covered in gore.

Before Rich could break the surreal shock he was rooted in, Gina collapsed to the floor. Her eyes stayed open.

"Well, this was fun," Vincent said with a smile on his face and a gaping hole in his neck.

The Graverobber. Now Richard jumped back, knocking over his chair. He called fire to his hands.

The Graverobber casually waved a few fingers and Rich's fire went out. "No need for that, Razzleblad. I just wanted to make a dramatic entrance. Have a seat," he said extended his hand to the upturned chair.

He had called Rich "Razzleblad." Rich looked around the room and saw Jason was missing. A familiar queasiness hit Rich as he returned his attention to the megrym.

"Richard Bates."

Vincent smiled. "There's no fooling you, is there, clever boy," he said pointing a greenish brown finger. "Sit down. It's been so long since we've talked. I've missed you."

Rich brought the chair upright and faced the cost. "You've come to see me way too soon. Don't you have to wait a few hours after I go super mage before making me pay?"

"You're talking about your wild ride to Suusteren? That payment won't come until later and, believe me, I'm working on something especially fiendish. No, I'm afraid this one is about all that fire you played with a while ago in Olukent. You can settle up now that your vacation's over, and..."

Vincent looked down to where Rich was looking. He nudged Gina's head with a boot. Her dead eyes seemed to look at Rich in accusation.

"Is she bothering you?"

Rich was afraid to answer that. He looked up at Vincent, who was looking back like the penultimate host, a host more concerned about his guest than the massive chunk torn from his own neck. Blood dribbled in lazy spurts.

"Uh..."

Vincent held up a hand. "Say no more." He rose, his leather apron streaked with blood trails down the front. He grabbed one of Gina's legs and dragged her like a bag of rocks.

Rich looked as Gina was dragged away, her legs split into an unflattering "V", her eyes locked on him the whole while as her head slid across the floor. Once Vincent got to the end of the waiting room pier, he chucked her like a boomerang. His strength was far beyond megrym sized and she flew thirty feet before splashing into the water.

When he turned back around, Vincent was wearing a face Rich had come to hate, despite it being his own Earthly teenage face.

"There we go," Richard Bates said, sitting back down across from Rich. "Now, where were we?"

Rich pointed to the placid surface of the water where Gina was slowly sinking and at Richard Bates sitting in front of him in Vincent's bloodied apron. "Was all this really necessary?"

"Hey, I'm just showing you what's bound to happen to these two if they keep hanging out with you and yours," Richard Bates said. "I think they need more experience first. You know, level up."

"Thanks," Rich said dryly. "You're being awfully helpful for a guy that seeks my imminent insanity."

Richard Bates winked at him. "Don't get me wrong, your mental health is still one of my chief concerns. I like you Razzleblad, you're one of my favorite playthings. But you're no longer my newest plaything."

Rich didn't like where this was going. There was always a twisted reason behind the things Richard Bates did. Jason didn't appear in this cost because this was about the new pendulum rejects.

"You're going to torture the new gray robe," Rich said.

"And how!" Richard Bates exclaimed, his eyes wide with glee.

The cost leaned in close, like he was confiding in an old friend. "Can you imagine his face when I'm finally able to get at him, and he sees me looking like his old self and demanding payment?"

Richard Bates leaned back and draped an arm across the back of his chair. "Let's just say I'm glad he's embedded in a body that's much younger than yours. I'd hate for his heart to give out, like yours almost did."

Rich stared deadpan at Richard Bates. "You know, you really are a cunt."

"Hey, no one's forcing magic spells to shoot from of your sleeves," he said with a shrug.

Rich had had Rew to guide his power and teach him about the cost. Without that, he didn't know how he would've reacted to Richard Bates' sporadic and horrific visits. He would've thought he was going crazy, which is the last thing anyone needs when they're trapped in this crazy world.

Richard Bates was pointing a finger at Rich, smiling like a fox. "I know what you're thinking, Razzleblad. You're thinking you need to find the new gray robe, tell him all about me and help guide his hand. And yes, you're right. This is what happens if you don't."

At the snap of his fingers, the roof of the clamshell started to burn away to cinder, like so much parchment paper. The roof fell away to reveal a nightmare scene. Under a sky stained orange with fire and smoke, Suusteren's beautiful buildings were broken. Fires plagued one half of the city which belched black, oily smoke into the sky. The other half of the city was under water, with taller buildings jutting out out of the brackish water at haphazard angles. Floating bodies and debris surrounded the submerged, blasted buildings.

"He calls himself Moloch, after an ancient god from your world," Richard Bates said. "And this Moloch, just like the god of his namesake, will come to demand the burning bodies of children as sacrifice. See for yourself."

Rich looked to where Richard Bates pointed. A brown haired man sat on gleaming bone. Small bones—little skulls and legs and ribs—were fused together and dipped in silver to form a sadistic shining throne. The armrests were flat skeletal palms fused into a bridge that reached up in open acceptance.

The man looked with a cruel smile at a colossal statue in front of him. The statue was an effigy of himself, looking imperious in his robes. At the base of the statue a tunnel had been hollowed out and in that hollow tunnel, fires burned.

On the other side of the statue, a line of people stretched to forever. Dirty, miserable, wretched looking people, who clutched wailing children and dragged them a step at a time towards the idol.

Rich's eyes went to the fore of the line, where a woman was a second away from feeding the fire.

"Nooo!" Rich screamed as the woman pushed the child. His scream followed him into the waking world, where Gina jumped back and away from Rich.

"What the hell, man!?" she asked, looking at Rich like he had just lost his mind.

"Don't mind him," Jason said. "He just does that sometimes."

Jason looked at him, his expression wry. "I'm glad you're back, Rich. We may need some crowd control."

Rich couldn't fathom Jason's meaning. He was still busy trying to shake his cost. "Crowd control?" he asked.

Jason pointed with his bone hand toward the door of the clam.

Five blue robes formed a line to bar entry, but a crowd was forming, bigger than it looked like they could handle. Dozens of aians, with droves more coming from the city to the beach. The closest ones waved and shouted at Jason.

"In our rush to get here, I forgot about my anonymity," Jason said. "And these folks wanna meet the Chosen One."

CHAPTER 8
Rockstar Messiah

Melvin didn't care about ensuring a proper arm mend. He wanted to see his brother.

He sat up on the bed which was really more of an altar of yellow sea sponges. The whole room was nothing but sponges of assorted colors, giving the clinic a cave-like appearance. Water fell from the roof sponges and pooled on the floor sponges.

Melvin grimaced as he moved his once broken arm. It hurt like a sprain. The muscles felt stiff and swollen. But he could move it and that was enough.

"I can't sit here any longer." Melvin said, making a move to get off the sponge bed. "You have to take me to the megrym. I need to see him."

The elderly turquoise-robed man smiled warmly but held up his hands to kill Melvin's protests.

"Just as it took both my hands to guide the water and the greater part of my focus to mend your bone, know that his restorative journey will equally require full hands and dedicated minds. Interruptions and distraction will only impede his healing path."

It was a nice way of saying stay out of the surgery room.

Melvin's water treatment had only ended five minutes ago. It entailed the blue robe shaping sea water he called forth from the sponges. The cleric gave the water substantialness like it was silk cloth before he wrapped it around Melvin's broken arm. His chants made the water glow and throb.

The blue robe had cut Melvin's leather sleeve away at the shoulder seam to work his magic. Now he was wrapping gauze around Melvin's arm at the elbow.

It was hard to just sit there.

In a moment, sitting there became impossible. Rich screamed from the waiting room. Melvin got up and rushed to the door, barely hearing the water cleric's protests.

Melvin's first thought was of the Graverobber barging into the water clinic. They were in no condition to fight that bastard again. Ruki seemed alright, but Mike and Runt were probably still being treated. Melvin had barely managed to recover his sword and even in Zhufira mode, he wasn't sure he could manage a fight in his condition.

When Melvin got to the waiting room, he saw a crush of aians outside the door. The blue robes forming a line at the entrance could hardly keep them back. Jason shrugged, a sheepish smile on his face.

It should have been fear on his face. Word didn't take long to travel when the House of Yol had built-in wireless Internet thanks to their hive mind. There was no doubt the High Fane already knew where they were.

"Any ideas?" Rich asked him.

"Only thing I can think of is stall," Melvin said. "Jason, you need to get out of sight. Go check on Mike and Runt, get an idea of when we can leave here."

Melvin pointed at Rich. He tried to point at Gina and Vincent, but they were in a furious discussion of their own.

"Hey!" he cried, waving his hand to get their attention. They both looked up like Melvin was a teacher springing a pop quiz on them.

"You two, Rich and I need to help those blue robes with crowd control."

Gina looked at Melvin like he had asked her to eat roadkill. "Bump that," she said.

"What she means is we appreciate your help earlier," Vincent said, "but we're done."

"Done?" Melvin asked. "What do you mean done?"

"Do you see yourselves?" Vincent asked. "I mean, have any of you taken serious stock? Cause me and Gina have and we're not on board."

"What are you talking about?" Jason asked. "We're kinda awesome."

"Ok, let me see if I can cover it all," Vincent said. "One of you takes random spazz-naps and wakes up with the Big No. Another one is the Chosen One of Prophecy. Half your group is hospitalized. Meanwhile, there's some crazy bodysnatcher dude actively trying to kill you all. He's probably on his way here right now, hell bent on rooting you out in this city. Only he doesn't have to look very hard seeing as how half the town's mobbing like you're rock stars. This about sum it up?"

Jason raised his eyebrow in consideration and conceded a nod. "Sounds pretty summed."

"Yeah," Vincent said. "We're out."

"Nothing personal," Gina said. "But you all are dangerous. We'll find our own way out of this mess."

"Wait," Melvin said, putting his hands up to stop them. "It may seem bad, but trust me, you do not want to go wandering around in this world without support. Tell them guys."

"They should go," Rich said. "We'll wind up getting them killed."

"Seriously?" Melvin asked. He couldn't believe that was all Rich could say on the matter. Melvin looked at Jason for back up. Jason just shrugged his shoulders.

"I got nothing."

Jason looked at Vincent and Gina. "Remember what I told you when Rich was spazz-napping. Find your character triggers. Knowing those will get you out of jams."

Gina nodded and put up the peace sign. "See you all on the other side," she said.

Melvin had no choice but to watch them go. Gina seemed competent, even without the twin daggers that sat on her hips. Melvin didn't know if Vincent had any weapons stowed in that apron of his, but it seemed he had a keen mind on his shoulders.

Gina pushed through blue robes and the throng of aians at the entrance with Vincent following close behind. Melvin was glad they had gotten the opportunity to explain all this a bit before the Graverobber attacked. Gina and Vincent at least knew how they came to be here and how to get back, which was more than Melvin and his gang got when they first arrived. Hopefully soon, they'll find their triggers and their way.

That still left a growing crowd to deal with. Stalling was no longer an option. Melvin looked at his friends, himself freshly tapped on ideas.

"There's only one thing to do," Jason said, smiling. "Give the people what they want."

Jason walked towards the crowd, holding his arms out like he was the living version of the Christ the Redeemer statue in Rio.

"My people!" he yelled. "Your Chosen One is here!"

Any hope the blue robes had of maintaining order crumbled as the crowd cheered. Encouraged by their messiah's words, the aians pushed their way through to Jason. Soon, Melvin could barely see his best friend in the midst of all these people.

"Think he's alright in there?" Rich asked, looking at the teeming crowd from the outskirts.

"He's going to have to be," Melvin said. "You should probably head outside and keep watch for the Graverobber. Let's hope Jason has a way with the masses while I corral everyone."

Melvin followed a couple of distraught blue robes, who led him to Ruki Provos. Apparently, they looked at him as the leader of their band, which had earned him a similar, if smaller, crowd of unhappy water clerics. They surrounded him demanding he restore order, peace and tranquility to their clinic... all things Ruki had no way of providing.

"Why the anger?" Ruki asked. "Ingrates, I should be getting a discount for all the potential customers we brought your way."

Ruki looked a lot better for the water treatment. His eyes were still a bit bruised and puffy, but he no longer suffered from a broken nose and busted lips. He looked at Melvin with relief on his features.

"We should go," he said.

"I was thinking the same thing," Melvin said. "They need to take us to Mike and Runt."

Ruki Provos got nowhere with the blue robes. They gave him the same line about interruptions and distractions impeding the healing path. Instead, they kept steering the conversation to the bedlam in the waiting room and how he needed to quell the mob.

"Look, we'll go and take the crowd with us if you just take us to see Mike and Runt!" Ruki said, his voice full of exasperation.

As if speaking his name summoned him, Runt burst out of a sponge room. He looked healthy, the only indicator of the battle being reddened skin on his face and neck that looked akin to sunburn. A blue robe followed behind the big man, holding up gauze.

"But sir, I need to wrap your head. It's procedure."

"Away with you," Runt said, annoyance furrowing his brow. "Or you will need the gauze yourself."

Runt walked over to Melvin and Ruki and his chattering blue robe entourage. "Mike Ballztowallz," he said.

Ruki Provos looked at some of the blue robes surrounding him. "You can either take us to see the megrym or tell the half-weagr here no."

That opened some doors. Specifically, it opened the door to the sponge room Mike was in. Many of the ceiling and floor sponges had been stretched to reduce light, which filtered in through cracks between sponges. Even with the wan light, Melvin could see what the Graverobber had done to his brother.

"Oh, Mike," he said.

Half of Mike's face looked like sludge, like lava after it had finished flowing and cooled. The eye on that side of his face looked drained of color, a pale ghost of its twin on the other side.

The lips on Mike's good half turned up into a smile.

"It wasn't like I was beating the groupies back with a stick before," he said.

"How do you feel?" Melvin asked.

"Exactly how you supposed to feel after taking an ass whipping. The pain's nothing to that. My boy Runt knows."

Runt nodded. A cold, steady anger burned in his eyes.

None of this was good enough for Melvin. He turned to the blue robe. "Can't you do anything more for him?"

The water cleric shook his head. "I'm afraid we've reached the extent of our healing prowess," he said. "The damage was cruel and extensive. We were fortunate enough to save his eye. He can see, albeit his megrym sensitivity to sunlight has been greatly sharpened."

"Well, how about you get more healers in here?" Melvin asked.

"Mel," Mike said.

Melvin wasn't hearing Mike right now. "You just stop when you get tapped out? Ever hear of teamwork, as in get another robe involved?"

"Mel."

"In fact, how about you get that whole fucking staff you had out there complaining in here and do something goddamn useful?"

"Yo, Mel, chill already," Mike said. "They did what they could. Sometimes when you get an asswhipping you take an asswhipping. It's that simple. Now get over here and help me off this stupid sponge bed."

Melvin's anger melted into worry as he saw his brother struggle to get down. He rushed over and helped set Mike on his feet.

"Least I'm not as ugly as Ruki Provos," Mike said. "That guy scares children."

"Yes, so full of wit," Ruki said scowling. He handed Mike his goggles. "Unlike you, I don't mind having a face only your brother could love."

"If I felt up to it, I'd be whipping your ass right now," Mike said, putting the goggles on. He half smiled, either from the banter or from having the light reduced. Either way, seeing it made Melvin's mood lighten.

"It's time to get out of here," Melvin said. "We've got a huge crowd of townspeople out front. If the Graverobber finds us that's a lot of innocent fodder we'd be feeding him."

Melvin led the way, expecting to have to push his way through a madhouse to get Jason. When he turned the corner, his steps faltered in disbelief.

All the aians were sitting down, mostly cross legged, looking up at Jason as he spoke. All of them were dormouse quiet, their faces rapt. Melvin could see all the way to the entrance, where Rich stood guard. Rich looked back with a smile and shrugged.

Jason spoke like he was a televangelist. "We're living in an exciting age, aren't we? Soon, there'll be twelve houses. Not eleven... twelve! Such an awesome, round number. I know you all feel limited with the choice of houses available. I mean, what if you didn't want to float like a butterfly... what if you wanted to sting like a bee? Now your kids will have an extra option, that's more choices for a fully realized future... and some pretty kickass family reunions."

Jason turned his head and saw the whole gang formed up behind him. He looked out over his people and spoke.

"One more question and then I have to insist that you all leave so I can commune with some Onesource."

A drove of hands shot up. Jason pointed to one hand, a clawed hand of the burrowing house that Melvin still hadn't placed.

"What will the mark of your house be?" the aian asked.

"That is for the Onesource to decide," Jason said. "It could be anything from the mighty jackalope to the majestic invisible pink unicorn. We will know when the time comes, not before."

More hands shot up.

"No one dare question the invisible pink unicorn," Jason said.

All the hands lowered.

"Before you all go, tell me the first rule of the Chosen One," Jason said.

In unison, the aians sitting cried out. "Don't talk about the Chosen One."

"Excellent," Jason said with a wicked grin. "Now, please leave me in an orderly fashion."

The aians obeyed without protest. A little aian girl, unmarked as all small aian children, pointed her finger at Jason when her mother hoisted her up.

"I hope when I grow up I get your mark, Sethrin," she said with a lisp, her eyes dancing with delight.

"How extra special cute!" Jason said with a smile. "And what's your name?"

"Rida," she answered. She smiled back, revealing dimples.

"Maybe you will, Rida," Jason told her. "I'd like that."

Jason whispered to Melvin as he waved to Rida and the rest of the people leaving with smiles on their faces.

"Dude, leading a cult kinda owns."

Jason, standing in the caravan, waved like a prom queen to the aians on the beach as Ruki sped them away. When they finally made the street, Jason pulled his hood up and resumed his anonymous status as best he could. He couldn't stop smiling though.

"Well, now that we got Rich back and everyone's here, I guess it's time to conduct Operation End Odyssey," Melvin said.

"I thought we agreed it was Operation Stealing Home," Jason said.

"Operation Choky Smurf, Operation Whiskey Tango Foxtrot," Mike said from the side of his mouth. He looked battle hardened with his scars and goggles. "Who cares as long as we pull it off?"

Mike was right. Sneaking into the Hierophane and using the Rift Pendulum undetected seemed like a monumental task now that there was nothing left holding them back. Besides thinking of operation names, not much planning had been put into it.

"Wait," Rich asked. "Why are we sneaking into the Hierophane to use the Pendulum?"

"Are some of your brain cells still stuck in stone?" Jason asked. "We failed the Hierophane's mission to trap the Death Null. And the mages tried to kill us for it. That doesn't exactly spell hero's welcome when we show up."

Rich shook his head. "The Hierophant had nothing to do with what Druze tried to do. I can talk to her, you know, get a feel for how we'll be received."

"How?" Jason asked.

Rich tapped the side of his head. "Magic."

"Find out as soon we've got some distance from Suusteren," Mike said. "It'd be nice to know what we're dealing with. If there's no beef with the mage leadership, it'll make for an easy trip back home."

Ruki drove the caravan through Suusteren streets, making his way to the Provos Trading Company. There, they'd prep their packs and get on the road.

"No one tell Uncle we're going to Ardenspar," Ruki said. "He'll try to load the caravan with enough goods to sink a trash barge."

Tavis was his usual cheerful self when they all walked into the store.

"Boy!" he cried, eyeballing Ruki and Rich. "You leave with merchandise and come back with one more bloodsucking security goon? You've got all the business sense of a burnt brick."

"Bah!" Ruki replied with a wave of his hand.

This was the beginning of a back and forth exchange, with Tavis Provos shouting random questions upstairs and Ruki Provos shouting answers back down as he went from room to room packing.

"Boy? You got some aians down here asking about the Chosen One. You hiding inventory from me?"

"Tell them the Chosen One makes housecalls, but only if they have one of our pewter tea sets imported from Kirda!"

"Boy? You got a man and a woman down here willing to pay premium for that mage statue. Where'd you put it?"

"It was a display loaner!"

"Boy, I'm getting swamped down here! Come down and help the lady at the counter. You can count it as a date, but only if you can actually manage to sell something other than a depressing future with you."

"Bah!"

Melvin didn't take too long to pack. He lay his steel bikini out on the bed. He had a strange sense of nostalgia for it. Even though he had to admit the cat suit looked fierce, especially now that he only had one sleeve. Besides, it was getting a bit cold for steel bikinis.

But he had room in his pack. Images of previous adventures with the gang flitted across his mind. What the hell. He stuffed it in.

He was shaken out of his memories by the worst kind of shaking. Earthquake sized shaking, which made the building rock violently. It lasted for what felt like forever. He could hear dishes and other stuff crashing below. He put his pack on and ran downstairs, filing in with everyone else going to investigate.

A massive mound of earth dominated the view of the street from the windows. The dirt had broken through the cobblestones, forming what looked like a volcano.

A lone aian jumped out of the volcano, landing with a flourish at the entrance to the store, his crimson cape billowing in the wind like he had summoned the gust just for that purpose. He stood up and smiled broadly.

Melvin recognized the aian man. He had seen his picture in the Temple of Houses. This wasn't a volcano, it was a massive anthill.

They were face to face with the god Yol.

CHAPTER 9

Yol

M ike had had enough surprises for one day. His face would've shown that if it wasn't numb on one side.

"Yol?" Mike asked as everyone stared at the aian making strides toward the store. He wore a bronze breastplate that shined like a new penny with a red cape attached at the shoulders.

Jason and Mel both nodded in answer to his question. They had filled him in on their adventures getting to Olukent, to include their Interview with the Gods. If all the gods rocked like Yol, they knew how to make an entrance.

"Think he'll go for your Jesus routine?" Mike asked.

"I've been wondering that same thing," Jason replied.

They were about to find out. Yol stepped into the doorway.

"Bring forth your Chosen One so that I may see him!" Yol boomed.

The ant god talked beyond loud, like he was auditioning for the part of a 1960's movie superhero. He stood in the doorway, with his fists on his hips, chest out, ready to save the day. Who does that?

Yol's dancing eyes lit up when he saw Jason. He pointed a gray, meaty finger at the kid. It was intimidating. His forearms were Popeye big from the natural ant armor of his house.

"Ha ha!" Yol started his words with a laugh. "You, boy! Nadi did not jest when he told me your appearance would underwhelm me! Nevertheless, prepare yourself. You are about to receive the greatest honor that I, Yol, can bestow upon a mortal."

Yol said his own name with passion, like it just sounded plain good to him. He raised his fist in the air when he spoke it, stressed the "y" and raised his already loud voice another octave as he rolled through the long "o" with lingering gusto.

Mike couldn't believe this guy was for real, even in fantasy land.

Apparently, Jason didn't know how to react either. "Uh... what honor is that?" he asked.

"The glorious honor of doing battle with I, Yol, the Pillar, the Strength of Will, Champion of the Valorous."

Yol smiled a broad display of perfect teeth, like he was a game show host giving Jason a brand new car instead of a potential ass whipping.

Mike had been inching his hand ever so slowly toward his diskbow. While Yol was in the middle of cheesing and bestowing his greatest honor, Mike popped off a shot.

Yol's armored forearm flashed up, and the disk plinked harmlessly away into a pottery jar.

"Ho ho!" Yol cried. "I like you, little melted twee! You have a warrior's spirit!"

Yol raised his hands up, an emperor making a speech to his people. "You all are invited to share in Cephrin's glorious moment! There is nothing dishonorable to added numbers or sneak attacks. Remember, you fight a god!"

"Excuse me," an unfamiliar voice said behind the gang. They turned and saw a small woman, her hand raised and shaking in the air.

"Can I go?" she asked. "I'm merely a customer."

"If you stay, you would rise above the appellation of mere customer," Yol said. "You would be forever remembered in the paint of my murals, the poetic verse of my epics! Here's your chance to be one of the many who stood with a false god and met their collective demise by the Strength of Will!"

Yol finished with a shake of his fist as he said "will." His "can do" nature almost made you want to jump on board. He'd be a natural if he was selling anything other than an untimely death by his hand.

The customer shook her head rapidly. "No, I just want to go home," she said.

Yol grimaced and then turned to the side with a flourish of cape, allowing the customer to scurry-run past him and out of the store.

"Whatever this guy's on," Jason whispered to Mel, "it's the cure for low self-esteem."

"Dude," Mel whispered back, worry all over his face. "How are we going to beat him?"

Mel had a point. He clearly wasn't in Zhufira mode and even if he was, they had already had a pretty grueling day between Bramblefen, the Graver-obber, and the water clinic. Wasn't that enough for one morning?

Yol pointed fingers at Mel and Jason. "Now is not the time for hushed mumblings. It is the time for loud, brazen battle cries!"

"Wait! Wait! Not yet," a voice said behind Mike. Mike turned and recognized him as the dude who had come in earlier, the one who had been digging Statue Rich.

"I'd like to request leave as well. I have no affiliation with any of these people, false gods or otherwise," he said.

Yol, visibly upset by the dwindling numbers, glowered. He held up his arm toward the door. Before the man left, he turned to face Tavis Provos, who had been behind the counter and glowering himself this whole time.

"May I inquire about the status of the mage statue?" the man asked.

"LEAVE!" Yol bellowed. His voice made the man jump like it was a cattle prod to his ass. He ran, probably faster than he imagined he could ever run before.

"Is there anyone else here who doesn't want the glorious honor of battle with Yol, the Pillar, Master of the Sixth House?" he asked in a boom.

Jason raised his bone hand.

"What?" Yol asked with disbelief. "What kind of sniveling false god are you?"

"It's the same thing I told the High Fane," Jason said. "I wasn't making any claims to be the Chosen One. I'm just trying to mind my own business."

Yol's brow furrowed. "You should have thought about your business before you had the audacity to conduct it without a mark!" he roared.

The god kneeled and punched the ground. An earthquake rumbled out. Everyone rocked from the shockwaves. Pottery and dishes fell off shelves. Hell, the shelves themselves fell over. A cloud of dust mushroomed up.

"The last false Chosen One, Denaldus, now that was a fight," Yol said rising. "It lasted four hours and destroyed half the town of Golreyer. Even after three hundred years, the songs they sing of that day still stir my breast."

Yol looked at Jason with sadness in his eyes.

"You disappoint me greatly, Cephrin," he said. "Not only are you easily half Denaldus's size and missing swaths of meat on your arm, but you do not even rise to the honor I came personally to present you."

"What do you want me to say to that?" Jason asked with a shrug. "I'm not the one who sold you on how awesome this moment would be."

"Bah!" Yol waved his hand. "Everyone knows the prophecies. The Chosen One is foretold to best any god who challenges his claims. The very least you could do is act in accordance with the prophecy."

"Sorry, Yol, it's just that it's already been a long day," Jason said. "We've been rumbling all morning, with like zero break. I mean, we haven't even had lunch yet. We're not gods like you, we need food and sleep."

The ant god looked at Jason with disdain heavy on his face. "Your ignorance is almost as appalling as your cowardice," Yol said. "Gods require both sustenance and rest. Yet I tunneled here ceaselessly when I got word of your appearance. My tiredness is great, yet you don't see the mighty Yol making excuses, do you?"

Yol shook his head. "This is sad, but no matter. They will still sing songs of how the Strength of Will rooted out Cephrin the False and took him and his wayward followers back to the Temple of Houses to meet justice!" Half a smile returned to his face as spoke. Maybe he was thinking of what the song lyrics would be.

"Sure, I'll go," Jason said. He held one hand up to silence the protest starting from his friends.

"I'll never be able to beat Yol," he said. With the other hand, the bone one, he reached behind his back and pulled his dismembered arm out of its quiver.

He walked slowly through the debris of the Provos Trading Company, holding the arm aloft with both hands. Anyone in his path instinctively stepped aside and gave him a wide berth. He placed the arm gingerly on a countertop and turned to face Yol.

"Alright," Jason said. "Let's go."

Yol raised an eyebrow. "What are you doing?"

"That stupid symbol of power's only gotten me in trouble," Jason said. "I'm leaving it here."

Yol laughed a deep, throaty guffaw. "Incredulous! How is a cleft arm a symbol of power?"

"That's how all this Chosen One business kept perpetuating," Jason said. "The ones who claimed I was chosen said the Onesource blessed my severed arm. They said only I was strong enough to hold it. I've been carrying it around, attracting attention. I think it's true what they say. But it wasn't worth it... it brought you down on my head. So I'm done with it."

Jason took a few steps towards Yol but the ant god threw a hand up to stop him.

"You do not understand the nature of the god before you, Cephrin," Yol said. "I do not just destroy false gods, I destroy all belief in them as well."

Yol strode over to the counter and grabbed Jason's severed arm by the hand. He turned it over one way then the next, appraising the severed appendage with a skeptically raised eyebrow as if the reason it was revered as a symbol would jump out at him. Finally, Yol hoisted Jason's arm in the air as if it was a victory celebration.

"Behold, errant mortals! Yol destroys all unworthy claims! Let no one hold stock in this false one's symbol of pow..."

Yol fell back, stumbling, and landed on the floor with a crash of trade goods. After the dust cleared, he looked peaceful as he snored loudly. He still gripped the sleep-inducing arm in a handshake.

Jason looked at Mel and Rich.

"Can we keep him?"

Mel exhaled bated breath. "I didn't think it was going to work. I mean, he got off like three sentences before it hit him."

"I wasn't sure either," Jason replied. "But he said he needs sleep, so I figured my arm may just be what the doctor orders in a world without Tylenol PM."

"Aight," Mike said. "Time to pop smoke. We definitely don't want to see how long he'll stay this way. Knowing our luck, he'll come to just as the Graverobber's stepping through the door."

The Graverobber could come any moment. It wasn't like they'd be hard to find with a giant anthill in the front of the store.

Jason took a second to retrieve his sleep arm. They all ran between top-pled shelves and fallen trade goods to the back of the store, where the caravan was parked. Ruki turned and waved to his uncle but never broke his stride.

"I have to run, Uncle. I'll pay for the damages, swear to it."

If looks could kill, Ruki Provos would've been a dead man.

"You think your uncle's gonna be aight in there with Bug Hercules?" Mike asked as they all loaded up into the caravan.

"I don't know," Ruki said, pulling gears and pushing levers. "I just know no creature damned or sanctified could compel him to leave."

No sooner did Ruki get the engine started did a giant roar erupt within the Provos Trading Company. The voice shook the caravan.

"Cowards!" it shouted.

If that was an accusation, Ruki didn't mind proving Yol right. He put the caravan in drive and tried to make tracks as fast as he could from the store. Mike looked behind them for signs of pursuit.

There was one sign. Tavis Provos was running at track star speeds for them. He may have been running for rescue, but he still had that murderous look on his face.

"Yo, your uncle, man!" Mike told Ruki. He didn't stop the caravan, just slowed it. Even then, he only slowed it enough to where you really had to want a ride to catch them.

Runt stuck out his hand and grabbed the running tradesman, hauling him aboard. Just as soon as Tavis Provos landed on board, the caravan lurched with repressed speed down the street.

A shock wave rolled out from the store, making the building and the two on either side of it collapse inward like someone stole the foundation.

Ruki turned the corner. That was the last they saw of the Provos Trading Company.

CHAPTER 10

1,000 Destriers

Rew Majora had to remember her diplomatic smile as she looked at the King of Runember in the communication mirror. Even the thought of asking this chauvinist ham-head for help made her smolder, let alone the deed.

"If you had a proper king up there, you wouldn't need a king's army, now would you, lass?" King Edge Runember asked, a smug grin behind his scraggly brown beard.

"Perhaps not," Rew said with a tight smile. "But then the free states of the Merkez wouldn't be free, would they?"

"Pah! Freedom's overrated," King Runember said with a dismissive hand wave. "One only has to look at the people of Runember to see that. Here, they love their king."

Rew wanted to say the people of Runember hadn't loved their king since the days of Edge's grandfather, Maris Runember. Instead, she kept the smile, which felt frozen in place, and remembered her tact in diplomacy.

"I'm sure they love their king, just as the free peoples here enjoy their autonomy. The Holy Aian Empire threatens that autonomy, and, if left unchecked, will tip the balance of power should they decide to continue their expansionist agenda. Do you really relish the idea of the eleven houses marching towards your doorstep?"

"Ha! Let the ash-skins come," Edge Runember said. "Do you think one such as I have anything to fear from those beast men?"

Edge was a strongman, as was his father Brenden. It was the biggest reason why their people held more love for Maris Runember than both Edge and Brenden put together. Sending two generations of a nation's youth off to die in unnecessary wars with Goshen and the Land of Nod would do that to a country.

But that was also a ranking reason why Rew wanted Edge's help. Those wars had produced veteran soldiers, a needed commodity against the looming aian force. It was reason enough to keep her smile and diplomatic flattery.

"I'm sure you fear nothing, King Runember, from aian and man alike. Likewise, I'm sure the men under your command are equally fearless. Now, how many of them can you spare for this noble endeavor?"

"You've quite the nerve, don't you, lass?" he asked with a grunt. "Tell me, what will your tower of frocks do to repay the nation of Runember?"

Rew swallowed the urge to tell this spoiled, middle-aged boy she was no lass. She was old enough to remember a real king of Runember. Maris would have been wise enough to realize the import of this threat, kind enough to send more units than Rew would've asked for, and charming enough to do it all with a winning smile on his face.

"We'll do what we've always done, King Runember," Rew said. "Your nation will continue to enjoy the free trade environment the Hierophane provides. The bulk of your war steel comes from caravans here. Likewise, when was the last time Runember sought the help of quest-mages and we did not answer?"

"Ha!" the king spat, "You ask for the bravest men in the world, and all you're willing to do is what you've always done? Only a woman would so undervalue the strength of Runembrian men!"

Rew had had enough.

"The Hierophane will defeat this threat, Edge Runember, with or without your help. If it's without your aid, we will remember what our friendship meant to you. This lass has a long memory. I'll give you a day to decide."

She snapped her fingers and killed the mirror-link spell. The link flickered and died just before King Runember's undoubtedly arrogant response.

"Arrgh!" Rew roared at her own reflection. She was glad the mirrors could only carry image and sound. The temptation to hurl a fireball through it and roast that pig would have been too great to ignore.

She went over to the other end of her office, where a decorative map hung on the wall. Her eyes roamed over the human kingdoms of the south. It was expansive territory. Such a waste.

These lands were ever renaming themselves as the kings perpetually conquered, treatied and subjugated one another. Some kingdoms lay small and fractured, scarcely as big as the High Veldt. Others stretched wide from one ocean coast to another.

Rew had seen this map change so many times in her lifetime. Unless she got more firm promises for aid, it would likely change again. Out of the four kings she had talked to this morning, only Drumayjin of Kirda had guaranteed men to bolster the tower.

"Hierophant," Brigitte's voice said. Rew turned to face her security chief.

"I have grim news," Brigitte said. "Breunan, keeper of the Nasreddin Mage Delegation Tower, reports the aian Chosen One was seen in Suusteren. The High Fane has sent the Armsguard on destriers to seize him."

"How many Armsguardsmen?" Rew asked.

"Breunan reports one thousand."

"What?!" Rew cried. This was madness. The fact that the Armsguard rode outside the border of the High Veldt already broke two agreements. One thousand Armsguardsmen on those giant warhorses was a slap in the face to every covenant with the Free States.

Rew stormed over to the mirror. She spoke the words for a spell link between her mirror and the official reception mirror in the High Fane. Her reflection shimmered for long moments until Rew stood face to face with Ananna. Behind the Queen of Spiders, the temple's mountain waterfalls fell in a brilliant cascade of spray.

"Lady Ananna, I have reports that the Temple of Houses sent a thousand Armsguardsmen beyond the border of the High Veldt."

"Your reports are accurate," Ananna said coolly. "Our action is warranted, backed by intelligence from the House of Yol."

"Warranted?" Rew asked in disbelief. "Sending one thousand warriors of your Armsguard through free lands is impossible to warrant. Our foremost governing doctrine will not abide standing armies in this region."

"That is your governing doctrine, Majora, not the Temple's," Ananna said. Her spider locks curled tightly around her face. "Besides, those thousand are a drop in a bucket compared to the full force of the eleven houses. I would hardly call them an army."

"I have no patience to consider what you would call them," Rew said. "I call them breaking the Free States Convention, the Rule of Peace and the Merkez Doctrine. Call them back."

"My my, child," Ananna said, a smile creeping up across her lips. "And here I thought your long-enduring years had taught you to not saunter into someone's home and make demands."

"This is invasion," Rew replied. She wasn't smiling. Her words smoldered with cold anger. "It will not stand. Call them back."

Ananna's tendrils shot out, as if the spider was raised up and hissing. "Call them back to what end? To watch your tower do nothing? How many mages have you dispatched to Suusteren to capture these renegades?"

The Queen of Spiders gave Rew no time to answer. Her spider tendrils lost their tension and fell to frame her youthful face. Her words matched Rew's in their cold, measured anger.

"We will not stand idle. I give a damn about your doctrines. And you had better mind how you speak to me, Rew Majora."

A silent moment stretched as Rew glared at Ananna. When she spoke again, her tone was flat, decisive.

"I know how I speak to you, Ananna. Trust what I have said and what I will say to be fully weighed. Call the Armsguard back home. Or I will send them home."

Ananna looked back at Rew, her composure regal, her eyes impassive.

"I, like you, take neither threats nor orders from anyone." Ananna turned her back to the mirror and walked away.

Rew snapped the mirror-link off. She looked at her own reflection. Behind her, Brigitte stood, concern etched into her features.

Rew turned to face the destruction mage. Wordlessly, she beckoned Brigitte to her with a finger as she walked back to the wall map. Brigitte dutifully followed and looked where Rew's finger rested on the map, to the East, on the city of Nasreddin.

"When did Breunan report seeing the Armsguard leave?" Rew asked.

"Less than thirty minutes ago," Brigitte replied. "I came directly to you once I received his full report."

"Destriers can cover an unbelievable amount of ground," Rew said, mostly to herself as she looked over the map. "They'll likely stop for only short periods, more rest for saddle hardened soldiers than for the horses themselves."

Rew drew her finger from Nasreddin through the High Veldt and beyond, into the grasslands of the Merkez. As her finger moved, Rew imagined a thousand destriers at a hard gallop and translated their speed to distance covered on the map.

"I imagine they will treat this mission as a cavalry rush," Rew spoke more to the map than anyone else while her finger traced the route. "This means the Armsguard will take a ten minute break every hour and feed their horses rusk," she said, referring to the enchanted bread the Fane used to restore stamina.

It was difficult and costly to make, but Rew counted on them sparing no expense to get to Jason quickly. A destrier on rusk could run all day and well into the night before its body demanded rest.

Rew's fingers fell over the rockier country of Central Anadol. This would be where they would make camp for the night. Her finger stood one third of the way to the coastal city of Suusteren.

It was a good place for ambush, but not optimal. There was good reason why an aian warrior camp was called "a living fortress". Well dug trenches and traps thanks to the mole house of Zemishirus, invisible wardens of the chameleon house of Sen, aerial reconnaissance from the houses of Demir and Eula, and every inch of the camp in constant communication because of the house of Yol.

Rew's eyes flickered further West. She saw the perfect place, half a day's ride from where she had anticipated the Armsguard to camp. She put her finger on Dreft Esker.

"Define our need to the Rift Pendulum," Rew told Brigitte. "Tomorrow, midday we need pendulum heroes at Dreft Esker to rout the Armsguard. I want the maximum."

There were limits to the power of the Rift Pendulum. It could only call into the world one hundred pendulum heroes at any given time. Any more beyond that and the heroes would be unreliable. Their weapons and spells could pass harmlessly through foes as if they were made of smoke or whole groups of heroes could disappear mere minutes after being summoned.

"Twenty-five full groups, tasked to rout the contingent of Fane Arms-guard along Dreft Esker," Brigitte said, summarizing her orders back to Rew. "Are you sure they will pass along the esker, Hierophant?"

Rew looked at the wave-like curve of Dreft Esker on the map. The esker, like all eskers, was a raised ridge of stratified rock. And Dreft Esker was huge, easily able to accommodate the aian warhorses at ten abreast. The valleys on either side of the esker were home to inhospitable ground—rocky, uneven and pocketed throughout with sporadic trees and deep plunges.

"I'm sure," Rew replied. Dreft Esker ran through rough country like a raised natural highway. It was the only choice for anyone who valued expediency.

Brigitte nodded. "Then it will be done as you specified."

The security chief turned to go but a question lingered in Rew's mind.

"Brigitte?"

"Yes, Hierophant?" the black robe asked, turning to face Rew.

"I recall telling you earlier to pull the mage delegation from Nasreddin. Why is Breunan still there to report the temple's movements?"

"I modified your order, Hierophant," Brigitte answered. "The rest of the mage delegation is safely away but I asked Breunan if he would stay on in Nasreddin. The added value of his intelligence potential seemed necessary in this time of crisis."

Unlike a subordinate afraid of being discovered breeching protocol, Brigitte spoke like an equal. She was full of confidence, seemingly unafraid of how Rew may react to her words. Rew's reaction was to raise an eyebrow in surprise of her acting security chief.

"Kindly notify me the next time you would like to modify my instructions," Rew told her.

"Certainly, Hierophant," Brigitte said with a curt nod. "It's just your concerns are bigger in nature. I didn't see the need to worry you with trifling details. Not when I'm here to handle the minutiae. Leaving Breunan in Nasreddin was a matter of regional security, and I am acting security chief after all."

"So you are," Rew said, returning Brigitte's nod. Rew couldn't help but smile at Brigitte. The black robe was proving to be especially competent and reliable.

Brigitte bowed her head and departed. Druze had chosen the girl among all other black robes to be his second in command. It seemed a wise choice.

Still, Rew missed her father. Living several lifetimes had a way of muting the immediacy of now. He could be gone for another two years and then show up one day like he'd only missed a few days. She hoped when he finally came back there'd still be a Hierophane standing to come back to.

Rew set about preparing for another mirror link with her fifth king of the day. King Hiru from the Land of Nod seemed a slim possibility, but his archers were fiercely respected enough to warrant her trying. She went over to the mirror.

Rew stopped in her tracks. A voice she hadn't heard in what felt like forever was buzzing in her head, asking for permission to scry. Her heart skipped a beat, and all thoughts of King Hiru dissipated as she sat down to grant the request.

CHAPTER 11

1,000 Excuses

Rich had thought of this moment, the heartfelt reunion with Rew Majora, a dozen times since getting free of stone. Of all the visions he entertained, the hot seat he was getting now hadn't made any of those versions.

"So," Rew said as she paced through her Hierophane office, "moments before you fight a being that has complete control over death itself, you decide to fall off the world for a whole week." Rew stopped her pacing and put her hands on her hips. Glowering, seething, she silently waited for Rich to answer.

"Um..." Rich began.

"Do you have any idea how beside myself I was?!"

"But..."

"You don't do that, Rich!" she cried, cutting him off. "You don't cut your scry abruptly and then go missing moments before a life and death battle. What insane world do you come from where this is seen as acceptable?!"

Now Rew was quiet. She just stared at Rich, as if she seriously expected an answer to that last question. Only Rich didn't know how to answer that question. Hell, he didn't know if answering it would even help.

Inexplicably, an image of his dad and one of his many arguments with mom, before the divorce, came to mind. "You're right, I should have called... er, um... scryed," Rich said.

"Yes, you should have," Rew said. They shared a moment of silence. She looked at him with a softer expression, her eyes rimmed with concern. "I was worrying myself ill about you. I was starting to think you fell to the death creature."

"What? And be the only gray robe in the zombie army? I was way overdressed for that, Rew."

Rew smiled. Finally. Rich thought he was never going to get back on her good side.

"Where are you?" she asked, scrunching her nose up as she looked at the blurry background behind him.

Rich knew they were headed toward the Hierophane. The actual path to the mage tower he wasn't clear on or concerned with. Rich guessed it showed in his scry. The only objects that showed up cleanly in his side of the scry was the caravan wagon and his customary bowl of water. The conjured bowl was a totally unnecessary one which stemmed from his first scry with Rew, back when he thought scrys were two people looking at one another through bowls of water. But even after she had demystified the process, he still brought the bowl along as his trademark. Behind the caravan, the trees blurred. It was akin to motion blur but weirder, more like the distortion grew on the leaves themselves—where the trees would look this way even if the caravan wasn't moving.

Funny the things you learn on the go. Rew had told him scry was a form of sleep. Rich guessed his mind was doing its best to reconstruct an area that he hadn't paid much attention to and was in the process of speeding past when he began the scry. Meanwhile, aside from the glut of papers on Rew's desk, the Hierophane looked the same as always.

"I'm not quite sure where we are," Rich said as he looked at the eerie blur-trees, which kept their same blur despite changes in caravan speed.

"But you're headed here, yes?" she asked. "To return home?"

"Uh... yes," Rich said, unsure how their return to the Hierophane would be received once Rew found out he had let the Death Null go and killed Druze. "Is that all right?"

"Of course, how else are you going to return home, silly?" she said.

"Well, there's some things you may not li—"

"Wait, don't say a word," Rew said shaking her head. "Not another word about anything else. I want you to close your eyes and think about yourself. Concentrate. Tell me the word that you arrive at."

"Why?"

"Shhh! Just say the word."

Rich wasn't a fan of doing things in ignorance, but he figured protesting would just make her angry again. So he closed his eyes and thought about himself.

He saw the crazy path that got them there, the weight on his shoulders, how everyone had gone so far out of the way to save him. He saw Richard Bates and the burden of the cost. The word came natural.

"*Zorbela*," Rich said. He didn't even know what it meant.

Rew seemed to know. She nodded acceptance. "This is your attunement word for scrying," she said. "Now I don't have to wait on the edge of my sanity for who knows how long to hear from you."

"I don't think you have to worry about that kind of thing anymore," Rich told her. "Last week I was in a bit of a hard spot."

"Was it the death creature?" Rew asked. A new batch of worries advertised their arrival on her features. "You did capture it, yes?"

"No," Rich said. This time he held up his hand, keeping her from cutting him off. "I let it go home, which was the right thing to do. You could have told me the creature you sent me out to cage was a traveler from another world that got stuck here."

Confusion danced across her face. "I didn't know," she said.

So that bastard Druze hadn't lied about Rew's innocence of the Death Null. "You would think Druze would've told you after three hundred and fifty years," Rich said. "I was here less than a week and he told me."

Rew eyes grew wide at the mention of Druze. "You've seen him?" she asked.

"Seen that asshole?" Rich asked with a smile. "More than that..."

"Mind your tongue, Rich," Rew said scowling. "Name calling does not become you. And I won't stand for it. That's my father you disrespect."

"Your..." Rich began, his smile eroding as he found himself treading in water he hadn't imagined could exist.

"Father?" he asked for lack of anything else to say. His mind couldn't work around it, process it, fathom it. He had an easier time seeing Mel and Mike as brothers despite race and gender issues. How'd that maggot of a man manage to have Rew for a daughter?

"Yes, father," Rew said, a hint of indignation in her voice. "You said you've seen him?"

"Seen him, I killed him," Rich thought. How do you tell a woman you care for that you killed her father?

"Um... what?" Rich asked.

"You said you saw my father," Rew repeated. "You said you've more than seen him."

Crap. No images of his dad popped into Rich's head. Dad probably never had to tell mom that he took a road trip and killed her father along the way... sorry about that.

Rew was looking at him, expecting an answer. What answer? He was drawing blanks. Any answer, just not the truth. Nothing came to him, much less something plausible.

He had to be looking suspicious by now. What would dad do? Rich didn't know. He just started talking, which might have been the same thing his dad would've done.

"Yes!" Rich said, before pausing to clear a throat which didn't need clearing. "I said I more than saw him and I did. That's because he... helped me! I did more than saw him, I got help from him."

"What manner of help?" Rew asked.

Rich didn't know if she was being shrewdly skeptical, innocently curious, or if the question was just instinctual. All he knew was he felt transparent right now.

"Druze, um, helped me with... the... Death Null," Rich said. "He talked to me through the ring he gave me. You remember that ring don't you?"

Rich didn't care if she remembered the ring or not, he just didn't want to face any more of her questions. Better to have her answer his.

"Yes, I remember," Rew said. "He told you the ring would reduce the cost. I knew that was a lie. But I reasoned he said it to bolster your confidence."

"There was much more to the ring than a confidence booster."

"So what did he say?"

"Oh, just words to live by. It got the Death Null back home," Rich said with a smile. The smile was hollow. Lying to Rew, looking at her with his face full of phony smiles, it made him feel like a crumb under the oven.

"I should probably go," Rich said, looking back at his stop-motion trees. "I don't know what's out there. I'll scry again when we stop. When it's safe."

"You had better," Rew said, giving Rich a warm smile. "I know your attunement. Don't make me come after you."

Rich didn't know if the emphatic voice in his head came from an angel on his shoulder, a devil, or Richard Bates tormenting him. The feeling gnawing at him was murky at best. The words were clear though.

Dude, you killed her father. You can't leave and not tell her.

But that's exactly what he did, managing a sickly smile at her as he waved goodbye and killed the scry. He just couldn't bring himself to say it.

His own father was often a jerk, full of excuses and broken promises. It was one of the reasons Rich's mom got the divorce. Still, despite the pain and trouble that man had caused, all the tears mom had cried when she thought Rich wasn't around to see, Rich still wouldn't have wanted somebody to kill him.

Rich opened his eyes and saw that the landscape had changed slightly. There were fewer trees dotting hilly grasslands, giving the afternoon sky an expansive openness all around them. Jason smiled and nodded at him.

"Glad to see you're back without all the screaming," he said.

"That wasn't the cost," Rich told him. "I was talking to Rew. She said it's cool to use the Pendulum and go home."

"Cool, definitely beats trying to ninja," Jason said. His lips curled up into a wry grin and his eyes danced more than usual. "You wanna know how you look when you take your spazz naps and conferences? Check out Slumberstilskin." He pointed a bone finger at Tavis Provos.

If Rich didn't know better, he would've thought the tradesman was dead. Tavis Provos lay in a near fetal position near the back of the caravan, his body rocking in gentle sync with the bumps on the road. His eyes were not fully closed, giving Rich a faint glimpse of exposed, unmoving eyeballs. A trickle of drool oozed out of his mouth and glistened on his chin.

"Do I really look like that?" Rich asked. Tavis' not-quite-there, slumber-of-the-homeless-man vibe was disturbing. If this was what it looked like to onlookers, Rich was glad he always scryed in semi-secret.

Jason nodded. "What's up with you geriatrics and your nap attacks?" Jason asked. He crossed his arms and slouched down in his seat. "It was bad enough dragging you around with your wheezing and shuddering. Now we got this guy and his brittle bones to worry about. And he's not just faking at old, he's like a career geezer."

Rich didn't pay any attention to Jason's harassment campaign. Jason must've been bored. Sure enough, Rich noticed Mel up front, where Ruki was trying to show her how to drive the caravan and Mike and Runt were both catching naps on separate benches. Jason was always the type to get bored by himself.

From the front, Mel said something to Ruki before turning over the driver's seat and darting to the back where Rich and Jason were.

"Don't listen to Jason, Rich," she said. "He's terrible at giving props, can't admit how well you cleaned up after that shave and haircut. He knows good and well you look far from geezer status."

Jason shrugged. "Can't exactly rib a guy by calling him an attendee at the Handsome Boy Modeling School."

Rich's brow furrowed. "Isn't that a band?"

Jason looked up at Mel. "Did you want something other than to swoon over Rich? How many boyfriends does a warrior girl need?"

Mel put her hand on her hip. "Funny. I just wanted to see if anyone else wanted to drive the caravan. It's a little complicated but kinda fun once you get started."

Rich nodded. "Maybe in a minute."

Mel smiled warmly, her eyes dancing as she looked at him. "See you in a bit," she replied before heading back up.

Jason leaned over to Rich, bouncing aian eyes gleaming like knives. "You know going up there to get driving lessons makes you a major cockblock in the eyes of one Ruki Provos," he said.

"You have any idea how long it'll take us to get to the Hierophane?" Rich asked. Might as well put Jason's overly active mind to good use.

"Two days. Maybe three," Jason said, eyes studying the horizon as if he could actually see the towers in the distance. Maybe his eyes could. "We're taking the direct approach..."

Jason's words trailed off as something in the back of the caravan got his attention. Not something... someone. Tavis was awake, glowering at the two of them.

"Rest well, Tavis?" Jason asked.

No words came from Tavis, just baleful stares with his pitchfork malice eyes.

Rich hadn't had the pleasure of knowing Tavis in the time he had spent in his stone prison. He leaned over to Jason and whispered. "Um... is he always like this?"

Jason smiled at Tavis and nodded as he whispered his response through clenched teeth. "He was always a bit on the vinegar side. I imagine it's exponentially worse now that he's seen his business collapse due to ant god earthquake." Jason finished by waving to Tavis. "Glad to see you're in a good mood."

Tavis cut his eyes even more, as if he was trying to develop laser vision.

"Like I was saying," Jason said, looking at Rich, "a couple days, direct approach. Then back through to the burbs, where you'll have no more crazy gods, crazy spells, crazy world."

Being back in the burbs sounded like heaven. So why'd the thought carry such guilt? Rich thought about crazy spells in a crazy world. His mind went to an errant, gray-robed reject running around unchecked in the world.

"Dude, do you think it's OK leaving like this? I mean, the Rift Pendulum just spit out another gray robe. Shouldn't we, I don't know, try to rein him in? What if he goes crazy?"

Jason scrunched his nose up like he smelled something ripe. "That fits distinctly into the category of not our problem. In fact, that sounds like the Hierophane's problem, the same Hierophane that employed us to chase down their premium supply of infinite life. We've done enough crap quests for them. It's their pendulum; they need to fix it when it breaks."

Rich nodded, mostly to himself. Like always, Jason made sense. Maybe it was just the suddenness of everything. A week had gone past for everyone to come to terms with their agenda. For him, it had only been a day since they had gone from their initial goal of saving the world from the Death Null to heading back to the Hierophane and using the Rift Pendulum. They were leaving in their wake a dead former Hierophant and a loose gray robe they had let get away. Neither one of those facts contributed to a feel-good ending for the storybooks.

Yes, maybe it was the suddenness of everything. Or maybe it was Rew, whose face Rich imagined when she finally learned the news about her father.

He wouldn't be there to comfort her or break the news even... no, he was going to scurry home to his television and cans of Mountain Dew and leave her to deal with the loss of her father, the one constant she's had for over three hundred years.

Tavis Provos inadvertently brought Rich out of his self loathing. The tradesman's V-neck shirt got Rich's attention. Near Tavis' heart the white fabric gave way to a red, blotchy stain.

"Is that blood?" Rich asked. He pointed at the stain.

"Of course it's blood," Tavis spat. "What else would it be?" he asked, eyeing Rich with distaste. "Think it was easy, getting away from the vengeful god you left in my store?"

"Sorry," Rich said. "If it's bothering you, I can cast a heal on it, take some of the sting out of it."

"Last thing I want is some of your rubbish magic," Tavis said. "I just want you all out of my life. For good."

With that, Tavis rose and made his way to the front of the caravan, where Ruki and Mel were both laughing as they drove the tank train together.

"You're quite done with your tutorial services," Tavis told Ruki Provos. "I'm driving."

Ruki smile dissolved. "Are you... sure, Uncle? I've never seen you drive one of these."

"I've been around more than you think," Tavis said. "And this is possibly the last fragment of my trading company. I'm not about to trust you with it. Now move."

Ruki nodded and got up for the old man. Tavis sat and in the space of a few choice lever pulls, the tank train lurched with newfound speed.

"See?" Jason asked. "We're not the only ones who think we've overstayed our welcome."

Rich didn't know how Jason could smile about it. Personally, he was starting to feel everywhere they went destruction followed.

CHAPTER 12
Status of Friends

Melvin's mind was made up. He was going to give up the drawers, chain-mail steel as they may be, to Rich.

It wasn't a decision he came to lightly. After all, it was a girl's first time, or a boy's first time in a girl's more experienced body. But seeing as they would soon be back in their original skins, it was kind of a once-in-a-lifetime opportunity. Why shouldn't he take it?

The quiet time on the road helped settle the matter. There was promise on the road, a promise in the air as everyone either enjoyed light naps or mirthful conversation under the afternoon sun. Stirred by a cool autumn breeze, the promise spoke of a well-earned ticket home, and soon thanks to Hierophant Majora's hassle free acceptance. No sounds of pursuit threatened to ruin it.

If he was going to ever act on wild impulses, he'd have to act now.

Well, not right now. The trick was getting Rich alone, which was impossible on a moving caravan full of people. Half the party was pre-occupied. Runt napped. Mike looked over the landscape, his eyes safely hidden behind blue-tinted goggles. He sharpened the blades of his disk shooter, the scrape of steel on sharpening stone adding punctuation and rhythm to a conversation he didn't bother joining. Tavis Provos drove silently, keeping all the negative energy in the caravan up front with him as he steered in a world all his own.

Melvin sat in the middle of the conversation, only halfway listening as he pondered things of a more personal nature. Jason and Ruki were both talkative people, so they didn't miss Melvin's input. They chattered about geography and myths and rumors of monsters that roamed in various corners of the land. Right now Jason talked about the misafir, a cult of humans who legend says grew envious of the aian animal houses and contrived a way to gain animal skills themselves.

"They say the misafir's dark descent into witchcraft and the ritual consumption of aian flesh twisted them all up," Jason said, his eyes dancing with delight. "It turned them into these weird animals with human faces, still hungry for aian flesh."

Melvin wondered how his best friend would react if he knew. If anything, Jason was the one who had convinced Melvin to go for it. He had talked about how great it was, skipping the worst parts of growing up to inhabit beautiful bodies. The thought had marinated in Melvin's mind. Now Melvin realized when they finally got back to their real bodies, he'd have nothing to show for his time as Zhufira. He'd lose his sword skills and he'd still be a virgin.

"That's only one of the legends," Ruki chimed in. "Sure, everyone's heard of the misafir with human faces on animal bodies. But then there are the ones they say have human bodies with animal faces. They eat human flesh, trying to get back to the way they were. And still other legends talk about the hidden misafir, the ones that look like men but can become complete animal at will."

Melvin had always envied women and their ability to get laid anytime they wanted. Now he could take advantage of that. There was no point not to. Soon enough he'd be Melvin as Melvin, stumbling and blubbering through awkward social interactions with girls more fascinated with college guys or the seniors that were more popular and/or more dangerous looking than him.

Ruki looked at Melvin, a smile on his face. He grabbed Melvin's hand. "You never know, my dear, I could be a vicious beast, ready to pounce."

SCRAAAAPE.

The prolonged dragging of steel against sharpening stone arrested everyone's attention. Mike was no longer looking at the landscape as he scraped the wicked disks against the stone in loud, purposeful strokes. There was no doubt the eyes behind the blue lenses focused on Ruki Provos. Mike's scarred face stayed emotionless and ominous.

SCRAAAAPE.

"Heh, well not quite that ready to pounce," Ruki said, taking his hand off of Melvin's.

That was a good thing. Melvin wasn't so sure he was ready for Ruki Provos and his pouncing. Ruki wasn't a bad guy. He was nice and carried a quirky, old school kind of charm. But he wasn't for Melvin, for reasons Melvin couldn't quite explain.

Maybe it was because he didn't know Ruki all that well. Or maybe Ruki seemed to like Melvin too much. Or maybe it was because he simply wasn't Rich. Ultimately, Melvin just wanted to end his curiosity about sex. To do that, he needed to feel safe with someone just as curious and inexperienced. He felt safe with Rich.

Rich was busy, eyes and focus buried deep into his book. It was kind of fun looking at him read. Melvin could almost feel Rich's excitement as he watched his eyes pore over spells and symbols and histories.

"We've got less than an hour of daylight, it looks," Ruki said, looking up at the sky. "It's a good time to stop and camp, I think."

Besides that, after all this time in Zhufira's skin, Melvin was starting to become hot. And bothered. He would have to read her stat sheets when he got back to see if any of it talked about her naughty factor.

Either that or all his naughty thoughts as he had played Zhufira were coming back to bite him on the ass. Speaking of, an idea of how to get Rich to bite that same spot would be useful.

Ruki Provos got up to talk to his uncle about a possible camp site, but not without a smile at Melvin first. It made Melvin realize he was a bit out of his depth. Rich certainly didn't look at Melvin the way Ruki did. Melvin figured all it took to get male attention was to smile and maybe bounce a little; he remembered that working on him. Obviously a little more was needed because Rich should be eyeballing him. The lack of attention left Melvin with a hard question.

How the hell do you seduce a guy?

JASON LOOKED OUT FROM a camp in progress to a horizon full of the reds and purples of a sun already out of sight. Everyone worked bringing supplies from the caravan to a campsite marked by a couple of trees, their autumn leaves a vibrant display of oranges, reds and purples to match the sky. Pretty soon, night would be upon them and his vision would devolve into dim-lit suck.

Still, even with his night vision, he saw more than apparently everyone around him. There was no going back to the burbs. This fact was so obvious it practically screamed at him.

It wasn't so much that they couldn't go back as what they were going to do once they got back. Nothing. They were going to finish high school then go to college to get a job so they could afford a wife who could spit out some kids who then got to repeat the process ad nauseum. Whose dream was this? And why did his friends want it?

Speaking of friends, Rich was under one of the trees looking visibly relieved that Runt didn't want a magic fire. The half weagr had a tinder box out and was making big sparks with adroit hands.

"You sure you don't want me to conjure one up?" Rich asked.

"Magic flame burns at strange temperature," Runt said, shaking his head as he chipped at the flint. "Hard to cook on it."

"I wouldn't be so happy about that if I were you, Rich," Jason thought, *"because in a couple days you won't be able to cause a fire without a Bic and some kerosene."* Rich was easily the biggest disappointment. His eyes should be glowing. He should be levitating, burning down legions of baddies, living life in God mode. But no, Rich was penny pinching his spell casts, trying to get the least amount of spell for the least amount of cost. All the real danger in this world, and here Rich was scared of dreams.

The camp was coming together nicely as the last remains of daylight darkened into deep purples and blues. Mike was setting up a cook stand. The thing looked like a collapsible card table, only half the size and made of steel mesh. Mike unfolded it and set it over the fire Runt had built into a decent blaze. Pretty soon, the surface would be hot enough to cook the supplies Ruki Provos was bringing from the caravan: salted meats, beans and ground meal for quick biscuits.

Jason could understand Mike's desire to punch out of here early. There probably wasn't that big a difference between being in the Army and being a wandering megrym. At least the Army came with a paycheck and the G.I.

Bill. Being megrym just came with diminutive height and bad skin, and in Mike's case, scarred skin.

Mike looked up at Jason, the campfire light reflecting off his blue lenses. "Hey, kid, make yourself useful. Get the dish pack." He pointed behind Jason to the parked caravan.

Jason swore under his breath as he managed the walk to the caravan. Night was in full bloom, the moon was just a sliver and his back was to the campfire, making his visibility craptastic. Without fixed light sources, night for aians was like looking through a bowl of churning oil. The walk was mercifully brief and he found the dish pack with a little rummaging about. Even in the darkness, he felt eyes on him.

Faintly illuminated by the distant fire, Jason saw Tavis Provos. Just his eyes really, staring at him from the caravan's driver seat as Jason handled the box of dishes.

This guy. It wasn't like they brought Yol down on his store on purpose. How long was he gonna sulk?

"Hey, Tavis," Jason said, nudging his head towards the camp as he held the dish pack. "Fire, food, fun. For free!" Jason had an errant thought about the killing he'd make if he worked in advertising out here. He wouldn't even have to work that hard; he could just use old ads from home.

"Go. Away."

Jason shrugged as he walked off. He had bigger concerns than the tradesman's hurt feelings. Like his friends' hurt feelings... how were they going to take it when they stepped through the Rift Pendulum and didn't find Jason with them on the other side?

There was no real way to tell them, at least no way that felt right. Jason pondered their possible reactions as he set the dish pack down behind Runt, who was slapping salted steaks onto the cook stand with a satisfying sizzle. If Jason told them before they activated the Pendulum he'd hear nothing but protests forever. Melvin would probably try to do something crazy like force him through the Pendulum for his own good or some crap. He would never be able to forgive his friend for that one-way ticket.

The smell of the meat wafted to his nostrils, mixing with the clean air of the open country. If anything, it confirmed he was making the right decision. Out here was substance, adventure. Life.

Maybe some other idea on how to break it to them would come to mind. Right now the plan was simple: express desire to return to stave off suspicion, share in the task of getting back and when the Pendulum opened, make sure everyone got what they wanted. Jason knew without a doubt what he wanted was to stay.

RICH DIDN'T KNOW CAMPFIRE food could be so good. Maybe anything would be great considering this was his first hot meal all week. He didn't care enough to work through the difference as he took another bite of steak.

He set down his plate, as he had a dozen times already and went over to one of the stone markers he had arranged. The stones sat in a circumference ringing the campsite in a diameter of about twenty yards. It all looked right.

"So, are you going to finally tell me what we're doing?" Mel asked as she handed him some smaller stones to feed the arrangement. If she minded setting down her plate to come play with rocks with him, she didn't show it. She was all smiles.

"Enclosure wards," Rich said as he chewed his steak. "I figure we're most vulnerable to attack from the Graverobber while we're asleep. So I'm setting up a barrier."

"How's it work?" she asked.

"It's actually a combination of two creation spells I saw in my book," Rich said. "But once I create them, it will act as a dampening field for everything within the stone circle. Magic projectiles will fizzle at the border and it'll burn any dead flesh that tries to enter the circle. Total protection."

"Smart," Mel said smiling.

"Not that smart," Jason said from a few feet away. He popped a piece of quick-biscuit in his mouth with his bone fingers. He pointed with his flesh fingers behind his back, where the hand of the severed arm protruded, looking as if it was about to grab Jason on the shoulder. "What about my arm club?"

"It's not dead. It's in sleep stasis, remember?" Rich said.

Jason held up his bone arm to let the brown robe sleeve fall down and expose the two long bones of the forearm. He flexed his skeletal fingers. "And what about this?"

"Um," Rich shrugged. "Should be alright?" he ventured.

"I'm with Jason on this one," Mike chimed in. "I mean, a lil while ago he had to wake himself up after getting his arm lopped off just to give you spell lessons. Now all of a sudden you Merlin?"

"Guys, seriously," Rich said, his indignation rising. "I've been studying. It'll work."

"Hello?" Jason said, pointing to his severed arm with his flesh hand. He wagged his skeletal fingers. "I'm not worried about it not working."

"Hell," Mike said. "I'm not worried about it not working either. I'm worried that I'll wake up with another head sticking out of my neck because you turned this patch of grass into a cell tower powered by a microwave oven."

"What's a microwave?" asked Ruki Provos.

"People!" Rich cried. "What's worse, us being woken up by a fireball rocketing at us faster than the guy on watch can scream or the remote risk of tumors and cancer?"

"True that," Mike said with a nod.

"What's a cancer?" Ruki asked.

Rich's observation about surprise attack in the middle of the night won out against any more dissent. Jason stood outside the circle as Rich spoke the words to finalize the enclosure wards. The ring of stones glowed purplish-blue. The quarter steak remaining on Rich's plate caught on fire and burned to ash. Great.

Jason took a tentative step inside and was relieved when neither his bone arm nor the severed one on his back started smoking.

"Hey Uncle," Ruki called out to the caravan. "You should come to the camp... it's safer here."

"Rather risk rabid strandwolves than fool magic!" a voice shouted back.

"All right, Uncle," Ruki yelled back. "Good night!"

Silence answered. Ruki looked out at a caravan surrounded by darkness. "Uncle may not believe it, but I'm going to see him up from this ruin and have him at the helm of a sprawling business empire." He faced Rich, leaned closer and talked in a low hush. "You wouldn't happen to have some kind of magic tether in your spell book, would you? It'd be nice if you could tie down the caravan, because I really can't put it past Uncle to not drive off in the middle of the night."

If there was a tether, Rich hadn't run across it yet. They would just have to watch the caravan as they took turns on night watch.

The camp spent the time before first watch winding down by swapping stories. Ruki told the legend Alora, whose heart was transmuted into a flawless pink diamond when her husband and powerful mage couldn't stop her from dying. Mike talked about some of the pranks him and the guys in his unit pulled on each other in Afghanistan. Jason talked about the monsters of the modern era, chiefly excessive litigation, which he illustrated with the story of when Kellogg's sued Exxon because the tiger in the tank logo looked too much like Tony. Mel finally answered Ruki's question of what a cancer was and offered that Alora of Ruki's story had probably died of it.

Rich closed his eyes. He felt a buzzing in his brain. No, it was more a voice calling his name, asking his name as if it was a question.

The voice was Rew's; more than the sound, the feeling of it belonged to her. So this was what it was like to have someone asking for permission to scry with you.

Excitement mixed with a certain sense of dread. What if she started asking a bunch of questions about her father? What if she had already found out?

Still, it had been a long first day back, and his reservations came nowhere near his desire to see her again. He answered her voice with his own voice and the imagery behind his closed eyes began to change.

He sat at the base of one of the trees of the camp. Nearby, the fire burned low with a soft crackle of dried branches. In the distance, the caravan sat like a sleeping iron caterpillar. Past the dividing line, the scene was one of lit candles and paper lanterns that caused shadows to play about the Hierophane chamber. Leather bound books sat on shelves, the flickering light making the golden gilt of the lettering down their spines twinkle. A giant map of the region hung on the wall with animated markings of destriers and mages drawn on top of the map in an enchanted ink that flowed as if it had a life of its own.

Rew was breathtaking. Her dark tresses framed her face in thick curls. She wore a nightgown of cream colored silk. More than anything else, what she had brought with her made him smile.

She held in her hands a bowl of water.

"It has been a long, trying day for me, Rich," she said, "and I would very much like to spend what remains of it with you."

CHAPTER 13
M.O.A.R.

(S omething Especially Fiendish)
Rich woke up in a good mood and not just because he smelled bacon frying.

He sat up in his bedroll to see Runt at the cook stand, rummaging through the food stores. Runt had set up the cooking fire and stand a small ways from the camp, to keep Rich's wards from disintegrating the meat before he could cook it. The distance did little to keep the smell of sizzling bacon from wafting to Rich. The rest of the camp stirred in their bedrolls, not quite ready to rise with the sun.

Breakfast was the capstone to a great night Rew had started with her bowl of water. Neither one of them spoke about their long day because once they were together, none of that seemed to matter. They picked up where they left off from their last long scry, when Rich was in Triptoe. And the night had melted away.

It was a great day to be alive. The morning air carried a brisk chill the others were trying to stave off as they hunkered under their blankets. Rich rose from his bedroll and got closer to Runt and the cooking fire.

"Morning, Runt."

"Rich Razzleblad," Runt replied with a nod. He pulled an orange squash out of the food stores and got to slicing.

Runt had picked last watch expressly so he could make breakfast. He could have it; cooking was nothing but more work to Rich. But Runt's persistence at the cook fire made Rich curious. "Do you like cooking or do you just not trust other people's food?" he asked the big man.

A small smile played across Runt's lips. "Perhaps both, Rich Razzleblad. Mostly weagr upbringing. Weagrs cook and eat as a village. Good cooks are revered." Runt spoke without looking at Rich, putting the sliced squash into a pan of brown sauce. "Short life span, weagrs; our days are numbered like our meals. So first meal to last, they all should be feasts of our own making."

Behind Runt, Mike's purple head popped out of his bedroll, nostrils flaring, his blue lenses regarding the big man and the fire. "Butternut squash?" he asked.

Runt nodded.

"With Runt Sauce?"

Runt gave another nod, grunting affirmative as he stirred the squash.

"Word!" Mike exclaimed getting out of bed to hang out at the cook fire. He took off the lightning gloves he had slept in and cracked his knuckles. Not just Mike: Ruki, Mel and Jason also rose at the mention of what was for breakfast.

One taste and Rich understood why everyone got up so quickly; you'd be crazy to miss it. All at once sweet and salty, nutty and savory, Butternut Squash with Runt Sauce was ridiculously good. Instinctively, Rich asked what was in it, which only earned him a stonewall look from Runt. Apparently, Runt wasn't keen on giving away his cooking secrets, so Mike had dubbed the big man's signature sauce after the cook.

"Uncle!" Ruki called out to a still caravan covered in road dust and morning dew. "Breakfast!"

"Ha!" Tavis' voice called back from the caravan. "Try choking on it!"

Ruki grimaced. A touch of sadness made his eyes tighten at the corners. "I don't think he's ever going to forgive me."

"Yo, he'll come around," Mike said around mouthfuls of squash. "Fam can't stay mad forever. That's what makes it fam."

Ruki Provos gave a half-hearted nod as he looked at the caravan. Tavis wasn't visible behind the train's iron sides, but Rich got the feeling the old man was seething, impatiently waiting for them to finish breakfast so he could drop them off and out of his life for good. It only took a few minutes after eating to break down camp, pack it all up and climb aboard the caravan, where Rich could see Tavis Provos looking dire.

It was obvious last night wasn't the most fitful night of Tavis' life. His skin looked pale and clammy and his eyes, still full of angst, sank a little more into his skull. Rich pointed at the red splotch on the old man's tunic, which had doubled in size over the course of the night.

"Tavis, I really should take a look at that," Rich said. The merchant had a right to be angry, but getting physically sicker and turning down help was plain dumb.

The look Tavis shot at Rich said it all; he would rather be stupid and stubborn than get help from him. Fine... maybe a fever-inducing infection would give the former store owner a new batch of issues to worry about than a ruined storefront. Rich took a seat next to Mel, who seemed to be in a good mood judging from her smile as she looked at him.

"Hey," she said with bubbly cheer as the caravan lurched forward.

"Uh... hey," Rich replied, his tone making his words sound like a question. They were of a sort; why was she saying hi when they had seen each other all morning? Did he miss something?

"So," Mel said before pausing to contemplate the caravan deck flooring as if she didn't know what came next. Finally a question emerged. "How'd you sleep?"

"Good," Rich said in the form of another question, looking for hidden meaning in her eyes. To not be a native woman, Mel sure confused him like one. Rich was stuck with a lingering feeling he either wasn't saying enough or wasn't saying it right.

"That's good," Mel said, sounding genuinely relieved. "I went to wake you for your watch and I couldn't. I assumed you were having a cost dream, so I tucked you into your bedroll and took your watch."

Now it all made sense. He had forgotten all about watch while he was with Rew, which meant Mel got stuck covering for him while he was having fun on an out-of-body date.

"Aw, Mel, I'm sorry. I didn't mean—"

She covered his hand with her own. "No need to apologize," she said with a smile. "I mean, that's what friends are for, right? To be there for one another, you know... help each other out."

"You're right. Still, you shouldn't have had to cover for me."

"No worries," she beamed back, full of more warmth than the morning sun. "I'm sure there'll come a time where I'll need you. And you'll be there... to, you know... help me."

Rich nodded with slow suspicion. It was a given; of course he'd be there to help her. Mel nodded back vigorously, like she was verifying some unspoken contract now in effect. Was he being paranoid or was she plotting on him, being all nice before she got him back for the lack of sleep he put her through?

Mel wasn't saying as her attention changed to the scenery. Her eyes danced as she took in the passing countryside, flitting from trees full of leaves stained in yellows, oranges and reds to the giant cottony clouds drifting lazily through aqua blue skies. Mel was an amazing beauty; the thought that she would soon be a sixteen-year-old boy was weird even though Rich had known the guy version longer. He felt closer to Zhufira-Mel than Melvin Morrow, a camaraderie forged by near-death struggles versus the simple roles played when they had thought it just a game.

But very soon now, it would all be over. No more magic and monsters and mayhem. No more life and death battles. And most importantly, no more cost. Nothing left of this world but memories; it certainly wouldn't be a game he played anymore.

"When do you guys think we'll make the Hierophane?" Rich asked to a caravan gone silent. Melvin and Jason sat looking at the changing landscape while the others leaned in their seats, eyes closed as the caravan jostled them in rhythm with the engine's chug.

"Should be in Ardenspar in a few hours," Ruki said, popping his eyes open to survey the area. Finding the back of his eyelids more worthwhile than nature's bounty, Ruki closed his eyes again to explore the darkness.

Rich reached into the library pocket of his mage robes and pulled out the *Birleshik Arcana*, the Unified Theory of Magic. Idle time meant study time. Until he actually set foot on a manicured suburban lawn, the last thing he wanted to be was unprepared. Unpreparedness fed fearful circumstances. Fearful circumstances fed Razzleblad.

He got lost in the book. The *Birleshik Arcana* was like a pocket professor, giving him exciting lectures on how magic worked. Today's lecture concerned blue mages, their mind powers, and the premium they placed on establishing psychic links. Rich wondered how you could tell them apart from the blue-robed sea clerics. Probably a different shade of blue. The spell to create a mental twin was insanely complex, like netherfire. Thinking about netherfire made him wonder how Druze had been able to call it into existence at a moment's notice, which in turn got Rich thinking about how much a man could learn in five hundred years.

Forever seemed to have passed when Jason's voice broke the book's hold over Rich. "Heads up, guys," he said pointing to some fuzzy smudge in the distance. "This doesn't look good."

The countryside had changed. The caravan traveled on a raised road, a naturally occurring ridge rather than a built highway. This elevated path was the only real option for the caravan; either side of the ridge was home to inhospitable terrain—hills and potholes and sporadic trees. Jason pointed to where the ridge stretched and wound its way to forever in the distance.

Ruki opened his eyes at Jason's announcement. He seemed more surprised at the scenery than anyone. "Uncle, why are we on Dreft Esker?"

Tavis Provos called back over the noise of the engine. "See for yourself." He pulled down on a lever and the train lurched with increased speed.

"What the hell?" Jason asked as the momentum tossed him back into Mike. "That's a more! We need to turn around, not race into it!"

Tavis careened forward heedless of Jason's warnings. It only took a few moments for Rich to see what Jason saw. Temple Armsguardsmen on destriers, column after column—hundreds of them, held their ground on the esker as if waiting for the caravan.

No, the riders weren't waiting; they were facing down another force. Between the speeding train and the horsemen stood a much smaller band, dozens of people, an absurd collection of armored or robed humans and tattooed nasrans, aians of every house and megryms holding strange gadgets.

Only the Rift Pendulum could bring this much diversity together. The summoned warriors stood before the larger, looming force without a hint of fear or wavering. Now Jason's words made sense... he called it a moar, not more. M.O.A.R. was something gamers talked about with wide-eyed reverence, when game conditions allowed for more than one, two or even five groups of four players, when serious carnage ensued because of "moar" players. They were heading into the Mother Of All Raids.

Mike stood up. "Turn this bucket around! Last thing we wanna do is crash into the back of a Hollower swarm."

Tavis Provos turned to face his passengers, leaving the driver seat empty, their collision course set. "Speak for yourself, twee. This is exactly what I want to happen."

Behind Tavis, Rich saw the summoned warriors take their first steps, moving in single-minded focus, toward the aian riders. Their back ranks were growing close.

"Uncle, stop this," Ruki said, moving toward the driver seat. "This is madness!"

Rich recognized the flow of spellcraft on Tavis' lips. The old man kneeled into a crouch, smashing his hands into the deck of the caravan. The trailer shook and flame erupted, separating Tavis from the others with a wall of deadly fire.

A short distance away, and getting shorter by the second, a war horn sounded within the Armsguard. The cavalrymen moved with precision, stirring their horses into action. They charged.

"Brutal preparation really is a bygone art," Tavis Provos said with a sick grin behind the wall of fire.

The caravan was so close to the pendulum army Rich could no longer see the charging Armsguard on the other side. He could hear their battle cries, the thunderous storm of hooves.

Mike fired his diskbow at Tavis. The disk shot into a gut made soft with age before exploding out the other side. Tavis kept his smile, unfazed by the mortal wound.

Tavis Provos had become the Graverobber. And in this guise he had driven them into a trap.

The sea of pendulum heroes was almost upon them.

"Jump!" Mel cried, diving off the side.

Everyone followed her example, ditching the caravan for one side or the other. Rich hit the dirt and watched as the caravan ran over three pendulum heroes on the back row and three more ahead of them before disappearing into the crowd.

Wordlessly, the men and women that had gotten run over by the speeding caravan got up, turned and looked at the new threat behind them.

Rich scrambled to his feet along with everyone else lying along the esker. Instinctively, they all backed away slowly. A dozen or so pendulum heroes took steps towards the train jumpers. The rest of the pendulum heroes, the ones who hadn't had a train rammed into their backs, continued unfazed toward the Armsguard.

"It looks like they know we're here now," Mel said, brandishing her sword. "Any ideas?"

"We're flagged," Jason said, nocking an arrow as he retreated. "And to a gamer, there's nothing sweeter than the taste of freshly flagged meat."

A clattering of steel resounded as hollow pendulum warriors drew weapons. They advanced without care or caution. Beyond Rich's vision, he could hear the sounds of weapons clashing, horses neighing and people screaming on a battle line being forged by pendulum warriors and Armsguardsmen.

"Hollowers don't feel shit," Mike said, cranking his diskbow taut with gloved hands as he backed away. "Just watch your backs and keep cracking at them until they turn ghost."

But it wasn't just them. Somewhere in this crush of hostility, the Graverobber lurked.

As if on cue, an explosion boomed behind the pendulum army, shooting a geyser of fire into the air. In that fiery stream, shrieking aians, squealing horses and Ruki's burning caravan shot up and out in all directions.

After that, moments, people, actions blurred—a machine with a hundred moving parts. Mayhem descended.

A cat aian, gray with black stripes, charged at Rich. The cat moved impossibly fast, bounding to a point where he was moments away from bringing his scimitar down on Rich's head.

Runt intercepted with his Z-blade, the clang of steel on steel harsh enough to cause sparks.

Without a blink, the aian's free hand shot up and he buried his cat claws into Runt's neck. The big man bellowed in pain.

A male version of Zhufira rushed to join the aian fighting Runt. Brown skin, chainmail loincloth, dreadlocks, huge sword—his face was impassive as he ran. The Khermer warrior raised his sword over his head for a killing blow.

Mike shot his disk at the Khermer warrior's legs. The bladed disk buried itself into the warrior's kneecap. Silently, the warrior kept running, unaffected by the crippling shot.

Rich did the only thing he could think of; he bent his robes. The sleeves smacked into the Khermer warrior and the black-striped aian, sending them both flying back. Runt yelled as the aian's claws ripped flesh from his neck as the aian flew away.

Another five pendulum fighters filled the gap: a nasran Hexenarii, a black-robed destruction mage, a male aian archer whose arms were tentacles, a female from the spider house of Ananna bearing a whip, and a megrym tinkerer in a steam powered suit.

Mike smacked his gloved hands together, creating arc lightning that shot out at the summoned warriors. Despite the electricity rippling and sizzling between them, all five continued moving toward the gang without pause. Ruki Provos followed up with his own arc lighting, which did nothing in terms of stopping the pendulum warriors.

The Hexenarii, destruction mage and squid archer all stopped. The nasran pulled a hex, the destruction mage started chanting, the squid archer, holding bow and arrow with tentacles, aimed his arrow. He turned his legs into more tentacles which he used to grab two more arrows.

Must be casting range for gamers. Jason loosed an arrow, which embedded itself noiselessly into the destruction mage's skull. The black robe kept casting his spell. Jason followed up with another arrow through an eye.

Between getting run over, a double dose of lethal electricity, and two arrows through the skull, the black robe finally ran out of hit points. He started unraveling, crumbling into dust like old parchment paper. The striped cat aian and Khermer warrior sprinted through the gap left by the crumbling mage, quick to get back to the action.

"Focus on the clothies," Jason said coolly, aiming an arrow at the Hexenarii as the nasran hex warrior lobbed his hex high into the air.

Jason loosed the same time as the squid archer. Jason's arrow found a home in the Hexenarii's neck. The squid archer's arrow sped toward Jason.

Jason reached out with his bone hand, grabbed the deadly missile out of the air, spun the arrow around and fired it off at the Hexenarii. Rich wasn't sure if the bone arm had a mind of its own when Jason was in full Cephrin mode.

While Jason was clearly Cephrin, Mel struggled without the benefit of Zhufira. It was all she could do to dodge and parry as the megrym tinkerer assailed her with relentless blows made even more powerful by his steam suit. She gave ground fast to his tireless strikes.

Rich spoke to bend his sleeves and knock the megrym back but was forced to divert his focus as the squid's arrows came speeding at him. He smacked the arrows out of the air.

Mike couldn't help Mel neither. He was doing his level best to stay one step ahead of a warhammer bigger than he was. The aian wielding it, a buff member of the horse House Otam, continuously smashed it into the ground as Mike rolled or dived out of its path.

Runt had his hands full with the cat aian. They both struck at each other with dizzying speeds. But Rich knew only one of them could keep this kind of pace up indefinitely.

Ruki Provos' only weapon was his diskbow, which he cranked out round after round into warriors who apparently pursued bigger profile kills.

Another wave of mismatched warriors were bearing down on the already overextended group. Beyond them, battle raged between the bulk of the pendulum warriors and the Armsguard. The cavalrymen were ill-prepared to fight these unfeeling demons, and they struck at random targets, yelling as they charged back and forth or cried in desperation as pendulum heroes pulled them from their horses.

Out of this carnage strode Tavis Provos, his body burned black by fire, his eyes sparkling with glee.

Another of Jason's arrows found its home in the Hexenarii warrior, making him dissolve on the spot. Without pause, Jason swiveled to refocus on the squid archer.

Before he could fire, a spider lady of House Ananna cracked her lash across Jason's face. A hard snap, sounding like a peal of thunder, the whip made Jason drop both bow and arrow as he cried out in pain.

The ground opened up under Ruki Provos and gray hands shot up from the broken earth. Burrowing aians, either the house of Yol or Zemishirus, seized Ruki's feet and dragged him screaming into the sinkhole.

"Ruki!" Rich yelled.

There was no time to help. The spider woman had broken Jason's Cephrin mode. She brought her whip back just as the Khermer warrior dashed at Jason.

Rich made to bend his sleeves. Again he had to divert them as the squid archer's arrows came careening toward him.

The Khermer warrior drove his sword through Jason's stomach. Rich saw the blade emerge on the other side of his friend's body, blood-soaked and gore covered.

Rich tried to cover the distance between him and Jason, but the whistling sound of something falling from high up, like a bomb falling, forced him to look skyward. Rich remembered the Hexenarii had lobbed his hex up into the sky and it looked like the hex had changed into a glowing, pulsing metal ball. Covered in wicked spikes, it looked like a sea mine. Rich had no illusion as to its purpose.

The metal ball struck the ground and the world exploded in blinding light. Rich felt himself being thrown into the air, being bathed in the most searing heat he'd ever known. He felt the ground rip and tear his robes as he landed among unforgiving rocks.

Rich struggled to rise, to open his eyes. From without, he heard the Graverobber laughing, cackling with certainty that victory was his.

CHAPTER 14
Bodysnatching as a Fine Art

A day before he would spring the perfect trap, Druze Wozencraft walked. He wore a delightful sundress, yellow with a floral print fetching enough to warrant being buried in. Not so delightful were the heels; he had discarded those miles back, preferring to make Suusteren barefoot. Why anyone would subject themselves to such awkward footwear was beyond him.

The city came into view on the horizon, gleaming dully in the noonday sun. He could have made a wind channel and gotten here much sooner, but little good would've come of rushing. Spellcraft was hard on a manipulated corpse in ways he had never had to contend with before in living tissue. The last thing he wanted was to face his enemies in a half-broken body without any replacement hosts on hand. Without a body would his consciousness disintegrate? Or would he linger in a place, waiting an eternity for someone to die close by? He didn't want to find out.

Besides, they were easy enough to track with the warrior girl's clasp betraying her. He attuned to it as he entered the city proper and felt it chiming close by, North and West. The Trade Quarter. Druze strolled down the wide avenues looking at the brick buildings that hadn't changed much since he was last here, over eighty years ago. He made his way to Clover Street, where the warrior girl's clasp called to him from a modest brick building with a large garish sign: Provos Trading Company.

Inside, an old man, thin and miserable looking, walked from shopper to shopper telling them the prices of everything they looked at. If he was a Provos, he wasn't Ruki. The old man turned and saw Druze staring back from the counter. Immediately, he turned and started yelling at the empty stairway.

"Boy, I'm getting swamped down here! Come down and help the lady at the counter. You can count it as a date, but only if you can actually manage to sell something other than a depressing future with you."

"Bah!" from upstairs, a familiar voice shouted back.

Obviously, the old man was in charge of Provos Trading, which made him family to Ruki Provos. Father? Druze hoped so. He smiled and waved the old man over to the counter.

"Didn't want to wait for these deals?" the old man asked. "I don't blame you. What can I do you for?"

"I want one of these knives," Druze said, looking down into the glass case that was home to a dozen field daggers. His gaze swiveled up to regard the old merchant. "Which would you recommend, Mr..."

"Provos. Tavis Provos," the old man filled in. Tavis walked around the counter, reached into the case and began pointing out various daggers. The one Tavis said was "good for cutting vegetables" was actually a Runembrian infantry poniard and the one he recommended for filleting steak was a ceremonial bloodletting dagger from the defunct cult of Io. Druze went behind the counter with Tavis and put his small, slender fingers on the hilt of a large Kirdan dagger, a blade referred to as a Sword Breaker.

"Expensive," Tavis said in a whistle, either out of salesman habit or ignorance that his suggested fillet knife was much rarer. "But a great choice, my lady. It'll surely handle anything you cross in your kitchen."

"Tell me," Druze said, admiring a dagger regarded as the first choice of assassins along the Azure Coast. "Is this blade sharp enough to quietly kill an unsuspecting shop keep?"

"Of course," Tavis said immediately, nodding as he stood by his product regardless of the query. Tavis' eyes widened as understanding took root. Druze's hands shot out, one clasping the tradesman's mouth and the other thrusting the assassin's dagger into Tavis' heart.

Druze guided the dying merchant's crumpled fall. Hidden from prying eyes behind the counter, he lied down beside the merchant. Soon as the corpse emanated its presence, Druze jumped into Tavis' body.

The first order of business was stashing his secondary host. Since the woman was petite, he had no problem stuffing her into the cubby space under the counter. He tore a swath of fabric from the dead woman's white shift to facilitate the next order of business.

Second order was preparing for the surprise attack. This meant taking the dagger out of Tavis' heart and bandaging the wound. In a fluid motion, he pulled out the blade and applied pressure to the wound with the swath of fabric. Standing up, Druze rooted around the counter space. Tavis Provos had been a collector of all things: curiosities and oddities and rarities and junk. Most of it was worthless garbage. He found some sticky pads, apparently designed to catch flies or rodents, which he used to fasten the makeshift bandage in place.

Now onto the third order of business: killing everyone. He sheathed the Kirdan dagger and affixed it to his belt. His simple plan involved walking casually upstairs, sticking this same knife into Ruki Provos' chest and taking over his body. He'd go from room to room silently murdering the entire lot. No need for theatrical battles... he only had one back up corpse at the moment, which wasn't a whole lot of breathing room.

Before he could take a step in that direction, an earthquake forced him to hold onto the counter for support. Dishes and trinkets fell from shelves with a crash and clatter as the street erupted directly outside the store. The mound ascended upwards, breaking through the cobblestones to form a giant anthill.

Great... Yol. You only had to experience Yol once to get your fill of him for the rest of your life. Disgusting, how he stayed so enamored with himself. Druze turned to find everyone he was heading upstairs to murder had made their way downstairs to him.

Yol burst through the door. Of course he would. "Bring forth your Chosen One so that I may see him!" the god demanded, his voice booming out like a weapon against eardrums.

As much as Yol annoyed Druze, the ant god could finally prove useful. Throughout history, one god or another had singlehandedly crushed false prophets or rebel leaders, including the small armies they commanded. This ragtag bunch of pendulum rejects would never be able to defeat Yol; he exemplified the martial prowess inherent in the rulers of every house.

The ant god would easily kill everyone. All Druze had to do was wait behind the counter. The only thing Yol had to do was stop talking.

Druze seethed in Tavis' skin as he waited for a battle he figured was inevitable. Leave it to a god to miraculously turn inevitable into evadable. The megrym tried to shoot Yol and the aian god sent an earthquake through the storefront, knocking the rest of the shelves down, but no real conflict came until Yol picked up Jason's severed arm.

Yol answered Druze's long-held questions about why the aian boy held onto that lopped off appendage. Scrying at them through Rich's ring had never shown him a purpose outside of macabre attachment. Apparently the boy mage had enchanted it with a sleep spell derivative Druze didn't recognize... something powerful enough to cause even a god to slumber.

Just as suddenly as Yol fell to sleep, everyone Druze wanted dead started making for a hasty retreat. This left him with a quandary: It was criminal to let Rich and his friends get away, especially since Druze had pilfered the perfect skin. But he had never seen the ant god in such a vulnerable state. He recalled all the ceremonies, peace conferences, and official functions of state where the mighty Yol graced the affair with his loud-mouthed presence. Gritting his teeth, Druze realized his hatred for Yol had been growing, smoldering, festering for centuries... aging and ripening into a heady, lavish bouquet of utter loathing.

Yol was too well armored for Druze's dagger. And casting netherfire would take forever in this skin. Druze didn't have that kind of time if he wanted to catch the boy mage. But this was the mighty Yol as helpless as a baby, and passing up the chance to kill the smug bastard pained Druze's everliving soul.

"I have to run, Uncle," Ruki Provos said, waving as he ran towards the back of the store. "I'll pay for the damages, swear to it." On his way to the back, Ruki passed a stove, a pot-bellied behemoth that looked like it could heat a building twice this size. Even the exhaust pipe extending up through the ceiling was massive. The stove reminded Druze of his harrying escape from Vanderfal, which in turn gave him a glorious idea.

Druze summoned magic chains to wrap around Yol's wrists and ankles. His chains wouldn't hold the god for very long but he didn't need very long either. Next, he approached the stove, casting a pressure spell that crushed the exhaust pipe. On the outside of the stove he wrote a hardening spell in its dusty surface, temporarily making the iron stronger and hardier.

He opened the door to the stove and inscribed two creation spells. In the heaping pile of ashes, he wrote a combustion enhancement spell. On the back wall he wrote a wind spell of his own design he called The Maw.

No sooner did he finish inscribing The Maw did the spell become active. Tornado strength winds howled out of the stove, pulling everything in the room towards it. Little knick-knacks and trinkets flew off the floor and into the stove.

Over the suck of wind, Yol's voice boomed. "Cowards!" he yelled, glaring at Druze while pulling at the chains that bound him.

Good. Druze preferred Yol to be awake for this. "*Ateshlemen!*" Druze cried, summoning fire that he hurled into the stove. He waved goodbye to Yol before running out the back of the store.

Druze chased after Ruki Provos' caravan, which had already gotten a fair ways down the street and away from the store. He ran faster than he felt was believable for a host this old and frail, determined to catch his prey. Fortunately, they saw his pursuit and slowed down, allowing him to catch up and get aboard with the big man's help.

Druze looked back to the store, which sat there deceptively quiet. If his spell layers were working properly, The Maw was sucking everything not nailed down into the stove, which was burning through everything thanks to the fire enhancement spell. The exhaust tube was closed and The Maw didn't allow for gases or much else to escape. Pressure was building quickly, and the hardening spell on the outside of the stove wasn't going to let the pressure escape because of structural weakness. The heat energy and pressure was gaining critical mass until...

The building collapsed, bringing down the neighboring buildings with it as the shock wave rolled out of the store. All anyone would be able to see from this spell is the resultant shock wave. Impossible to see was the fiery explosion ripping through the store for a brief instant before the wind magic took over and the explosion got pulled into The Maw. An implosion followed, the destructive repercussion of consuming so much energy and pressure as The Maw pulled even itself out of existence. This shock wave was like a fifty-foot giant's clenched fist slamming down, powerful enough to make the store and both buildings on either side of it collapse inward like a house of cards.

Hopefully, somewhere in those destroyed buildings was one crushed ant. With no way to confirm, Druze refocused to the task at hand. He was in a moving caravan with half a dozen people he wanted to see drown in their own blood. No replacement bodies on hand meant biding his time; possibly murder them all in their sleep.

Druze steeled his nerves for a long day's trip with hated enemies. He forced himself to listen to their pedantic conversations, just in case their chatter held information of some value. The green grass and changing leaves of the trees brought a measure of peace as the countryside rolled by.

There was a merciful lull in their conversation when he felt Brigitte's request for a scry. He closed his eyes and entered the meeting with a woman on edge.

"Druze, we face invasion," Brigitte said as she paced back and forth in the Hierophane security office.

"Has the war already begun?" Druze asked.

"It may as well," she replied, stopping her paces to explain fully. "The Temple of Houses has sent one thousand Armsguards through free lands to intercept the renegade Cephrin in Suusteren. Destrier cavalrymen."

Druze grimaced. A specialized team, composed of House Demir high flyers, or burrowers from House Zemishirus would have been more effective in retrieving their errant messiah. But one thousand destriers sent a clear message to the Hierophane and the Free States at large: You exist solely by our good graces. We do what we will.

"And Majora's response?" Druze asked.

"An ambush of twenty-five pendulum hero groups along Dreft Esker, set for tomorrow at midday."

Druze nodded. It was a good plan, probably the best plan under such circumstances. Doing nothing invited tyranny. Calling the mages would be a logistical nightmare when trying to catch destriers which would undoubtedly be running on rusk. One hundred pendulum heroes should be enough to deal with the threat, but without any mages present it was akin to sending a self-powered hammer and trusting it was smart enough to pound down all the nails.

Forcing an ideal outcome was always better than hoping for the best and Druze had little faith in self-powered hammers. He looked away from the

Hierophane's security offices, to his side of the scry. A perpetual blur sprouted from the trees, caused by memories of a caravan moving at good speed. A caravan that could likely move even faster if he had somewhere to be.

"Excellent work, Brigitte," he said. "Keep me informed on any changes. I'll be making my way to Dreft Esker to oversee the assault."

Brigitte nodded, fading away as the scry ended.

Druze came out of the scry to find little had changed on the caravan. Ruki Provos still manned the controls, trying pathetically to seduce the warrior girl while he drove. Runt and Mike slept, their bodies recovering from a hard morning of getting blown up and melted down. The fake robe and Jason talked.

"You have any idea how long it'll take us to get to the Hierophane?" the boy mage asked.

"Two days. Maybe three," Jason answered. His eyes panned the horizon as he talked. "We're taking the direct approach..."

Jason's words trailed off as his eyes met Druze's. "Rest well, Tavis?" Jason asked.

Druze made no attempt at pleasantries. Hiding in a body meant not having to hide his contempt. Instead, he got his bearings, looking to the horizon to ascertain current direction and travel speed, working on a best guess on how far away they were from Dreft Esker and best routes. He had a route mapped out in his mind when the boy mage said something that stole Druze's attention.

"I mean, the Rift Pendulum just spit out another gray robe. Shouldn't we, I don't know, try to rein him in? What if he goes crazy?"

The Pendulum pushing out more rejects was alarming news. The last incident was three years prior with Samedi and his band. Now, within the space of a less than a month the pendulum had suffered two known malfunctions. Granted, there could always be more rejects at large than Druze knew about, some who died immediately from hostile environments or never made the Hierophane to report their circumstances. Still, this many occurrences indicated a deeper issue with the Rift Pendulum.

The boy mage brought Druze out of his musings. "Is that blood?" the fake robe asked pointing at the bandaged spot where Druze had silenced Tavis' heart with a knife.

"Of course it's blood!" Druze spat, blaming the wound on his escape from Yol. He got up before anyone could grow too curious. Making his way up to the front, Druze took control of the caravan from Ruki Provos. He pulled the accelerator and the caravan leapt with a burst of speed.

Being in the driver seat meant not having to notice the others. It also meant total control when faced with forked roads. He veered the caravan onto the northeast route. They'd make Dreft Esker in no time.

Well, he'd make Dreft Esker at any rate. Once everyone settled into their bedrolls tonight, he'd go from throat to throat, cutting from ear to ear. He'd jump into Runt and use his overstuffed muscles to dump the other bodies into the caravan. Nothing like having a corpse surplus when he arrived at the esker.

He made good time driving. Being only nominally attached to a body meant forgoing things like fatigue and hunger. Thoughts like this were some modicum of comfort, but he'd much rather be in his original skin. He had gone from a perfect system of immortality to a squatter—body hopping—and all because of the boy mage and his friends.

By the time Ruki Provos wandered back up to the cockpit and asked about a campsite, the sun was nearly on the horizon. Druze brought the caravan to stop near a couple of massive oaks where everyone piled out to stretch. The sound of their collective good moods darkened his.

He stayed in the caravan while they prepared to eat and drink and cry into each others' arms because they were so homesick and whatever else they did before going to sleep. It was an insufferable wait. Night had barely arrived when the aian boy made slow strides towards the caravan.

Druze looked at him from the driver's seat. The boy was away from the others. He could slit the boy's throat while the others were prancing around their campfire. Druze felt the handle of his dagger. Look at the boy, shuffling around in the darkening night. He'd never see Druze coming. And two corpses against the remaining five were decent odds, odds that increased by the number of foes felled.

Suddenly, the aian boy looked up. He squinted at Druze from the back of the caravan.

"Hey, Tavis," the boy said, nudging his head towards the camp, arms wrapped around a box. "Fire, food, fun. For free!"

There was no more getting the drop on him. "Go. Away." Druze stated. The boy walked off and Druze steeled himself to wait a few more hours.

Illuminated by the glow of the campfire, Druze watched as the fake robe started setting down wards. Did he learn that on his own? Anti-magic and anti-necrotic wards by the looks of them. Druze swore under his breath. This was a horrible way to end the night.

They even had the good sense to keep watch. No getting at them now, but he was only midly upset by this turn. He had to admit, there was something poetic to driving the unsuspecting group into an impossible battle. He passed some of the night making a few magic inscriptions on the caravan, little enhancement and barrier spells that even adept mages would be hard pressed to notice, much less the fake robe. Then he waited, watching stars twinkle until the light of dawn came creeping up over the horizon. The sun was still freeing itself from the corners of the world when he heard a voice call out to him.

"Uncle, Breakfast!"

Unbelievable. "Try choking on it!" Druze yelled back.

Luckily, these people had some sense of urgency. After finishing breakfast, they broke camp quickly and got on board. The boy mage looked at Druze, concern plastered all over his face.

"I really should take a look at that," he said, pointing at Tavis' death wound.

Druze didn't bother to answer him. Instead, he got into the driver's seat and set the caravan to a fast cruise. He had plenty of time to make Dreft Esker. With any luck, he'd get there ahead of the pendulum calling.

He drove them through the changing countryside for hours without much notice or fanfare. If they were smarter, they would have noticed the area getting hillier, the trees sparser instead of the flat, grassy lands that are more prominent around Ardenspar. They never even protested when he steered them onto Dreft Esker. After half an hour of travel along the esker, the aian boy jumped up, alarmed by what he saw in the distance.

"Heads up, guys. This doesn't look good."

"Uncle," Ruki Provos called to Druze a moment later, "why are we on Dreft Esker?"

"See for yourself," Druze responded. He couldn't see what the aian boy was seeing, but he knew what awaited the lot of them. He pulled down hard on the accelerator and the train shot forward with all the speed it possessed.

It only took a few moments at this speed for the train to eat up enough ground to reveal what Druze knew. The Armsguard was there, straddling their destriers as they ascertained the threat before them. The numbers weren't intimidating so much as the eclectic mix of warriors in opposition: human warriors from the farthest reaches of the Southern Kingdoms, Megrym Hegemony wolfriders, Hexenarii of several nasran nations, every color of mage robe imaginable and even their own kind, aians of each house that stood defiant to the riders of the Temple of Houses and their holy purpose. How this force against them had come to be had to give the Armsguard pause.

Mike stood up. "Turn this bucket around! Last thing we wanna do is crash into the back of a Hollower swarm."

Druze activated one of his magic inscriptions and the metal controls of the cockpit rusted over. Now there would be no slowing down, no turning away. Druze got up and faced his enemies. "Speak for yourself, twee. This is exactly what I want to happen."

Ruki Provos tried to approach the cockpit. "Uncle, stop this. This is madness!"

"*Atesh engel*!" Druze cried, smacking his hands onto the caravan deck. It activated a hidden inscription, allowing a barrier of fire to erupt from the floor. The boy mage would have to work impossibly hard to counter the fire.

Druze looked up and smiled. The fake robe wouldn't be working at all. The boy sat immobile on the seat, eyes darting erratically behind closed eyelids. Of all the strokes of fortune possible, Druze hadn't begun to think this would happen.

The boy, like all unbound casters, had no say over the time and place he paid the cost, and it had come to claim him. Vainly, the warrior girl shook the boy. He was beyond help. They all were.

Druze began to speak, activating his remaining inscriptions. An intricate spell, the inscriptions along with his spoken spellcraft would blow the caravan sky high, provided nothing stopped his speech.

The twee fired off his disk shooter. Grimacing, Druze suppressed a groan as it flew through his guts. He kept his voice level, his tone even. More inscriptions sparked to life.

"Jump!" the warrior girl cried. She grabbed handfuls of the fake robe and hauled him over the side along with herself. The rest followed suit.

Druze turned around, still keeping the spell alive with his words, just in time to see the caravan run down the back row of pendulum heroes. The caravan jumped haphazardly as it navigated a trail made bumpy with row after row of plowed over bodies. Druze held onto the rocking caravan, being careful to speak the remaining spell slowly, dragging it out.

Within moments, he emerged out of the pack of pendulum heroes and now faced a charging cavalry bearing down on him. Druze's spellcraft slowed to a crawl.

More cognizant of the careening caravan than the pendulum heroes had been, the cavalrymen split their forces, parting for Druze's runaway engine. Once safely past the caravan, the first waves of Armsguardsmen filled in the empty lane behind the vehicle and kept their charge.

Now.

Druze finished his spell and felt a blistering burst of fire. Blinding light and searing heat consumed him. Around him, he heard the aians and their horses scream as the explosion claimed them as well. Druze laughed through the pain as a world on fire rushed around him.

A hard, jarring stop told him he was finally back on the ground. He opened his eyes to find himself in the midst of skirmish between the pendulum force and the Armsguard. His host's body was missing his shirt, his skin charred black. He felt the welcoming presence of freshly dead bodies all around him, too many to count.

Rising to his feet, he made his way towards the back ranks of the pendulum heroes. If the summoned warriors hadn't already killed the fake robe and his friends, Druze would. He had too many hosts at his disposal to fail.

Druze reached the back ranks and his eyes widened with shock. Of all things imaginable. The pendulum force hadn't killed a single one of them. They were beyond reach.

Winged aians from the house of Demir had them all airborne, carrying them away from the danger of battle. None of them looked wounded, except for the fake robe who twitched in the midst of his cost. Even Runt had an aian on each arm, flapping their wings as they made distance even Druze couldn't reach using spellcraft.

Druze all but ignored the sounds of combat and men dying behind him as he watched his prey turn into specks on the horizon. He couldn't recall the last time he felt such raw, burning rage.

A strange sound behind him got his attention. The closest thing he could equate it to was the sound of wind gusting only to die a second later then gust again at gale force. He turned to find the pendulum force flickering, going back and forth from substantial to transparent. They all stood rooted, many of them in mid-strike, while the Armsguard in their midst looked on in fear and confusion. The flickering got faster until the whole host of remaining pendulum heroes disappeared completely. The aians looked around, looked at one another.

A grimy, dirt-streaked Armsguardsman raised his sword and let out a throaty cheer. The others picked up the cheer, a resounding victory chorus.

One group of enemies was already beyond his reach. Druze would be damned if another enemy celebrated good fortune while he watched. His anger bubbled over.

Druze strode over to the nearest celebrating aian and grabbed him by the breastplate with both hands. "*Zirhin silahim! Ve harap etmek, ezmek istiyorum!*"

The aian screamed as his own armor collapsed into itself, crushing the man who occupied it. Druze held onto the breastplate, the strength of his will and anger manifesting itself through the violent action of the spell. In seconds the armor of the legs and arms crumpled and folded into the torso and, as the aian's screams abruptly choked to nothing, the torso crunched and compacted into a dense ball of metal, meat and bone.

"*Demear fuze!*" Druze cried, and the ball that had once been a soldier careened through the sea of remaining Armsguards, smashing into heads and chests as it tore through their midst at breakneck speeds. If the dying man's screams hadn't gotten the rest of their army's attention, his deadly exit did.

"Who among you leads?!" Druze shouted to the silent throng.

One aian, a belly crawler from the House of Marad stepped forward. "I am Mors," he said, "Knight-Marshal of the Temple of Houses. Surrender and know our mercy."

Druze pointed his burnt-black finger at the snake. "When you return to your temple, tell them a demon lives in this land. And he is coming to devour all houses."

That was all the dialogue Druze's anger gave patience for. A sea of bodies beckoned to him, hundreds of corpses—more in number than survivors it seemed. Druze had an army at his disposal.

He got to work.

CHAPTER 15
Hell of a Rescue

Flying by aian bird-dude reminded Mike of flying via Blackhawk in Afghanistan. The pressure in his ears combined with the up and down from the wing flap, surprisingly similar to rotary wing turbulence, made him slightly queasy.

He looked down at the landscape, laid out like a carpet five thousand feet below. The carpet was dusty, with pockets of rocks huddled in places, hills turned bite-sized with distance. Clumps of multi-colored autumn leaves dotted here and there as they flew over forests and glades.

Speaking of flying, that was a hell of a rescue. Mike had no doubts without the bird folks swooping down everyone would've died by Hollower hands. Except maybe Rich, who had already been playing dead. Every now and again the kid would twitch in the arms of the flyer holding him.

"What's up with your boy?" Mike asked his brother.

"Long story," Mel said grimacing as he looked at his sleeping friend. "I'll explain when we land."

Landing was a nice thought, considering Mike's nausea and the constant need to swallow to clear his ears. The ten flyers occasionally swapped passengers, allowing three flyers at any given time free hands and a rest break. Partially due to these rest breaks, they had been airborne for awhile now. Mike wasn't trying to complain or nothing, but safely away from the danger of both aian riders and Hollowers, where the hell were they going?

As if on cue, one of the empty-handed flyers flew ahead of the pack and turned to face everyone. The rest flapped in place.

"We must learn to meet under better circumstances, Cephrin of Prophecy," he said to Jason with a bow of his head.

"Targhos," Jason replied with a bow of his own. "Until those better circumstances, I appreciate your saving throw in dire times."

"Of course, Chosen One. It is the wish of our house's god to see you safely to your destiny, just as it is his wish to counsel with you. Will you attend him?"

"Uh..." Jason said looking around like it was a trick question. "Sure," Jason finished. Bird dudes probably talk casually from this high up all the time, like it was natural or something. Unlike standing on the ground, getting asked if you want to meet the boss takes on a different meaning while suspended from bone crushing, organ liquefying heights. If Jason hadn't had sad yes, Mike would've said yes for him.

"Excellent," Targhos smiled. "Garol, with me," he said and the aian carrying Jason broke formation to move behind Targhos. "Sevollian, see the others safely to the village of Mere. Protect them all as if they were the Chosen One. They are extensions of him."

"Your will done," Sevollian replied with a nod.

The band separated, with Jason getting carried north while the others went south. Mel craned his neck a few times as if he was trying to memorize where Jason was headed. Rich twitched. Runt sweated buckets, despite the strong, cool winds up here, looking back and forth at the two eaglemen who held him aloft.

"You aight, Runt?"

"No."

First-time flyer. Mike leaned a little closer, keeping his face serious before speaking in a calm whisper. "You know sweating just makes you more slippery, right?"

Runt looked away from the hands that carried him to glare at Mike. A growl rumbled in Runt's throat like thunder rolling.

Mike let loose a toothy grin. "See? Now you got other things on your mind, like how you wanna smoosh me flat when we land."

Runt's glare was deadpan.

"No need to thank me, homey. You too big to be scared of freefall. It ain't a good look. You don't see Ruki..."

Damn. Ruki.

The tradesman dangled despondently, looking like he didn't care either way if the flyer dropped him. Pain and despair clouded his features. Mike's good mood, brought on by their narrow escape, disintegrated. They hadn't escaped, not everyone.

"Sorry about your uncle."

"Don't." Ruki shook his head. He didn't even bother to look up. Mike kept quiet. Better to give Ruki some space and time to deal.

It was a quiet, uneventful flight, the silence broken only by the rhythmic flap of wings. A small village came into view on the horizon. It must've been Mere. From way up here, the town looked quiet, peaceful, beautiful in its battle-free tranquility.

Then Rich woke up, hollering his head off. His yell gave everybody a start.

A start was the last thing anyone needed suspended a mile above ground.

The flyers holding Runt lost their rhythm, which made Runt panic and jolt. One of the flyers lost his grip, which made Runt grasp and claw at the remaining flyer holding him. They started falling from the sky.

Rich's flyer pulled back abruptly, almost colliding into Mel and his flyer. Rich got jostled roughly as he stared in stark, open fear at the ground so very far below.

Runt and his lone flyer were still descending pretty fast. Another flyer flew to meet them, and Runt reached out for the newcomer in desperate swipes. He looked like a drowning man whose panicked lunges did more to drown the rescuers than help keep himself afloat.

"Rich!" Mel cried, trying to get his friend's attention. But the old dude looked a world away, his eyes bulging in fear, his mouth moving in a blur as he spoke gibberish.

The skies darkened. Howling wind tore at them from all sides. Rich's robes expanded, forcing all the other flyers back and away. The robe kept growing until the material easily had ten times more volume. The robe caught the wind, like a gigantic kite.

"Rich!" Mel yelled, competing against wind that had grown to a roar.

The flyer holding Rich was no longer in control. The wind pushing against Rich's robes drove now, and the flyer flapped in vain against its stronger pull.

The wind batted at Mike's little frame. He tightened his grip and forced himself to stay calm despite the imagery raging in his mind of gale winds blowing him away. Looking down, Mike no longer had eyes on Runt. Looking up, the storm clouds above them started to swirl, churning into a funnel.

The funnel descended, a tornado heading straight for them.

"Rich!"

Mel's last yell must've jarred the kid out of his spell trance, because Rich shook his head as he looked back at Mel and stopped gibbering. The tornado funnel retreated back into the clouds and his robes shrank.

"Mel! What's going on?" Rich asked.

"It's OK," Mel replied. "Stay calm. Everything's fine."

Rich listened, staying calm for the two minutes or so it took to land on the outskirts of Mere. They landed to find Runt already down there, having had a head start on his descent and all. He looked relieved.

Mike made strides across the field to where Rich and Mel had touched down. His brother had his hands on Rich's shoulders, concern etched in girlish features as Mel asked his friend if he was OK.

Fuck that noise. Mike closed the distance to Rich and shoved the living shit out of the gray robed kid, hard enough to make him stumble, fall and tumble backwards. Rich looked up just in time to catch Mike's boot in his face. The kid yelped and landed on his back.

"That's for trying to kill us," Mike said pointing a lightning-gloved finger at the kid. Rich just stared, rubbing his bruised cheek.

"Mike!" Mel cried in surprise.

"Mike, nothing!" Mike shot back. He turned to face Rich again. "It's bad enough, you got my brother hauling your dead weight around when we got an army of Hollowers up our asses. But then you wanna wake up from your powernap and play wind games at splatter heights. Next time you pull some shit like that, fuck boots to face... I'm putting a disk through the back of your head. We clear?"

Rich just lay there, massaging his bruised cheek as he glared at Mike.

"I ain't speaking in tongues like you. If you got beef, you can go head and stand up so we can cook it. I ain't hard to find. Meanwhile, you better acknowledge what the hell I'm telling you so I know understanding's taking place. We clear?"

Rich nodded. "We're clear."

JASON ENJOYED THE RIDE enough to regret not having rolled a flyer as his character. Soaring through the clouds totally owned over walking—every day of the year plus leap day. If he had it to do over, Jason would trade being a badass archer for being a decent archer with wings.

A mile or two above ground felt like absolute freedom. Then they started descending, and Jason's heart leapt in his throat. Sitting atop a plateau, an ancient fortress grew in size as they approached. The place was decrepit looking. Fort Law looking. Flashbacks of his first night here assaulted him, complete with weagrs, strandwolves and the undead.

"Demir's here?"

Targhos, flying level beside Jason, turned and smiled serenely. "Openly meeting you is not safe, Lord Cephrin. Our god opposes the Temple of Houses through his actions. His desire to see you fulfill your destiny is not one held by the other gods."

They landed on a parapet. Jason felt as if he was still suspended in the air because of the view. This plateau fortress towered over the surrounding countryside, making it seem as if it floated under its own magic.

"Garol, you have the watch," Targhos said, folding his wings behind his back. "Pay careful attention to the east."

Garol nodded and flew to the eastern tower. Targhos motioned for Jason to follow him inside the weathered fortress. Jason shook away his fears and followed. He tried to think about other things to keep his mind off of creatures that lurk in abandoned forts, like Death Nulls and strandwolves.

The aians had all come from the east. Garol was watching that direction in case of pursuing Armsguard. Jason looked at Targhos, who was easier on the eyes than the netherfire torches that tinted the walls blue in that familiar Fort Law fashion.

"Doesn't the act of you rescuing us incriminate Demir?" Jason asked.

"No need for concern, Chosen One," Targhos said with a smile. "The High Fane has stripped me of my titles and functions as First Flyer of the

First House. It has been thus ever since I helped you escape the temple. My actions will not tie back to Demir."

The sound of their boots clinking on stone seemed to punctuate the silence they shared as they descended a stairway. Jason hadn't thought about what problems his escape could've caused for Targhos until now.

"Sorry to hear that."

"It is of little consequence," Targhos replied. They came to rest in a huge room, an audience chamber. Rows of slit windows allowed slivers of sunbeams to cut through the gloom. Dust motes danced in the air. Targhos turned and faced Jason.

"Demir is the lost god. He has not been seen among mortals in centuries. The Temple of Houses will know he did not aid me. Truthfully, I have not followed him for years, which is just as well. Demir could not have spared me the temple dungeons, or better still, given me the power to escape."

Jason raised an eyebrow. Maybe it was the way Targhos said the word "truthfully." A creeping sensation started growing in Jason.

"What do you mean you haven't followed Demir in years?" A little over a week ago Targhos was Demir's Elevated. And dungeons. "You escaped the temple dungeons?" Jason asked.

Targhos smiled. "Escape is possible when you're blessed with the power of my god. A true god."

Targhos spread his wings. His magnificent feathered wingspan seemed to take up half the audience chamber, the many slivered sunbeams making the aian look angelic. Then a dark aura spread over the wings, emanating from within. The feathers fell out or were pulled into the dark aura. The wings grew even bigger and when the darkness subsided Jason felt a wave of fear as he took in Targhos. He had leathery bat wings, sharp boned and powerful looking, terrible in their massive size.

"Ah! I see you have arrived," a deep voice said behind Jason. "You are well received here at Fort Truth, Cephrin of prophecy."

Jason turned to face the voice. Standing before him was an aian in a blood red robe with pitch black trim. The stranger was like him, an aian unlike any other. The most alarming feature was the stranger's eyes. Jason had grown accustomed to the aian dancing irises, but the stranger's eyes remained still, unnatural and cold despite his smile. Jason could barely tell he was of the House of Yol with the open sores covering his temples and forearms. His antennae were gone, as if whatever sickness he had was actively trying to eat away any signs of his house.

Jason realized from his time in the Temple of Houses that it wasn't a sickness eating away at the stranger's house marks. The stranger was the sickness.

He was face-to-face with Onus.

CHAPTER 16
The Adversary

Jason took an involuntary step back in shock. The last thing he ever expected was to be standing face-to-face with this world's equivalent of the Devil. The slit windows leaked sunlight over Onus, and his red robe seemed to come alive like fire where the light struck. From the stories Jason had heard, he halfway believed this being would turn to ash in the sun.

"I see you know of me," Onus said, a sardonic smile playing across his lips. "Of all the things the Temple of Houses could have done with a youthful amnesiac who may be the Chosen One, they decide to fill you with fear of me and try to kill you. Brilliant."

Jason kept his eyes locked on Onus, trying to quell the growing panic. Wasn't there something he could do? Running seemed like a stupid idea; he was in a fortress sitting on a sheer plateau guarded by flyers. Fighting the God of Power seemed an even stupider notion. The fact that Onus had the ability to beef Targhos' wings up to such a sick and predatory degree quelled any notion Jason had of winning that fight. Besides, he was so far from the calm he needed to function as Cephrin that he'd likely shoot himself in the foot with an arrow. In the absence of any idea on escape, Jason stared.

"Allow me to introduce myself properly," the Corrupter said. "I am Onus, the Maelstrom, Bringer of Chaos, the Fuel of Driving Fire." He ended his words with a flourishing bow.

Jason held his hands up like he was being robbed. "I'm nobody," he said. "Believe me; you've got the wrong guy. I'm not your Chosen One."

Onus rose from his bow, a grimace etched on his face. "No need to be modest," he said, pointing a finger at Jason. "I detest such humility. It does not suit you, one with such promise, so much more potential than Denaldus and Avilram and Mavus and the parade of all the Chosen Ones who have come before."

He looked at Targhos, whose giant bat wings still dominated the space behind the aian despite being folded. "I won't keep you any longer, dear Targhos. Please, join your brothers at watch while I council with Cephrin."

Targhos nodded sharply and took a step back toward the slit windows. Violently, he unfurled his wings. The force of the action powered through the fortress stone, blasting bricks in an eruption that left a massive hole in its wake. Targhos stepped backward through the opening left in the fortress, where he fell out of sight briefly before he flew up and away on wings that had returned to the semblance of an eagle.

"You must forgive Targhos his display," Onus said as Jason stared at the open hole. "It isn't easy for him, or any of his brothers for that matter, keeping all that power locked up inside, a secret from the world."

Jason dry swallowed. Being here reminded him of the time his gaming buddies tricked him into taking a portal that ended in the middle of a dungeon boss's lair. Only this particular dungeon boss wanted to chat Jason up instead of ripping his heart from his chest and eating it in front of him. Or maybe Onus wanted to chat *before* eating his heart. Butterflies swarmed in Jason's stomach. He looked down through the newly opened space in the wall. It was a long way down.

Onus grabbed the back of Jason's shoulder, which felt like a push to Jason instead of a clap of camaraderie as he looked at the ground far below. He jumped out of his skin. Onus maintained his firm, fatherly grip on the boy.

"Be at ease, young Cephrin," Onus said. "I have not brought you here to harm you. Verily, you and I want the same thing."

Jason looked down at the ground tentatively before looking at Onus and his unnatural, unmoving eyes. "We do?"

"The Chosen One seeks to restore the glory of the Twelfth House. I, too, long for this same restoration. How could I not see an ally in you?" Onus asked.

"Um... from what I've heard of the prophecy, the Chosen One ends your house," Jason replied. He took another look down. "Not that I'm the Chosen One or anything."

Onus's face straightened. His dead eyes panned smoothly to a spot behind Jason before coming back to stare in Jason's oscillating eyes. "I must ask," he said. "Your fleshless appendage is perturbing enough in itself; why do you carry a severed arm on your back? It's rather freakish."

Jason craned his neck to regard the hand behind him, looking like it was waving "hi" to everyone. "I'm pretty attached to it," Jason answered. A wave of indignation rose in him. He was getting commentary about freakish appearance from the evil incarnate with chewed up house marks and eyes that stood still.

"The fact that it took the High Fane this long to find you when you roam the world with fleshless fingers, no marks and a cleft arm strapped to your back should be a testament to their competency," Onus stated with a smirk. "They couldn't find their way through the prophecies with a road map while the ghost of the Prophet Zona himself shouted directions."

Onus sighed; a look of sadness fell on his features as he looked out over the plains below. "But that was always the chief shortcoming of my brothers and sisters, the other house masters. Short-sighted, the lot of them. They were so busy looking to stop the chaos of the Maddening Times they never took stock to think what it truly meant to save aiankind."

Jason found himself relating to the Devil, as weird as that was for him. His friends, like a family to him now, all wanted to hurry up and return home so bad they weren't stopping to think about what they were really going back to.

Onus's gaze returned from the view outside to regard Jason, giving him a warm smile. "Do you know the difference between my siblings and me?"

"They're not hiding out in a ratty fortress," Jason thought. "No," he answered.

"When we communed with the Onesource millennia ago, they all asked for an end to the maddening, a request so predictably short-sighted. Me? I asked for dominion over the madness, the power to control the gift of magic that ate away our minds. They asked for the easy escape. I asked for the strength to endure the hard road. And their choice collectively destroyed aiankind."

"How'd they destroy aiankind?" Jason asked. From what he saw, aians were in no danger of making any endangered species list.

"Can't you see, Cephrin? There is no such thing as an aian. Not anymore. My siblings brokered with the Onesource and allowed it to pervert our nature into those of filthy beasts!" Onus looked down in disgust at his armored forearms, halfway chewed threw with decay to where they were scarcely recognizable as belonging to the house of Yol.

"That's why I like you, Cephrin," Onus said with a smile. "Despite your humble manner, you are a true aian. A markless aian. Not simply hiding your marks or trying to work them into the prophecies like Denaldus or Avilram or the other false Chosen Ones gone by the wayside. You are what we are supposed to be. Outside of your openly exposed skeleton that is, which is nothing short of gruesome."

This dude had some nerve. While Jason bit his tongue to prevent telling the Corrupter not to throw stones from his glass house, Onus went to stand in front of the open wall made by Targhos. He held his hands outside the fort, where they began to glow red. Jason ventured another step and saw the stones Targhos had knocked out of the wall rising up from far below. Onus commanded the stones, compelling them to adhere and stack against the side of the fortress with a series of hand gestures. When he was done, the stones formed a stairway leading up to the fortress battlements.

While Onus was performing construction feats impossible for an aian, Jason watched the rotting spots on Onus's outstretched forearms. The corruption seemed to grow, spreading further up his arms while he worked the magic. Once the stairs were in place, Onus let his arms fall to his side where the fiery robe covered the cost of his display.

"Walk with me, Cephrin," Onus said as he stepped outside onto the steps.

Jason kept a hand groping the lichen-encrusted exterior wall as he traversed the stairs, trying his best not to feel nauseated by the dizzying look down. They made their way up to the battlements, where the panoramic view of the surrounding countryside lay before Jason, spread out so far and stretched to all four corners of the world that he felt like a god himself looking down at it.

Onus seemed to know what Jason was thinking. "You feel powerful right now, the master of all you survey. I feel it emanating within you. The High

Fane preaches to feel this way is wrong; that you should seek humility. Be humble.

"Utter tripe," Onus said with a scoff. "Lunacy! It is unnatural for us to desire less power. What surges through you is one of the most wonderful intoxicants ever tasted. Can you imagine, eschewing the glorious taste of power for the meager scraps of meekness? It is a paltry plate, Cephrin, one that fills the mouth with ash and vinegar, the bitter aftertaste of dreams decayed as you content yourself to remain in your place. Yet the eleven houses would have you eat your fill of it. 'Stuff yourselves,' say the hypocrites! Do you see the gods chewing on this same cruddy fare as they sit in their lofty thrones high above Nasreddin?

"I think not," Onus said smiling as he nudged Jason with a friendly elbow. "To hell with their famine rations. Their followers chew on thrown bones, happy to serve, to count their own exposed ribs. Feast I say! Glut yourself on power and control, means and influence. Anyone who says otherwise surely has a full plate, one they are loath to share with you."

Onus pulled up his robe sleeve, showing Jason the severity of his rot under the rays of the afternoon sun. His arm was pocked with pustules and lesions, many places the skin was black, dead from necrosis.

"Unlike my siblings, I am more than willing to share my power. Before I can, my house needs a home. That's why I need you, Cephrin."

"Me?"

Onus nodded gravely. "Abandoned by my siblings to absorb the Onesource's gift of power alone, the communion destroyed my original body. Since then I've had to rely on my faithful followers as the conduit through which I act. Unfortunately, my followers all come to my house from other houses. I am a god, Cephrin, I cannot make my lasting home in another's house."

"And you want me to be your lasting home," Jason said, the blanks finally filling in for him. Onus wanted a marks-free Chosen One for nothing short of a demonic possession. That's why the god wasn't ripping out Jason's heart for dinner despite the supposed threat the Chosen One held for him.

Onus smiled. "Think of it, Cephrin; we would rule the Twelfth House together. Our power would know no bounds."

"Uh…" Jason stumbled, trying to say exactly the right thing. He definitely didn't want to say "yes" and become Onus's meat suit. Saying "no" might get him pulverized by a vengeful god. "Can I think about it?" he asked.

Onus's smile evaporated and he fixed Cephrin with a serious look. "You would do well to address me with candor. I am several thousand years old, young Cephrin, not a fool who burst forth from a cabbage sack two days ago. Obviously you would have some reservations about the amount of autonomy you'd retain as my conduit, yes?"

"Well, yeah," Jason replied with a shrug. "You're kinda asking me to share something I've grown used to enjoying alone."

"My dear boy," Onus said, returning his fatherly hand to Jason's shoulder. "What I propose is a partnership, nothing more. You'll see, by the time you invite me to join you, you'll find our mutual interests are so aligned it would be impossible for you to tell whether I am performing an action or if you are. We shall be as two halves, complete. I want you to have something."

Onus reached in his robes and pulled out a brass colored pendant on a chain. The pendant looked like a heart. Not one of those perfectly symmetrical "I heart NY" hearts, but a real one cut from a chest and miniaturized. Instead of valves, eight maggots protruded from the top.

"I move over the world and through it; trust me when I say you can never have too many allies. Change is upon us, Cephrin, for human, nasran and aiankind alike. War is smoldering, like embers thirsty for fuel. When it gets that fuel, this whole land will be swept up in its destructive path. I offer you the power to persevere in these trying times," Onus finished, holding the necklace out to Jason.

Jason looked at the necklace like it was an uncoiled rattlesnake. He made no move to take it.

Again, Onus seemed to know what Jason was thinking. "I assure you, accepting this gift does not constitute an open invitation for me to jump into your skin. Believe me when I say when you accept my partnership it will be of your own volition and foreknowledge. This is the way it must be. My lasting house must have a firm foundation. Think of this merely as a hint of how joining with me will empower you."

Tentatively, Jason reached out with bone fingers to accept the gift. Onus looked at him patiently, expectantly as Jason put the necklace on. Once Jason had it on, Onus smiled warmly.

"Should you ever need power, all you need do is call on me," Onus said. "Let me show you."

Suddenly, Onus grabbed Jason by the shirt with both hands. In a fluid motion, Onus whirled and hurled Jason off the castle battlement.

Jason's desperate scream filled his own ears as he found himself hurtling fast to the ground below. He flailed his arms and legs in panic as he looked at the castle speed past in a blur followed by the rocky cliff it sat on. His fumbly fingers found the necklace and he stopped screaming long enough to cry out.

"Onus!"

He looked at the necklace as one of the maggots wriggled into the heart. But nothing else came, nothing happened to stop his fall. The ground sped at him relentlessly. He closed his eyes against the impact.

The crash sounded like an earthquake in his ears. But the sound was all there was to it. After a moment, Jason pushed against the ground and opened his eyes.

He found himself kneeling in a depression made by his impact, shaped in a rough outline of his body. Beside him, Onus stood.

"In these times of famine," Onus said smoothly, "you, dear Cephrin, have license to feast."

CHAPTER 17

Waypoint

Melvin felt like running after Mike and tackling him as the megrym walked away toward the town, taking Runt and the flying escort with him. Exhaling slowly, Melvin let the anger pass. Instead, he focused on Rich, offering the mage an arm to help him off the ground.

"Are you OK?" Melvin asked. "Mike had no right to do that."

Rich shook his head, rubbing the bruise on his cheek from Mike's boot that was quickly purpling. "No," he said, "he had every right. I'm falling apart and it's putting everyone in danger."

"We're all fine," Melvin offered. "You didn't mean it."

"That's the point, Mel," Rich said with a grimace. "Magelord magic is something you're supposed to mean. You don't fire off a nuke and say 'oops, pressed the wrong button.'"

Melvin put his hand on Rich's shoulder. "We're almost through this. We'll be back home where you won't have to worry about Magelord magic—accidental or otherwise. C'mon, let's find the pub in this burg and wait for Jason."

Rich nodded and gave Melvin a wan smile. They turned toward the town and saw a brown-skinned man leaving the outskirts of the village, walking their way. An older guy sporting black lanky hair, his features looked East Indian to Melvin. He walked with a cane and wore a long brown tunic and white pants in a style that seemed very Shaolin monk-like.

No, this old man did more than walk with the cane. He used it to tap the ground from side to side as he walked. Melvin and Rich stood transfixed as the old man tapped his way to them until he was about ten feet away and sat down on a nearby rock.

"Which one of you was responsible for the tornado on this otherwise sunny day?" The old man asked. He looked at neither one of them; his head was turned so his right ear faced them while his eyes remained still, unfocused on anything.

"Well?" he asked when neither Rich nor Melvin answered. "I know you're there. I can hear you breathing."

Rich looked at Melvin. If Rich was thinking the same thing Melvin was, he was wondering if he should answer at all. This didn't feel right to Melvin; his short time in this world had bred a sense of distrust when conversations started off with demanding questions.

"Suit yourselves," the old man said in the short space of their silence. He hoisted his cane up and in an instant the cane became a dagger. With incredible speed, the old man threw the dagger at Melvin.

"Whoa!" Melvin cried out before Rich bent his robe and knocked the knife away. The old man reached out and the dagger sailed in the air to come back to his hand, where it became his cane again.

"So it was you, Mister Bendy Sleeves," the old man said leaning forward on his cane. "Now tell me why."

"It was an accident," Rich said.

"You call on levels of magic most mages die before they reach by accident?" the old man said with a shake of his head. "Do you have any idea what your accidental tornado would've done to this village if it had touched down?"

"Look, mister, I'm sorry about that," Rich said rubbing the back of his head. "I mean, I woke up after the cost with an eagle man dangling me miles up in the air. I panicked. Sorry."

"Hmph," the old man grunted, rising from the rock he sat on with the help of his stick. "How are you so brown-robe wet yet powerful? Is the Hierophane skipping classes on practicality and pragmatics now? Did you fail to pick up the simple life lessons available all around you on your way to gray?"

He answered his own rhetorical questions with a harrumph. He rolled up a sleeve and turned to face Rich directly. "Repeat after me; *parmaklarinda murekkepi kurumadan havaya olan el*," he said.

The old man pointed his cane at Rich when no words immediately came. "Hey!" he shouted. "I don't hear anything, Bendy Sleeves. If you're going to almost obliterate a town on accident, then I'm going to take you back to school. Say the words."

Rich did what the old man asked. Once Rich was done speaking, the old man said, "Let your ink flow," and started tracing a pattern in the air. Liquid black hung in the air where the old man traced, as if his fingers had ink in them. Rich traced his own pattern to mirror the old man's. Melvin watched as the two men drew what looked like spheres that had crowns on one side and funnels on the other. Here and there, they'd scrawl small squiggly lines.

"*Tuttur*," the old man intoned and Rich echoed. Both their hovering ink symbols glowed white. When the light faded, the symbols were gone.

"There," the old man said nodding to no one, his head turned again to where his ear faced them. "That's a portal root, Bendy Sleeves. Everywhere you go, you make one until you run out of places to visit. That's how mages travel; they don't dangle like a rabbit over a pot while some eagle man flaps them places."

The old man sat back down on his rock. "You're welcome," he said after a moment as Rich and Melvin looked on.

"Thank you," Rich said.

"You can thank me by not wind-blasting hapless villages into debris," the old man said.

"Are you a quest-mage?" Melvin asked. He was still puzzled by this whole turn of events. It was obvious the old man knew magic, but he dressed differently than any mage Melvin had seen. Even the quest-mage they'd hired to free Rich from stone wore a robe.

"No," he said. "I've got no need for quests and I see a lot better than any robe I've ever run across." He said no more than that and simply sat on the rock, unmoving as if he was part of the scenery.

Rich grabbed Melvin by the arm and nudged his head towards the town. It was time to go. The old man made no move as the couple walked past him.

As the name suggested, Mere was small. Melvin found it very reminiscent of Triptoe with its festively colored houses, built with a combination of wood and mud brick. The buildings lined the neat dirt roads in a more or less orderly fashion, which made this town feel about as close to the suburbs as Melvin was going to get in this world.

"That was kind of weird," Melvin told Rich. "You know, with the old dude."

"Tell me about it," Rich said. "I am kinda glad he showed me how to make a portal root, though. The diagrams and instructions in my books were all confusing so I was scared to try it. It reminded me of trying to put together IKEA furniture, and a portal root's probably not something you want have extra screws left over after you build it."

"You put your own furniture together?" Melvin asked with a laugh. "Is that why your wardrobe has that crazy slant to it?"

"Crazy nothing!" Rich said. "I wanted to make it more aerodynamic. You know, avant garde."

"Mmmm-hmmm," Melvin said from the side of his mouth, regarding Rich with a raised eyebrow.

"You know what? You try assembling a PAX Uggdal before you judge me! No one can put that thing together right; that's science."

"Can't argue with science," Melvin said smiling.

Rich's smile made Melvin's smile grow. As they strolled past quaint cottages, Melvin realized the two of them were finally alone together. Time to try his feminine wiles.

"Hey, Rich? Remember at the Temple of Houses, when you... um... helped me when my body... ah... changed?"

"Course I do," he said.

"See... ah... my body's changed a lot more since then. Well, I guess you can't tell, I mean, it looks the same right? But I'm able to get into Zhufira mode a lot more easier. Plus, um... some other stuff..."

Rich's face scrunched up. "Stuff like what?"

Melvin could feel his cheeks getting hot. Real girls didn't have this kind of problem talking with guys about sex, did they? Where was all his charm and allure hiding, that stuff he'd seen in all the girls he'd ever liked... was there a Zhufira mode for that?

"Well... um... it's the kinda stuff that I guess every hot-blooded warrioress feels..."

"What, a need for steel swimwear?" Rich asked with a smile. "You miss your bikini bottoms?"

Melvin laughed, which sounded a bit too loud and nervous to his own ears. Before he could specify what it is a hot-blooded warrioress feels, Rich pointed to a large building on the adjacent corner. Upbeat music emanated from it.

"Looks like that's our tavern," Rich said. He looked at Melvin. "You wanna get a drink and finish telling me about your body changes?"

In the bar, with the whole world listening? Melvin shook his head vigorously. "That's OK. It's nothing; I was just making small talk until we found this place." He forced a smile.

"Consider it found," Rich said smiling back. He bowed slightly and offered his arm for Melvin to take. "Shall we?"

Melvin took Rich's arm and allowed himself to be escorted. Acts like this confused Melvin; offering an arm made it obvious Rich saw him as a girl on some level. So if Rich could see the girl why didn't he *notice* the girl? Why was he making this so hard? Melvin answered his own questions with a deep, wistful sigh.

The mood inside the bar wasn't in keeping with the lively sounds coming from it. A lot of that had to do with Melvin and Rich's travel mates. Mike and Runt sat at a table, the two of them sharing grimaces between draughts of beer. The aian escort occupied a singular table bereft of beverages or conversation; they all sat erect and stoic as if they anticipated a life or death bar fight despite the fact that the tavern only entertained a handful of townies. Ruki Provos sat alone at the bar, his head down and eyes staring into his short, squat glass as if he was divining his future in the murky brown liquid. Rich and Melvin went with the most inviting option of Mike and Runt.

"Can we join you?" Rich asked Mike.

Melvin sat without waiting for a response, pulling Rich by the arm into another unoccupied seat. The last thing Rich had to do was ask Melvin's dumb brother for permission.

Mike merely raised an eyebrow to Rich's question and Melvin's display. He pointed a little gloved finger at Rich, his blue goggles refracting light as he leaned towards the mage.

"Understand you and I are square now. We already had our words. No need to go asking polite-ities and tiptoeing around me. That shit'll just get on my nerves."

"OK," Rich said visibly relieved. He signaled the barkeep for a beer.

Mike put his hand up. "We cool; that's you and me. I don't speak for Runt."

Rich turned to address Runt but the half-weagr shook his head. "No need to explain, Rich Razzleblad. It was a height I would not want to wake up to, either."

"You probably would've done better up there asleep," Mike told Runt with a laugh. "You looked about as comfortable as a cat in water. Hell, that was first class compared to a CH-53. They got these hammock seats and the damn roof leaks hydraulic fluid all over you, no matter where you sit. I remember one time when a pipe burst—"

"Mike," Melvin interrupted his brother, who had his hand in the air to simulate the helicopter he was describing. Melvin pointed a thumb at Ruki. As if on cue, Ruki knocked back his drink in one large gulp and gestured for another. "Should we go talk to him?" Melvin asked.

"I already tried," Mike said. "Some shit people need space to deal with. So give him space."

Another look at Ruki was enough to make Melvin disagree with his brother. The tradesman sat at the corner of the bar, his jaw clenched and skin tight around his eyes. He looked like he was wallowing in despair. Whatever the space was doing, it wasn't helping.

"C'mon, Mike, let's try to talk to him again."

Mike scrunched up his face and grabbed his glass. "Didn't I tell you—"

Melvin gave him a look that stopped him short.

"Aight," Mike said, setting his glass down. "You wanna see for yourself, let's see." He got up from the table and walked with his brother towards Ruki. "I don't appreciate you cutting your eyes at me like Mom used to do, though," Mike told Melvin.

Melvin and Mike took seats on either side of Ruki with Melvin taking his seat casually while Mike's short stature compelled him to do what amounted to a pull up on the bar before pushing off to get into his seat. The tradesman didn't affect to notice; instead he studied the dark contents of his glass until he upended it.

"Hey Ruki," Melvin said, his voice soft, full of concern.

"This is wrong," Ruki replied, looking down as if he addressed the empty glass.

"What's wrong?" Melvin asked.

"This," Ruki said, finally looking up from the bar to take in the whole room. "All this."

Pushing the glass away, Ruki began to speak, answering Melvin's unasked questions.

"He raised me, you see, took me in after my parents died, taught me everything he knew about business, what it meant to be a merchant. He had fierce pride in his profession. He used to say, 'Success in trade isn't like love; you won't have to wonder.' And he was right. I never wondered. He was never one to smile, but I got the only grins I've ever seen him make when I brought back huge contracts, deals he didn't think to make along the routes that I secured. I was good.

"So when I say 'this is wrong', I'm referring to a tradesman being in a town without trade goods to trade. Wrong is a business man on a bird-baked adventure to the Hierophane instead of doing something—anything—of business worth. Indeed, there's nothing right about a merchant who's knocking back drinks when his flagship store sits in ruins."

"Yo, Ruki—" Mike began.

"This is where we part ways," Ruki interrupted. "I've gotten too far away from who I'm supposed to be, what my uncle wanted me to be, and it got him killed."

Both Mike and Melvin made moves to protest, but Ruki held his hand up and shook his head.

"I don't blame you, any of you, for what happened to Uncle. If anyone's at fault it's me."

"You can't blame yourself for what happened, Ruki," Melvin said.

"I can," he said with a sardonic smile. "But it's not about blame, not really. Mostly I want—no, I need—to go back to something I'm good at, something I feel good doing. That's business, not leaping from one deadly ordeal to the next."

Ruki splashed a handful of coins across the bar and rose from his seat. "Goodbye, Morrow Brothers," he said, looking at the two of them. "Good luck on your travels."

Melvin was speechless. He wanted to tell Ruki it would be OK, that he shouldn't go, but the words weren't there. Mike leapt off his stool and held his hand out.

"I understand, Ruki," he said. "I appreciate all your help, homey. Know that I always got your back, hell or high water. Stay up."

Ruki grasped Mike's hand and nodded. A faint smile creased both of their mouths, a knowing smile borne of sharing high stakes on an unpredictable road together.

"Goodbye, Ruki," Melvin managed to say.

Ruki Provos made his way to Runt, where he held his hand out in parting. Runt rose from his seat and took out his bladed staff. He disassembled the staff into twin axes and crossed them over his chest.

"My blades are ever your blades, Ruki Provos. Fare you well."

Ruki smiled at that. He gave Runt and hearty clap on the shoulder, shook Rich's hand and left the tavern.

"You should get a drink, Mel," Mike said heading back to the table.

For lack of better options, Melvin got a beer. He was halfway through it, with Mike recounting the Maltep heist for Rich, who had missed the first telling of it for being trapped in stone, when Jason strolled into the bar with Targhos and Garol in tow. Targhos and Garol joined their aian comrades while Jason sat down with everyone else. He leaned forward conspiratorially.

"Dudes," he said, "we're in the middle of some serious deep shiz."

"Ruki Provos left," Melvin said.

"Good," Jason said. When the faces of the guys around the table turned sour, Jason waved them off with his bone hand. "No, seriously, that's good. Our escort, guys, they're not House Demir."

"You're not making sense," Rich said. "Don't you see the wings?"

"That's what they want you to see," Jason said. "They keep hidden, just like they told us at the High Fane." Jason leaned even closer and spoke in a harsh whisper. "These guys are Twelfth House."

Melvin leaned toward Jason in disbelief. "Onus?"

Jason nodded slowly. "Who do you think I just spent an hour shooting the breeze with?"

Targhos seemed to know what their group was talking about; he got up and came over to the table bringing half the winged aians with him.

"Undoubtedly, Cephrin has informed you on certain aspects of our house and nature," Targhos said. "As Cephrin can attest, the lord of our house wants no harm to come to the Chosen One."

Everyone at the table looked at Jason, who shrugged and nodded.

"So what's he want with you?" Melvin asked.

"Let's just say his envy of my six-pack goes well beyond normal," Jason replied.

"We have been charged to protect the Chosen One," Targhos said. "Naturally, that courtesy extends to his comrades as well. Know that the orders of the Chosen One are second only to our House Lord. We stand ready to fly all of you to any destination you choose."

"What happens if we decline your services?" Jason asked.

"We eat your hearts," Targhos said flatly.

Everyone at the table looked at each other. Abruptly, Targhos filled the room with laughter.

"Forgive my humor, but the look on your faces was worth the prank. The uninitiated tend to believe such foolish things until they've learned to shed the infantile preconceptions the High Fane feeds them," Targhos replied. "We would respect your decision and leave you to your own means. But know that we would surreptitiously monitor your travels and stand ready to intervene, as we did at Dreft Esker, if necessary. In us you'll find no better vassals."

"Can you give us a minute to talk?" Jason asked.

"Certainly," Targhos said with a bow before taking his entourage back to their table.

"I don't like this," Melvin said. He recalled the picture hanging in the Temple of Houses, the one of Onus' body being eaten away by maggots. Whatever infantile notions the High Fane had of the Twelfth House, it was likely grounded in some truth.

"You know what I don't like?" Mike asked. "Walking. I don't care if these dudes are dropouts from the Wicked Witch of the West Flying Monkey College or original backup dancers for MC Hammer; their wings trump my shoes. I say we fly."

"I trust my boots," Runt said with a grimace.

"You would say that cause your heart turns mushy at cruising altitude," Mike said. "You'll be aight, just do what I do before I fly and get drunk."

"I'm with Runt and Melvin," Jason said. "I don't want these dudes tailing me, flying me anywhere, nothing."

"No, I think Mike has a solid point," Rich said. "I mean we've got things chasing us: the aians, the Graverobber, who knows what else. We should get to the Hierophane as fast as possible. That means flying."

"That's easy for you to say," Jason said. "You don't have Onus looking at you like you're what's hot to wear to prom."

"No, it's easy for us all to say," Rich said. "Once we make the Hierophane and take the pendulum back, there'll be no pursuers, no Onus, nothing trying to kill us. We don't have to worry about any dastardly evil overlord plots if we're not here, you know?"

Melvin nodded. "Sooner we get back, the sooner we'll be trouble free, Jason. And you don't have to worry about Onus sweating you if you go into the Hierophane and never come out."

Jason chewed his lip, as if the answer didn't quite sit right to him. But he didn't speak on it, which wasn't typical at all for him. Jason loved to point out the angles no one else had thought of. If there were any other angles to consider, he kept them to himself this time. Finally, he nodded.

"So... we fly," he said.

"Word," Mike agreed.

Runt grimaced before draining his glass hastily.

Their travel arrangements settled, everyone filed out of the tavern. Only a few townspeople milled about the town and fewer still turned to look at their motley ensemble. Melvin looked at the sky; they still had a few hours of daylight left.

They all held their arms up in the air and an aian—in Runt's case two aians—came behind them to grab their wrists. Before they lifted off, Melvin heard a shout behind them crying "Wait!"

Melvin turned and saw Ruki Provos walking up to him, his hands behind his back.

"I've heard a few times about who you are and what you are," Ruki told Melvin. "All the same, I'll remember you fondly as who you apparently aren't but I see plain as day. I've gotten you something."

He pulled his hands from behind his back and presented Melvin with a small, pink stuffed strandwolf. Unlike the ones that swarmed them back at Fort Law, this little strandwolf had large white eyes and a toothy grin that was full of glee. A little mane of pinkish-red hair ran down its back.

It was made for a girl. And it was pink.

It was unbelievably cute.

Melvin hugged Ruki tight. "Thank you," Mel breathed. "I love it. Thank you so much."

Ruki hugged back. "If you should ever find your way back to Suusteren, do look me up, pretty brother."

Melvin nodded. He made it a point to stow his pet strandwolf in his pack so he wouldn't drop her in flight.

Then they were in the air, getting carried off by winged agents of Onus while Ruki Provos waved goodbye until he became a small dot in a town that was increasingly shrinking from sight.

CHAPTER 18
The Barons

Rich had an easier time with being suspended in air now that he wasn't waking up from a living nightmare. The aians flew at a low altitude thanks to Runt's insistence, so while Rich couldn't see a lot of the countryside, what he could see seemed close enough to touch. They soared over a vast forest canopy, spread out beneath them as far as the eye could see. The leaves splashed in a beautiful clash of green, red, yellow, purple and golden brown as they battled against the coming winter.

The thought reminded Rich of another battle, the one the cost had recently manufactured for him. The horrific scenes of all his friends being killed systematically flashed in his mind. It was a brutal cost, but then again, they all were.

The *Birleshik Arcana* talked about the Rites of Ascension, which started when an acolyte took an oath that bound magic potential, preventing access to higher command magic until the mage could pass certain tests. The benefit of the Oath of Binding was that while it was increasingly difficult to ascend to access the highest levels, the levels a mage had passed carried with them reduced costs.

Unlike real mages, Rich had effectively cheated his way to gray, without the Oath of Binding or passing any of the rites to ascend to higher levels. He could access insanely high levels of magic, especially when mortal terror tripped his Razzleblad trigger, but the downside was that all magic, whether he created a category five tornado or a simple bowl of water cost the exact same.

It didn't matter if Rich knew the nature of the cost and why his costs were so exacting. None of his books, in their infinite wisdom, decided to print the Oath of Binding; otherwise he would've opted out of gray already. So the only thing that mattered now was getting to the Pendulum and escaping this world and these robes. If he didn't, he knew it would only be a matter of time before Richard Bates broke him down, before the cost claimed his sanity.

Well, they were certainly on their way to ending his torture. The eaglemen were making good time over this vast forest, and even though it sprawled endlessly before Rich, he felt good for the speed they flew. He knew even endless forests had an end, and with it came the last leg of their journey. Things were looking up.

Overhead, the sun's light suddenly grew in intensity, like a light bulb being fed more voltage. Rich had to turn his head down and away, squinting in discomfort. Before he could ask what was going on, the sun's light discharged in a pulse and mayhem descended with its blinding rays.

THERE WAS A REASON the Army constantly briefed soldiers about trips, slips and falls; those bitches hurt. Mike picked himself gingerly off the ground, feeling the sting of a dozen bruises, batters and cuts. He pulled off a few broken tree branches that had gotten stuck to him during the hard crash down. Other than topical wounds and a harsh skin treatment, Mike was all right.

Taking stock of the forest floor, he considered himself lucky. He had landed next to a thick, brambly blackberry bush. Unlike most forests he had seen back on the East Coast, this forest's understory was home to a parade of big, inhospitable plants. He recognized the strawberry and blackberry bushes for the fruit along with the rose bushes. Vine plants grew up the bark of trees and hung down from branches in tangles. Coupled with other bushes he didn't recognize and a moss-covered, fallen tree here and there, this forest looked hard to navigate. He didn't see any of his people in this mess.

"Glad to see that little light show didn't kill you," a strange voice said behind Mike.

Mike turned and saw an aian from the house of snakes leaning against a vine covered tree, smoking a hand-rolled cigarette. His head was down as if he was either trying to nap standing up or the act of looking at Mike wasn't worth bothering with. He wore black leather armor with diamond patterns of white and blood red. One of his hands held a machete that looked bigger than Mike. The other hand took the cigarette out of his mouth and he spoke as smoke fumed out.

"See, I want you alive when I cut your little pecker off."

"Word?" Mike asked. "Lemme ask you something, Slithers, you come way out here just so I could tune you up, or do you live here and was waiting for a miracle asswhipping to rain down on you from heaven?"

"Heh!" Slithers spat. "We made it rain. Well, more like he made it rain." He pointed his machete upwards, where a blonde-haired human dude sat high up on a branch of the same tree the snake leaned against. The man, wearing gleaming white robes, fingered a necklace chain that hosted a pendant of a radiating sun. He waved cordially and flashed a smile.

"Little purple lizard negro," the snake aian said, "you ain't got a good goddamn clue who we are, do you?"

"Keep talking," Mike said nodding as his ire rose. "Cause you starting to look like a new pair of snakeskin boots to me," Mike said. "Dude in the white wedding gown must be your boyfriend."

"He's clever," the man in white purred. "And saucy."

"Let's see," the snake aian said. "Let's see if he's clever. You know the thing about this game, friend?" he asked Mike. "Ain't nobody playing it by themselves."

Slithers had called this a game. And he had called Mike a negro, something Mike was sure wasn't what they called brothers around here. Now the pieces were starting to fit.

"Y'all are boys with purple dress," Mike said, referencing the purple robed pendulum reject he had killed in the Sprawl.

Slithers looked up at the white robe. "You were right, darlin'. Sumofabitch is clever. And here I was thinking I was gonna have to start speaking ape!"

Before Mike's indignation could flare, White Robe tsk'ed sharply. "Babe!" he scolded. "That is abhorrent, the very antithesis of progressive."

"For fuck's sake, darlin'!" Slithers called up. "We fixing to kill him. Can't I have a little fun?"

White Robe turned his head up and away in answer. "Goddamit!" Slithers swore and looked back at Mike, chagrin on his face.

"Forgive my lack of couth," Slithers said. He took a drag on his cigarette and breathed out smoke as if he was exhaling exasperation. "How bout we start over, this time with some nice introductions and how do you do's? I go by Kriminel. Up there is La Croix. We already know you as the megrym who killed Samedi. Now, you can give us a proper name if you like, but it don't make much a difference—we ain't gonna be erecting no headstones or nothing."

"Your boy had it coming," Mike told him.

"I don't doubt that, friend. Samedi was a right ornery fucker. Mean-spirited through and through to speak truthfully about the dead. Still, there's a reckoning to be had. You killed a baron, one of our own."

"Babe," La Croix called down, "the Khermer girl is on her way and I don't know how many she's bringing with her."

"Well, you heard him," Kriminel said, flicking his cigarette into a nearby bramble bush. "And me and La Croix are sensible; we don't see the need of slaughtering the whole herd cause one bull trampled where it ought not trample. You best settle up now before your pals get involved and get murdered on your account."

"Aight," Mike said, "this is your last chance to roll out, go on home to Brokeback Mountain and live your life out. You sure you want some of what Samedi got?"

Kriminel smiled. "With sugar on it."

Mike grabbed his club, transferred it to his left hand, his weaker hand. He smacked the ground with it a couple times, pointed it at Kriminel.

And fired his diskbow.

The diskblade whirled, moving in a blur like a sprung mousetrap. It hit Kriminel in the gut.

Mike had seen the wickedly sharp diskblades cut off arms, hit a man in the gut and erupt out his back. This time the blade barely broke skin, coming to a dead stop as if Kriminel's abs were made of concrete. Kriminel reached down and plucked the harmless disk out of his skin, looked at it like he was impressed with the craftsmanship before he tossed it aside, and raised an eyebrow to Mike.

"Heh, you *are* a clever one, ain't ya? But you're gonna have to work harder than that. I got me an angel on my shoulder."

Mike holstered his club and smacked his glove hands together. He pulled them apart and the electricity arced between his hands, ready for him to cook whatever he directed the blast at.

Yellow lights, a stream of energy slivers, shot from La Croix's extended fingertips as he popped his hands in imitation of twin pistols. The energy stream cascaded through Mike's arc lightning, disrupting and dispelling the electricity before Mike could blast it out at Kriminel.

"Now, now," La Croix said with a shake of his head. "If you wanted to play with energy, you had your chance during the character creation phase."

Kriminel ran at Mike, his machete hoisted behind him to strike. Mike brought his club up. With a hoarse, angry yell, Kriminel swung.

Mike blocked the blow and stumbled. Another swipe came, just as hard. Mike was ready. He pushed his weight into his club as he blocked. Then he turned and lashed out.

Kriminel, fast as a cobra strike, dodged in a whirl. The machete lashed out again like a fang.

Mike managed to block, barely. Kriminel came down with his free hand, delivering a vicious left hook to Mike's face. Mike stumbled back.

Not letting up, Kriminel whirled again, backhanding with his machete in a swipe aimed to take Mike's head.

Mike hit the dirt, falling on his back as Kriminel's machete cut across empty air. On his back, Mike kicked out with both legs, aiming for Kriminel's knees. The impact forced the snake aian to stagger and drop to his knees.

Mike came up from the ground, his club leading the way. It scored Kriminel's chin, like an overpowered uppercut, knocking Kriminel on his back.

Kriminel didn't stay down for long. Before a full second had passed, he had flipped off his back into a crouch. If he was stunned or otherwise hurt from Mike's vicious club swing, he wasn't showing it. In fact, he smiled at the megrym.

"You got some fight in you, I'll give you that."

"What you got in you—steroids?" Mike asked. This guy seemed invincible. Meanwhile, his own face stung bitterly from the left hook.

"Heh," Kriminel said as if that answered the question. He rose from his crouch into a battle stance, his machete poised above his head and pointing at Mike like a scorpion's tail. Mike knew if Kriminel's obscene endurance held, it would only be a matter of time until he felt the sting of that blade.

Of all possible saviors, La Croix was the one who stayed the battle. He had come down from his branch and was running to meet Kriminel. "Babe," La Croix said pointing to a quiet patch of thickets across the clearing. "We're out of time."

Kriminel kept his battle stance but backed away slowly from Mike, La Croix in tow, his dancing eyes alternating between Mike and the silent space of forest brush. Like some sort of short term prophecy, the thickets started rustling. The rustling grew in intensity until two mighty swipes of double-edged sword brought Mike's brother into the clearing with a sizeable backup.

Mel led Runt and Jason along with Targhos and six of his flyers. Visible relief flashed across Mel's face at the sight of Mike. It was quickly replaced with confusion then anger as he saw Kriminel's machete in strike position.

"I don't know who you are," Mel said, raising his sword with Zhufira grace to mirror Kriminel's same stance, "but you picked the wrong megrym."

Kriminel displayed a toothy grin and let his forked tongue flicker. "We're just playin' a lil game, sugar, some 'slice the tail off the monkey'. Now you welcome to play, but it ain't exactly a favorite for girls with pretty faces."

Kriminel's words made Mel's brow furrow in rage. Mel may look like a pretty girl, but he'll be damned if you called him that.

Targhos came to stand beside Mel, drew his sword and pointed it at La Croix. "Sun cleric," he spat, "you are responsible for the deaths of at least two of my brothers."

La Croix frowned as if the facts presented stung. "Well," he said, "your grumpy attitude certainly won't bring them back."

With a roar, Targhos flew at La Croix. His wings flapped furiously as he sped towards the sun cleric, his sword held out to impale the man.

Almost in a blur, Kriminel shot out and intercepted Targhos. His free hand grabbed Targhos' sword arm while he swung his body into a cartwheel-like leap to land on top of the flying aian. Moving with the fluidity of a snake, Kriminel's legs wrapped around Targhos', he wove his body and arms under and around Targhos' where it looked like the flying aian could only move his wings, which still flapped towards La Croix.

Kriminel contracted his muscles. As he did so, Targhos' body bent backwards, as if his head and feet were trying to touch his wings. With a choking gurgle as Kriminel applied pressure with an arm across Targhos' throat, the flying aian's wings lurched and he landed with a crash, Kriminel still wrapped around him as they tumbled across the clearing.

Once they came to a stop, Kriminel was under Targhos. But he still had Targhos horribly bent backwards. Targhos had dropped his sword by this time and was clawing futilely at the air, his head and neck bent so far backwards he couldn't even see where he was clawing at. Kriminel flashed his grin once more and brought up the hand he wasn't using to pin down Targhos.

It held the machete. And he brought it down without ceremony into Targhos' gut.

"Holy shit!" Jason swore as Kriminel buried his blade to the hilt. Targhos' clawing hands went spastic, then went limp.

"Bastard!" Sevollian spat while Kriminel smoothly untangled himself from Targhos' dead body. The rest of the flyers fanned out in a half circle to face La Croix and Kriminel.

"There is no need to maintain pretense for these dead men, brothers," Sevollian told his warriors. "Let them tremble with fear as they look upon their doom."

Mike took an involuntary step back as the flyers unfurled their wings and a throbbing darkness enveloped them. Feathers fell and the darkness grew in pulses. When the blackness faded Mike was left staring agape at monstrous, leathery bat wings.

"Holy shit," he said echoing Jason.

Kriminel and La Croix looked at each other for a long, wordless moment. Then in unison, they both started laughing.

A collective rage consumed the mutant flyers. The derisive laughter of the two barons was both a challenge and insult to whatever menace the sons of Onus believed they possessed. They surged toward their enemy as one, a dark tide rushing to destroy.

La Croix grabbed the radiating sun pendant dangling from his neck and shouted, "Sun for truth in light, for life in day. Burn through darkness, let none cast shadows!"

Light blossomed out of the sun pendant in all directions as if it was the epicenter of a nuclear explosion. Mike's goggles shielded his eyes, allowing him to watch as the light blasted out into the clearing. The light didn't affect Mike and it didn't seem to hurt Mel, Runt and Jason, who only moved to shield their eyes from the brilliance. The same couldn't be said of the flyers; just like a nuke, he saw them all disintegrate into the light.

The light died and a surreal, quiet peace filled the clearing. Mike, Mel, Runt and Jason were left facing Kriminel and La Croix. The flyers, their weapons and the dead body of Targhos had all disappeared as if they had never been there. Even the blood that had stained Kriminel's blade had been washed clean; it gleamed as it rested against his shoulder.

"What you think, darlin'?" Kriminel asked La Croix as he looked at his remaining adversaries. "Them's bout even odds."

La Croix shrugged and nodded noncommittally, looking the newcomers up and down as if Kriminel had stretched the truth by overestimating the opposition. The sun cleric held his hand out and circular bands of yellow light coursed twin paths down to the ground and up to his head. Gleaming white wood coalesced where the bands passed until La Croix held a thick staff that was crowned with a radiating sun symbol which mimicked his pendant.

"I'll take the aian boy," La Croix said, "and your pretty Khermer girlfriend."

"What about it, big fella," Kriminel said to Runt. "Care to dance? I'm wagering you ain't got the moves like chocolate lizard over here... he's got what they call natural rhythm."

Mel struck first. Mike wasn't sure if it was the pretty girl remark or the chocolate lizard thing, but he was all Zhufira as he lunged at Kriminel with a growl. Kriminel blocked, his machete meeting Mel's sword with clang and sparks. Their blades met two more times as blurs so fast it was impossible to tell who was attacking and who was parrying.

La Croix's staff came down at Mel's head. Runt rushed in and caught the staff with the head of his Z-blade. It didn't matter; Mel had whirled past the blow like it had been telegraphed to him a month ago and brought his sword across to swipe at Kriminel. Kriminel matched with his own rapid fire parries and strikes.

Jason nocked an arrow and watched, waiting for a clear shot at either combatant. Mike wasn't about watching, not when he had a new pair of snakeskin boots to claim. He came at Kriminel.

Kriminel altered his dance with Mel to dodge Mike's club, taking swooping steps and exaggerated bows as his blade rang out time after time against Mel's.

Strobe-like flashing made Mike aware of Runt's precarious situation. The half-weagr handled his Z-blade deftly as he traded staff blows with La Croix, but the sun cleric sent sporadic energy pulses through his staff, making the sun emblem at the head of the staff flare out with painful, stabbing light. It was forcing Runt back and affecting his aim as he tried to fight through temporary blindness. It was all Runt could do to block crushing staff blows while trying to manage a few errant strikes of his own.

Mike's club scored the back of Kriminel's knee, a blow that should've knocked him down. Yet Kriminel stood, deflecting more of Mel's blows, his knee giving little to the club. Kriminel rolled away from both Mel and Mike's dual strikes.

The high pitched twang of a fired arrow sounded as Kriminel stood up from his roll. He caught Jason's arrow in the neck, but just like Mike's diskblade, it hardly broke the surface of his skin. Kriminel pulled the arrow barely hanging on out of his neck as if it was a nuisance more than anything else.

"These guys are buffed!" Jason shouted.

"What the hell's buffed?" Mike asked Mel as they both faced Kriminel.

"Shielded," Mel said, meeting Kriminel's smile and flickering tongue with a level gaze and a snarl.

"Even a blind kid could've seen that," La Croix said smirking as he sidestepped Runt's clumsy, half-blind swipe. "Let me show you."

La Croix hopped backwards and flicked his fingers at Jason like he was giving the peace sign. Two energy bolts flashed from La Croix's fingers and shot into Jason's eyes.

Jason dropped his bow and grasped his eyes howling. "Son of a bitch!" he cried.

Kriminel ran at Mel and Mike. They charged in to meet him halfway.

The deadly dance resumed. Mike tried to score a hit, any hit against the incredibly agile Kriminel while dodging the occasional machete side swipe, or lightning fast kick or punch. Mel's offensive was just as ineffective as their blades clashed.

This deck was stacked, high enough to fall over and kill Mike and Mel with a stiff breeze. All Kriminel needed was one opening, one well placed blow to end either of them. Kriminel and La Croix had a running surplus of second chances with their shield up.

Mike swung his club at Kriminel's ribs.

Kriminel brought his blade down hard on Mel's blade, deflecting Mel's strike. As his machete rebounded back from the force of the blow, Kriminel swung it down at Mike.

There was no time to block as the blade came down.

Mel lunged, his sword catching the machete inches above Mike's head. Kriminel threw an elbow, smashing into Mel's face. He cried out more from anger than pain. Mike pressed his attack, giving Mel a chance to recover. Kriminel kept his poise, unfazed by Mike's angry strikes.

Mel tried to circle around Kriminel but was thwarted as the snake aian retreated in measured steps to where he and La Croix were back-to-back.

Out of nowhere, Jason shouted "Onus!" Mike saw Jason moving unnaturally fast, quicker than the diskbow blades. He ran through the melee and grabbed both La Croix and Kriminel by their backs. Lifting them off the ground as they struggled and shouted in protest, he spun in circles while clutching two handfuls of killer enemy. After a cyclone of whirls he released them as if he was throwing the discus.

Mike watched in mute shock as both La Croix and Kriminel shot upwards, breaking tree limbs and branches as they blasted a hole through the forest canopy. They streaked what seemed like a mile in the air, becoming small dots before the arc of their flight path descended and they disappeared completely from view.

Mike, Mel and Runt looked at Jason like he was a dead relative at the front door who showed up for Thanksgiving dinner.

"What?" he asked defensively. "You don't go messing with an archer's eyesight. Everyone knows that."

Mike pointed up at the unnatural hole of broken and splintered branches left in the barons' wake. "So you gonna act like tossing folks past Jesus' window is just another Tuesday, huh?"

"I'll explain on the way," Jason said. "But right now we should move. I have a strong feeling they survived that trip."

The kid had a point about their survivability. Why take chances? "Word," Mike said, "so how do we get out of this forest?"

"It's not out we're going," Jason said. "Look around. Rich is missing."

CHAPTER 19
Clash of Gray

When Rich came to, he was lying on the forest floor. The first thing he recalled was the unbearably bright light, yelling, screaming and finally, falling. He bolted upright, knocking broken branches and twigs off his body as he scanned the area for his friends. Only the occasional rustle of bushes made by chirping birds greeted his eyes.

What if this was a cost? This scenario certainly started off like a heinous Richard Bates plan. He could be in the middle of living through a nightmare while in reality he was peacefully drifting in the skies. He had no way to be sure.

Just don't wake up scared of falling, he thought. Without much recourse, Rich picked himself up, groaning as his body painfully informed him of the many bruises it had collected on the way down from heaven. If this wasn't the cost, he'd best find the gang. If it was the cost, no way Richard Bates would stand back and let him nap it out. Either way, it was time to get a move on.

He didn't get much of a move on. This forest wasn't hospitable to visitors. The blackberry and rose bushes caught on his robe in a dozen places and the calla lilies, netted in places with thick spider webs, made him wary as he tried to navigate through the dense understory. He looked to the sky as if there was an easier way out of the forest up there. An eerie afternoon fog loomed over the forest, causing the trees to stretch silently into the veil where their foliage hung as figments and ghosts.

It would be dark soon, and this was no place he wanted to spend the night alone in. He turned his attention back to escape and pulled his way through the brambles that clawed at him to stay.

After pushing through a wall of ferny bushes, Rich emerged in a clearing. No, not a clearing so much as a wide trench that had been blazed and bulldozed. The crudely dug chasm ran perpendicular to his present path before disappearing into places hidden by detritus. Uprooted, charred plants and felled trees littered either side of the trench, as if the digger had raged against this forest and its lush understory.

The way Rich looked at it, he didn't have much in the way of options. Every one of the dozen or so steps he had taken towards getting to this crude clearing had been impeded by plant life. Besides, it wasn't like he had a map; wandering around aimlessly was the easiest way to stay aimlessly lost. He looked at the scorched, upturned earth, stepped down into the trench and headed in the same direction the trail blazed. The path had to lead somewhere, and judging by the raw haste in which it was made, he wasn't entirely sure he wanted to go where it had started.

He made his way around a massive strawberry bush that had fallen into the trench after an unknown portion of it had been burned away. Once he cleared the bush, his breath caught in his throat.

The trail ended in the worst way imaginable. Rich stared at the ravaged ground of a massive clearing. In the middle of the clearing an obscene pile of debris gathered—huge, burnt chunks of countless tree trunks, a mass of twisted brambles, caked up piles of raw earth, and all of it crudely formed into a dome. What remained of the standing trees immediately surrounding the clearing were bent toward this dome of devastated nature. Whole branches and parts of their trunks had been ripped off savagely, as if some malevolent, pulling force compelled the trees to bow in homage.

Here, Rich saw what became of the flyer that had carried him. He dangled from one of the trees bent unnaturally toward the debris dome, impaled through the gut by a treetop that had become little more than a jagged spike from whatever had caused this.

The trench made the cause apparent. Rich's eyes followed the carved gash running through the ruined ground until it terminated at the dome. It ended with a figure Rich had seen before, only briefly back in Bramblefen.

Clemson the gray robe. Eyes closed, he lay motionless at the end of the trench, nestled in the debris of the dome.

The feeling that Rich was knee deep in the middle of a cost came back strong. Even in a land of magic, the likelihood of the two of them meeting here was too unbelievable for coincidence. Richard Bates had to be messing with him.

Then he saw Clemson twitch.

Richard Bates was indeed messing with Rich, but not through any cost of his own. Clemson's cost was what had brought him here. Richard Bates must've tripped Clemson's character trigger and the poor kid cast a spell of apocalyptic magnitude to get away from whatever plagued him.

Rich shook his head, revolting against the idea. He remembered costs where Richard Bates had scared him into Razzleblad and he had caused all manners of atrocities, but waking from the cost he had found none of it had happened. The cost should not be able to influence the waking world, which meant Clemson had been awake, got his trigger tripped and blazed this path of destruction—coincidentally right where Rich would be.

That made even less sense. No matter how he tried to slice it, all the parts added up to Richard Bates driving Clemson here to Rich. Having paid his fair share of horrible costs, Rich knew that bastard well enough to see this as something right up his maniacal alley.

Rich took a seat in the trench, staying well away from Clemson to make sure he didn't startle him when he woke up, and watched the new gray robe as he twitched again. If this was a game to Richard Bates, he was about to lose big. Now that Rich had eyes on Clemson, he'd wait until the kid woke up and explain to him what was going on—with this world, the nature of the cost and how to get back. He'd make sure Clemson wouldn't have to cast another spell before they opened the Rift Pendulum, depriving Richard Bates of his newest plaything.

As he waited several minutes, Rich couldn't help but smirk. He was actually looking forward to his next cost, where he could taunt Richard Bates for a change. Well, provided that he wasn't actually living a cost right now, a thought that still intruded from time to time as he watched the conveniently placed Clemson.

Suddenly, Clemson's eyes popped open and he shouted, "Get it away! Get it away from me!" The look on Clemson's face freaked Rich out, an expression he could only describe as perfect disgust. Clemson followed his emphatic shout with a barrage of more words: clear, precise, poetic.

Spellcraft.

"No! No, Clemson!" Rich stood up and waved his hands, trying to derail him from what could only be a spell of insane magnitude coming from a gray robe with a tripped trigger. Clemson ignored Rich. The words kept coming.

Clemson ended his spell with a shout. A legion of tree trunks groaned and blasted out from the debris cluster, all in Rich's direction. One massive trunk careened head on toward Rich.

Rich felt his own mouth move through his terror, heard words he didn't understand. "*Paramparcha eden eli ah-ir!*"

His hands moved on their own accord, coming up to meet the flying trunk moments before it plowed him down. When his hands touched the trunk it stopped as if he had caught a beach ball instead of a log whose diameter was three times his size. A ripple of energy coursed from the two places his hands held the wood and emanated down towards the distant end of the trunk, the wood bulging out as the ripple made its way. Once the shockwave reached the far side, the trunk exploded into a million slivers, all of them headed back towards Clemson.

Clemson was still in character mode after the five second exchange of drastic magic. "*Kurt duvari!*" he cried as the rendered trunk came at him in a million sharp points.

A sound similar to bubble wrap popping came from the debris dome as dime-sized holes exploded all over the place in the large clumps of earth. Pinkish roots—no, earthworms—shot out of the holes and began to stack directly in front of Clemson. In moments he was behind a writhing, pink wall six feet high and three feet thick.

Rich's splinter barrage hit the earthworm wall, stopping the onslaught. But the force of impact pushed through the wall of living matter, causing an explosion of earthworm bits all over Clemson.

The wall of worms collapsed into a squiggling mess. Rich found himself face-to-face again with the newly awakened gray robe. Clemson was busy looking over all the gore he was drenched in. Rich saw his expression change from utter shock to complete revulsion.

"No, Clemson! Wait, hear me out," Rich tried to talk him down. But the spell was already coming.

As he spoke mindlessly, Clemson thrust both hands through the mass of earthworms into the ground. The worms that hadn't been blasted into bits snaked with unnatural speed over the ground. In a moment they had covered over half the distance to Rich, filling a massive square, each worm an inch apart. There they stopped, dug their heads into the dirt and stuck their tails in the air with extreme rigidity.

It was a pink, living bed of spikes.

"Clemson!" Rich called, but the guy was still a world away, lost in spell-craft. Clemson rose from the ground, bringing the ground he still held in his hands with him. The entire earthworm-filled square lifted with a rumble like a giant yawning, a huge sheet as thick as a megrym was tall. And it kept rising.

It was no longer a bed of spikes. It was a spike wall two stories tall. Rich watched as the wall as big as a building stopped rising and began to fall on him.

Rich didn't know what he was saying; the words falling from his lips were both fast and foreign. But as the looming shadow of the spiked wall grew ever bigger as it fell, he knew what he was thinking.

"*Shit.*"

Instinctively, Rich drove his fist into the ground as he finished speaking the words. The ground rocked back and forth like sea water. As if in imitation of his hand, a giant rock pillar, meticulously carved to show the five fingers of a closed fist, sprang up to meet the descending wall.

When the two magical forces collided, a burst of gray light blossomed and blew itself out with a boom. Then it felt like the whole world shattered. A power akin to an explosion without heat and fire pushed him across the clearing as rock, dirt and worms showered everywhere.

Rich picked himself up from the debris strewn field, feeling more than battered, as if he had been smooshed somewhat flatter by some unseen hand. He saw the debris dome had exploded, its contents littered across the field. On the far side of the clearing, Clemson lay on the ground, groaning and clawing the dirt to find purchase.

"You idiot!" Rich yelled, taking hurried strides toward the gray robe. "You'll kill us both, never mind the costs we'll have to endure later."

"You don't understand," Clemson shouted. "I'm trying to kill me! Clemson Goodchild is coming after me, and he's everywhere!"

"Calm down," Rich said as he stepped over burnt brambles. "I can explain all this."

"Explain!" Clemson shouted with a laugh that was more of a cackle, something sick and off kilter. "He's who I was, who I should be. I'm no one now, a character. My own imagination creature. Now characters who look like my character are going to explain!"

"We're real," Rich called halfway to Clemson, who was still scrounging in the dirt. "You're real. What you saw with Clemson wasn't. Hear me out."

"A fake man tells another fake man the real man coming to kill him isn't real. Clemson Goodchild doesn't exist; the man he built is. Ha ha ha!"

"Rich!" a familiar feminine voice called him from behind. He turned and saw Mel making her way to him with Jason, Runt and Mike.

"What the hell happened here?" Mel asked as she ran towards him. "Are you hurt? Were you fighting? Did the barons attack you?"

"I'm fine," Rich said, holding his hands up as she neared him as if showing her he still had five fingers on each hand was proof. "There's nothing to worry about. I can explain this; it's all because of him."

Rich pointed toward Clemson, but wound up pointing at nothing. Only an empty patch of razed forest clearing presented itself. He looked around frantically, futilely.

Clemson Goodchild was gone.

CHAPTER 20
Cornered Quarry

Mel led the chase for the pendulum reject. Not that Mel needed to clear much pathway; this guy's trail plowed through the forest with the haphazard abandon of a seizure. The reject obviously didn't know where he was going and didn't care; he just didn't want to be where he was a moment ago.

Ahead in the distance, a gray light winked in and out of existence. The forest filled with a subsequent boom. Mel whacked through the bush presently in their way, cleaving a makeshift trail toward the commotion.

Mel stopped, speechless as he emerged in the clearing where the gray light must've appeared. Everyone else had to walk around him as he stared at the unnatural display.

Everything festered. In a huge, perfectly circular space, all the plant life was beyond dead, locked in a stage of impossibly exaggerated rot. The blackberries and strawberries hung overripe and bursted on bushes whose leaves were crowded with fungus. The trees stood despite gaping cavities and soft rot cracks throughout their trunks, their multi-colored leaves listed slick and slimy. The trees and plants that stood halfway in the circle of decay were half vibrant and half rotted, looking every bit as freakish as the carnival sideshow performer who had a man's face on one side and a woman's on the other. Even the ground squished as the guys stepped on putrid grass.

"What the hell did he do?" Mel asked still stuck absorbing the obscenity of it all.

"Exactly why we have to find him," Rich said, scanning the ground for footsteps. "He's volatile, extremely powerful. And cracking."

"And gone," Mike said, scanning the forest with goggled eyes.

"We need to de-gone him!" Rich cried, looking around at the putrescent wasteland. "We have to stop him. Look at what's he's doing."

"Yo, what you want us to do?" Mike asked grimacing. "You the one with the special effects up your sleeves. Can you de-gone him?"

"There has to be something we can do," Rich said.

"Yeah, we can bounce," Mike said, nostrils flaring. "This place stinks."

Rich was about to protest but Mel came over and placed a hand on his shoulder.

"Mike's right. The trail ends here, Rich. We can't afford to traipse through this forest turning over stones, not when the barons could be anywhere looking for us."

Rich's face scrunched up in confusion. "The barons?"

Mel explained as they headed away from the rotting zone. Poor Rich had been stuck in stone for the telling and retelling of Mike's exploits after they had gotten separated in Fort Law. A lot of those adventures featured a purple robed mage named Samedi, a terrormancer that originally hailed from Chicago. Mike thought he ended Samedi's terror campaign with a disk to the face, that was until Kriminel and La Croix showed up.

"But why are they called the barons?" Rich asked. He was behind Runt, who was helping Mel clear a path through the forest with his Z-blade.

"Cause baron everthing else, they're annoying as all hell," Mike answered.

"No," Mel said with a calculated swipe at some brambles. "They're named after *loa*, spirits of Haitian Vodou. In Vodou, they believe these *loa* act as intermediaries between humanity and God. There's bunches of *loa*, so many that they're broken up into families. The Ghede family of *loa* embody the powers of death, and that family is run by the barons."

A moment of silence hung in the air. "Ok," Jason said, "is anyone else weirded out by Mel right now?"

Both Mike and Rich sounded an emphatic "yes."

"Screw all of you," Mel said, punctuating the words with a whack of foliage before looking to his right. "Not you Runt."

"I don't mean anything by it," Rich said, "but how do you know this kind of stuff?"

"Wikipedia," Mel replied with a shrug. "Like if I saw something interesting that day or if I ran across a term I had never seen, I'd go to Wikipedia, read about it and a lot of times click on the links that would be on those pages and wind up finding other cool pages. I could lose a good hour or two doing that sometimes. I mean, I can't be the only one here that used to go to it just because, right?"

No one answered. Mel whacked at some overgrown calla lilies. "Screw you guys. Not you Runt."

The reason Mel hadn't studied much of the game lore or stats or whatever else was because there was so much to the real world to get lost in. Haitian Vodou, Mayan calendars, Egyptian pyramids, Mongolian steppes. Cultures and concepts that rung with intrigue and adventure, places Mel had always harbored an unspoken promise to see. The game had been fun and, for a couple months now, the only real way to hang out with Jason, who had immersed himself whole hog. But what was an imagined realm compared to all the real world had to offer?

Mel whacked at a tangle of hanging vines. Guess it was a moot point now. But the research did provide some insight that may be useful.

"There's a fourth baron," Mel said. "Baron Cimetière."

"That makes sense," Rich said nodding. "After all, a standard party is four. I wonder why we haven't run across him yet."

"Maybe he's dead," Mike said. "People don't do so hot when the Pendulum firsts rejects them."

"Maybe we have run across him," Jason said musing. "Maybe he's the Graverobber."

"I don't think bodysnatcher is a playable class," Rich said.

"Neither is bone armed aian," Jason said flexing his skeletal fingers. "Who knows what could've happened to him out here? All I know is he hates us. What do you think, Mel?"

"Anything's possible," Mel said with a nod. "Baron Cimetière translates into Baron Cemetery. And the Graverobber was waiting for us at one."

"Listen," Runt said stopping.

They all stopped in their tracks. Mel heard a constant whisper under the occasional bird chirp and rustle of leaves from squirrels, something that sounded like it was perpetually trying to shush the rest of the forest.

Water.

They made their way toward the sound, and it grew from a whisper to a rush. They emerged from the brush to the banks of a large river. It cut through the forest with authority, splashing over rocks as it ran its turbulent course to places unknown.

"This must be the Arden," Jason said as he looked with appreciation at the coursing whitewater. "I know you guys know what that means."

They didn't.

Jason sighed like he was tired of teaching cats to fetch. "If we follow this river, the *Arden* River, it will take us to *Arden*spar."

"Man, you talking like you had a plan we wasn't gonna do anyway," Mike said indignantly. "Why wouldn't we follow the river? Improved visibility along the bank, no trail to make, no rustling through the brush to give away our position, access to fresh water. Thanks for pointing out our only option."

"But you didn't know where it went," Jason said, pointing in his palm with a bone finger to prove his point.

"I would've seen where it went eventually, since it's the only option," Mike responded. "If you wanna tell me something I don't know, you can explain how you got the juice to toss people around like they're sacks of flour."

Jason explained as the group made their way along the Arden. He talked about the disturbing deal Onus wanted to make along with the free trial of power he offered in the form of the necklace. Jason brought the necklace out and showed them the six maggots protruding from the heart as if it was cool. Mel thought that thing absolutely disturbing—even more so than when Jason first presented his arm of bone.

"So what happens when you run out of maggots?" Mel asked. Even the thought of them wriggling into the heart was gross.

"I guess I run out of god-mode sauce," Jason said.

"This doesn't sound like something you should be guessing at," Mel said. "You should throw that thing away."

"I will once I know I won't need it," Jason said tucking the bracelet underneath his shirt. "I'd rather have one less maggot sticking out of it than be maggot food. Right now, there are too many people whose mission in life is to see us lifeless."

He had a point, but the point wasn't worth much to Mel. Onus was the closest thing to Satan himself this world had. Any gift the god gave couldn't be good. Just the fact that Onus' minions had been banished by light should be proof enough that Jason should be putting as much distance between Onus and his gifts as possible. Mel wanted to argue this but knew they'd be empty words. Jason was going to be Jason, treating his new toy like some kind of gaming cheat code.

A bend in the river caused a change in their direction. When they rounded the bend they were greeted by a late afternoon sun barely peeking above the treetops. Its light played across the surface of the Arden, which had over time turned peaceful, making the water shimmer like sequins as the river coursed.

They made good progress along the river. But they didn't have a lot of time towards making their way, as this long day—with its Hollower battles, Graverobber, magic tornadoes, dialogs with Onus, mage duels and barons—was quickly becoming evening. Not even an hour into their walk, and the sun had already disappeared behind the trees and the sky overhead was changing from orange to red with deep streaks of purple.

No one talked about anything, meaning the subject of making camp never came up. Even when the shadows grew in thickness and Jason had to stare at the ground directly under his feet to ensure his footing was sound, he didn't broach the subject. Mel figured everyone silently agreed this was not a place to make camp in. After the sun set and darkness muted eyesight to where the peaceful gurgle of the Arden alongside them was the strongest signal to guide, they didn't stop. Mike barred Rich from casting fire so they wouldn't advertise their presence to potential pursuers. Instead, he removed his goggles and placed them on his forehead. His eyes glowed green, one a sicker, paler light than the other.

"I'll lead," he said.

They spent an immeasurable time this way, with Mike at their front, a legion of stars overhead, the Arden beside them and all around them the shadowy shapes of a forest steeped in darkness. Mel recalled this was how they spent their very first night in the world, with Mike leading them to Fort Law through the darkness of night, the threat of weagrs behind them. It seemed like so very long ago.

Mike stopped, forcing Mel back to the present.

"Yo, Rich," Mike said. "Gimme some fire."

"Illusion fire or the real stuff?" Rich asked.

"Whatever'll help y'all see this stuff, bruh."

Mel gasped as Rich called fire into existence, exposing a scene both beautiful and unexpected. They were in the midst of ruins so ancient hardly anything was left besides foundation. Powder blue granite walkways and steps extended everywhere, even down to the riverbank where they all stood. The remains of regal marble columns, whittled down over time to knee or waist high, dotted the expanse. Here and there, what had been the walls of this place staggered like pale blue steps, eroded to where even the tallest ones stood at Runt's height. Droplets and flowing ripples were intricately carved into the stonework.

"What is this place?" Mel asked breathlessly.

"Look like camp to me," Mike answered.

Mike had a point. They could only walk so far before exhaustion would claim them; better to pick your spot to rest and not have it pick you. Besides, Mel wanted to explore. It reminded him of places back home he longed to see: Petra, Caesarea, Ephesus.

They made their way up beautifully inlaid granite steps to a place that looked like a promenade. A bowl-like depression dominated the square, which is where Rich set his magic fire to illuminate the makeshift campsite. As everyone else besides Mel sat down, it became apparent this was also where they all wanted to stop their exploration.

"Doesn't anybody want to see what else this place has to offer?" Mel asked indignantly.

"Once you've seen the Sprawl, you get your lifetime fill of ruins, bruh," Mike replied as he brought out his bedroll. Runt seemed to concur with a grunt as he rifled through his pack.

"Meh," Jason said lying with his head propped against his pack turned pillow, seemingly more interested in looking at his little maggot necklace than checking out the ruins.

Rich got to fumbling with his robe, probably to pull out a stupid book. Not this time; Mel grabbed him by the arm and kneeled down to look at Rich with pleading eyes.

"Please, Rich. I can't see this place without you."

Rich seemed to consider a moment then acquiesced with a nod. He removed his hand from his robe, a hand blessedly free of reading material, and stood up while Mel pulled on his sleeve with insistence.

Mel led the way while holding onto Rich's arm to keep him close. Rich lit their path with illusionary mage fire glowing softly in his palm. Together, they walked between and around waist high walls, uncovering a thousand different stories carved into sunken relief on the floors. Images of epic battles and heroes fighting monsters, solitary figures tinkering with vials or scrawling on scrolls, lovers embracing.

It became obvious the builders had lovingly incorporated the waters of the Arden into the design with meticulous care. The powder blue stone extended to embrace the banks of the river, drawing the river deeper into the ruins to form circular pools and oval grottoes. River water flowed into the pathways, running in chiseled grooves that would curve and flare around each other in patterns similar to both Arabic script and French fleur-de-lis. An expansive stone room hosted water the builders had somehow coaxed to flow upwards, and the couple found themselves walking in a water garden, where ankle high granite tiers hosted water that flowed, sprayed, flowered and played in delightful patterns. The fact that the water hadn't eroded the stonework was either a testament to the builders' skill or the lasting power of wonderful magic.

"I'm glad you talked me into this," Rich said, the skin around his eyes wrinkling at the corners while a playful smile creased his mouth.

Mel still held onto Rich's arm, and had been for the duration of their tour through the ruins. Although the place was decidedly different, the electric vibe and carefree feeling reminded Mel of their tour through Nasreddin. They had gotten happily lost in that city together, exploring and enjoying what the aian capital offered. It was nice to feel that again.

"I'm glad you came," Mel said, returning Rich's smile.

The water garden gave way to a pool ringed with rough hewn stone. The pool sat on the edge of the river, overlooking the Arden as it flowed, the pool's rough stonework making it look like a natural outcropping. The difference between this pool and the others Mel had seen was the steam rising from it. Mel kneeled and reached for the water with tentative fingers.

Deliciously warm.

"It's like an onsen," Mel said looking up to Rich with delight.

"What's an onsen?" he asked.

"It's a Japanese term," Mel said. "It means a hot spring, one that people have built structures around so they could incorporate the spring as a sort of natural spa."

"You know, the more you talk," Rich said with an appreciative grin, "the more fascinating you become."

Mel couldn't help but smile. His cheeks grew warm. Tonight had a special magic in the air, a spell mages couldn't cast by reciting textbooks. Tomorrow would be the day where their plan came to fruition, where they'd be home again. Before life returned to normal, he could experience love from a woman's perspective. It was something he would never be able to experience again, and the time do so was fleeting.

Still kneeling, Mel took off his pack, sword and cloak and set them down next to the pool. The onsen provided the perfect excuse for an idea that couldn't miss. Mel rose to face Rich, sly mischief in his smile.

"It's bath time," Mel said. Without warning or ceremony, Mel reached for the hem of his leather top and pulled up, exposing perfect breasts. Crisp shock struck Rich's countenance, and he stared for a long moment until he turned hurriedly to face away from Mel.

"Uh, um... yeah, good idea," Rich stammered.

Mel affected nonchalance while he continued to strip. If Rich had any problems noticing the girl before, he didn't now. "You better believe it," Mel said in agreement.

Taking off his boots and leather pants, Mel turned to face the onsen. "You can look now," he announced devilishly.

Mel didn't have to see Rich to know he had turned around and was getting heaping eyefuls of Mel's bare bottom. Mel relished the attention, taking slow, measured steps down the stairs built into the onsen.

If there was ever a Zhufira mode without sword wielding anger, this was it. Mel was Zhufira, felt her in all her glorious proportions: the curve of her breasts, the sway of her hips. She was dainty as she took each small step to descend deeper into the warm water. She stopped, the water pooling around her calves, and her slender fingers brushed a lock of raven black hair from her face as she turned her head to regard a stuck, staring Rich.

"Coming in?" she asked.

Rich lost whatever slight focus he needed to maintain his fire spell. The light winked out of existence, leaving the mage to stammer in the dark.

"Uh... um... but... oh, wait... fire... ah..."

When Rich finally got through the spell and brought light back, he could she was comfortably in the onsen. The water came up to her chest, framing the two mounds like low cut cleavage.

She looked at him expectantly.

"Oh... um... getting in..." he began.

"It's been a trying day," she said, "with warring and flying and fighting; it's been a day steeped in stress and sweat. Come." She beckoned to him with a curling finger. "Relax."

Rich looked at the onsen then down at himself then back to the onsen as if trying to figure out the process on how to get into the water. Mel could see what he was thinking, causing her to smile at his sense of modesty.

"I'll turn around," she said.

"OK," he said with a nod. "But none of that sneak peek stuff."

She turned. Behind her, Mel heard the fumbling rustle of clothing being removed followed by splashing that sent warm ripples of water to wash against her back.

"OK," Rich said when he was settled. "You can turn around now."

"See?" Mel asked as she faced Rich. "Isn't this relaxing?"

"It does feel good," Rich said with a contented smile.

Mel looked at Rich for long moments. The silence stretched. Surely, Rich could see the invitation in her eyes. Yet, he made no move in her direction. He just stood there, enjoying the water.

Mel wasn't about to waste this opportunity. She closed the space between them, set her hands to drape across his shoulders.

"I want you to sleep with me," she told him.

"What?!" he cried. His face scrunched up like he had misheard every letter in her simple sentence. Then his eyes turned shrewd, like he had figured out her game.

"Richard Bates," he said his own name like an accusation.

"Huh?" Mel said, confused by this bizarre tangent. She didn't know what Rich wanted or what he was asking or even if he was asking. "I know who you are," she told him.

"I..." Rich began shaking his head, "I don't know what this is anymore."

"This is me," she said, her hands on his shoulders pulling him closer. "Asking you..." she felt his chest against hers, the pressure pushing her breasts in a way that sent tingling warmth to her extremities. "Will you sleep with me?"

She kept her gaze level and they stared into each others' eyes for a silent moment stretched taut. Rich broke the silence.

"Don't you have... I don't know... reservations, considering who you used to be?"

"I used to be a guy," she said, "and with any luck, I will be one again someday. But I'm not now. Now I'm in a world filled with danger, where any given day could be my last. I don't want to not know, maybe never know, what it's like."

"You're a woman," he said. "It'll be different from that side, I would think."

"I don't think so," she said. "I've thought about it a lot. I imagine when two bodies are intertwined, moving together in unison, it would be hard to tell where one person ends and the other one begins."

Under the water, Mel felt Rich's hands reaching for her, grabbing her waist.

"Are you sure?" he asked.

She answered by leaning into him. His lips met hers. Bursts of hot electricity radiated through her as they kissed. She felt his hands questing, one gliding along the arch of her back, the other grabbing her bottom with a firm, passionate grip. She moaned as she stepped closer, eager to close the remaining scant space between them.

Suddenly, Rich pushed her away.

"I'm sorry," he said. "I can't... for reasons I can't explain."

Shocked beyond protest, Mel watched as he climbed the stairs leading out of the onsen, grabbed his robe, and worked to don it as he hurriedly left.

She finally found her words. "Rich!" she called. But he was gone, far enough to where his firelight died without his presence.

"I need your light," she said to the empty, silent darkness.

CHAPTER 21
Bedside Manners

Rich felt like a jerk, no, the ultimate jackass. First, he had rushed halfway back to camp before he got the mind to realize Mel would have to stumble through the ruins, lost in the dark without him. So he had rushed even faster back to her. When he had finally returned to the onsen, his light exposed a woman seething, smoldering in wet clothes, pulling boots over wet toes.

She stayed silent the whole way back. Rich was scared to say anything. He had seen what she could do while angry, and this was the angriest he had seen her yet. Besides, he didn't have a fricking clue on what to say.

His feelings were convoluted. Rich had zero problem seeing Mel as a woman. He had only gotten to really know Mel as Zhufira, not the kid that came before. And he really liked the woman he had gotten to know. She was level-headed and insightful and at the same time dynamic and feisty. And beautiful and poised and graceful, and, dammit—beautiful! In ways that made his blood rush hot.

It wasn't like explaining all that to her would've helped. Even if he knew what to explain, when would he had been able to say it? When they had arrived back at camp, Mel had stormed past everyone as they stared at their damp comrades, pulled out her bedroll and signed off for the night.

Her back was still turned to Rich, who wondered if she was really asleep or just quietly seething as he sat tired, awake and alone in their slumbering camp. He had chosen first watch to get it over with, having found himself extremely exhausted after setting up the anti-Graverobber wards. Now torturously awake and on guard, he had plenty of time to explore his own hang-ups. As he looked at her curves, he cursed himself yet again.

Rich knew honesty was bound to fail. He couldn't wake her up and say, "When I was kissing you and touching your body I wanted you bad. Then I pictured Rew and it felt wrong."

The thought pattern was stupid. Him and Rew weren't boyfriend and girlfriend, dating, nothing. She was Queen of the Mages, over three hundred years old. He had killed her half a millennium old father and hadn't told her. Plus, he was a day or so away from literally leaving Rew's world forever. Whatever they were, they were not an item.

He shut his eyes and rubbed his temples, trying to massage out the stupidity. All thoughts amounted to a hot girl in a hot tub throwing herself at him, only for him to grow cold feet. What guy says no to a girl that fine? If there was ever going to be a colossal "do over" moment in his life, the thing he'll think about and wince with regret until the end of days, he was sure this was it.

When he opened his eyes again he saw Mel had turned to face him. She was staring at him. It felt like she stared right through him.

Wordlessly, she got up and approached. He shambled to his feet in a rush to meet her. She stood before him, still silent, her eyes searching his for meaning. He wanted to apologize, to tell her she was beautiful, that he regretted walking away; he said none of these things.

"Why?" she asked, her eyes filled with hurt.

He caressed her cheek, the feel of her smooth, flawless skin sending electric tingles through his fingertips. There were no words he could speak to satisfy her question, because all his answers left him unsatisfied. He had been foolish, too busy looking to the horizon to notice what had been in front of him the whole time.

She moved her mouth to speak again, to perhaps ask the same question he couldn't rightly answer, perhaps to confess something deeper. He would never know because he pressed his mouth against hers. All thoughts of Rew Majora vanished as he reveled in the warmth of her tongue and her full lips on his.

Their hands found each other as they kissed. Passion made them move with urgency as both Mel and Rich fumbled and grasped at his robe, removing it with clumsy haste. Mel smiled slyly as Rich finally pulled the robe off and tossed it aside.

"No underwear?" she asked.

"I don't think they're hip to the elastic band here," he said with a shrug.

She closed the space between them. They kissed again, this time with Mel guiding Rich down to his bedroll, until she lay on top of him in his embrace. She broke contact with his questing lips, smiling slyly again. Then she began to kiss his neck, his chest, down his stomach, past his navel. Rich closed his eyes as his body tingled with each kiss. Behind the darkness of his closed eyelids, he heard her voice call to him.

"Razzleblad, you really are gullible."

Rich jerked his head up to find Mel grinning. There was nothing sly about that smile. He had seen that same expression a few times on a few faces, but they all boiled down to the same douchebag. Unlike the hot tub, there was no mistake this time.

"Richard Bates," Rich said.

"You don't sound happy to see me," she said. The cost-in-costume looked over Rich's body. "But you definitely *look* happy to see me."

Rich got to his feet and grabbed his robe with earnest. "I should've known," he said as he dressed. "It was probably you in the onsen playing your games with me all night."

Richard Bates made no move to change what he was wearing, which was Mel's face and body. The warrior girl shrugged. "No, that was her. If I had contrived the whole scenario, I would never be able to delight in your self-imposed misery. Just how frustrated do you feel right now?"

"Can we hurry this along?" Rich asked, his brow furrowed. "Bring out the parade of giant spiders and the scenic tour of burning villages already."

Cost-Mel raised an eyebrow knowingly. "That's pretty frustrated," she said nodding. "But that's why I like you, Razzleblad. You're so new at this, so naïve. This is my second visit in a single day. Do you have any idea why?"

"Because you're a sadistic bitch with a lot of free time," Rich fumed his answer.

"I am the cost, Razzleblad. There's no such thing as free time," Cost-Mel said. "More to the point, I exist to bring restorative balance back to souls, pulled by that direct contact with the Onesource you mages are so fond of. After our first session today, you went and stretched your soul pretty thin—what, with all the tornadoes and a full on gray duel and all. I had to come back."

"No, you didn't," Rich said. "My cost is the same, no matter what spell I cast."

Cost-Mel shook her head. "The cost's not the same thing as damage to your soul. Say you get hurt and you go to a healer who charges a uniform exorbitant price for services, no matter how small. I'm that greedy healer, charging you an obscene yet flat rate whether you've stubbed your toe or had all your skin flayed off. This time, Razzleblad, you've got no skin left. Your soul needed some emergency care."

Rich didn't know how to take Richard Bates' words. He felt fine, albeit tired. He would think that if his soul was in some sort of trauma condition it'd show. Cost-Mel seemed to know what he was thinking and filled in the details.

"Novice magic, gray magic, it all adds up. Without this visit your soul would've likely snapped on the next rudimentary spell. You would've been stuck in a coma, forever paying the cost in a nightmare for which there is no escape. It doesn't happen often, because the body will normally falter, the mind pass out. But in rare instances a mage in the heat of constant spellcraft can push past their exhaustion points and break their souls before I can reach them. It's a shame, really. As an enforcer of natural balance, it gives me no joy to see someone paying a perpetually empty debt."

Cost-Mel snapped her fingers and the scene behind her scrolled to the right, as if stepping through a slideshow, the Arden River and ruins replaced by an unfamiliar village on fire. From the doorway of a building writhing in flames, a seemingly endless line of humongous black and green spiders marched toward them, their eight legs in synchronous step with one another. A few seconds later, the scene changed again to another village on fire. And again. The only things persisting through each scene were the ever-growing line of spiders and the doorway which hosted them.

Rich scowled. "Seriously?"

Cost-Mel shrugged "I'm just giving my customers what they want." She patted the ground next to her. "Have a seat."

"No thanks," Rich said, "I'm weaning myself off gullible."

She beckoned with a hand. "The harm's already passed, dear Razzleblad. I mean, if I wanted to see you physically squirm, I would've just traveled a few more inches south on you," she said, following the words with a vicious clamp of teeth. She held the display, a beautiful smile which made Rich shudder.

The cost had a point. Even if only a temporary loss, that kind of loss would've been the type of trauma to cause nightmares for years. Rich took a seat next to Cost-Mel, where they both watched the ever-changing roasting villages and the cavalcade of spiders. The procession of spiders reached mage and cost and filed past them, heading noiselessly to destinations unknown. They all walked with their heads turned towards Rich, compound eyes reflecting red light from the distant fires, mandibles dripping venom.

"This is the kind of cost the average mage sees," Cost-Mel said as she looked off into the distance. "Some mages never even reach a level where they interact with me directly. I decided to use this quick patch job on your soul to show you what you've been missing. Not too bad, right?"

The hungry looking spider eyes, the eight hairy legs marching in sync, the dripping mandibles, it all freaked Rich out. But compared to other costs this was a regular trip through the circus funhouse.

"Why are you showing me your softer side?" Rich asked. If he knew anything about the cost, there was always something behind his displays.

"A few reasons," Cost-Mel said. "One is because you have a good soul. If anyone's going to draw upon the Infinite All, it should be people like you. I can't say the same about other recent gray robes."

She clapped her hands and the faces of the spiders all changed into Clemson Goodchild. The Clemson spiders still regarded Rich with black compound eyes and dripping mandibles as they continued their orderly march past him.

"You should have killed him when you first happened upon him," Cost-Mel said, a wry smile creasing her mouth as she stared at the burning village vista. "I delivered him to you wrapped like a birthday present.

"But I knew you wouldn't." She turned to look at Rich. "It was your last chance before the innocent among you start dying."

"He just needs someone to sit him down and explain what all this is," Rich said as he spread his hands out to the burning village. "What you are."

"Razzleblad, I think you're the one in need of an explanation of the whos and whats while you sit. You speak highly of strangers I know better. Clemson Goodchild was a darkly brooding neurotic in your world, a man driven to escape his miserable existence through game. And just as your young, clever mind occupies the older gentleman in Magelord gray, so too does Clemson's dark, brooding mind occupies a seat of obscene power. His neurosis had a physical manifestation in the form of sleepwalking. This, too, has followed him here."

Rich thought about what that could mean to a mage and whistled sharply. "He can cast real spells while he's in the cost." Now Rich understood how Richard Bates had manipulated Clemson's arrival in the forest.

"Oh, it gets better, Razzleblad. Are you familiar with the nature of the green robes?"

Rich nodded. The *Birleshik Arcana* had introduced him to all the color disciplines, which he had associated to scientific branches to remember them better. Green robes were the equivalent of biologists, their magics influenced and infused by flora and fauna.

"Glad you've been studying, leaves me to get to the meat," Cost-Mel said. "Mages, of course, don't start at gray; they have to ascend to Magelord. That means spending the bulk of your spellcasting career in another color. The robe that Clemson created and now occupies, like every other gray robe, didn't just go from nothing to gray without a pedigree. His was green, specifically the dark, morbid biological magic found at the dying end of the life cycle."

Cost-Mel laughed and shook her head. "He's as close to what you would call a necromancer this world has, with all its decay and rotting meat and putrescence. But the man behind the robe is compulsively neat. Do you know what his character trigger is?"

"Disgust," Rich said in a whisper. Now the plant and animal magic Clemson had used in the duel made sense. Anytime this neat freak found something disgusting, he'd respond with worms and rot, which would only disgust him more. Even though Rich's fear trigger on Razzleblad was bad, Rich generally only had to cast one spell of ridiculous magnitude to remove whatever threat was causing his fear. Clemson's Moloch trigger was perpetual, feeding perfectly on itself.

"I will break his mind soon," the cost said. "In a day or two, a week at the most. When that happens, he'll no longer hold onto to himself as Clemson Goodchild. He'll be Moloch through and through, with no need for triggers. And all these villages in front of us really will burn."

"Why don't you stop tormenting him?" Rich asked looking at Mel-Cost as she stared at the flames. "Don't you care? That people will die?"

"No," was her flat response. "I am the cost, mage, not a conscious. You, Clemson, everyone. Everything pays what they owe. Everything must." Cost-Mel turned to face Rich. "Don't *you* care, Razzleblad, or are you already too short for this world?"

Rich had a right to leave; he didn't belong here—he wanted his old life and body back. More than this, he absolutely needed to get away from being a mage and paying their costs. He had put his friends in danger when he awoke scared in disarray. He was beginning to confuse reality. He was deteriorating, same as Clemson Goodchild, losing pieces of himself in slow drips until he wouldn't be able to tell day from night or who it was suffering under the crazy spells he fearfully uttered.

"This must be another one of your reasons for showing your softer side," Rich told his cost. "You think I'm going to feel bad for leaving this world in danger."

"You do feel bad," Cost-Mel said with a smile. "Good souls feel bad for poor souls, lost souls. You've seen him and know as I do. Many will burn under Moloch."

Rich looked at the parade of spiders and the flaming village slideshow. "This is starting to feel more and more like a regular cost," he said.

"Sometimes the worst torment is leaving someone grim realities to consider," Cost-Mel stated. "Here's more for your consideration. This cost was a stabilizer, a minimalist patch job to get your soul back in some semblance of usable shape. I'm coming again tomorrow, to take remaining payment on a soul stretched well past what you've ever known before. It will be lasting and brutal, the stuff of your nightmares unfettered and rampaging."

"So, guilt-ridden if I go, mind-raped if I stay," Rich said.

"I don't see your choices so clearly cut, Razzleblad."

"You wouldn't," Rich scoffed. Then Cost-Mel's words took on a new meaning to him. "You don't think we'll be able to escape tomorrow."

"What I think is irrelevant. The possibility of leaving is there, tossing about in a raging sea of other possibilities. That's all the future is really, a sea that's never calm. What I know is the same as you; the only way to make the possibilities you want reality is to fight for them, to seize them squirming from that tumultuous sea."

Cost-Mel stood up. She gestured as if she was bowling and the presently burning village and marching line of spiders whooshed away like a hurricane gale had blown them into oblivion. The scene returned to the quiet ruins along the Arden. She looked down at Rich.

"Like I always have, I'll be watching you, to see what kind of fight you have in you."

One blink later Cost-Mel was gone. Another blink after that and Rich found himself face to face with Jason, who was shaking his head at Rich.

"You're about as useful on watch as a blindfold."

"Sorry." Rich didn't know what else to say.

Jason held up his bone hand for Rich to talk to. "Save it. I'm up. Go back to sleep. Just don't spazz me awake with your dream sequences after I'm done with watch."

Rich didn't protest because there was nothing to protest. He had let the guys down yet again. He lay down on his bedroll, too weary to contemplate the hundred things on his mind.

CHAPTER 22
Wake Up Call

Rew Majora started her day with good news and no news. The initial reports on Dreft Esker indicated a successful rout. A massacre really, to the point that the mages on site were unable to tell how many survivors, if any, had fled. With this victory, the Hierophane had upheld their promise to never allow standing armies within the Free States. The battle should give Ananna and the rest of the Temple of Houses cause to pause if they believed marching brutishly through the Merkez would be an easy task.

The good news didn't mix well with the lack of news. She had not heard from Rich last night. Her call to scry went unanswered, leaving her with a forlorn little water bowl and a mountain of worry which persisted well after Brigitte's morning security report. "*Surely, he must have been tired from his travels and slept through my scry,*" she told herself. Maybe she could have listened to her own consolation if not for the fact that she didn't know where he was or when he would arrive.

It was her own fault, really. She should have asked him all these pertinent questions the last time they scryed. But Rich had an uncanny knack for disarming her. He was truly otherworldly, unintimidated by her ageless symbolism or in awe of her power as the head of Seat Esotera. They talked person to person, free of labels and the trappings of status. When she was with him she seemed to forget about her responsibilities, her troubles, her life as Hierophant.

High in the upper reaches of the Perihelion Tower, Rew looked out from her bedchamber to the horizon. The sun was slowly pulling away from the land's embrace, pushing the shadows of last night back in a measured wave and causing the distant landscape to glow amber. It advertised the promise of a beautiful day.

Rew sighed, not for the sunrise but for her worry. She stood fully dressed, without an appetite for breakfast and well before the time the rest of the counselors other than Brigitte would be active to query for updates. There was nothing to do but worry.

She sat on the bed and looked at the water bowl on her nightstand. The magic had persisted, through her restless sleep, Brigitte's battle assessment and the start of Rew's day, like a tangible link to Rich that refused to succumb to the ether.

That's when she realized what she felt for Rich was more than worry. She was worried about the looming possibility of war and securing military aid. She worried about trade agreements with Fhayrsea. Those issues made her pace and plan, but they didn't make her wistfully sigh and stare out of windows. She missed Rich.

"Perfect," Rew said to the water bowl. The first time in a lifetime where someone excited her heart's beat and that someone was a man destined to disappear from her world altogether. Rich would go back to a realm of switch powered lighting and flying steel vessels. Her world would return to one of business as usual.

She looked at the placid surface of the water and saw her reflection staring back. Placid was boring. For a while, even if it was only the briefest instant, she wanted to do more than manage mages and treaties. She wanted to enjoy the new rhythm of her heart's beat. The time was now, within the flare of that brief instant. She opened her mind and sent a request to scry.

A moment before she killed the scry and resigned herself to even more worry, she felt Rich accept. Half of her bedroom melted into a forest backdrop. Rich smiled at her in the midst of weathered stone.

"Hey," he said smiling.

"Hello," she replied, relief washing over her as she spoke.

The ruins were both hauntingly beautiful and immediately familiar. "You're in Deluvial," she said.

He looked around. "You know this place?"

"Most everyone knows of Deluvial," she replied. "It was a precursor to the Hierophane, an ancient kingdom that devoted itself to water magic. The kingdom ended abruptly and inexplicably. Most say it fell from within, some say an evil wind swept over the land. Water clerics claim their healing magics come from Deluvial, passed down amongst themselves through the ages. To this day, Hierophane mages still study the few scraps of parchments left behind."

"I'm just glad it was monster free," Rich said with a wry smile. "It seems everywhere we go something hostile's snatching up the welcome mat."

Even if all their time could only be spent in scry, Rew would welcome it. But Rich was at Deluvial, which meant he was a stone's throw away from the Hierophane, the Rift Pendulum, going home. She had the means to help. A big part of Rew, the part that enjoyed looking at Rich's lopsided grin and hearing his novel view of her world, screamed against niceties and the right thing to do; that part of her revolted against what she was about to say. It selfishly sought to hold every moment of their instant, to stave off the imminent approach of forever without him. She spoke despite her desire.

"Would you like me to portal you here?"

"You can do that?"

"I go to Deluvial at times to roam the stone pathways," she answered. "The solitude clears my head when I need peace of mind. In a moment, you'll be here to share breakfast."

His eyes lit up. "Great!" Suddenly, his brow creased in worry. "Give me a few minutes, Rew. I need to tell the guys and pack and stuff."

They broke scry and Rew set about the task of preparing for company. She went down to the veranda overlooking the gardens, where she put in a breakfast order the size of a feast. Then she oversaw place settings and décor, wanting the presentation to be beautiful. Finally, she looked herself over in the mirror to make sure her hair wasn't out of place and her robe was immaculate. Everything had to be perfect.

"DRUZE WAS HER WHAT?"

Rich wasn't sure if the question came from Mike, Mel, Jason or all three at once. The words came through a menagerie of expletives and gasps so intense Rich swore he could see the exclamation points above their heads. The only one who seemed unperturbed by the revelation was Runt.

"I guess it makes sense when you think about it," Rich said with a placating half shrug, "who else do you share the gift of eternal life with other than family?"

"Yo, 'when you think about it'?" Mike quoted incredulously. "You didn't have to think about it cause you already goddamn knew. When the hell was you gonna tell us about it?"

Rich held his hands out. "I just found out yesterday. When did I have time to explain all this... after the massive pendulum hero raid or before we chased after the lunatic king of rot-magic?"

"Man," Mike said batting a hand at Rich, "don't sit here acting like we should've had our people talk to your people to get on your calendar. How about when we was all hiking down the river? Woulda made a great topic for convo along with the voodoo. How about before you and my brother took y'all lil moonlight stroll or after y'all both came back soggy. Was it wet enough for you?"

"Uh..." Rich began. Mike's face was deadpan behind the goggles as he waited for the answer to a question Rich wasn't sure would go well no matter how he answered. Rich shot a furtive glance to Jason, whose aian eyes danced with knowing mischief. A sidelong glance at Mel revealed an angry scowl that was all Zhufira.

"Look, enough," she said tersely, "we take her portal, don't say a word about Druze and get this thing over and done. Nothing's changed."

Jason smirked. "This feels fairly reminiscent of when we collectively faked amnesia in the Temple of Houses. Don't get me wrong, I got sentenced to a public execution but it wasn't because they didn't believe our story. Just saying, in a place devoid of television programming, amnesia totally works here."

Mike nodded at Jason's words. "We was gonna run into this problem now or later so just as well hit it now. Everybody stay casual as we see the eternal daughter of the dude Rich killed and ask her for a ride home."

AS REW FUSSED WITH an errant lock of hair, she felt Rich's call to scry. An exciting rush filled her, not unlike the first time a boy knocked on her door to call upon her. She remembered her father's hard glare and harder questions for the boy more than the boy himself.

"*What's wrong with me?*" she thought, a question she only half-heartedly asked. She felt alive. Knowing the answer wasn't as important as enjoying the results.

Rew let the errant lock dangle and cast a portal recall, choosing Deluvial as her location. The blue and white rift swirled into existence. She stared at the inactive portal for moments that felt stretched to eternity. She wished the act of taking a portal didn't turn it into a one-way system because she would've already gone through and retrieved them. She contented herself to wait. And like the first time they had met, Rich emerged into the Hierophane via portal, bringing all his friends with him.

Jason hadn't changed since the High Fane rescue; he still wore the simple brown robe she had procured from the Nasreddin Mage Tower. The warrior girl had thankfully changed her barely-there outfit to something more covering if only slightly less provocative. A scarred, goggled megrym and a giant man came through the portal as well, people Rew had never met but had heard enough about to know instantly.

"Mike," she said nodding to the megrym, "and Runt," she said to the man, "If you were told half as much about me as I was of you, I will consider us already well introduced. I am Rew Majora, Hierophant of Seat Esotera. I bid you all welcome."

She looked at Rich, feeling her smile grow. "Welcome."

Rich smiled back. "It's good to see you, Rew."

They looked at each other for long moments until Rew found her manners.

"Please, have a seat everyone. I'm sure your trek here did not afford many amenities. Enjoy the hot spiced tea and chilled pear juice. Breakfast should arrive momentarily."

Not long after everyone had their seats, the servants treated them all to a traditional Hillander breakfast. Their plates hosted sizzling grilled mushrooms, small bowls of warm sliced bananas topped with cashews and sweet cream, and *borek*, hot pastries stuffed with minced lamb, mint and dill.

Her guests ate with hearty gusto. It had been awhile since Rew had traveled uncertain roads on adventures, but she remembered the meals being inconsistent at best and oftentimes unappetizing. Speaking of, even seated before this delectable breakfast, Rew had little appetite. She looked at Rich.

"So," she began, "your road and back to cage the death creature was not without its challenges. I want you all to know that I as Hierophant, along with the peoples of the Free States, thank you for your endeavor. I'm particularly thankful that you all devised a method to grant the creature due pardon while ensuring the safety of the realm. We all are in your collective debt."

Rich and his friends nodded and smiled at her, except for Runt and Mike who, outside of a cursory bob of the head, kept their eyes down on the plate and their forks in motion.

"Some things I'm aware of or party to," Rew said, "like freeing dear Jason from the confines of the Temple of Houses. However, some of your trials I know solely by vague inference and I'm sure there are parts I'm completely ignorant of. Please, I would be most honored if you regale me with the story of your travels."

Her guests looked at each other as if they didn't know how to proceed or where to start, a confused look that should not have belonged to people who had lived through what she was asking to be described.

"No need to be reserved," Rew said smiling. "Must I threaten you all with fire every time I want to hear of your exploits?"

Mike spoke around bites of *borek*. "Dig, it wasn't much to it. We wound up in the mountains at Cult Town, West Virginia. Monster dude pulled a last minute E.T. and went home. So we bounced."

Rew's brow furrowed up in fierce confusion. "Hmmm," she managed while she tried to unravel Mike's bizarre dialect.

"Word," he said, holding up the *borek*. "These biscuits are banging."

Rew had so many questions based on Mike's short explanation she didn't know where to start. Where was Cult Town, West Virginia in relation to the Eural Mountains? Was it underground? It had to be, why else would they have to dig? How much digging did they have to do? What was a "last minute E.T."? How high up did they bounce?

She didn't even know what word Mike was asking for when he said "word", or if banging biscuits meant the *borek* was overly crunchy or hard.

"Rather than bombard you with a million questions," Rew said at last, "can someone other than Mike tell me what happened?"

Jason came to Rew's rescue, explaining what had transpired in plain language. Tracking the Death Null to Olukent, the rendezvous with Mike, the death cult, the last minute surge of Maltep nasrans—it all made for riveting narrative.

"So, Jason, you all had to contend with locating the Death Null when your direction finding failed, while at your backs were cultists, undead warriors, and an angry tide of nasrans?" Rew asked. Jason nodded as he bit into his *borek*.

"Remarkable," Rew said. "The next part I understand well enough; after its countdown, the Death Null opened a portal and returned to its own realm. What I don't understand is you, Rich," she said, grabbing the mage's hand and looking him in the eye. "Why not simply return here once the Death Null departed? Why go to Suusteren?"

Rich seemed surprised by the question. "Well... hmmm... you see—"

"Hierophant, are you well?" Brigitte's voice called out. "It is unlike you to—" Brigitte came into the veranda and her words froze, her face impassive as her eyes roved over every guest.

"I am fine, Brigitte, happily distracted with friends," Rew said. "Rich here was just about to tell me how he wandered down to Suusteren." Brigitte's stoic stare locked onto Rich. Rew turned to face him expectantly.

"Here's the thing," Rich began. "The cult master in Olukent was a super powerful mage as well. I couldn't beat him, no matter what I did. So I had to use a spell from Kaftar Friese's spellbook and turn him to stone. But the spell turned me to stone too as its cost. The guys took me to Suusteren, to try to free me from the stone spell."

Shock flashed in Rew. He had been trapped in stone; that was why Rich had taken a week to talk to her. Why hadn't he just told her?

"Not trying to be funny," Mike said in the silent spaces left by Rich's confession and Rew's mute shock, "but I'd really like to get back home right about now. Kinda wanna catch up on being human, reaching the top shelf, that sort of thing."

Rew nodded. "Forgive me, you are right. You all have done the Free States a great service; it is unbecoming of me to keep you here longer than you desire." She turned to Brigitte. "Would you please escort most of our heroes to the Rift Pendulum?" As she finished her question, Rew's hand clasped over Rich's. "I'll be along shortly, bringing Rich with me."

"Take your time. I will have the area prepared for your arrival," Brigitte said nodding curtly. Everyone filed out behind the destruction mage, leaving Rew and Rich alone at the table. Rew felt their brief instant together slipping irrevocably into the past. She squeezed his hand. He squeezed back and smiled.

"I guess this is goodbye, huh?"

"Yes, I believe it is, Rich."

Wordlessly, she rose and gingerly pulled him to his feet. She led him into her personal library and pulled *Navigating the Rift* down from her shelves.

"This feels a lot like when you gave me the *Birleshik Arcana* to read," Rich said looking at rich brown leather and ornate gilding of the book.

Rew smiled at the thought. "I suppose this is similar. Although this time I'm not giving this to you to provide magical insights, but keeping it so I can steer the Rift Pendulum to your proper place and time."

Rich's eyes widened with surprise. "So that's the Rift Pendulum's instruction manual?"

She nodded. Rew barely heard him talk about the book's ornate appearance or thoughts on rift manipulation as her mind flashed back to when they had sat next to one another reading a love poem. That crisp image made her sigh and shake her head. She may have to use this book, but she wasn't going to spend the last of their time together talking about it. Instead, she grabbed his hand to escape a library that had suddenly become overbearing.

Hand-in-hand, they walked through the gardens, the scenic, indirect route towards the Turris Centrum, where the Rift Pendulum waited to take Rich away.

"There's a saying we mages have about scrys," Rew said as they strolled past blooming pink and purple chrysanth flowers. "They say that when a mage opens their mind, the heart will surely follow. I always thought it was a beautiful sentiment, even if it was lost on me. I've been using scrys for centuries for one sort of business or another. I've enjoyed the simple efficiency of a scry, nothing more."

She stopped and looked at Rich. "Until I met you."

He returned her gaze, a pained look creasing the corners of his eyes. "Some of my best times have been spent with you, while everyone around me thought I was asleep."

"You know, Rich," she said, "there is no proscribed time where you must depart."

"A big part of me wants to stay, Rew. But the cost is hard for me, and is slowly becoming too much to bear."

So that was it then. She looked down at some chrysanth flowers. The next words he spoke brought her attention back to him. They weren't words of sentiment but spellcraft. She looked up to see him drawing in the air, placing a portal root.

"Maybe it's nothing to you," he said, "But part of me will feel a little hope that there's a way back to you, even if it doesn't work in my mundane world."

He looked at her as he had right before escaping Nasreddin through her portal. Only now it was her turn to let go. She reached up to meet his lips with hers. Rew freed herself in his embrace, relishing the pleasure of his kiss and the warmth of his arms as only one could for the last time. Their brief instant together stretched taut in this moment.

At long last, they pulled away from one another. "I guess we shouldn't keep your friends, your world, waiting," Rew said.

She led Rich by the hand through the gardens into the Turris Centrum. Some strange, optimistic side of her believed he'd change his mind at the last minute, or at least wanted to believe it.

They entered the Rift Pendulum chamber and found a mutinous scene. A team of destruction mages had bound and subdued all of Rich's friends. Brigitte stood over them all as her team worked binds and gags.

"What is the meaning of this?!" Rew asked.

Brigitte turned and regarded her Hierophant coolly. "These people are wanted foes of at least two states, those states being the Temple of Houses and Seat Esotera. I have apprehended them, save the one you escort."

"Are you mad?!" Rew shouted. "We are not hounds for the Temple of Houses, to chase after who they perceive as enemies. Neither are these people foes to Seat Esotera. Release them immediately."

Her acting security chief's stoic look did not waver. "You are unaware of their trespasses against the Hierophane," she said. "Allow me to show you the powerful mage your dear gray robe turned to stone."

Brigitte went over to the Pendulum, where a mass taller than her stood hidden under a canvas tarpaulin. She pulled the tarpaulin to reveal a headless statue reaching out for someone or something. Next, she bent down behind the statue to grab the head, partially obscured by the statue's feet. Brigitte walked over to Rew before thrusting the stone head towards her.

The face was unmistakable. Druze. She looked at Rich, to ask for the meaning, some explanation, a confirmation that this was impossible to him, that he hadn't done it.

The look in Rich's eyes said it all. They confirmed what Brigitte was saying. There were few robes powerful enough to put Druze in stone. Rich had virtually told her how he had managed it.

Rich had murdered her father.

CHAPTER 23
Underthral

"I ..." Rich started. The word began a speech he had rehearsed no less than seven times in his head, his explanation to Rew of how her father had double-crossed them to ensure his continued immortality, and how the ancient mage was willing to kill and torture for it, and how the only escape Rich could find was Kaftar Friese's stone spell "Equal Hardship." But looking at her, the hurt in her eyes lashing out, a hurt both accusatory and bottomless, made his lone word sound foreign instead of practiced, an inadequate beginning for the pain he had caused.

"I had to," was all he could manage. His words could have been the blade of a knife he plunged into her gut for how she looked at the disembodied head in her hands then back at him. With her look came the hard reality that he had killed her father and lied about it; nothing he had prepared to say would mute such betrayal.

He reached for her. She jerked back like the hand was a snake striking. Brigitte reacted swiftly to Rich's outstretched hand, tossing a dull, metallic die at him. When it got close to Rich, the metal die glowed red and fiery tendrils blossomed out of it, enveloping Rich in a webbed embrace before the tendrils disappeared altogether. Rich felt all his energy evaporate like morning dew suddenly thrust into desert sun. He crumpled to the ground. Above him, the metal die shined a bright crimson. He knew what this thing was.

He'd seen the device before in Fort Law. It was a Majora Witchlock, the same magic that had trapped the Death Null. Even if he didn't feel completely drained under it, his memory of that powerful creature snared under it served to let him know there was no escaping the witchlock on his own volition.

"You need time alone, Hierophant," Brigitte said. "To absorb what has befallen you and us all. I will escort the prisoners to the Underthral." Effortlessly, Brigitte hauled Rich up by the arm, an act his body couldn't struggle against.

Rew didn't respond to Brigitte's words. She sank to the ground, her robe pooling around her as if she had melted into the floor. She held her father's head, Druze's face forever locked in a grim visage of pain and rage.

Brigitte snapped and signaled at her four-man team of black robes, who gathered all of Rich's friends to their feet. The mages shouldered all their packs and their weapons, a vivid testament to their helplessness. Runt initially tried to struggle against his bounds and gag. Brigitte waved off the destruction mage who attempted to quell Runt's rebellion. Instead, she grabbed Rich by the scruff of his neck with one hand, called a swirling storm of raging blizzard into the other and serenely guided Rich's face towards the hostile cold. Runt stopped struggling.

Everyone followed Brigitte's lead. She took them past shining towers, serene gardens, and gawking passers-by until the towers became less prominent, the gardens less kempt, the pedestrians non-existent. They walked toward a domed building that, despite its one story height, looked fearsome. Stone outcroppings erupted in strange angles from the sides of the dome, like the frozen legs of a spastic crab. The dome sat in the middle of a metal platform separated from the green grass of the Hierophane by a circular trench. A six-foot-long bridge spanned the trench between grass and metal; looking down over the bridge, Rich saw it was no simple trench but rather an abysmal chasm that disappeared into darkness. The perfectly sheered, raw earth framing the chasm perimeter stood in stark contrast to grooved stone and metal walls, descending like a giant screw in a hole that continued down to forever.

Brigitte let go of Rich's arm and he found his strength to stand gone with her. He collapsed unceremoniously onto the cold metal ground. Brigitte knelt beside Rich at the descending tower's entrance, where she began to speak for ink before she traced a pattern over the floor with a finger.

"*Anahtar uydurmasini lazim olsun,*" she intoned. The pattern she had traced glowed green in response.

She stood after her incantation, the doors to the dome opening with the jarring cry of groaning metal.

Brigitte picked Rich back up by grabbing two handfuls of his upper arms and steered him into the maw, down the narrow steps of the descending tower. During the descent, Rich felt Brigitte let go of his arms. The witchlock kicked in, the magic both pushing him down and sapping his strength to resist. He fell down the stairs, all of them, yelping and flailing as his body took the stairs the hard way.

Lying on the ground feeling the dull throb of bruises all over, Rich heard the steps of the others reach him eventually.

"Oops," Brigitte said flatly.

"Fuck... you." It was hard to even talk under the power of the witchlock.

She hauled him up roughly and push-guided him to a guardrail. The stairs had opened up to a tiered courtyard three floors high.

"Just be thankful my hands aren't clumsy now," she said.

Bridging the lengthy distance from floor to roof, four giant square columns stood, made of transparent glass. What was likely illusionary magefire shone inside the glass, roiling and rumbling inside its confines, filling the courtyard with yellow-orange light.

Many people milled about the tiers and courtyard. Bare-chested men wore bright yellow skirts and sandals, women, simple tunics of the same brash color. Rich didn't have to question why everyone was uniform in appearance or why weathered grimaces were plastered all their faces. This was prison. General population.

Brigitte took them down to the courtyard floor. On either end of the courtyard yellow garbed prisoners with golden bands on their upper arms congregated around what looked like foxholes. Utter darkness reigned in the foxholes, a pitch black that defied the gracious light provided by the fire filled columns. The arm-banded prisoners took turns casting rudimentary magic into the dark space, crude fire and ice and dirty light and smoke. The foxholes did not respond to their spells; they only sat there ever dark, ever hungry. Brigitte ignored these prisoners and their spellcraft, taking the group to a wall where a giant door stood next to a solid stone slab. A brown robed mage sat behind the flat slab as if it was a desk, yelling at three convicts who were tasked with shoveling hay from a giant cart into a furnace.

The brown robed mage turned to regard the five destruction mages and their prisoners with a raised eyebrow. "Going deeper?" he asked.

"Yes, Trevayne," Brigitte replied.

"Shame," Trevayne responded looking at the huge door beside him. "Could've used the gray robe to pump the Heart."

A pendant dangled from Trevayne's neck, the emblem looking like the sun emerging from the horizon, only the sun's half circle and pointy rays were upside down. Trevayne took the pendant off and placed it onto the stone slab. A stream of black light surged from the pendant, fell to the floor and ran a channel to the massive door. The door evaporated, leaving an uninviting darkness in its wake.

Thoughts of reprieve or escape seemed to evaporate with it.

The next section of the Underthral was dire. Miniscule, foot-long versions of the courtyard's glass fire columns hung on the walls in sparse intervals. There was no courtyard to speak of; a graduated slope wound down without end. The smell of stale sweat and dank iron permeated the air. Occasionally, the floor would level out and a passageway would present itself. Any yellow-garbed prisoners caught out in those passageways immediately retreated further into the darkness when they spied the black robes and their prisoners.

Their steps echoed in lonely concert through the dim expanse until they reached the bottom level occupied by another massive door and stone slab. Papers and books littered the surface of the slab and the bespectacled, red robed mage seated behind it didn't look up as he made notes from a heavy, open tome. Brigitte's nose scrunched up as if the books or man's robes were made of garbage.

"Have you no pride of office, Kerr?"

"Pride? Think it is lacking because your eyes seek order and cannot find it?" Kerr asked, head still down and hand writing notes as he talked. He looked up from the book to regard Brigitte. "The lacking is in your eyes."

"The lacking is in my patience. You've got prisoners to stow."

Kerr sighed as if Brigitte's words caused exhaustion. "If you bothered to read my security reports, you'd know I'm at capacity throughout the Castworks."

"Put them in The Fouls," she said.

"That part of the Castworks is off limits. Unless these black robes behind you are the detail I requested months ago to come down here and clear it."

"They are not. The prisoners will clear The Fouls."

Kerr adjusted his glasses and squinted at the prisoners, all of them bound and gagged except Rich, held up by Brigitte clutching his arm like a girl holding onto her favorite rag doll.

"Are you going to unlock the gray robe?" Kerr asked.

"No. He comes with me. Deeper. You get the others."

"Are you mad? This rabble can't possibly clear The Fouls."

"They can do anything," she said turning to her captives, her face unreadable, flat. "They're pendulum heroes."

"This is Residuum," Kerr said shaking his head. "Not a gang of roadside bandits. Save your—"

"They will clear it," Brigitte said over Kerr's protest. "In fact, they will clear it bound and gagged."

Kerr regarded Brigitte with a stonewall face, steady gaze. "This is nothing short of murder."

"Since when do you care about your charges?"

"I don't," he answered. "I care about the clearing of The Fouls."

"If they don't clear it, report directly to me and I will immediately dispatch a destruction team. Five black robes. Are you happy now?"

Kerr seemed to chew on her question, biting his lip as he looked over the bound prisoners and back to Brigitte.

"I'll take the rare occasion of your silence as agreement," Brigitte said. "Now fetch your block warden."

Kerr stood, gathered his red robe about himself and left, disappearing into the surrounding darkness. Only the knocking echo of his footsteps remained to fade into whispers. Brigitte turned to Rich's friends.

"Kerr's right, you know. Normally, Residuum requires at least three mages. But you guys are almighty pendulum heroes!" she shouted. "The same wonder team that brought Druze low."

She looked at Runt then focused a baleful stare at Mike. "And killed Samedi," she said. "A baron. My baron. For that you all will die mangled and chewed."

Runt and Mike rushed at Brigitte. Dropping Rich in a split second, her sleeves lashed out violently, striking Mike and Runt midstride in their guts.

They hit the ground on their backs and skidded. Two destruction mages followed up with their own bent sleeves, holding them to the ground.

"You may have eventually found reprieve with Majora. Maybe. Forgiveness was never a question with me. She will live with your accidental death in The Fouls. And I will rejoice in it."

Kerr returned from the shadows, bringing a brown robe in tow. The black robes set down their captives' backpacks and weapons and followed the brown robe, pushing Rich's friends out of sight while he sat helpless on the floor.

"No..." Rich managed to say.

"At least you got the opportunity to know you're seeing them for the last time," Brigitte said. "More than what they gave me with Samedi."

She gave a brief nod to Kerr. The red robe went over to his stone slab desk and pushed papers away from the center. He brought a pendant necklace out from beneath his robes, placing it on the cleared oasis of stonework. A channel of white light ran from the slab to the massive door, dissolving it.

The next section was clinical, well-lit. White light illuminated the roof, making the white walls shine bright enough to cause Rich to squint. The hallway ended quickly, turning at a sharp right angle. There was no color. Their footsteps made no sound.

They turned the corner and a longer hallway, identical to the first in its aseptic starkness, met them. This hallway had open apertures spaced equidistantly down its length. Brigitte and Rich passed the first opening. Inside, a man in white lied on a bed, twitching in sleep. The next aperture they passed held the same thing, a man in white twitching on a bed.

"They call this part of the Underthral 'Broken Alley'," Brigitte said. "Do you know why?"

She stopped at the next open aperture and turned so Rich could squarely see. A woman, elderly with coarse gray hair, twitched on the bed. Her brow was heavily furrowed as if whatever she saw behind her eyelids tormented her relentlessly.

"They were mages," Brigitte said. "Now they're cost broken, spending the rest of their lives paying a cost that never ends."

The sight of someone cost broken did no justice to what Rich knew he couldn't see. He imagined any one of the costs he had endured and thought about having to live through it for untold years with no escape, no pardon. It was the worst torture imaginable.

"Why..." Rich began.

"Why keep them alive? Why not kill them?" Brigitte seemed to know his question. "We do normally, as a mercy. You're looking at demented mages. Or criminals such as yourself. We keep them alive to study them. Experiment on them. If they can tell us anything about how to break this cycle, then they would've been more useful to the world twitching in bed than they ever were awake and causing harm."

Brigitte led Rich away from the woman, further down the hallway past a dozen others suffering in silent agony. "I know what you're going through, Razzleblad. I used to be a gray robe myself. Big spells. Big costs. Too much to bear, really. The only thing that saved me was the Oath of Binding."

They turned the corner. At the first aperture Rich saw a man in white sitting on his bed. As soon as the man saw Brigitte and Rich he rose and launched an assault of spells at them. Fire and ice and bent white sleeves; all of it dissipated as soon as it touched the aperture threshold.

"He's demented," Brigitte said. She panned her head casually down the row, where several apertures sat in wait. "They all are."

The force field in place between the aperture and the hallway failed to deter the man, who kept lobbing magic elements and forces in an attempt to kill the black and gray robes on the other side.

"If you pay enough big costs, or if you're an unbound mage such as your-self, the dementia will come. It's just a matter of time."

Brigitte took him further down the hallway. The next aperture hosted a man who lay on the floor, whispering to it and stroking it like a pet. The next held a woman who conjured rain, danced in it, then looked down and be-came enraged at her wet floor before summoning fire to cook the water away. Then she summoned more rain.

After that, Rich stopped looking.

"I've found the neatest thing about a witchlock is the way it works," Brigitte said as she took Rich through the madhouse. "It nullifies a spell's de-livery, not the spell itself. Why, a mage under the lock may not see any results, but they're free to cast to their heart's content."

Abruptly, Brigitte pushed Rich into the aperture beside them. He fell down in front of a bed. A man was sleeping on it, face scarred, his hair dyed blue and spiky as if it was mimicking netherfire. Rich turned to look back at Brigitte.

"His name is Delv Vereyn. He used to be a blue mage, one of the best mentalists the tower has ever known. Then he cracked, started playing very sick mind games on others. Things that made people want to claw their own faces to shreds, bite their own tongues out. Very scary, terror-inducing stuff."

Rich looked back at Delv then back at Brigitte. All the things she had spoken as if it had been idle chatter made horrifying sense.

"Don't..." he started.

"Shhh." She put a finger up to her mouth and smiled. "I wouldn't want to wake him if I were you."

CHAPTER 24
Foul Deeds

Jason couldn't believe it. The bastards had really put them all into The Fouls bound and gagged. All his friends struggled at their binds, their backs to the entrance, their eyes looking into the murky dark depths of the gargantuan, industrial-sized pipe they had all been thrust into.

Luckily, the mages were too busy being magical to bother thinking about simple physics. You can't handcuff a guy with a detachable hand.

He popped his off bone mitt, letting it fall with a *sploop* into the grimy water puddling the pipe floor. His hand free, he retrieved his skeletal hand from the murk, took off his gag, and got to freeing the others.

"Why didn't you do that before they tossed us in here?!" Mel asked in exasperation as he rubbed his wrists.

"Like when we had a whole cadre of destruction magic specialists up our asses?" Jason asked. "That was a better time?"

"Dude, now we're stuck in here!" Mel cried in a harsh whisper. "With something even the mages don't want to tangle with."

Mel had a point there. Jason threw up an open handed shrug. It was the only retort he had.

"Look," Mike said, "we can stay here trying to wedge all our thumbs up Jason's asshole or we can get Oscar Mike."

Jason wasn't quite sure what the second option was, but it sounded better than the first. The megrym took off his goggles, the low light making his eyes glow. He took a step toward the gloom of the tunnel and Jason reasoned Oscar Mike was military for get a move on. Definitely better than option one.

"Wait," Jason said. "I know a little bit about the Underthral. We may wanna talk first. You know, pre-brief."

"Ok, game nerd," Mike said turning to face Jason, his one scarred eye glowing pale and ethereal next to the other. "Pre-brief me."

"The Underthral isn't just a prison, it's a labor camp," Jason said. "More like a mine for magical energy. That's what that first part was. The Heart. There the convicts that know even a lick of magic throw spells into the collection system, what they call 'pumping the heart'.

"Second level is the Castworks. They put the folks that couldn't scrape enough magic together for a card trick here. This is where they do prison maintenance work, probably some odd jobs for the Hierophane proper too like hava-chaise repair and spellbook binding. Right now we're in one of the prison maintenance wards, the waste disposal unit."

Mike cast his eyes about the huge pipe, grimy from different collections of yellow-brown rust and water stains.

"Glad we got you here to help us figure out we in the sewer. Anything else?"

"It's not just human waste disposal in The Fouls," Jason said. "That magic collection system in the Heart processes magic spells into raw magical energy so it can power the Hierophane; you can't juice those floating sidewalks and whatnot with crappy ice spells. But like most factories, it's not one hundred percent efficient, so waste products from the Heart get collected into The Fouls as well. Normally, The Fouls are an efficient waste disposal system but you guys can guess what happens sometimes."

Jason stopped talking and looked at everyone. Surely they'd get where he was going. When the looks turned from expectantly waiting to angry, Jason let out a defeated sigh.

"Magic has a strange nature, even when it's magic waste. Every now and again that nature manifests into... something. Something bad."

"Residuum," Mel said.

"Finally," Jason said relieved.

"Yo, let's bounce," Mike said.

"Wait," Mel said, "we're just going to go traipsing through here without a plan?"

Mike grimaced at his brother. "Do I look like Super Mario to you? I ain't trying to hang out in a pipe all day. This a sewer, which means sewage intakes.

We find an intake and make it an outtake." Mike looked up at Runt. "Tell him why else we traipsing."

"Dead end," Runt said, looking back at a door that wouldn't open. "Get cornered here, few options left to us."

Mike led the way into the gloom of the large pipe, his head panning as his eyes scanned the darkest recesses. Jason walked beside Mel while Runt brought up the rear. The Fouls was a horrible place to have aian eyesight, as Jason could only see a few feet ahead before it all melted into uniform, impenetrable black. The dark unknown creeped him out, a feeling exacerbated by the hollow drips and splashes of water, the random creaks and groans of metal.

Eventually they came to a five-way junction, the pipe pathways radiating out like a star. Typical Mike, he started trudging down the middle pipe, like the choice was completely arbitrary. Jason grabbed his shoulder quickly.

"No, dude. Left. We have to go left."

"Man, what is this?" he asked, visibly annoyed that Jason had stopped him to tell him where to go.

"He's right, Mike," Mel said. "I'll explain later. Trust me on this."

Mike looked like he was ready to say something smartass to both of them. Instead he shook his head and proceeded down the left-most tunnel. Jason exhaled relief; Mike never struck him as a guy he could reason with, especially when it came to the rules of dungeon crawling.

The pipe was more like a line of several pipes, linearly connected by circular flanges that jutted out in seams every forty feet or so. It got increasingly smaller every time they passed a flange, shrinking from gargantuan to huge to big to a point where Runt could put his hand flat against the top of the pipe. That's where it ended, with them all facing absolutely nothing but bare metal wall.

They turned to double back. Only now there was no back. The last flange was not a mere pipe joint but a circular door; they watched their escape route shrink out of sight as the flange door swelled shut.

"Great," Jason said, "we had to stumble past the only metal that doesn't creak around here."

"I don't know a whole lot about plumbing in either world I've lived in," Mel said staring up at a ceiling grate made of thick iron bars. "But this can't be good."

Among the distant echoes, Jason heard a yawning groan, followed by a whoosh. He looked at everyone.

"You guys don't thin—"

His words were cut off by a deluge crashing onto them. A flood of water rushed out of the grate, pounding their bodies, quickly filling the small chamber. In less than a minute, all of them were treading futilely against water rising to their necks as more water poured on their heads. Panic made Jason's heart leap and his mouth open wide for desperate breaths. The onslaught of water overhead filled his mouth, making him choke and splutter as the water below rose rapidly to reach his mouth.

Moments later, they were all submerged.

There was nowhere to go for air. Runt pulled angrily at the iron grate. It did not budge. "*The hell if I die in this damn sewer,*" Jason thought. Frantic, he felt for his heartworm pendant floating on the chain around his neck.

Suddenly the floor slid away. The water dumped out of the room, carrying them all with it. They all tumbled down and up and around in the raging rush until Jason lost all sense of direction. A few moments later his legs hit a hard surface and they crumpled. The force of the water pushed him out of the still rushing cascade and Jason found himself on his back staring up at a moss covered ceiling. All of his friends had been similarly deposited, sputtering on the floor as drainage roared into a sluice gate behind them. Jason sat up and saw in front of them were stairs. The lichen and lime crusted stone steps kept rising until they disappeared into darkness.

"Go left they said," Mike grumbled as he pushed himself off the floor.

"At least the stairs go up," Jason said. "Up is good."

"Let's hope so," Mel said looking at the stairs with a slight grimace. "Because there're no backsies anymore."

Mike led the way up the stairs. Darkness reigned, with light coming in rare bursts through rusted gas lanterns affixed to the walls. Jason groped his way through the dark as the stairs wound their way up, the slimy grime on the walls disgusting enough to make him wish both hands were sensationless bone.

"This is bullshit," Mel said to no one in particular. "We were almost home. Can't anyone else see we should be at 7-Eleven right now, not roaming a goddamn fantasy sewer? What the fuck?!"

"Shut it, bruh," Mike said. "Losing it only attracts attention. I hear ya, believe that. But right now, nothing out there in the dark need to hear ya. Feel me?"

Mel nodded even though Mike was in front and couldn't see him.

The stairs eventually leveled off into a narrow passage. They walked until they came to a "T" intersection. Mike looked left with baleful disdain on his face before turning right. Jason didn't bother to argue, even if Mike was going about dungeon-crawling dead wrong.

They hadn't made it far down this wrong hallway before Mike called an abrupt halt. He stared out into the darkness, at something Jason didn't stand of chance of seeing. But he could hear whatever it was in the form of a dull, repetitive pounding.

"Big ass muscle rat," Mike whispered.

Jason made a brief check through the bestiary in his head and was about to ask what the hell a muscle rat was when it answered the question for him. The pounding sound bumping out from the darkness gave way to a harsh cracking. A sliver of wan light filtered into the darkness to expose the muscle rat and the cause of the noise.

The thing was banging on the walls—with fists. It looked like a rat for the most part, brown furred, worm-tailed and as big as a possum. That's where the similarities died. Muscle rat had human arms and hands, as big as Mike's, which it used to beat the wall. The creature's back appeared broken; while its top half bent upright awkwardly as it focused on the wall, the hind-quarter sank as if crushed and its little rat legs splayed out uselessly on the floor.

Mike stood there watching it. Muscle rat freaked Jason out. A part of him wanted to tiptoe back the way they had come, but there was a huge reason to stay. Muscle rat had broken the wall to allow light in, which meant there was something behind the wall. A way out.

Muscle rat stopped its fist mid-swing. The sliver of light fell across the rat's face, exposing a whiskered snout that crinkled and sniffed the air as if it had picked up the promising scent of peanut butter. It put its meaty palms on the ground and used them to swivel, turning to face the four onlookers.

"If it don't turn back around and get back to business, we shoo it away," Mike spoke softly, "then try to widen that gap ourselves."

"Um..." Jason said too busy engrossed with the head-on sight of mutant muscle rat. He had no intention of going near that thing.

The muscle rat's tail snaked up into the air. Suddenly, the tail shimmered as if was oscillating. Blue bubbles of light coalesced in the space around it. A moment later the tail stopped shimmering and they found themselves looking at least a dozen incredibly long, impossibly thick worm tails.

Jason took an involuntary step back. This was no mere mutant freak. It was magic. It was—

"Residuum," he said.

Without warning the tails shot out at the group. Fast like lightning bolts, the huge wormtails reached them in a blur, wrapping around the four of them. With strength well beyond what should be in any rat's arsenal, the tails hoisted them all up.

The Residuum turned its head at a slight angle as if it was curious about the four captives now struggling futilely against its thick tails. It crawled on its hands toward them. Jason dry swallowed. The feeling of floating mixed with fear as it pulled them toward it.

The worm tails didn't stop when they got to the Residuum. Instead, the tails moved them beyond the creature and gently set them down in front of the barely broken wall. There, the tails unwrapped and shrank back to their owner. The Residuum looked at them, whiskers bristling.

"Do we... fight it?" Mel asked.

"With what, our good looks?" a scarred-faced Mike answered. "You felt how strong those tails were. It ain't obvious to you?"

The Residuum made it obvious. The mobile half of it rose up like a cobra and it pounded one meaty fist into the palm of the other. It wanted them to take over the dirty work of pounding the wall.

"Wants are same," Runt said. "Makes us allies of a kind."

They all turned to face the wall. The sliver of light came from a crack in the top right corner, exposing the wall as a round iron cover held there by stone and mortar. The Residuum had beaten on the solid iron enough to crack the stone support, which looked like no easy task.

Runt balled up two big fists and slammed them into the iron cover. A dull throb came back and little else. He did it again and a few stone crumbs from the crack above the iron flaked off.

"We'll be here for days at this rate," Jason said.

"What makes you think we'll last days?" Mike asked. His eyes were on the Residuum, which didn't look too pleased at its new workforce. It smacked its hands restlessly on the ground as it watched Runt's lack of progress.

"We're gonna need more strength," Mike said. "I'm talking stupid strength." He looked at Jason.

In fact, they all looked at Jason.

"Can't we just take turns beating at it?" Jason asked.

There was a reason he didn't just power up at the first sign of danger back when they were in the water tank. The first time he had used his heartworm pendant, Jason had been too scared to feel anything else. The last time he hadn't been scared, and it had felt good—a little too good. Jason was savvy enough to see the writing on the wall; the last thing he wanted was to be curled up in a cave somewhere stroking the emblem and calling it 'Precious'.

"I'm the last person who's a fan of Onus-wear," Mel said, "but this time we have no options. We need to get out and the Residuum will mangle us if we don't do it the way it wants."

Mel was right, annoyingly so. Jason turned to face the iron cover. No use stalling; the Residuum was only going to look at them idle for so long. He touched the emblem and called on the God of Power.

No sooner than he spoke the word, his body prickled all over, an electric sensation that tingled sharp and hot in every nerve he had. His muscles seemed ready to burst forth from the constraints of his skin. He could hear his heart beating like an engine revving, feel his blood surging, coursing, rushing.

He felt impossible. Godly.

Jason brought both hands back and launched them at the heavy iron cover as if the metal he wanted to push through were paper mache. The strike of his hands sounded like thunder booming, followed by cracking, splitting and a torrent of dust. When the dust cleared the small crack had widened and stretched to cover a quarter of the perimeter around the iron cover.

The Residuum clapped its hands together and chattered excitedly. Jason braced himself. This time, he put not only his arms but his whole body into the swing.

Walls, ceiling and floor shook with a jarring clang at the moment of impact and a violent eruption of dust swallowed Jason. The dust cleared in seconds because Jason was falling, his hands still holding the giant metal disc as it plummeted.

A moment later it hit the ground and rang like a gong. Jason looked up behind him to see his friends peering down from the huge hole he had created a story up. He looked around to get his bearings. That's when he saw the mages. The brown robe looked stupefied, his arms holding one of their backpacks that he had apparently been dumping into a wheelbarrow along with their weapons. Kerr sat across the room at his stone desk, looking up from a book with a face that advertised complete shock.

Kerr didn't take long to recover. He stood up and spoke magic, pushing out with a hand. One of the books on his desk shot out at Jason. The book shimmered as it whizzed toward him, turning from pages and leather binding to gleaming steel.

Jason ducked fast, barely dodging as the metal book flew by to crash into the wall with the fury of a cannonball. Before he could begin recovering, he looked up to see two more metal books barreling down on him.

There was no time to react.

The books impacted with crushing force to his face and chest. Unbearable pain mushroomed out in nauseating waves as the velocity of the missiles took him off his feet. He landed on his back, his ears ringing like church bells.

Those blows would've killed most anyone. Not Jason, not in his state. He wasn't just powerful. He was power. He rose to his feet, fueled by seething rage caused by the pain this mage had dealt him.

Something akin to instinct took over. Jason lashed out in a blur with his bone fist. At the moment where his arm was fully extended, he quickly uncurled four fingers. The fingers at the knuckle shot out from his outstretched hand, like bullets, and covered the distance between him and Kerr, burying themselves into the red mage's robes. Kerr crumpled with a yelp. A moment later Jason jerked back on his bone hand and the finger bones embedded in the fallen mage came flying out in small eruptions of red mist to rejoin his hand.

Gore dripped from Jason's bone fingers. He smiled as he turned the hand to look it over. Then his eyes drifted to the brown robe, keeping his satisfied grin as he did so.

The brown robe dropped the backpack and summoned fire in his hand. He hurled the small, pathetic fireball. Jason almost laughed. The sorry spell barely moved at half the speed of Kerr's books.

Before Jason could side-step the fireball, the Residuum landed directly in front of Jason. It reared up on its broken spine, its rat mouth opening wide to swallow the fireball in a single gulp.

The Residuum seemed both angry and pleased by its meal. It pushed off the ground with its hands into a position where its half-broken body sat atop its many tails, which curled and coiled like a dozen rising snakes. A red glow radiated from its core down its human arms to its fingers. The glow intensified in its fingers until they burned as if each digit was a sword being forged. Heat waves rose from them.

It went after the brown robe, moving quickly on its writhing tails, fiery fingers extended. The brown robe shrieked and ran into the darkness of the Castworks. The Residuum disappeared in pursuit.

Mike and Runt were at Jason's side a moment later. "You aight?" Mike asked.

Mel ran past Jason to reach Kerr. The red robe leaned against his slab desk a hand clutching his gut.

"Where's our friend?" Mel asked, shaking the mage by his robe. "Where!" he shouted enraged when Kerr shook his head no.

When Kerr shook his head, Jason immediately thought the "no" meant "no more". The bastards had killed Rich. It ignited a rage unquenchable in Jason's gut. He stalked toward the goddamn mage to bury his bone fingers into Kerr's worthless neck.

Mel apparently didn't hear the same thing. And he wasn't giving up. He rooted around Kerr's robe until his hand emerged holding a necklace, the same kind the prison warden in the Heart had. Mel pushed books out of the way and set the necklace down on the stone slab. A white light bloomed and the giant doorway melted to reveal the clean, clinical hall of another part of the Underthral.

Mel looked back at everyone. "They took him deeper," he said. "Let's go."

The white hall, Mel's words, they gave Jason hope. His friends all ran to the wheelbarrow to gather their weapons and gear. They didn't question. They weren't about to consign Rich to doom.

Letting his anger evaporate, Jason rushed to join them. He grabbed his bow, backpack, and quiver of arrows and severed arm. Together, they took to the bright white hall wordlessly.

Silently, Jason prayed they weren't too late.

CHAPTER 25
Binding Minds

Rich stared at the demented blue robe asleep on his cot, afraid to breathe too deeply as if the mage was a bomb ticking down.

For all intents and purposes, the mage was.

Rich likened the blue robes to the psychiatrists of magic. They were mind readers and brain tweakers; the dominion of blue magic lay in the heads of others. Useful in discerning the truth or helping someone overcome irrational fears, blue mages could even implant subtle receptors to make a person feel stronger, more confident, or keen at remembering details.

But Delv was demented, bent on playing sick mind screws. "Very scary, terror-inducing stuff" Brigitte had said. How she knew Rich's weakness to fear pointed back to Druze.

In the quiet spaces between Delv's slumbering breaths, understanding came to Rich. Obviously Brigitte was more than a destruction mage or an assistant to Rew. She knew what was happening to Rich with the cost and knew Baron Samedi well enough to want revenge. She said she had been a gray robe before going black.

Brigitte was the fourth baron, a group of pendulum rejects transported here who knows how long ago and had opted to stay.

Maybe they didn't opt anything. The Rift Pendulum brought people here by tragic accident. Where was the proof that anyone could even leave once the pendulum glitched?

No. Rew said they could go back, so they can. She wouldn't lie.

She's not like me, Rich thought. Under the draining weight of the Majora witchlock, stuck in a cell in the lowest depths of a magical prison, Rich's thoughts turned to how Rew was doing. She had just lost her father. That's hard enough for most people, but unlike most people, Druze's end was not something guaranteed. The look on her face when she had learned what he did... he would never be able to find the words to describe it. That look shook him to the point that Rich didn't care if Rew ever forgave him; he just wanted her to stop hurting.

"You look like a man with a lot on his mind."

Rich looked up to see Delv awake, lying on his cot and looking at his new cellmate. Delv's eyes were a fierce blue to match his spiky hair. The scars on his face crinkled as the man smiled at Rich.

"It's a gift," Delv said sitting up on the cot. "I can always tell when someone's burdened. Yours is more than the witchlock, even though they are oppressive, aren't they? *Sorgulama*."

Rich felt a prickly heat at the back of his brain, a sensation akin to feeling groggy or dizzy yet still coherent. Delv kept his smile and eyes friendly.

"What... are... you..."

"Doing?" Delv filled in. "Not much. Rich, is it? I'm just getting to know you a bit better. The real you, without all the lies and garbage that invariably spews out of a person's mouth." Delv smiled. "I find people sickeningly dishonest in conversation."

"Stop..." Rich began.

Delv shook his head and held up a finger to silence Rich. "*Dushunjeye dalun*," he intoned.

The white of the cell seemingly exploded in all directions, leaving Rich and Delv in a place that was without anything. Even the witchlock was absent. Rich immediately felt the crushing weight of it gone. Delv sat down in a flop of blue robes next to Rich.

"You were saying?"

"Where are we?" Rich asked.

"No place scenic, apparently. Think of it as a scry, only without all the troublesome sharing. You'd probably not want to have a piece of my mind, at any rate. I've been told the nastiest things lurk there."

The unfamiliar blue magic he was casting, the mage's words and his everpresent smile, all out it creeped Rich out. What was a scry without the sharing?

"We're in my mind," Rich said.

"And a keen one at that," Delv said with a nod. "The only place you have freedom from the witchlock. Sparse as it may look, it is a haven where we can have discussions at civilized speeds as well as thrilling mage duels."

Rich didn't like this. A demented blue robe was sitting in the white space in his head. Telling Delv he didn't like him there and to leave his new playground didn't seem like a successful plan. Rich tried a different tact. "I'm not interested in discussions or duels. I'm interested in freedom. How about you crush the witchlock and we find a way out of this dungeon together?"

Delv frowned. "But if I crush the witchlock, your innate mental defense would come back and you'd be able to actively refuse this tunnel into your mind. Not a lot of fun in that. Dueling a gray without a safety net seems an obscenely stupid thing to do, don't you think? Plus, our conversations would be reduced to mere talking, which means you'd just be lying and lying and lying, spewing whatever nonsense came to you. No, I'm afraid escaping with you just doesn't have the same appeal as playing with you."

Rich shook his head. "I'm not going to duel you, not when my entire being wants to be free. Besides, it's all in my head, not real, nothing to be gained from any of it."

The blue robe smiled. "That knowledge won't stop you from casting though. I've seen it. There is something beautifully broken about you. You believe a monster lives in your fear."

Delv's smile deepened. "Let's see, shall we?"

MELVIN LED THE PACK, trying to keep a hurried pace as he frantically looked from cell to cell. He felt precious time dissolving whenever he had to pause and verify the person in a cell wasn't Rich. Every aperture hosted the uniform sleeping, all of them twitching and thrashing. Their unrest was the only sign they were still alive.

"What'd they do to these guys?" Jason asked. No one answered. He spoke again. "How are we gonna save Rich if he's on the Hierophane Epilepsy Program?"

"Shuttup!" Mel snapped. Last thing he needed was Jason in his ear, adding more worry to the mountain already there.

Mel turned the corner and jumped back in a jolt as the nearest cell's occupant threw fire at him. The fireball hit the seemingly open doorway of the aperture and disintegrated. The prisoner threw his sleeves next, which fell limp and shriveled at the doorway. Finally, the prisoner ran at Melvin. Once he touched the aperture threshold, the same unseen force hurled him violently against the back wall. He crashed with a dull thud, fell awkwardly on the bed, and rolled off it to land on the floor in a heap.

"Forget the sleepers," Jason said. "What they'd do to that guy?"

"Let's keep moving," Mel said.

They did just that, working their way through a bizarre prison ward that was nothing short of an asylum. Every cell was its own separate slice of tragedy, the occupants fighting hopeless battles against logic, sense or their very selves.

Despair about Rich chipped away at Mel with every aperture he passed. He began to fear what he'd find in the next one, what Rich would be doing. Finally, he came to the latest aperture and stopped short.

Seated on the bed was a man with a blue robe and blue hair to match. His eyes were closed, a look of serenity broadcasting from a scarred face. On the ground next to him was Rich. The witchlock hovering above Rich throbbed violently in crimson bursts. Underneath it, Rich's face twisted in abject horror, his eyes glazed, his mouth moving in a blur. No words came out.

"What the hell is going on here?!" Mel shouted.

Abruptly, Rich fell out of his tortured state and started panting. The man on the bed opened his eyes and looked at Mel.

"Curious," the blue robed mage said. "Are you here to visit me, or the fellow whose mind I'm making merry in?"

"Step away," Mel said drawing his sword, "or I'll end you."

"Quite the fury you are," the blue robe said smiling. He turned to Rich for a moment before looking back at Mel. "He seems a touch old for you, wouldn't you say?"

Mel tried to take a step forward but Mike grabbed his wrist.

"Bruh, you saw what happened to Ragey Hands back there. Even if you can just walk right in, you know you there ain't no walking back out again."

Mike was right. Mel looked around, trying to find some sort of switch or trigger for these magic barriers. Everything was clean, white, featureless.

The smooth walls lacked buttons, the uniform floors lacked panels, the ceiling glowed its serene white light.

But this wasn't exactly back home. No buttons on the wall meant no light switches. How did they power the lights? More importantly, they were all in the belly of a magical dungeon. Forget about what powered the lights... what if the lights powered other things?

Guided by impulse, Mel thrust his sword up into the ceiling. Instead of the shower of sparks he expected, Mel got a rush of darkness. A patch of shadow coalesced on the floor and ran up the walls in front and behind Mel, meeting together at the ceiling. The light flickered, went out, and a rain of glowing black pinpricks fell, bringing an unnatural gloom with them to the square they stood in. While on either side of them the hallway maintained its surgically clean, white glow, the walls and floor in the space they stood had changed to drab, concrete gray. The air in the aperture doorway seemed to shimmer.

"Think that did it?" Jason asked.

"*Sahtekar olajaiyim,*" the blue robed man said, his grin deepening. He wagged a finger at Mel. "You have a clever mind, girl. One I would love to frolic in."

Mel's anger at this man quickly changed to shock as he heard the twangy release of Mike's diskbow. The disk shot past Mel and buried itself into the gut of the blue robe. The man looked at the ever-spreading dark, wet spot spreading over his robes as if he was curious about what it was. He looked up at them.

"That's... new."

He leaned forward, falling off the bed and landing in a crumpled heap beside Rich.

Mel wasted no time. He ran up to the floating witchlock, put a hand over it and squeezed. Mel both felt and heard the witchlock getting crushed as a shock wave boomed out of it, making the walls shake.

"Mel," Rich breathed.

Mel helped Rich up, hoisting one arm while Jason rushed to get the other. "We're here, dude," Jason said. "Time to go."

When they emerged back into the hallway, it looked like an entirely different building. The shockwave had destroyed many of the ceiling lights, causing random pockets of darkness throughout the hall. Gray walls and floors stood in contrast to the smattering of remaining white ones. In some places the white light flickered and underneath those lights gray and white spazzed back and forth in a nauseating war.

"We need to put some pepper on this breakout," Mike said. "I think we just freed a whole village worth of crazy-mage."

Mel led the way, although not exactly with pepper in his step. The place had turned in an instant from futuristic hospital hallway into post-apocalyptic horror basement. The dance of flickering light and abject shadow made the apertures along the wall grow and shrink in size. The apertures were all mouths of the mad, howling at them. And lurking in every one was someone not in their right mind.

Mel kept a firm grip on Rich in one hand, a firmer grip on his sword in the other, peering closely at each aperture as he proceeded cautiously back the way they had come. None of the prisoners seemed eager to escape or accost them. It seemed their greatest prison was their own mental state. The gang turned the corner without incident and made their way down the next hallway without any surprises. Once they were back in the Castworks, they could pick up the pace, perhaps even get out of here without bringing a swarm of mages running.

They turned the next corner and saw five people standing at the far end. The flickering, sporadic light played across their black robes, making them seem like the expanding shadows of angry wraiths. Gone was any chance of a clean exit.

Leading the destruction mages, Brigitte's baleful glare spoke war.

RICH FELT LIKE CRYING, like lying down and giving up on the spot. The only thing that kept him from caving completely was Mel's reassuring grip on his arm. He fought waves of nausea and vertigo, parting gifts of the crushed witchlock. It sickened him to swallow, and all he wanted to do was swallow away the acrid taste on his tongue. Instead of quitting, he leaned into Mel's grip a little more and steadied his gaze down the hallway at Brigitte.

"Before this, it would've simply been a joy to see you motherfuckers die," Brigitte said. "But now, I promise you, it will be the source of my next orgasm."

She took a step toward them, stopped and spoke in a blur. A fireball came shooting out of the aperture beside her. In one motion she thrust her hand out, caught the fire in it and threw it to the ground where it evaporated in a blossom of fiery tendrils. Brigitte kept walking as if that attempt to fry her was inconsequential. Without word or hesitation the four mages flanking her descended into the aperture. A flurry of exploding lights ensued, greens and reds and yellows, followed by a piercing scream. As suddenly as they rushed the room, all four mages fell back in step behind a quickly approaching Brigitte.

There was only one word for these guys: elite.

"Guys," Mel said. "Um, run?"

"I see your attempt to escape has already strained you," Brigitte said. "Allow me to cool you off. *Terini bana gel!*"

Rich felt a pull unlike anything in his life, like placing a vacuum nozzle an inch away from his skin only the nozzle was everywhere. The sweat from his forehead and the sweat that had gathered on everyone else flew from their skin, clothes and hair towards Brigitte.

"*Dur,*" she intoned and held her hands up. The countless droplets stopped to hover in the air. "*Terini donduran,*" she said and under the flickering light, Rich saw the sweat grow shinier, reflecting light with sharp facets that spoke of unnatural hardness. Ice.

Brigitte spoke again and pushed out with her hands. The newly formed ice daggers flew at them.

Out of nowhere, Runt stepped in front of the group, his arms up in an "X" across his face. His large body took the brunt as the onslaught met them. The zips and zings of the ice whizzing past sounded like bullets. Even with his weagr skin, Runt growled and grunted as the ice bombarded him.

Runt put his arms down once the ice wave passed. Those arms dripped blood from countless cuts.

"*Buuz duvara!*" Brigitte cried. Behind the gang, the ice daggers littering the floor and stuck in the wall came together, growing into a thick ice sheet that rose all the way to the ceiling. The wall of ice blocked any retreat back into the adjacent hallway. There was nowhere to run now.

The two black robes directly behind Brigitte bent their robe sleeves, hitting Runt with a four-piece that sent him crashing back into the ice wall and putting him on his ass. They were closing the distance fast.

Suddenly, one of the black robes in the rear yelped as he was snatched backwards into darkness. The other mages turned toward the commotion and the one closest to the darkness launched a fireball. Rich saw in the brief, fiery light a rat monster holding the destruction mage in the air by a dozen tails. The rat monster grabbed the fireball with a human looking hand and shoved the flame into its mouth.

"Sparver. Dein," Brigitte said and two of the mages broke formation and retreated into the dark, casting spells at the rat monster. Brigitte and the man on her right turned back towards Rich and his party. They kept pressing forward.

"Can you cast?" Mel asked Rich.

He could barely stand. His brain was clouded, seasick. His mouth felt stuffed with cotton. "No," he said. "Too weak."

"It's the witchlock failsafe. We gotta give him time," Jason said. "Here's hoping to me having some godsauce left." To Rich's amazement, Jason spun and punched the ice wall with his flesh hand. Instead of coming away with broken knuckles, the ice wall shattered.

Rich didn't ask. No one explained. They took off down the hallway, retreating from the black mages as fast as possible. Rich ambled on clumsy feet.

"You think running deeper into our depths will save you?" Brigitte called after them once she turned the corner. "There is no miraculous ladder, no emergency escape hatch waiting for you there. You will die as dogs, begging in a dark, forgotten corner."

"Perhaps not," a male voice said from a place unseen in the flickering light. "*Tavuk gibi korkuyorsun.*"

Instead of fleeing Brigitte, everyone turned. From the dark apertures they had already passed without incident, the crazy inmates rushed out towards the black robe next to Brigitte. He tried vainly to bend his sleeves and push them back but they swarmed relentlessly, a frenzy that swallowed him as a tide. In a matter of moments there was nothing to see but a roiling mass of bodies. His screams pierced the hall until they puttered into gurgles.

"Like my handiwork?" The speaker revealed himself by stepping out of the aperture. It was Delv. He smiled at Brigitte.

"If you can imagine, I had plenty of time to test the prison defenses," he said. "By all means, they're stout. But the lines tend to blur when dealing with blue magic and the power of suggestion. Did I give these stale bread-weary prisoners an insatiable craving for chicken or was that there all along for me to nudge? Who knows? But what I do know is that I just made your destruction comrade there smell like chicken. And by their apparent account, he's delicious."

"Delv," Brigitte growled through gritted teeth. "Aren't the scars I've already given you enough?"

Mike looked at Mel. "How the hell he live through you lopping his head off?"

"Me?" Mel said. "I saw you shoot him."

"Blue means mind screw," Jason said. "C'mon. Our best chance is now, while they're distracted." He looked at Rich. "Can you cast yet?"

Inside his head, Rich heard his own voice, the one from his old life, laughing. Richard Bates.

The cost was coming for him. The mother of all costs. They wouldn't be able to get through Brigitte and Delv without some magic, probably a lot of spell casting. Rich only had a few minutes at most before he'd collapse to the rest of the world. Meanwhile, he'd be stuck in the cost for how long... a day? A week? No, they needed out of here now.

An idea suddenly came to Rich. "Take me around the corner," Rich said. "Deeper."

"But—" Jason began.

"Do it," Rich said. "I don't have time to explain."

A brief exchange of looks later, they hauled him around the corner, down further into the Underthral. The sounds of frantic shouting and explosive bursts that come with magic duels began to dull into the background. Rich stood up and spoke the only magic he'd hope to cast before the cost came.

In front of him, the blue and white light of a portal coalesced.

"Aw, crap," Mel said.

"Beats dying in an underground deathtrap," Rich said.

Mike and Runt rushed in, followed by Jason, an obviously reticent Mel, and finally Rich. When the light subsided they were all back at the outskirts of Mere, where the blind man had taught Rich how to portal. The dying light of day made the town in the distance seem unreal, shining in the rusty orange of dusk. Everyone visibly exhaled and took in the fresh air heavy with the scent of grass.

An uncontrollable chill rushed down Rich's spine and made him tremble. Despite the cold, he began to sweat. It felt like it was pouring out of his face and hair.

The cost had never announced itself before now. Unlike all the fears he'd ever experienced, the fear of what was going to happen for this cost made Rich's blood turn to frost.

"See, Bendy Sleeves?" a voice said behind him. "That's how a mage is supposed to travel."

Rich turned and saw the blind man. He sat on the same rock he had earlier, as if he'd been in that same spot the whole time.

In his desperation, an idea came to Rich, inspired by the woman who had just tried to kill him. He ran over to the blind man.

"Give me the Oath of Binding," Rich said.

"Shouldn't you already have taken it, gray?" the man asked.

"I didn't. I need it. It's coming. Please!"

The blind man's eyes stood still while his nose crinkled as he sniffed the air. "I can smell the fear on you, the cold taint of spent magic in your very sweat. You don't have to tell me a cost of the furious kind is coming for you." He stood up. "Quickly repeat this:

"I have no magic. The Onesource is magic. Magic without guidance is power without control, rage without boundary, body without soul, intelligence without morality. If magic will lend itself to me, I will lend myself to magic. I will be its control, its boundary, its soul, its morality. Until I have mastered myself, may not a single spell flow through me. Such am I bound."

Rich repeated the words, sweat drenching him the whole time. An overbearing headache began to throb in his temples, making him feel dizzy and sick. Still, he kept speaking the oath.

"Speak your signature," the old man said after Rich was done.

"Signature?" Rich asked with trembling lips.

"The one word that defines you. If you don't know that, the oath is meaningless."

Rich seized his temples and screamed at the headache pounding its way out of his head. He had to finish. He knew the word. Rew had taught him.

"*Zorbela!*" he cried before his world turned to black.

CHAPTER 26
Grow

Mike summed up everyone's shared frustration best. "This some bullshit."

He sat on one of the inn's beds beside Runt. The big man watched Mel pacing back and forth. Jason stared out the window at sun filled streets.

Mere's inn was small, and largely unoccupied by travelers, allowing the guys to rent two connected rooms each with two beds. This is where they carried Rich after he had passed out. The old kid slept in the other room while everyone else congregated, sharing in that pissy feeling of defeat.

"So close," Mel said to no one in particular, still pacing with his eyes down. "So goddamn close."

"Maybe it wasn't meant to be," Jason said as he continued to stare out the window. "Maybe this world isn't done with us yet."

Mel stopped pacing at Jason's words and looked up at his friend. "What the fuck is that supposed to mean?"

Jason turned to Mel, his face serene, his eyes dancing. "The aians believe the Onesource is sentient. Maybe it's got its hand on this world. On us."

"So now you're divinely inspired?" Mel craned his neck and put his hands on his hips, looking every bit like their mom whenever she caught Mike in a lie. "Should I write that down? Wouldn't want to leave that out of the motherfucking Gospel of Jason!"

Jason held his hands up in surrender. "I get it. You were almost home. You're frustrated. I understand."

Mel looked at Jason as if he had lost his rabid ass mind. "You understand? Yeah, you certainly act like you understand that being stuck here blows, with you loving those top notch marksmanship skills and your oh-too-cool bone hand and your legion of devoted worshippers."

Jason shrugged. "Hey, if you want more devoted worshippers, put the steel bikini back on."

Mel shook his head. "You're such an ass."

"No, you're an ass," Jason said closing the distance between them to point his bone finger into Mel's chest. "All you do is whine and bitch. 'Oh, I'm a girl now!' 'There're no 7-Elevens' 'I miss Pop-Tarts and being an insignificant teenager.' Have you listened to yourself? You're a goddamn buzzkill. Yeah, it sucks you didn't get to pendulum hop so you could enjoy some cable TV and mediocrity tonight. But don't get shitty with me because I've been making the most of my time here while you've been busy singing the blues."

Mel looked at Jason with cold eyes. "You either move your fingers or we move furniture," he said with a level voice that was all Zhufira.

Nothing in the room stirred. Jason eyed Mel and Mel looked back, the two of them sharing a long, tense moment. Finally, Jason brought his bone fingers back and away from Mel's chest. Jason smirked.

"Looks like I'm not the only one who can enjoy the perks of being here when he has to."

Noiselessly, Rich entered the room. The old gray robed kid rubbed sleep out of his eyes before looking around at everyone.

"Did I miss something?"

"Yeah," Mike said, "you missed your two bullshit friends here fighting for the award for biggest jackass."

Mel spun around and looked at Mike as if his big brother had just betrayed him. Mike threw up a hand to kill whatever he was going to say.

"Your friend may be an arrogant asshole who's having a little more fun than he should be with this, but he's right about you. Nobody wants tickets to your pity party, especially me. You been so busy moaning about your life with tits that you haven't even considered if any of us got it worse. I'm a four-foot scarred-up purple lizard dude. And going home solves all your problems like algebra. But me? I wanna go home but I gotta worry about time. Did you forget I'm in the Army and was on R&R when this all started? Life is great if time stood still back home, but what if every second we've been here has passed on Earth, too? What if months have gone by? Either way, it don't matter; I'll be looking at federal lockup for being A.W.O.L. And all for a game I didn't wanna play in the first place."

Mike shook his head at Mel, his scowl deepening as he voiced all the circumstances beyond his control, the things he didn't want to think about because dwelling on it was a futile, worthless endeavor. "Grow up, bruh."

Mel closed his mouth and looked at his brother, the fire to fight leaving his eyes. Mike turned to Rich.

"Get enough sleep, Rip Van Winkle?"

"The most restful since being here," Rich replied with a sloppy smile. "You have no idea."

"Good," Mike said. "Now that you got your beauty rest, we can get to business. Time to be solution oriented. Crying about what happened back at the Hierophane'll only produce tears when we need to be producing results, hooah? Anybody got any ideas on how to get to that pendulum?"

After a moment of silence, Jason raised a bone hand.

"We sneak in, like we were gonna do in the first place?"

"Thought about it," Mike said, "but them are suicide odds. They know that's where we headed, so they're gonna lock it down tighter than a liquor cabinet on prom night." He looked at Rich. "You connected more than anyone else when it comes to the mages. Got any more people on the inside, you know, folks whose friends and fam you haven't killed?"

Rich's face darkening like storm clouds. "No."

"Well, if we can't talk our way in, and sneaking in is walking to our own deaths, I say we march in," Mike said. "At the head of an army."

"What army?" Mel asked.

"We rendezvous with Savvy," Mike said. "She up north, getting all the nasran tribes together. She's planning to come down on the Hierophane like a hammer, dismantle that bitch brick by brick. We need to be on Team Smash if we wanna ride that pendulum."

Mel shook his head. "There has to be another way."

Sometimes Mike wondered if they really had the same DNA. He gave Mel a deadpan look, something that was probably impossible to see behind the goggles. "I'm listening."

"I don't know," Mel said with a noncommittal shrug. I just don't feel comfortable fighting a war."

Mike guffawed. "Seriously? Did you just say that?" The megrym looked around the room at the others. "Did he just say that?" he asked before turning his head back to his brother. "I'm talking about war, not wardrobe. Comfortable is what you say about your socks. What I'm talking is an enterprise in which people die. Could be some of us doing the dying. You ain't supposed to find comfort in that, just the best, least suicidal path to getting home."

"But going to war is taking it too far," Mel countered. "I know the nasrans have their own axe to grind with the Hierophane, but that's *their* axe. My joining their cause is me saying I'm willing to kill whoever's in the way of my goal: foot soldiers, innocent mages, anyone. I'm not ready to say all that."

"I am, bruh," Mike said. "These fools got a grip on my freedom. I ain't sign up for this, and I damn sure ain't gonna let them bring me out here in the wilds only to tell me I can't go home. Not having it. But you'll have it, huh?"

Mel looked like he wanted to shrug again, like that would solve their ever-present problem. Mike jumped off the bed and held a hand up to kill whatever lukewarm milquetoast bullshit Melvin was fixing to preach. "I got a clear plan I'm gonna follow unless you got something worthwhile to say in the next few minutes. Meanwhile, you do whatever moves you. Me? I'm gonna go downstairs, drink to the blood of my near-future enemies, and head out of town to make it happen. Whoever wanna roll is welcome."

Mike opened the room door and headed down aged wooden stairs, followed by Runt and Jason. The inn's tavern held a handful of yokels who thankfully had enough of their own business to only spare the newcomers a short glance of acknowledgement. They all quickly went back to their own tables, their own world and conversations. When the barkeep's eyes met Mike's goggles, Mike pointed at the tap and brought up three gloved fingers before finding a free table.

Mike looked at Jason, who was busy looking at an antelope head mounted on the fireplace. "You rolling with us?"

"Meh. Who knows," Jason replied. "But I'm not exactly one to miss an opportunity to drink to the blood of near-future enemies." As if on cue the beers came to the table. Jason smiled with Cheshire fierceness as he raised his mug.

Runt raised his own glass as well. Mike looked at his big friend.

"You and I done came a long way from when we first stumbled on your house in the middle of nowhere. You've already went above and beyond for me, two or three times over. But this is war I'm talking. You don't have to come with, man. Like Ruki Provos, this ain't your beef."

"Hmm," Jason mused as he looked at Runt with dancing eyes. "Now that Mike brought it up he's got me thinking; why do you hang with us? We're nothing but trouble."

Runt set his beer down. "I am half man, but also half weagr. Man half enjoys peace, other thirsts for carnage. The two natures agree on little. Weagr in me wants my blades to soak in blood. If I can help noble friends for noble causes while that happens, then the man in me grins a happy smile. Two natures in agreement."

Mike picked up his beer mug. "Guess that means you're rolling."

"Yes." With nothing else to say, Runt picked up his mug again.

"Noble friends," Jason said with a chuckle. "The only noble I've seen from Mike is Chernobyl."

"Savvy should be in Maras," Mike said ignoring Mel's smart ass friend. "Hooking up with the Kahraman tribe." Mike knew most of Runt's old adventuring days had taken place in the human kingdoms to the south so he wouldn't have much intel. He looked at Jason. "Know anything about that region, game nerd?"

Jason's face frowned. "Had to do a quest one time up there for some stupid red peppers. Hill country, mostly. Nothing really cool, except I leveled up when I was there putting arrows in nasran faces."

Mike shook his head, more than a little unsettled by Jason's words. "Ever consider the real possibility that those nasran faces were more than just game visuals and you inadvertently murdered innocent folk?"

Jason shrugged and raised his mug to his face. "It's impossible for me to feel bad about being an awesome player," he said before taking a sip.

Mike didn't have a reply, so instead he focused on Mel and Rich, who were now making their way down the stairs. They were welcome to sit if they wanted to join the fight like Runt or drink like Jason, but Mike was in no mood to hear more talk about what constituted comfort. To their credit, Mel and Rich took their seats at the table and only spoke to order drinks.

Speaking of credit, Mike could use some. "How you dudes sitting on ends?" he asked.

Jason patted his pockets. "We're still pretty flush from when the Hierophane outfitted us to take down the Death Null," he said. "I guess they figured newbie kids from another world may take a lot more time and expense getting to it than your typical seasoned mercenary."

"Drinks on y'all," Mike said. "On top of that, we need to divvy up. It's a long trip to nasran country when all you got is two nickels to rub together."

"So that's it then?" Mel asked. "Long trip north, long time gathering up a bunch of nasrans, all for a long war?"

"Not necessarily," Mike answered. "I mean, we are in a world of magic... maybe pouting and crying big, salt-stained tears will open up a mystical portal to Arby's where we can celebrate with curly fries and horsey sauce. Wanna try that instead?"

"You want to try shutting up?" Mel asked. "Just because I don't have any better ideas doesn't mean I have to like yours."

Mike didn't bother to respond. He drank his beer. A silent moment reigned over the table, where everyone seemingly retreated into their own glasses and heads. In terms of where their futures were headed, there was a lot to consider.

Jason looked up from his beer. "Anyone else got a hankering for a roast beef classic with horsey sauce?"

Mike drained his mug. "No sense wasting daylight, time to make trails. Everybody follow me upstairs."

Jason made haste to finish his beer. Runt had already killed his. Mel and Rich left their mugs half drained, neglected while Mel fished out money to pay for drinks. Upstairs, Mel and his friends shaved off a third of their funds and gave them to Mike, who in turn gave half to Runt. Afterwards, they all shouldered their packs and made their way downstairs and out the door. Mike didn't know if any of these guys except Runt was about to follow him all the way to Savvy, but this path was the only one present for now. He'd worry about any new directions when they came up.

Outside, the bright sun did little to heat the brisk autumn air. Mike was going to have to get a coat, maybe a cloak like Mel's. The people of Mere milled about the dirt-packed roads and simple wooden buildings in long sleeves. Mike didn't envision the northern lands would be getting any warmer.

"So, the basic plan is to walk?" Rich asked.

"Basically," Mike answered. "Hoof it to a town with some traders, then maybe we can pay for a caravan ride."

"I think I may have found us a faster way," Rich said pointing.

Mike followed Rich's finger down the street to an Indian looking dude who was sitting on a stool in front of the general store, the same blind man Rich had had words with last night before passing out.

"What's up with you and that dude, anyway?" Mike asked.

"He's given me a few choice words, more than once. C'mon."

Rich led the way to man who sat with unfocused, staring eyes, sitting still enough to look every part the statue Rich had been.

"Um, excuse me?" Rich began.

"Want something, Bendy Sleeves?" The old man didn't bother to turn his head to address Rich.

"Can we pay you for a portal somewhere?"

"Course you can," the old man grumped "it's one of my many professions around here after all. Besides, it's not like you can anymore."

Jason raised an eyebrow. "What do you mean?"

"I recognize your voice. Didn't you listen last night?" the old man asked. "Bendy Sleeves here asked me to take his magic. He's gone from casting magelord spells to barely being able to cast a die."

Jason looked at Rich then back to the old man, a look of surprise and disgust stuck on his face. "Seriously?"

"I'll portal you for free anywhere if he can bend a sleeve and knock me off this stool," the old man said. "You game, Bendy Sleeves?"

Rich looked around tentatively, the expression on his face making it seem like he had just realized he had walked outside with no clothes on. After a moment Rich shrugged, raised his sleeve towards the old man and said a word that sounded like "aay". Nothing happened except for Rich looking stupid with his arm raised.

"You gotta be kidding me!" Jason exclaimed. "We're in a world teeming with threats and you decide to go all level one on us?!"

Rich looked saddened. "You don't understand—"

"I don't understand?!" Jason cried. "Here am I calling on dark gods and the encroaching threat of full on bodily possession to get us out of binds and you give up the power to literally move mountains because you can't handle a few bad dreams?! No, idiot, do you understand?"

"You can stop now," Rich said, his eyes narrowing.

"Or what?" Jason asked with a scoff. "You're a nub now. You've got no stats to shut me up. You gave up all your power."

"Maybe you should take stock of yourself," Melvin said, stepping in between Rich and Jason. "Since when do you discount a friend because he has less power to wield? Onus doesn't have to go too far to possess you, does he? Seems like you're almost there."

"Hey!" the old man shouted. "I didn't ask for an invitation to help you all carry your personal baggage. Buy a portal or get on already."

Mike nodded; dude was right. "Yo, man, can you hook up a ride to Maras?"

The old man nodded. "Been there a few times. You can be there too, for the right price."

The right price turned out to be more than steep. Mike had the mind to shortchange the geezer, but he seemed to have more uncanny sense than most sighted people. There was nothing sensible about cheating someone keen enough to get around without eyes and powerful enough to port you into a volcano.

"What's your name, old man?" Mike asked. "I like to know who I'm getting screwed by."

"Vylar Ginza," he said with a grin as he felt the fabric of the money he'd recently procured. Once he pocketed the cash, he stood up and walked into the street holding the cane without bothering to tap his way. He began to speak foreign sounding words.

"Hold up, dude!" Mike yelled. He ran into the general store, leaving everyone on the street staring at each other for a few long minutes. He came out wearing a small, brown leather coat, something that was probably made for a child but it suited his purposes just as well.

"Aight," Mike said, folding down his new collar. "Let's roll."

Vylar began the spell anew and after a moment the sound of air getting sucked into a vacuum started followed by the familiar sight of a blue and white portal coalescing out of air.

"Not this again," Mel groaned.

Mel was always a touch pessimistic. Mike was beaming; this beat days and weeks of walking and bumming rides. He was the first one in the portal.

Consequently, he was the first one to find the tip of a dozen nasran spears pointed to his throat. He found himself surrounded by hostile nasrans, grimaces on all their faces as if he was the king of mages. "*Should've thought through the whole use magic to go to mage-haters thing,*" Mike thought. Then came Runt, who found his neck similarly threatened. Then Mel.

"Fricking portals," he muttered looking down the spear tips.

Jason and Rich got the same treatment. Finally Vylar came through. Immediately all the spears lowered. "Abi Vylar! Abi Vylar!" a few of the nasrans cried.

Instantly, the nasran camp turned from hostile to friendly. Now the various campfires throughout the site seemed warm and hearthy, not something these folks were going to toss strange megryms in to burn. Nasran men, women and children came out of rounded, fur covered tents with smiles on their faces. Men wore tanned leather outfits, the women thick cloaks. The air smelled of meats being smoked, earth and sandalwood. Behind them all in the distance, rolling hills ringed the campsite, blue-tinged against overcast skies.

"It's a good thing you came with us," Rich said.

"Good thing nothing," Vylar said. "I had to. How else am I going to put down a new portal root?"

"Yo," Mike said to one of the nasrans who had the nerve to put a spear against his adam's apple. "Where's Savvy? Uh, Savashbahar?"

The warrior looked surprised. "Who asks for the den mother?"

"Mike Morrow. She knows me."

The warrior's eyes got big at the mention of Mike's name. Without warning, he grabbed Mike's shoulders and ushered him through the growing crowd jockeying around Vylar.

Mike really hated his current height at times like this. For what felt like forever, there was nothing but a sea of nasran waistlines that he got jostled and pushed past. The tall bastards blotted out the sky. The time he could actually see over a crowd seemed a far distant memory. All he could do now was fight the urge to punch dudes in their crotches.

Eventually he emerged in front of a massive tent, round like all the others, covered in a herd of furs. "*Kabile annejiyim*!" the warrior called. Moments later the fur draping the tent door rustled, and Mike saw her.

Savashbahar wore one of the gray-black leather outfits she had acquired in the Sprawl, with chrome and brass hardware stitched throughout, and had added a leather cloak similar to the Hexenarii Mike had first encountered at Maltep. More than just mere wardrobe, Mike noticed Savvy wore a hex belt with innumerable silver-tipped wooden hexes glinting and dancing on her waist. She looked good despite the age evident in her black hair heavily streaked with gray. She saw Mike and her lips creased into a deep smile.

"*Evah*! You have come to me, little one. How pleased I am!" She closed the distance to Mike, knelt down and embraced him tightly.

He returned the hug. "So am I, Savvy. It's good to see you."

She looked at him and a motherly hand went up to the scar tissue on his face. "What has happened to you?"

"It's nothing, all cosmetic," Mike said. "At least I'm still alive; I can't say the same thing about the other guy."

"Ah!" Savvy said standing up. "And Runt has come as well." That's when Mike notice the big man had appeared behind him. Savvy went over and gave him similar treatment, embracing the big man like a dearly missed son. After a moment, she turned to Mike.

"I can guess what brings you into the heart of these ancestral lands."

"I'm pretty sure your guess would be right," Mike said. "We aim to join the cause against the Hierophane. Got room for us?"

"Such stupid questions," Savvy replied with a smirk. "My hearth is always yours as well."

"I didn't just bring Runt," Mike said. "I actually managed to keep my brother and his dumb friends out of trouble this time. They're back this way."

Mike led the way back as best he could considering he went mostly by feel instead of sight. The nasran crowd parted easily for him now that Savvy was behind him. She commanded utmost respect here in Maras, a far cry from how it was when they first met in Maltep. Eventually the nasrans parted to where Mel, his friends and Vylar stood.

"You guys remember Savvy right?" Mike asked.

Savashbahar wasted no time for recollections. She immediately strode over to Mel and embraced him.

"Ah, the beautiful brother who caused so much fuss. How are you, my lovely?"

"Fine," Mel replied with a clumsy, happy smile. "Just fine. And you?"

"Never better, *kizim*." Savvy turned and simply nodded at Jason and Rich. "Hollow friends, not quite hollow," she greeted with a cordial, less than warm tone.

"So, here we all are," Mike said. "Your new house guests."

Mel flashed a wan smile. "Not exactly," he said.

Mike's confusion must've spoke volumes on his face. Mel rushed to fill in the gaps.

"Rich is going back. Vylar's going to train him to be a mage."

"Again," Jason spat with bile.

"For a price," Vylar stated.

Mel looked at the two of them like they were ruining an awesome surprise before turning back to Mike. "We're going to go back with him."

Before Mike could say a word Jason spoke. "Yeah, about that... I kinda like this scene. I'm going to stay."

Now it was Mel's turn to look perplexed. Jason waved his bone hand before Mel had spoken a single word.

"I'm into adventuring, seeing this world, not cooling my heels in a small, go nowhere town. I'd die a slow detention-style death there, Mel."

"But—but—" Mel began.

"Meh, it's pointless to fight it," Jason said. "We want different things now. Truth be told, I wasn't going to go back with you through the pendulum." He shrugged, his barely concealed cat out of the bag. "I like it too much here to go."

"Yeah, I figured that," Mel said. "Honestly, I was planning to push you into the rift as soon as it opened and just have you mad at me on the other side."

The two friends looked at one another, saying nothing for long moments. "You sure about this?" Mel finally asked.

Jason gave him a sloppy grin. "As sure as I am about anything, meaning I sound real sure while guessing in gross amounts. But I am confident in one area. It'll all work out," he finished with a wink.

Mel nodded with a certain finality and hugged his friend. Like that decided it all.

"Hey, hold up," Mike said, "I got something to say about you just up and leaving."

Mel looked at his older brother with that mom look. "Do you really think you're going to say anything that'll keep me here?" he asked.

In that moment, Mike realized just how grown up his little brother had become. And as much as he wanted to watch over Mel, he knew Mel could look out for himself.

"I guess not," Mike said.

"Wait," Savashbahar said. She pulled a hex from her belt. "Find," she named it before lifting up Mel's backpack and sticking it to the sword's scabbard.

"In case we need to locate you again," she said with a smile. "Next time, you won't be so much trouble, yes?"

"Yes," Mel agreed with a smile before they hugged again.

Finally Mel bent down to Mike and regarded him with softened eyes. "I want to go home bad, just not this bad. Won't you reconsider?"

"Fraid not, bruh," Mike said with a grin. "Be easy out there, aight? Watch out for pajama nerd; I ain't gonna rescue him again if he gets stuck in gold or Jello or something."

"OK," Mel said. He gave his brother a hug. Then he stood up, took his place beside Rich while Vylar worked his magic. A moment later, a portal opened.

A moment after that, Mel was gone.

CHAPTER 27
Tribal Ways

S avashbahar's heart warmed at the sight of Mike and Runt. She had missed them this passing fortnight. Not so welcome was their ally. She had come to grudgingly accept all of their hollower origins, but the aian's shimmer had taken a foul turn since their last meeting. Now it growled around him, an angry, throbbing red.

Besides, even if Jason wasn't truly aian he looked aian. No true member of her race held kindly to the continued occupation of Nasreddin.

Now that Mike's beautiful brother was gone, the little megrym looked about the town of Maras, teemed to bursting with the warriors Savashbahar had brung, and smiled a toothy grin.

"You've been busy," he said.

"It has gone as I have hoped," she answered.

She had already told Mike her plans before they parted at Olukent, to include sketching out a crude map of her projected whereabouts. First, it was short and easy trips to meet with the Antep and Kastamonu, the two tribes most closely aligned historically with Maltep. Both the Antep and Kastamonu tribes had shared so much blood in marriage and side by side on battlefields there was never a question in Savashbahar's mind that they would rally to avenge the fall of Maltep.

Next, it had been the trip into hill country, to the nomadic Kahraman tribe. Truly, Maras was the only permanent settlement the Kahraman had, a site as sacred to them as the mounds of Maltep were to her people. Despite its permanence, most of the Kahraman here lived in *yurts*, round fur-covered tents which could be quickly broken down and carried to another campsite.

"It is a good thing you came when you did," Savashbahar told Mike. "Good or bad, today is my last day here."

"I remember your plan," Mike said. "If I missed you here, I'd roll to Lake Bafa to catch you parlaying with the Balikesir." He tapped a finger to the side of his head. "It's all right here, Savvy. I even remember the map you sketched out. Not my first time at an ops briefing."

Savashbahar smiled. The sketching and telling of plans was not a matter of simply sentiment toward Mike. She remembered her blood whisper all too well, of seeing the little megrym at the fore of a dismantled Hierophane. She was prepared to bring the towers down without him; still she took comfort in his presence.

"It is good you have come," Savvy said, "If any foreigner can persuade the Kahraman elders to join with me, it is you."

"Why would they need convincing?"

"My tribe and theirs have not always been on the best of terms," Savashbahar answered. "Distrust remains. You will be able to state to them what I cannot."

"Word," Mike said thrusting a thumb into his chest as if to indicate his suitability, "I got your back." He turned and jumped back in surprise when he found himself face to face with a cat bigger than him.

The caracal stood waist high to nasrans, lean and golden furred, with long ears that seemed even longer because of the black tufts of fur which protruded from them. A slight tug on the caracal's leather collar brought the cat back to its master, one of the Kahraman *vashokadama*. The man was as lean and wiry as the cat he cared for and, as all other *vashokadama*, he had fashioned his hair to point up in two directions to mimic the caracal's tufted ears. The *vashokadama* and their war cats made for excellent scouts and were highly feared for both their guerrilla attacks and cavalry strikes. They were all the more reason Savashbahar wanted the Kahraman to take up her cause.

Savashbahar led them all through Maras back to her yurt. The town was swollen, close to bursting its seams with the many warriors of Maltep, Antep, and Kastamonu gathered there. She did not have to weave her way through the throng, the warriors and townspeople paid their respects by clearing a wide path for her and her companions. She had come a long way from being an outcast on the fringes of Maltep society.

"Looks like I'm not the most welcome face in the crowd," Jason said as he walked. There was no hiding the cold, hard stares of the nasrans they passed.

Savashbahar would have to keep the aian near until those looks softened a bit, lest he found himself with his throat cut.

"Pay it no mind," she told Jason. "We are not friends of the Temple of Houses. When they see you are one of the rare aians that do not stand with the temple, their eyes will soften."

"They'd better," Jason said looking around skeptically. "Because right now they're looking at me like I'm the old lady at the register still writing checks for groceries."

"*Ayvah*," Savashbahar muttered with a grimace. "Measure your words with care, Jason. It is difficult enough to parse what Mike says without you also saying incomprehensible gibberish."

"Word?" Mike asked looking shocked and offended.

"I see your point," Jason said.

The crowd parted to reveal Savashbahar's yurt. She led the way inside, into a cavernous space hosting nothing save a long oaken table and a bedroll. Maps, parchments and cups littered the table. A wooden ring framed a large hole in the center of the roof which let light in. Slender wooden support rods sprouted from the ring in all directions to meet the walls in a way that reminded Savashbahar of symbolic drawings of the sun.

Mike strolled over to the table. His fingers idly sifted through various parchments before tapping a wooden cup. "Having a book of the month club party?"

"Ritual feasts, then venerations to the ancestors," Savashbahar said. "Then more ritual feasts, followed by recounting of past glories, followed again by more ritual feasts, followed finally with discussions of current plans and strategies."

She was both sick and weary of ritual. Truthfully, she would have preferred to be in Balikesir country by now, securing promises of their support, but there was no way to rush the Kahraman. They held onto tradition with an iron death grip, refusing to be rushed into action no matter how urgent the matter. Not until all the observances were made.

Mike leaned over and sniffed a now empty cup. "Sounds like a party, but a slow ass way to start a war."

Savashbahar went over to the table beside Mike and started gathering a few of the maps and parchments, those few among the others that were important to her devised war against the mages. "The rituals are over at last," she said. "Soon, I will hold my last meeting with the elders of Kahraman, and there they will decide whether to support my cause."

"Am I the only one bewildered by this?" Jason asked. "I mean, you've personally verified the Hierophane has at its disposal a seemingly endless supply of magical warriors with nearly godlike power. These warriors can go anywhere, and literally appear out of nowhere. They destroyed the ancestral homeland of a nasran tribe but you're here *trying* to convince another tribe that stopping the source of the magical warriors is a good idea."

"If you knew more of our customs and traditions, this would not seem so bewildering," Savashbahar said.

"Hell, spend some time in the Army," Mike said. "After a couple years, you wouldn't question stupid-sounding procedures. You'd just get it done."

The fur walls of the yurt quivered as a ram's horn trumpeted, a dull throbbing that came down from the hole in the ceiling to fill the room. The elders were calling. Savashbahar rushed to gather the remaining documents.

"Jason, Runt, I ask you two to remain here," she said.

"Nope," Jason said with a smirk. "I'm going to find whichever fur dome that's serving as a bar."

Savashbahar shook her head. "Many here don't yet know you. It is unwise."

Jason made his way over to the entrance flap, looked back at them and grinned. "The best part of being a world away from mom is I'm one hundred percent sure you're not my mom." He shrugged. "Not obligated to listen. Gonna go drink now." With that, he disappeared with a flourish of the door flap.

Savashbahar looked to Runt, who nodded and took to the door before she could say anything. The door flap settled back into the place and Jason's muffled shouting emanated back into the tent.

"Clear the way! Chosen One coming through!"

Savashbahar grimaced. She wished the boy had decided to travel with Mike's beautiful brother and the mage. There was no time to corral him. She couldn't keep the elders waiting. Her one hand clutched the documents. The other grasped Mike's shoulder.

"Are you ready, little one?"

Mike's goggle lenses reflected her worried features when he faced her, an effortless smile creasing his lips. "Bet."

Together, they proceeded through the crowded streets of Maras to the council chambers. Not only did people nearest them clear a way as before, everyone stopped talking, stopped trading and hawking wares and laughing to look at the two of them make their procession. Even the caracals stared. It added a certain indelible weight to the upcoming decision.

Two warriors guarded either side of the council chamber. Their spears refused to move from the entrance as Savashbahar approached. One guard looked at Savashbahar with a face of stone.

"The foreigner, he is not allowed into the council chamber."

Savashbahar kept her voice calm and level. "Not allow the one who aided me in felling the factory mage towers? Allow him. He is *dost*."

"We will need to get approval," the guard said.

"Then get it," she replied.

The guard looked to the other, who retreated inside the yurt. Several silent moments passed until he emerged and nodded. The other guard wasted no time gathering the flap and pulling it so Savashbahar and Mike could enter.

This was Savashbahar's first time in the council chamber and it was much more ornate than the accommodations she had been afforded. Beautiful paintings stretched over the domed ceiling and curved along the walls, depicting legendary Kahraman battles. Large, colorful rugs adorned the floor. Dominating the center of the room was a crescent shaped table. There sat the seven elders of Kahraman.

The one in the middle of the table, known as Kayitsiz, had wispy white hair and a heavily lined faced. He beckoned her forward.

"You are welcome, Savashbahar of Maltep, First Hexenarii, War Chief of the Keepers of the Emerald Sun." His voice rumbled as if thunder lived in his throat.

"I am well met, Chief Kayitsiz," she replied. "May the roaming people of Kahraman ever find their way home to the hills of Maras."

"You seek to have my people cease their roaming," Kayitsiz said, "to pick up their spears and do battle with the mages, your former trade allies. Why should we do this?"

"It is true Maltep sought trade with the mage factory among others," Savashbahar answered, "but we did not seek hostility. When we limited trade with the mages, the hollowers came to our remote villages. When we ceased trade altogether, the hollowers came to the halls of sacred Maltep itself."

"After you destroyed the towers the mages hold dear," Kayitsiz said.

"After hollowers killed my son," Savashbahar countered.

"You say the mage factory produces hollowers. We say that while you may be First Hexenarii and War Chief, you are nonetheless a woman, one consumed in the worst grief a woman can bear. It is grief that can turn any sign of smoke into a raging wildfire. Do you have more than your belief that the mages make hollowers to move our spears?"

"I have him," Savashbahar said, presenting Mike to the council. She turned to face her friend. "Tell them who you are and what you are."

Mike took a moment to look at all the council chiefs. "I am not a megrym. I'm Mike Morrow, a man from another world pulled here by the Hierophane. For general purposes, I'm pretty much a hollower."

"Hollowers do not talk," Kayitsiz said.

"I'm broken," Mike said with a tilted grin.

Chief Kayitsiz turned to his left to Chief Gulbeze, the only woman on the council. Her gray hair was braided, with broken hexes weaved into the braids. Like Savashbahar, see saw things in people few others could.

"He does not lie," Chief Gulbeze said. "He is hollow, yet somehow full."

Chief Kayitsiz nodded. The confirmation of Mike's origins did not change the stoic expression on his face. "Do you know of Enverpasha?"

"Yes," she replied coolly. Talk of Enverpasha was all she had heard for a week now. Enverpasha was convinced war between the mages and the aians was imminent and inevitable. Rumors spoke he was further north trying to unite the tribes there, to take them to war against the Temple of Houses and liberate Nasreddin, believing the aians would be unable to fight a war on two fronts. Ironically, a possible war between the tower and the temple would also be a boon to Savashbahar's own effort.

Kayitsiz stroked his beard for a moment then leaned forward. "Do you believe your cause as noble as his?"

Savashbahar kept her composure and spoke calmly, evenly. "Nasreddin is home. Can there be a cause as noble as seeing it fully returned to our hands?

But as nasrankind has ever stood, Nasreddin will ever stand. My cause is not as noble, but I can say it is more pressing. Aians are not spilling nasran blood. Aians did not raze Maltep to ruin."

"Whether Maltep invited its ruin when it shook hands with mages is a matter of debate still."

Savashbahar felt raw heat surge into her cheeks. She swallowed her anger, but spoke through trembling lips. "What do you think will happen here when the mages run out of the hexes they stole from Maltep?"

"Their hex stores are not our concern," Kayitsiz said with a shake of his head. "We are far removed from the mages and their dealings. They do not invade Kahraman lands. Yet you seek to invade theirs, with our spears, our *vashokadama*. If we pledge to you we cannot back Enverpasha—"

"Enverpasha! Enverpasha!" Savashbahar spoke the name as a curse word. "It is all I've heard from the Kastamonu, from the Kahraman, and I expect I will hear it again from the Balikesir when I arrive there seeking aid. Enverpasha! He is coming on a white horse! He will ride like a howling gale to the gates of the Enduring City! Enverpasha! He brings an army the size of an angry sea. He will send them crashing against the Temple of Houses! Enverpasha! Look in the sky! He comes with the clouds, so every eye shall see him!

"Hang Enverpasha! You look for him as a savior but he is nowhere to be found," she said, pointing to herself. "I am here. And I make no great claims to be the next *Buyukata* or to restore Nasreddin. I come humbly, bringing with me the last of Maltep. We come to you with a simple plea, as your brothers and sisters. Help us honor our fallen. Help us stop this from happening to the other tribes."

Chief Kayitsiz nodded. "We have heard your plea, Savashbahar of Maltep. Now, the chiefs of Kahraman shall let our hands speak to your cause."

This was the final ceremony. If a chief raised a hand it meant they were behind Maltep. She needed four hands. To Kayitsiz's right, one chief raised his hand. To his left, Chief Gulbeze raised her hand. The chief next to her raised his hand. That was all.

Savashbahar felt empty. Numb. She had spent nearly a week here, trying to garner favor that never came. It was time Enverpasha was using elsewhere to spread his word and curry his own favor. How many tribes had she lost to him while she was getting spurned by the Kahraman?

Chief Kayitsiz looked to his peers and gave a nod of assent before turning his head to Savashbahar.

"Take this as a lesson. All the tribes do not and will not hold the same passion you have to your cause. Do not be discouraged. Uniting all the tribes is a task many feel can only be done by the next *Buyukata*. Although we do not all agree to your cause, we do agree a special fire fills you. Perhaps that fire is what makes a *Buyukata*. Those on this council will see firsthand."

Kayitsiz raised his hand. "Kahraman marches with Maltep."

CHAPTER 28
War

Rich's robe looked like flowing mud. It refused to stay one shade of brown under the treatment of deep dungeon shadow along with the yellow-orange light of illusionary magefire which roiled and tumbled in the giant glass column beside Rich.

None of the prisoners of the Underthral were here, no one worked now. An eerie quiet filled the lonely courtyard, the kind of intimidating silence that made whispers sound like roars. Rich looked beyond the orange and yellow fires blossoming in the glass column to find what had once been his own face glaring back, a teenage face more wretched and twisted in anger than Rich could ever imagine being in life. Rich gasped, his fear coursing like an icy fire through his gut. Nothing but glass and flickering illusion separated him from Richard Bates.

"You know my rule, mage," Richard Bates growled. "My one rule. Every one, every thing pays. Everything must."

Rich couldn't speak as he stared at an entity whose open rage seemed to bake off him in waves. Any words Rich could have summoned would've been frozen in his throat.

"Who are you to not pay?!" Richard Bates screamed. He stalked around the pillar of magefire, his eyes never leaving Rich. "If I could strangle you with these hands, I would. I would visit upon you an eon of nightmare. But I can barely stand to remain here because the piddling spells you cast now aren't worth my time." He stood face to face with Rich. "Who's to pay for the magic you devoured before you went to brown?!"

He stood there glaring, saying nothing, letting the question hang as if Rich had a reasonable answer for him. In the silent stretch between words,

Rich visualized getting punched in the face. When Richard Bates brought his hand up, it was only to push a finger into his own palm.

"It's magic you used, magic that can never be paid for. But you don't care; you've taken the Oath of Binding and cut out your ties to the debt. What's it matter that somewhere in the fabric a debt still lingers, a glaring lack of balance in forces you were never truly meant to dabble in? Who cares that now no one can set the balance right? Not you, you've gone and reduced yourself to near-nothingness so you could frolic uncaring of old obligations."

Richard Bates looked at Rich as if he was a leprous beggar. "Enjoy the rest of your meager cost, shit robe," he said before vanishing completely.

Rich was left alone in the belly of the Underthral. Without Richard Bates around to spew bile, crushing silence filled in the empty space. It was ominous in its completeness. Rich could hear the dull throb of his heartbeat, every breath in, every breath out, the friction of dry throat muscles constricting when he swallowed.

Crash! Rich flinched instinctively as the giant column next to him exploded in a shower of glass, vermillion sparks and fire. He looked up to see Mel hurtling through the broken column to land with a strangled yelp as she hit the floor.

Someone or something had thrown Mel through the glass.

Darkness closed in on the dungeon now that the column of light was gone. Rich panned his head back and forth to see someone, anything, but the darkness revealed nothing save Mel's prone form draped in shadow on the floor.

Rich couldn't see Mel's face because of the overwhelming darkness, couldn't tell if she was conscious at all. She wasn't moving.

From the recesses of the dungeon, a ball of magefire careened toward Mel. It hit her still body and flared up into a brilliant explosion.

When the light faded, Rich found himself looking at the back of Vylar's head. The blind man sat in a wooden chair. Rich was no longer in a dungeon, but lying on a bed in his new teacher's house. Daylight streamed through the open windows.

"Not so bad as a brown robe, is it?" Vylar asked as his hands felt across different collections of metal trinkets on the table.

"If you say so," Rich answered. It was true, he didn't bolt awake screaming in terror, but the cost was still far from pleasant. That's why mages never called the cost "the perk".

Vylar had been right about a few things. Now that Rich had taken the Oath of Binding, he could feel the cost creeping up on him, even stay its hand for awhile, much like how people stave off sleep when they're tired, until he was ready to pay. He no longer confused the cost with the waking world.

Rich sat up and pulled the brown robe away from his skin for ventilation. The wardrobe change had been Vylar's first condition to training Rich. The hot, humid air of Vylar's house made Rich feel stuck to the robe. Rich looked at his teacher, whose back was still turned away as he tinkered at a workbench cluttered with all manners of strange metal contraptions.

"You ready to teach some more?"

"Don't you need a break, Bendy Sleeves? You've been at it nonstop for three days."

"Can't stop now if I ever want to get back to gray."

"Heh!" Vylar laughed and put down a silver globe. "You're a good student and all, but you can go ahead and give up on that now. Few mages ever make it to gray once and you're trying to do it twice?"

It didn't matter if he ever made gray legitimately. Truthfully, with the cost in check now magic was a joy to learn. And with no opportunity to return home in the near future, he had nothing but time on his hands to learn it. He wanted to get to a place where he could hold his own in a street fight or mage duel. Jason's derision at his choice to give up gray gnawed on him a bit; the last thing he wanted to be was useless when everyone was ready to try to get to the Rift Pendulum again.

"Call me optimistic," Rich said.

"How about I call you leech," Vylar said, frowning as he rubbed fingers over the silver globe. "I didn't think you were going to monopolize all my time when I agreed. Why don't you go about some studying on magic theory?"

Rich had an advantage over most novices. In his desperation to understand the cost and get a better handle on it, he had consumed large portions of his spellbook and the *Birleshik Arcana*. Fear was a potent motivator to remembering the contents of what would otherwise be stale textbooks.

He strode over to the door and opened it, letting the telltale creak of hinges speak to Vylar on Rich's intentions on studying. "Care to quiz me on what you think is important for the next tier?" he asked.

Vylar grimaced and stood up as he chucked the globe. "Lead the way, Bendy Sleeves."

Vylar's modest house stood alone on a hill overlooking the town of Mere. The yard held a well built with large, bulky stones and a stout oak tree. The tree boasted a full complement of leaves which had turned several shades of red, orange and yellow but had largely refused to fall.

Mel leaned against the tree trunk, grabbing the only shade around. It was cooler out here than in the house, but not by much, with the sun beating down like it had forgotten these were no longer the dog days of summer.

She looked at Rich with a curiously raised eyebrow. "Back so soon?"

Rich shrugged. "How long was I gone?"

"Less than an hour." She smiled and the vision of her crashing through glass flitted across his mind. It must have shown on his face; her expression changed to one of worry.

"You OK?"

"Yeah," he said forcing a smile. "Cost wasn't as easy as my first one in brown, but it was definitely manageable."

She nodded slowly as if she wasn't quite sure if what he said washed. "Maybe you should ease up a bit," she said.

Vylar grunted. "Save your breath, lady. Bendy Sleeves isn't keen on reason and sensibility. Try putting your advice in the form of a spell."

Rich scowled at Vylar. "I can handle it. Why do you think I'm pushing too hard?"

"Let me see," he said. "It's only been three days and you're already Brown of the 5th Kind. Standard for that is two months. One month is accelerated learning. What's it going to take to satisfy you?"

"Today? Brown of the 6th Kind," Rich answered with a smile. "Maybe even 7th. Let's get started."

"All right," Vylar said. "You can bend in two directions, alter materials into similar but different materials, and can craft simple creation and mental support spells. Time to apply length, density and mass: bend every branch and the trunk of this tree."

"My shade!" Mel cried.

REW LEANED FORWARD in her chair, her hands folded on a desk littered with parchments, maps and treaties. She locked eyes with Brigitte. The destruction mage stood at attention in Rew's office, her face stoic, unreadable as Rew chewed on her update as if it was made of bitter roots.

"So, you let Rich and his companions escape a prison no one's escaped from in over a century," Rew said, "where they've been at large for three days. Now, out of this blank page you tell me they're in the village of Mere. And you want me to authorize sending a contingent of pendulum heroes. Yes?"

"Yes," Brigitte said with a curt nod. "It's the only reasonable option."

"How is that reasonable?" Rew asked incredulously. "Pendulum heroes don't distinguish between fugitives and innocent villagers. They would obliterate the whole town."

"Every other option reduces our chances of success. Mere is a town lacking note, so none of our robes, quest-mage or otherwise, have a portal root there. There are few red mages present I would trust to properly creating a wind tunnel, and none of them completely. Slower travel methods present the real possibility of the fugitives fleeing before we even arrive. When we arrive, provided they are still there, our forces will have to contend with a powerful gray robe. Not only is time a critical factor, the danger inherent with this mission is very high. Sending a force that is instantly available, extremely deadly and completely disposable is the best, most reasonable option."

Rew sat in raw disbelief of Brigitte's gall. The black robe was not only untroubled with the prospect of killing an entire village of innocents to get a handful of escapees, she thought enough of the idea to recommend it to Rew. Brigitte's presentation of options left Rew angry. More than any one of those options—more than all of them put together—Brigitte's unflinching demeanor made Rew livid.

Rew stood up, her eyes never leaving Brigitte's. "Were you sleeping with my father?"

Brigitte's face registered shock, the first emotion Rew had seen since Brigitte entered her office. "Excuse me?"

"That is what I'm trying to do, excuse you," Rew said. "Excuse you from your gross lack of propriety for even suggesting to me that we destroy an entire village because five fugitives may be there. Perhaps the excuse is you're blinded by a vengeance fueled by lost love. I ask again, were you sleeping with my father?"

Brigitte looked at Rew as if she was the one speaking absurdly. "It's my job to present you with tactical strategies for your consideration," she said. "So consider, Hierophant, the facts. These fugitives broke free of the Underthral, causing the deaths of two black mages and critically injuring Kerr the Red Warden. They also released the most demented blue robe I've ever had the displeasure of knowing. Finally, they turned arguably the most powerful mage of the modern era into stone. They are beyond dangerous. My feelings about Druze—my employer, my friend, my mentor in black magic and whatever else he may have been to me—are none of your business."

"Massacre isn't an option."

"If you won't listen to the facts, listen to your emotions, the same ones you accuse me of having too much of. He was your father, Rew Majora. We may never get an opportunity to find these fugitives again. You're letting them get away with Druze's murder. Does he mean nothing to you?"

"I don't need reminding, Brigitte. My father or no, I will always act for the good of the Free States. And it seems the best decision I can make for that good is to remove you from the post of security chief."

"I've done nothing wrong."

"You've changed my orders when it suits you, you propose plans that would lead to wholesale slaughter, and, although I can't prove it, I'm quite confident that you disregarded procedures while handling the prisoners, presenting them with the very conditions that allowed them escape. If you've done nothing wrong, you've certainly done enough. That will be all."

Brigitte's expression remained stoic. "I must remind the Hierophant that security chief is an essential post. Once you get the approval of the Chamber of Colors, I will be more than happy to honor your decision, as I have all your decisions."

"Then I will assemble them," Rew said. "Until then, the last order you will carry out is to dispatch a mid-tier brown robe to the town of Mere. He is to investigate, report back to me and wait for an opportunity when our fugitives are away from civilians before establishing a portal. We will capture them responsibly. Now leave."

Brigitte nodded briskly and left without a word.

Alone now, Rew felt utter solitude in the quiet space of her library. She sighed when she really felt like screaming. Who did Brigitte think she was? The last thing Rew needed was a reminder of what the fugitives had done. Plus, her "plan" was absolute lunacy.

But Brigitte was right about time being critical. Even though Rew gave the order, she didn't really expect the brown robe to make it to Mere in time to find anyone. Rew was grasping at straws, but what choice did she have?

Perhaps. Perhaps she could appeal to Rich to come back and face justice. There had to be some decency in him, or was everything she believed him to be a complete illusion?

There was no harm in trying. Her heels clinked on the marble floor, echoing like chains as she went over to her chair. She sat down, took a deep breath and exhaled slowly, then closed her eyes and sent out a request to scry.

Intolerable moments passed without response. She resigned herself to being balked, even in this simple measure, when suddenly the room opened. Her library office joined with grassy countryside. A small house sat lonely in the distance. Between her and the house stood Rich. He stood awkwardly in a silly brown robe and waved with an apprehensive hand. Waved! Rich looked at Rew with all the concern he should have shown before his crime.

"How dare you wave at me!" she screamed, her rage erupting as if a pipe had burst. "You've lost any right to greet me as you would a friend."

"I'm sor—"

"You killed my father!" Rew glared at Rich through the tears streaming, burning her eyes. She made no attempt to wipe them as she pointed her accusing finger. "And you lied to me about it! You think your apologies are going to change that? They change nothing!"

"I had to," Rich said, his voice an anguished moan. "He tried to kill me, Rew!"

"After all your lies, I'm supposed to believe you now? This, from the same person who cut through the Temple of Houses when it suited him? I've seen what you do when you're scared. You're irresponsible, reckless with your power and you put my father on the bitter end of your carelessness."

"Rew, you need to believe me..."

"Believe you?" she asked, "What? Now that your lies have been caught, believe you? Believe you now that I have no more family left for you to take?"

Rich hung his head down, his jaw clenched. The skin around his anguished eyes was tight and he scanned the grass as if the perfect thing to say lay there waiting for him to root it out. But Rew Majora was beyond his words. She spoke more of her own.

"You know, I was going to ask you to come back here and face trial, but I see the pointlessness in it. I used to look at you and see something wonderful, something that defied your youthful years. But, really, you're nothing more than a scared boy. Scared to be honest, scared to come here to face justice for what you've done. I don't care how long it takes, how far you flee, I will see you before me in chains!"

Rew killed the scry. Only then did she wipe her tears with her robe sleeve. Suddenly exhausted, she reclined in her chair and exhaled. She dabbed her face with her robe until she felt no more wetness and abruptly, uncontrollably exploded into tears. Her body racked with sobs, she put her face into her hands and wept, letting the pain take its course.

She didn't know, didn't care how long this lasted. When she finally lifted her head, she saw her communication mirror shimmering. A Hierophant's duties are never done, even in times where running felt like her only recourse. Hurriedly, she cleaned her face, checking carefully, before heading over to the mirror and opening the channel.

Annana stood before her, cold baleful eyes behind a level gaze.

"I send one thousand Armsguard on a peaceful mission to safeguard the security of our empire and you have the audacity to ambush them?"

"You were warned, goddess," Rew answered.

"It wasn't enough that you bar them from passage or even rout them in combat," Annana growled around her clicking mandibles. "Instead, you claim nine-hundred ninety-nine lives and send back a lone soldier to tell me of your dastardly act. There is no debate among the eleven houses the Hierophane seeks to protect the criminal gray robe and promote the sacrilege inherent in the false Chosen One. All I will say is ready yourself."

Annana's hair tendrils locked like a spider hissing about her face as she spoke. "The Temple of Houses comes to break your towers."

CHAPTER 29
Anatomy of an Ambush

Druze did not feel any of the exuberance which should have been present in the teen boy he inhabited. Instead he felt wrath. It showed on a face drained of color, with lips burst open and cheeks home to festering wounds. He cut his eye at Brigitte.

"And you explained to Rew that pendulum heroes were her only real option?"

"I pointed it out to her exactly as you specified," Brigitte answered. She sat behind her desk in the security office, looking at Druze in his latest guise. The marble floors of Hierophane became grass as the ground crossed the hard line of the scry. "Despite all my arguments, she refused to deploy them."

"What did she say when you reminded her that they murdered me?"

"She refused to send pendulum heroes even then. All she said was, 'father or no, I always act for the good of the Free States'. Then she tried to fire me as security chief."

Druze's ire burned like molten steel. The boy robe had gotten that far under Rew's skin that she'd betray her own father to protect him. A knife across the throat was the standard way to repay that kind of loyalty.

"She is no daughter of mine," he told Brigitte. "You know what to do."

Brigitte nodded and killed the scry, taking the Hierophane with her. The countryside returned to surround Druze. He looked with hatred at the lone house sitting on the hill in the distance.

"So, what's the word on back up?" Kriminel asked.

"We are without," Druze said.

"*C'est la vie*, darling," La Croix said with a shrug.

"Well, if it makes ya feel any better bout it, I ain't seen nobody exceptin' the warrior girl and them two fogies," Kriminel said, looking at the house with his bouncing eyes. "Granted, you can never tell who's lurkin' about, but I don't see all them fittin' in that tiny house, specially that big feller they call Runt."

"No, Kriminel, it does not make me feel any better," Druze said. Not getting the pendulum on his side this time was the capstone of a rough journey that began back at Dreft Esker. Once Tavis Provos' body had been rendered unusable, he had to jump into aian skin to finish off the other Armsguardsmen. That's when he had learned how truly inferior aiankind were; he was completely cut off from magic, as if the spells he uttered were snuffed out the moment he'd speak them. He had to kill them all by hand, all save the captain who identified himself as Mors.

That was a long, tedious job. He spent an even longer time on the back of a destrier, riding through open country towards the warrior girl's clasp signal until he ran across a human, any human. Fortunately, he stumbled across a traveling family of four. That's when he became a kid again.

"Are you two ready *this time*?" Druze asked the barons. Once he had rendezvoused with them, he had made it no secret his displeasure of their failure.

"Rude," La Croix said with a cluck of his tongue as he summoned a staff of light. Kriminel unsheathed his machete and looked at Druze with a sneer.

"I don't recollect hearin' any of your success stories when it comes to killin' them boys," he said. "Unless you fixin' to regale me now with one of 'em, how bout I ask you: are *you* ready?"

"Almost," he answered. Druze turned his back on the house and walked over to the wagon cart. A man sat on the cart, visibly exhausted. He was the head of the family of four Druze had encountered. He was also the workhorse who had pulled this cart after Druze had run the destrier dead.

"Your name is Yant, yes?" Druze asked.

Yant nodded. A glimmer of hope returned to his desperate, pleading eyes. "It's not too late, Yanthrum," he said, "We can fix what ails you."

"How about I fix what ails you," Druze responded, "by showing you the way to your son."

In a fluid motion, Druze unsheathed his dagger and thrust it into the man's heart. Yant died with an expression of shock and betrayal on his face as he looked at his son. Druze could relate.

"Jesus," Kriminel swore, "I'm a snake man, and even I think that's cold-blooded."

"It's nothing," Druze said. After living half a millennium, he found it impossible to hold value in this peasant's insignificant, fleeting life. Meanwhile, he had spared the woman and toddler; Yant's family name would remain intact, which is more than better men than Yant sometimes got.

Druze felt the comforting presence of Yant's newly dead body. Comfort stood in stark contrast to being inside the son's long dead carcass. Druze felt the worms writhing in the open wound through the heart, chewing at dead flesh and organs. He had to swallow the worms down when they began to creep up his throat. This body was far from comfortable.

It only had to hold for a little while longer. He gripped the dead man by both hands and hauled him off the wagon. Druze dragged Yant face down by his shirt across the field toward the house.

"I'm ready."

MEL SAT UNDER THE TREE trying not to think about the heat, how sweat seemed to percolate on his brow or how the tight black leather clung to him, baking his skin. At least he had his shade now that Rich had bent the tree back to a close proximity of its former self. Of all the things Mel thought about, it wasn't creature comforts from home, but rain. It had been forever since it rained, and he would welcome those drops from heaven with open arms and a lover's kiss.

"Specificity is key as Brown of the 7th Kind," Vylar said. "None of that overexaggerating or wild guessing's going to do you—"

He stopped suddenly and sniffed the air. "There's a strange taste in the air. People. One sweetly of honeysuckle, sunflower and sweat. Another." He sniffed. "Of oiled leather. The last reeks of death."

Mel remembered one of those scents intimately when he and Mike were fighting for their lives. "The barons!" he cried, launching himself to his feet and drawing his sword. He looked at Rich. "That oiled leather is Kriminel. And you can guess who the death reek belongs to."

"The Graverobber," he said dry swallowing.

"I take it this won't be a friendly reunion," Vylar said, "with the way you're drawing your sword, the anxiety in both your voices."

Far from a friendly reunion, this was going to be the death of them. The whole gang together was hardly a match for the Graverobber. Now he had help from the barons and they weren't exactly easy pickings either.

"There's no way we can win this," Mel said grimly.

"Any of them use magic?" Vylar asked.

Mel nodded, forgetting in his worry that Vylar was blind. "A sun cleric and this unkillable, undead... thing... that uses magic like we use air."

"Settles that," Vylar said. "I don't fight out in the open like this unless I'm the only one casting. I've got no time for lengthy mage duels or useless notions like fair play."

Vylar spoke spellcraft and the blue and white pool of a portal opened in front of him. "Follow me," he said, disappearing into the light.

Rich went in second followed by a grimly reluctant Mel. They emerged in near total darkness, with only the glow of the portal behind them shedding light to the abyss. Eyeless insects scurried away in a small stampede, their legs sounding like water cascading, their skin so translucent Mel could see through to their organs.

Vylar walked past the horde of insects, beckoning them to follow. As soon as Mel took another step away from the portal, the smell of this place assaulted his nostrils. It carried an overpowering stench of rotten eggs.

"Ugh!" Mel's cried, his face scrunching up instinctively. "Why are we going deeper into this?!"

"Silly girl," Vylar said. "That portal won't close before they follow us through. We need some distance."

A surge of panic rushed through Mel. He had thought this cave was an escape route, not a battleground. Hurriedly, he turned his head at the glowing vortex. No one had come through. Not yet.

Vylar led the way through a maze of stalagmites and crags, his every step sure as Rich and Mel's began to falter under the failing light from an ever more distant portal. "No fire from you, Bendy Sleeves. Grab my shirt for guidance. Girl, grab his robe."

Mel complied, grasping Rich's robe as if it was a security blanket. The stalagmites and jagged rock walls had done wonders to block the portal's light, leaving only a dull halo behind them. Now everything in front of him was shades of black.

"We're outside?" Rich asked bewildered. Mel saw the shaded silhouette of Rich's head looking up so he followed suit. Above them shined, unbelievably, a blue starry night sky.

"No," Mel answered in awe of seeing something he'd had only read about. "That's arachnocampa."

"What?" Rich asked. Mel felt him shiver in a clutched handful of robe. "Spiders?"

"No. Fungus gnat. It lures prey by mimicking the outside sky. Has these poison silk threads—"

"Shut up!" Vylar hissed.

The darkness was near complete. Mel bumped into Rich, indicating that Rich had stopped moving, which meant Vylar had stopped. Mel felt a hand on his shoulder. At least he hoped it was a hand and not some cave bug or a vampire bat. Another hand grabbed Mel's other shoulder and guided him to turn around and crouch.

"*Arcana goster*," Vylar's voice intoned from the darkness. Immediately, Mel could see everything within two feet in front of him in a harsh red light. Rich crouched beside Mel, looking at Mel with puzzlement on his face. Vylar stood in front of them both, head slightly craned as he listened.

"Is anything around you two glowing?" Vylar asked.

"Yes," Rich said, "Mel's clasp."

Vylar's hand reached for Mel's shoulder, felt its way down quickly to Mel's neck, and deftly removed the jewel from the clasp.

"Where'd you get it?" Vylar asked.

Crap. The memory hit Mel and he felt four flavors of dumb. "The Hierophane," he said with a shake of his head. That was how they were able to find them.

"There's good magic in it," Vylar said. "No more talking. You're about to get your first lesson in layering spells."

Vylar clenched his fist, snuffing out the red light the jewel made. Submerged in darkness once again, Mel's eyes strained for substance, but it was like looking through a blindfold.

Long, tense moments passed as Mel stared into pitch, to the point where he began to question whether he was staring in the right direction at all. Then he saw a white light, just the halo of light really, which outlined the craggy spaces of jagged rock walls and thick stalagmites. The halo moved with a slight bounce, winding its way through the cave, coming slowly, slowly closer.

The light illuminated the many rough surfaces of the cave, covered in several places with a white, slimy film that hung like small stalactites but looked as if a giant had blown his nose all over the rock. That snot-like look made them easy for Mel to recognize. They were snottites, extremophile bacteria that actually ate harsh toxins like sulfur and hydrogen sulfide and excreted an acid waste as strong as battery acid.

Mel took a strange sense of comfort in knowing some of the weird and crazy things he had spent hours reading and learning about his own world carried over to this one. That comfort mixed with butterflies and a sense of dread as the white light approached. Everything felt surreal, as if he was in a movie theater watching it all unfold.

The light rounded a corner, exposing the source as the tip of a staff. Holding the staff was Baron La Croix who walked slowly through the maze with Baron Kriminel on his left and a strange boy on his right. There was no doubt who the boy was; he looked every bit the zombie without the shuffling and moaning.

The men, the light, crept ever closer, revealing more and more of the cave. Mel and his friends were still bathed in darkness. He wondered if Vylar knew the light was coming to expose them, if he was going to do anything before it was too late. A small part of him wondered if he was all alone, that both Vylar and Rich had left him there. Was he the diversion, stuck there to aid their escape? Was this his payment for bringing this wrath down upon their heads in the first place? He reached a questing hand out in the darkness where it found Rich's hand. It gave a reassuring squeeze.

The barons and the Graverobber crept closer still. Mel could see the whites of their eyes, their pupils questing for their quarry. Their light drank in the darkness. In a moment, Mel and his friends would be exposed.

Now, in a blur, Vylar chucked the clasp's jewel at them, a glowing red dot. But these people were skilled and wary. La Croix pointed his finger and shot a quick dagger of light.

The light dagger hit the red jewel, magic hit magic, and a small, red spark ignited.

The Graverobber yelled out "No!" in a kid's voice. He was still yelling no, as the spark turned blue and the floor of the cave came alive in an explosion of blue flame. The flame seemed to rush into the kid's gut.

The kid exploded in a red ball of fire as he was still screaming his warning for La Croix. The barons went flying into the air. Before the explosive fire squelched out completely, Mel saw Vylar bound off into the falling darkness.

There was nothing but sound now, the shrill pitch of voices screaming, the whine of a sword cutting through air. Then nothing.

Moments later, a portal opened close to Mel and Rich. It illuminated Vylar, who looked as calm as he ever did. He motioned for them to follow before stepping into the portal.

Rich, still holding Mel's hand, rushed to the portal, with Mel following close behind. Once he emerged, Mel found himself looking at a house very similar to Vylar's house on the outskirts of Mere. Only now the house was in the base of a valley of dry, brown grass. The sun beamed down on them, and while there was a well beside this house like Mere, there was no tree to shade them. Vylar sat down on the brown grasses, his face toward the blue and white portal as if he was watching it despite unfocused eyes. His expression unconcerned about pursuers, Vylar patted the ground next to him, inviting Rich and Mel to have a seat.

"Do you know how I did that, back in the cave?" Vylar asked.

"Not a clue," Rich said. "I heard your spell, and all you did was expose the magic already there in the jewel. How'd you make it explode?"

"I didn't. The cave did."

Suddenly, it all clicked with Mel. The snottites that live on toxic materials, the overwhelming smell of rotten eggs, it all made sense. "There was gas in the cave," he said.

"Exactly," Vylar said. "When magic comes into direct contact with other magic, it causes some friction—a lot of friction when the magic is imbued in an object. For my purposes, I could've enchanted a piece of bat guano to be a compass, or a rock to sound like chimes. But I figured while we were walking through the cave that the trouble of making a magic object was already taken care of, I just had to find it."

Rich shook his head as he looked at the still open portal. For a good while he just looked at the magic swirl in front of them. Then he looked a Vylar, a question on his face. "How'd you know they were going to stop the magic jewel with magic?"

"Mages, clerics, most magic users have an overwhelming dependence on spellcraft," Vylar said with a shrug. "They'd use it to tuck themselves in bed or clean their soiled butts if they knew the right spell. It's one of the reasons I don't see eye to eye with the mages."

He stood up as the blue and white light of the portal dispersed into nothingness. "That and, unlike most honorbound mages, I believe the best fights are the dirtiest you can make them."

DRUZE STOPPED SCRAMBLING to reach the portal, only a mere few feet away, as it evaporated. It had taken him too much time to get his consciousness back to Yant's body, too much time to find his way with only illusionary mage fire, without the aid of the clasp to guide. He grit his teeth, feeling nothing but rage as he looked at his chance to finally get his enemies disappear.

To his left, he heard crying, a faint, desperate sobbing. He turned and saw La Croix, kneeling. The sun cleric held Kriminel in his arms. Druze approached to see them both in bad shape. La Croix's once all white robe was now a charred, tattered mess. He sobbed over the snake man, who lay prone. A severe gash ran across Kriminel's face, where it looked as if it had been completely split open then crudely held together and healed. Small wonder, La Croix wouldn't be able to get decent sun magic to heal in this dank cave.

"Wake up, baby," La Croix said tearfully. "I promise I'll fix you better once we're out of this cave. But first, you've got to wake up."

La Croix noticed Druze standing beside him. He looked up at Druze with pleading eyes. "We need to get him out of here."

Druze had other needs. "Do you remember when I helped you all—Brigitte, Samedi, Kriminel, you—when you first arrived from the Pendulum?"

La Croix nodded, a bit of confusion clouding his tear-streaked face.

Like a bolt, Druze's hands shot out. One covered La Croix's mouth, the other held the back of his head in an iron grip.

"I am through helping you, tender. Especially when you ruin my plans with your stupidity. No, it's time you help me. Help me have a body of pure magic."

La Croix's eyes went wide with the realization of what Druze intended. He tried to struggle, but Druze kept his iron grip on the sun cleric.

"You know the fatal mistake you made when we first met, don't you?" Druze said while La Croix clawed and shook his head in muffled protest. "You told me all about the real you, Scotlin Bowers. You gave me the power to unmake you."

For centuries, Druze had worn the black robes out of respect to his original calling moreso than his limitations with magic. He started off as a destruction mage. True to his roots, the words of destruction flowed from Druze, fast and flawless. He added to the destructive wind the man's true name, where he was born, what he despised and who he loved most in life.

He said the last of the destruction spell and a bright yellow light emanated out of La Croix's eyes, nose and mouth. Just as Druze had suspected, unmaking the identity of the man behind La Croix did not unmake the body. As soon as he felt La Croix's death presence, Druze jumped inside.

Yes. The body had so little time to stop, it picked back up. This time, in this body, Druze could feel the heart beat, feel the blood flow, sense the tingle of nerves not quite so dead and distant, but close and raw. As opposed to the aians he had lived in, the magic in this body was overwhelming. Exhilarating.

He laughed in the blackness of the cave.

It wasn't such a dark day after all.

CHAPTER 30
War Measures

Brigitte, with a heady combination of sadness and intrigue, kneeled between Druze's tattooed legs and traced a deft finger over his exposed chest. From her finger flowed both a mild destruction spell meant to penetrate the epidermis and black ink. The two layered spells caused a pungent sizzle as she traced spell fragments into skin.

Her sadness came from the body Druze occupied. She kept her eyes focused on the chest, etching in the spell augments which defined heat protection. "Are all the barons dead?" she asked.

"Only you remain, Cimetière," Druze replied.

It was a name she had forsaken a long time ago, shortly after the Pendulum deposited them here. Despite the others' protest that the four barons was more symbolic, she had opted to be known as the female Voudun *loa* named Maman Brigitte. Brigitte clenched her teeth, willing anger to replace sadness. They all had been through so much together after the pendulum had thrust them here. The fact that they had all been killed was a heavy weight.

"I know it is hard for you," Druze said, "but the ambush that killed Kriminel and La Croix also destroyed my former body. Assuming this body was my only escape."

Brigitte nodded without looking up and began to work down to the stomach.

Her intrigue lay in what she was doing. Using a weathered parchment diagram he had provided, she had filled up his back, legs, shoulders, then chest, and now his abs with spell fragments, spell augments, but not a complete spell. Would a complete spell even work if tattooed into skin? Their magic was largely meant to be spoken. What good were these fragmentary pieces all over his body?

Finally done with the magic words that spoke of intensity, she double checked the parchment on the ground next to her. With no more work to focus on, she looked up at Druze's face, a face that had once belonged to a dear friend, and nodded.

Druze rose from the chair. He went over to the wardrobe mirror, one of the few furnishings in his minimalist bedchamber, and began to scrutinize Brigitte's handiwork. He spent several minutes giving each section hard gazes, turning slowly and inspecting the elegantly flowing words from every possible angle. At last, he smiled.

"A magnificent tapestry," he said as reached for the black robe lying on his bed.

Brigitte nodded. It was off-putting, seeing La Croix in black robes, so foreign and unnatural, no matter how many times she told herself this was Druze now.

He seemed unaware of her discomfort. "Would you like to know what this was you've been working on?" he asked with a grin. "This process isn't exactly to be found in any textbook in existence."

"Yes."

Druze opened both his hands and brought netherfire into existence. It was not illusionary; the two glowing cobalt fireballs made the room's temperature noticeably hotter. A spell that takes skilled mages hours to craft was crackling in his palms in a second, and he hadn't spoken a word.

So this was how he was able to have such supreme mastery over netherfire. Brigitte still didn't understand. She had only tattooed spell fragments. "How?" she asked.

"You're looking only at those fragmentary bits of spell you wrote," he said smiling a slick grin under the harsh blue light of netherfire. "You're forgetting the medium you used. It is etched into my skin; the spell will burst forth from my skin, thankfully protected now by the augments. The spell's beginnings are woven across my nerve endings; I can call it forth just by thinking of the spell catalyst.

Now it made sense. His entire body was the binding agent, bringing all the disparate fragments together as a whole. Brigitte was impressed. "How did you know, the first time you did this, that it would work?"

"I didn't." He clenched his fist, choking the netherfire out. "You have been steadfast in the execution of your duties. Still, it would be poor of me to not caution you against initiating someone else into this secret for the sake of having your own body tapestry."

"Have no concern about my discretion," Brigitte said. "You know I prefer ice."

Druze nodded, then looked out his window to the rest of the Hierophane. "Soon the Chamber of Colors meets to determine your fate, security chief. You should go. I'll be along."

Brigitte nodded and spun on her heels to leave. She always tried to maintain disciplined, unflinching composure in the face of all things. Silently, she was thankful Druze had returned, in any form, to see her through this.

REW STOOD UNDER THE impressive dome of the Chamber of Colors. Enjoying the peaceful respite that came with being early, she looked at the dais before her, at the ten empty chairs. They were thrones really, carved whole out of massive veins of varying gemstones to represent the color branches. Amber for the orange mages, amethyst for the purple, blood garnet for the red robes and lapis lazuli for the blue. The school of destruction sat in black onyx while the school of creation sat in white opal.

Rew took time looking over each magnificent chair before panning her head up to the dome, where her eyes got lost in a sea of colorful mosaic tiles. From this distance, it was impossible to see the individual tiles of solitary color, only the patterns in which they came together to display. They depicted some of the greatest moments witnessed by the Hierophane. She never got tired of seeing the Heroic Escort of Idleram the Last Megrym King or the Raising of the Rift. Her eyes wandered over to the Battle of Six Houses, where she saw her father depicted, looking valiant and fierce as he led the Hierophane to battle.

She fought down a wave of sadness. Now was not the time for grief. After all, a leader had to put on a strong face in times of war. Once she got past the first order of business of replacing her security chief, she'd announce the

Temple of Houses declaration of war and turn to the serious matter of ending the hostility as quickly as possible.

"Prompt as usual, Hierophant." Rew didn't have to look away from the dome to know the voice belonged to Brigitte.

"Brigitte," Rew said. After a moment she peeled her eyes off the dome to look at the black robe. "You really should resign your post. The Chamber of Colors has more pressing matters in its hands than you."

"I would, Hierophant, but there is no secondary on hand. I must remind you that I was your father's secondary, simply acting in his stead. The Chamber must approve both a primary and a secondary. This meeting is merely a formality to ensure you get exactly what you need."

"I would like for you to stay on as secondary," Rew said. "If nothing else, you have been extremely resourceful in most matters."

"No thank you, Hierophant. I no longer have any desire to be secondary."

There was little left to say as the two women looked at one another. Suddenly, the chamber doors behind the dais opened with a groan. A procession of mages issued forth, all of them wearing a robe from different schools. As custom dictated, they all wore their hoods, symbolizing how each person was not an individual but the embodiment of their school. One by one, they sat in the chair that matched their robes, orange then purple then red then blue. Black sat down followed by white. Green sat in a chair carved of jade and yellow sat in citrine. Even the novice brown robes were represented, by an unidentifiable mage who would soon undoubtedly graduate into another color, but for now sat in the chair of jasper.

It was time to proceed once these nine chairs were filled. The tenth chair, the one made of polished gray lodestone, remained empty as it had been for twenty-five years.

"Gathered heads of your respective schools," Rew began, "I have a few issues to address, the first being official replacements for the office of Hierophane security chief."

Before the councilors could reply, Brigitte took a step forward. "I must ask the council relegate this matter to a later time, as we must face an issue of utmost urgency. I speak of treason to the Free States, committed by none other than Hierophant Majora."

All the councilors turned to Rew. Two of the councilors gasped as if ice water had been tossed in their faces. All Rew felt was anger.

"What?!" she cried, storming up to Brigitte. "How dare you—"

"No, Hierophant, it is you who dare!" Brigitte turned to face the councilors. "This war we brace ourselves for is her doing. She colluded with the rogue gray robe who desecrated the Temple of Houses. When the High Fane requested she surrender this mage at the cost of war, she decided instead to aid his escape. Because of her, the Hierophane faces the gravest threat it's ever known and the future of the Free States is in question."

"This is madness, Brigitte!" Rew cried. "You twist events to suit your purposes."

The Chair of Green leaned forward. "Brigitte, you accuse our Hierophant of a grievous crime," he said in a gruff voice. "Words alone will not move us against her. What proof do you offer?"

"If you do not trust the words of her aide, who has carried out her requests during these trying times, then hear the testimony of one who bears direct witness to the Hierophant's actions in connection to the rogue gray."

Behind Rew, the main chamber doors groaned open. In swept a young man in black robes with a face unknown to her. There was familiarity in his walk, in a look that seemed to say he was the smartest person in the room. He strode up, past Rew and Brigitte and addressed the councilors.

"Esteemed Chairs, I come to you an old soul in new guise. I am Druze Wozencraft, Second Hierophant, and I say to you all Brigitte speaks true."

"Bastard," Rew said through gritted teeth. Her hands and lips trembled with the anger flooding through her. "You invoke the name of my dead father to fuel your lies?" she couldn't look at the charlatan anymore, so she turned to the councilors. "Chairs of the Chamber, remove this man lest I violate this hall's sanctity and roast him on the spot."

"Daughter, Esteemed Chairs," the man said, unfazed at Rew's obvious rage, "I am in this form due to the renegade magic of the rogue gray robe Brigitte described, but I am Druze Wozencraft nonetheless."

The Chair of Orange leaned forward, exposing brown skin and full lips. "How can you verify such a wild notion?" she asked.

The man smiled. "Besides my ability to answer any question both general and intimate regarding the last five hundred years of the Hierophane's history, there's this." He snapped his fingers and netherfire leapt into existence in his palm.

There was only one man who could do such a thing. "Father?" Rew asked. "How—how can this be? Rich can't do something like this."

"Your Rich has power he can neither control nor understand," Druze said. He turned back to the councilors. "He did this to me. He carved the Temple of Houses apart. And when I went to suppress the mage at Mere and turn him into the Temple, my daughter Rew Majora did not send the reinforcements necessary to procure this mage's death or capture. Now he is in the wind, and we find ourselves on the brink of war because our Hierophant has traded in our security for the love of a criminal."

His words felt like daggers in Rew's chest. She shook her head at her father's accusations. "Why? Why would you say these things?"

"The safety of the Free States demands more loyalty than you have shown me," he answered. "Chairs of the Chamber, you say words alone will not move you. So let Majora's thoughts tell you exactly as Brigitte and I have. Chair of Blue, will you not dredge her mind and see the muck yourself?"

The Chair of Blue leaned forward. "Will you permit me, Hierophant?" she asked.

"Delve into his mind," Rew said, "he is the one claiming ludicrous things."

"I am not the one on trial for treason," he said. "It doesn't matter if I'm a blond man in a black robe claiming to be the second Hierophant reborn or a talking slice of butter orange cake."

"He speaks true in this regard, Hierophant," the Chair of White said, his tone flat and unreadable. "Inside your mind lies the quickest way to ascertain the veracity of these charges."

"Trust me, Hierophant," the Chair of Blue said in a soothing tone. "I'll only go as deep as needed. Have I your permission?"

Rew held her head up high in defiance. "I refuse."

Spellcraft rushed out of Druze's mouth in a blur of words. He knelt suddenly, and a rush of chains blossomed from the marble floor around his hands and shot out to swarm Rew. Before she could speak countermeasures, Brigitte tossed a red cube at her. Rew crumpled in a heap as the Majora witchlock flared to life and drained her power.

All the councilors bolted out of their chairs. "Madness!" cried the Chair of Yellow. "Have you lost leave of your sense?" asked the Chair of Black.

"I have lost leave of my body," Druze said, "not my senses. War looms like a hammer raised above our heads and you ask about my senses? It is your sensibilities we've no time for, nothing to spare on discreet investigations. No, all our time will be spent preparing for an onslaught she caused. We will spend our days burying our own. Chair of Blue, my daughter can no longer refuse you. It will only take you a second to see the truth hidden there."

Druze dismissed the black chains surrounding Rew, now meaningless with the witchlock binding her, and held his palm out as if offering his daughter to the blue mage. The other councilors nodded and the Chair of Blue began to cast her spell. Over the fatigue of the witchlock, Rew felt the chair's probe through her mind, like butterflies dancing on her scalp.

"It is as Druze told us," the Chair of Blue stated. "She could have ended this dispute with the High Fane before it escalated, but chose to aid the rogue mage. Furthermore, the war is not coming, it is already here. The Temple of Houses has already declared as much."

Druze took a step toward the council. "We would not be here, Esteemed Chairs, if she had used the necessary force at Mere. Now I move that she stay under lock, indefinitely, while a Hierophant more suited to the task total war lead the Free States to victory."

He pointed up to the ceiling, at the mosaic of the Battle of Six Houses. "I humbly ask to be reinstated as Hierophant."

One by one, the members of the Chamber of Colors bowed their heads in consent. Rew looked on numbly, struck without the words to protest thanks to the witchlock.

Druze looked at Brigitte. "Take her to the Underthral, while I busy myself getting us out of her mess."

Brigitte seized Rew roughly by the arm and hauled her up. It was a long walk to the Underthral, where a Hierophane full to bursting with students, teachers, recalled quest-mages and field envoys stared at their former Hierophant being led away under lock. The witchlock deprived Rew of even the strength to hold her head high. She kept her head bowed, looking guilty even in her stance, as hushed murmurs rippled through the crowd of onlookers.

In due time, they came to the Underthral, a place Rew did not relish visiting even when she wasn't a prisoner. They worked their way down to the Heart, where all the convicts cheered at the sight of her. They passed the glowing columns of the Heart, passed the dark ghetto of the Castworks and went into Broken Alley. Here the scars of Brigitte's mage duel with Delv were everywhere. They walked past scorched walls, broken lights and pock-marked gray brick in silence. Without warning, Brigitte shoved Rew and she fell awkwardly into cell.

"You should be proud of me, Majora," Brigitte said. "As you can see, I'm following procedure to the letter, which, according to you, will not afford you the conditions that will allow your escape."

The dull clink of Brigitte's heels fading into nothing heralded her departure. Rew was left alone in her small cell. Outside these walls, the threat of war descended. It no longer mattered for her. She was captive, bound tightly by the device she had invented, the lock that bore her name.

What had once been grief for her father turned now to rage. He had grossly underestimated her. They all had.

"*Ör,*" she said. A lock of her black tresses interwove itself between another two. "*Ör,*" she spoke again, and the tresses wove themselves together again, lengthening the braid.

The witchlock wasn't flawless. She had designed it as such. It blocked virtually all magic, save this, a harmless, useless spell. Each successful cast of magic opened the witchlock more and more.

In the dim confines of the Underthral, she spoke the word. Again. Again. Again. It would take time, an extremely long time, to have enough strength to break the lock. But having everything stripped from her, time was all she had. She got to work. She braided her hair.

CHAPTER 31
The Lake Bafa Dialogues

Savashbahar realized when she arrived on the shores of Lake Bafa that she would not have to spend untold weeks of traveling and courting to gather many of the remaining tribes. Out of the seven tribes left to court, six tribes were already in Bafakoy. Five of these had come with Enverpasha.

She remembered the streets of Balikesir's ancestral capital well. The people treasured cedar and it showed in the construction of Bafakoy. All the buildings were round yet built of the hardwood, using lumber bending techniques the Balikesir craftsmen refused to share with any outsider. Even the streets were made of wood, many pieces of various sizes and shapes fit perfectly together like a puzzle and held tightly together with a clear coating.

But it was impossible to see such things now. The city was bursting with people. Banners of six tribes and their countless clans waved in the air everywhere Savashbahar looked. Once she was well into the city, those banners comingled with the banners of the four tribes under her. It felt like someone had cast a powerful spell. A prideful feeling warmed Savashbahar. This was what tribal unity was, something Savashbahar had not seen in all her years. She remembered the looks on the elders' faces when they told stories to her as a child. Even though the banners of the Jahnavar weren't present yet, and despite the fact that the lost tribe's banners would likely always be missing, this was what the time of the *Buyukata* must have felt like.

Only it wasn't unity. Many of these tribes had drawn their swords for Enverpasha. She made her way to the Chieftain's Hall now only to see if the Balikesir, too, had committed their steel.

Mike grumbled as he wove his way through nasran legs. "How the hell you know where you going in all this?"

"Long memory," she said. As she made her way through the streets, she realized she wouldn't need Mike this time. She had better history with the Balikesir than she had with the Kahraman.

Touching Mike's shoulder with one hand, she pointed to an *arikovana*, a round building easy to see being three stories high.

"The inn is there."

Mike wiped a purple finger across a goggle lens. "Ah, the big beehive building, like the ones y'all got in Maltep?"

"Yes, the beehive."

"Bet," he said. Without another word, he split off from the group with Runt and Jason close behind. Once again, Savashbahar made a silent wish for the aian boy to stay out of trouble.

In Bafakoy's town square stood the Chieftain's Hall. Magnificent, ancient cedar trees ringed the building, obscuring it with their evergreen, needle-like leaves. Through gaps in the foliage, Savashbahar saw the round *arikovana*, its highly polished wood gleaming like a new promise.

It would be easy, yes, to get the aid of those who had meant so much to her in times past. What was Enverpasha to that?

Before the giant doors of the Chieftain's Hall, a guard stopped Savashbahar.

"Show us your strength to enter without invitation," he said.

Savashbahar grabbed the chain around her neck and pulled up, exposing the signet rings of the four tribes that followed her.

"The strength is in the people," she said.

The guard nodded and pushed the giant doors open. She had no doubt about her level of access. The signet ring of a small clan chief would suffice in most cases, let alone a single ring that spoke for a whole tribe.

The guard led the way through the Chieftain's Hall. Not that Savashbahar needed a guide, the Balikesir had changed nothing in the days when she used to light up and down these halls giddy with learning, excited to be in Bulmak's company.

They came to the central audience chamber. The doors opened to reveal a round room, its walls made to look as if the room was inside a hollow tree. A wooden bench curved around the entire length of the wall. On the right side sat three strangers, whose smiling, cordial faces turned flat when they saw

Savashbahar. On the far end of the room sat the tribal elders, one of whom smiled fiercely at the sight of her.

"Savashbahar," Bulmak said. His Hexenarii tattoos had grown in number since the last time she saw him. They now filled his arms, shoulders and exposed legs, as befitting the tribe's Hex King. "The sight of you is most welcome. Please, honor us with your company." He pointed to the left, where the bench stood empty.

Savashbahar bowed her head, feeling surprisingly empty as she looked at Bulmak. "The honor is mine," she said as she sat.

Once seated, Savashbahar stared directly across the room at the three strangers. The one on the right was definitely Hexenarii, his many tattoos fiercely displayed across his bare chest. The one on the left looked to be a warrior, a big nasran with thick, corded muscle and leathery skin scarred in several places. The one in the middle, Savashbahar held no doubt was Enverpasha.

JASON FOUND HIMSELF restless after the second round of drinks.

"This kinda blows. I mean, I'm all for a trip to Sloshed City, but I didn't travel through time, space and who knows how many dimensions only to drink. I coulda just went over to my uncle's house for that. Besides, this beer tastes like breakfast cereal."

"Why don't you head outside, give these nasrans one of your Chosen One speeches?" Mike asked. "I've been dying to see a live crucifixion."

"Please," Jason said with a scoff. "Like I'm scared of them. Do you know my pedigree?" He leaned forward, his bone fingers rapping on the table. "I'm an escaped convict, dude."

"You stupid," Mike said as he took a drink.

"No, I'm bored," Jason said, collapsing back in his seat. "What's the point of traveling through these spots if I can't see any of the sights? First it was 'you're the Chosen One in Nasreddin, it's not safe.' Then it was 'you're on the run from the High Fane, wear this hood and stay indoors it's not safe.' Now it's 'you're an aian in nasran lands, it's not safe.' Safe is killing me, which is me saying safe isn't safe."

Neither Runt nor Mike even looked at Jason while he vented. Mike was busy trying to get the barkeep's attention. Runt had taken out the fist-sized Z-knives he had gotten in the Sprawl and was sharpening them.

Forget them. Jason pushed back from the table. "I'm going out," he said.

"Aight." Mike said. He didn't bother to turn around to look at Jason but changed the number of fingers he had in the air from three to two.

At least Mike didn't put up a fuss like Mel did. Without any resistance, Jason took to the door of the beehive.

The town of Bafakoy was packed. The last time Jason had seen so many people in one place he had been riding through Nasreddin. Despite the overwhelming numbers, only a couple of nasrans gave him the stink eye. Maybe stories of his unadulterated badassedness preceded him. He took to the streets, passing several throngs of nasrans, more beehive buildings and a few stalls where vendors peddled weird junk.

Eventually, he found his way to a less dense part of town. He could actually see beyond the city. A grand lake framed the distant visa beyond the squat rooftops, its sea green water reflecting the sun's light with a sparkle. Beyond the lake, a majestic mountain rose toward heaven, its crevices filled in with green grass among the rocky brown crags.

Something in him wanted to see more of that. He took steps in that direction, looking at the lake grow and the rooftops shrink, until a hand at eye level stopped him in his tracks. Behind the hand, a nasran stood with four of his buddies.

"Did you come from Laetmus?" he asked. "You are far from the trade district. You are in a place where there is no help for your kind."

"Oh, I don't need help," Jason said, shaking his head as he thought about it.

"When we finally get behind Enverpasha, the first thing we'll do is raze your city to the ground, kill all your people," the nasran said, sneering. "But I think, why wait until we join? We can start now, early, with you."

"Oh!" Jason exclaimed as realization struck. "You weren't really asking if I need help in a friendly type way, you were talking smack. This is you being a threatening alley-thug type. Now I get it."

The nasran looked to his friends as if he didn't know what to make of Jason. Jason, more than a little amused, talked to give the thug a helping hand.

"Here's how you talk smack. You see me, you see the bone hand," he said raising his arm to illustrate the sick sheen of it in the sunlight. "You notice the self-confidence. It's brought on by a supreme calm, which is bad news for you, weaksauce. It means I'm itching to put you and the Fisher Price My-First-Goon-Squad behind you there on your backs. It all depends on you. You can either make the right move and step to the side or the wrong move and get put to sleep. What's it gonna be?"

Jason wasn't lying about the supreme calm. In that calm, he saw the thug's face contort in anger, his arm draw back for a punch.

It was the wrong move.

In a blur, Jason reached behind his back, grabbed his severed arm, pulled it out and brought it down on top of the nasran's head before he could finish his swing. The thug's eyes closed and he began to swoon with his instant narcolepsy. Jason let the arm club bounce off the nasran's head, using the momentum to bring it across another thug's face.

Those two were falling out. Quick to react, the third nasran rushed Jason with a hard right. Jason ducked easily and swung the severed arm hand side up. The nasran stepped into the hand, caught the fingers all over his face and dropped a second later.

The fourth nasran backed up, shock and fear on his face, the rest of his team all sound asleep.

Jason's eyes grew bigger than his smile. "They stay asleep... forevah! Mu Ha Ha!"

The last thug tried to bolt. Jason chased him down the street with the arm, laughing all the while. His arm finally touched the thug when he tried to round a corner, making the thug drop and slide across the street as if he was stealing home plate.

Jason stopped and looked thoughtfully at the slumbering goon.

"I really gotta think of a catch phrase or something when I do this kind of thing."

His way now clear, Jason headed toward the lake. Tall green grasses and shrubs greeted him as he passed the last houses on the outskirts of town. There was scarcely a patch of brown as the greenery extended all the way to the shores of the lake. The water held a gray blue color that looked equal parts refreshing and icy cold. Without the buildings to obscure it, the single mountain rose large and dominating on the distant shore.

His keen eyesight told Jason there was another village on the other side of the river, at the base of the mountain. The structures were square, not rounded like most buildings here in Bafakoy. He walked along the banks of the river, toward the mountain, trying to get a better look. He went along the bank some way, rustling through grass and bush, squinting at the village. The inhabitants practically seemed to live at the lakeshore. Then he noticed they were aians.

"Fancy meeting you here, Cephrin" a deep, familiar voice spoke, bringing Jason's attention back to this side of the lakeshore.

Onus sat on a boulder which protruded out the water at the edge of the shore like a giant molar. Still garbed in the shimmering blood red robe, the god smiled, looking at Jason with those disturbing, unmoving eyes.

ENVERPASHA LOOKED NEITHER warrior nor Hexenarii, but instead wore a regal ceremonial tunic as if he was about to be coronated the *Buyuka-ta*, the chief of all tribes. His sword, a loud, golden color, looked ceremonial as well. Enverpasha's shimmer looked like bubbling mud. If that didn't speak volumes for his character, the rings around his neck did. Instead of protecting the signet rings, of keeping them hidden and sacred, to be shown only when needed, Enverpasha brazenly displayed the rings around his neck like they were costume jewelry.

She saw the rings for Sinop, Chorum, Erzinjan, Erzurum and Urfa paraded around his neck. The signet ring for Balikesir was thankfully vacant. Perhaps there was hope after all.

Enverpasha leaned back, a smug smile on his face.

"If it's not the great avenger of Maltep. You must be a fierce woman indeed for so many tribes to place their swords behind you. Either this or the avenging of Maltep is so easy a task many would consider it woman's work."

Savashbahar placed her hands on her belt, letting her fingers jangle the silver tipped hexes. "Well, I came to work," she said. "Because that is what it will take to bring down the mage factory. But perhaps you think reclaiming

Nasreddin is only a matter of having a parade and flashing your pretty golden sword."

"No, it is a matter of an army," he said, hoisting his chain up to let the rings clink against one another. "And I ask myself, why do you take away from that army with your little romp with the mages?"

"Do you ask yourself these things because even the two men you have brought with you here have no desire to talk to you?"

Enverpasha leaned forward. "You are disrespectful."

"You hoist the tribal rings you have earned like a prize stable. What would you do with my respect, that of which you haven't earned?"

Bulmak stood up before Enverpasha could retort. "This gets us nowhere," he said. "Your goals may be different, but I do not believe killing one another is on either of your lists. Savashbahar, come with me."

Savashbahar kept her demeanor neutral, her movements stiff as she followed Bulmak out of the audience chamber. He led the way through the Chieftain's Hall, past war trophies and displays of horns and paws taken from great hunts, until they were at Bulmak's private chambers. Once he had closed the doors, he spun on Savashbahar, looking at her as if she had lost all sanity.

"Are you trying to compromise your own position?" Bulmak growled.

"Are you trying to compromise it?" Savashbahar responded hotly, not bothering to hide her anger. "Why would you pull me out of the audience, as if I was wrong or a child in need of chastisement?"

"You already looked wrong!" Bulmak cried. "You're a strong woman, the strongest I've known, but still a woman. Those men in that chamber don't see a peer and equal striking back at another peer, barb for barb. They do not even see Enverpasha starting that worthless exchange. All they see is a woman who cannot control her emotional outbursts."

"Am I to let this man, neither warrior nor Hexenarii, talk to me as if he was superior?"

"Yes!" Bulmak growled. "This is a contest of causes, not character. I see Enverpasha as weak and soft as the fabric he wears and just as uselessly showy. But his cause, Savashbahar, his cause speaks to me, as it does all nasrans. You need to state your case, to speak for Maltep and of a danger that will not allow us to sit idle. It is what you've done for every tribe you've already visited. You do not win an uphill battle by rushing downhill."

Savashbahar let out a sigh. Bulmak was right. Enverpasha had baited her from the outset. Now she would have to work that much harder win the Balikesir's support. She nodded, conceding to the wisdom of his words.

"We should return to the audience chamber," she said. "Who knows what Enverpasha says to the tribal chiefs about me while we are here?"

"Of course," Bulmak said, managing a wan smile. "First, tell me of our son. What has become of Dushunmek?"

"He is dead," Savashbahar said flatly. "You know by whom. I did not come all this way for Maltep alone."

Bulmak nodded gravely. "Know that I grieve for him. The only thing I regret in Dushunmek was the tying of my hands."

Years ago it had been Bulmak, then only the Hex King's second son, who had shown Savashbahar the path of Hexenarii after she fled the repressive ways of Maltep. He had shown her a respect and care that she had never experienced. How could love not follow? It was the best time of her life, full of power and control and secret trysts as she blossomed as a Hexenarii and a woman.

Savashbahar conceived, which Bulmak took wonderfully as a blessing. Then the Hex King's first son died, a boy who was never really competent as Hexenarii, destroyed by his own misuse of hexes. It made Bulmak first in line for Hex King. He could not have his firstborn, possibly his successor, with a foreign woman. Bulmak was torn. Rather than see him abdicate or destroy their customs, Savashbahar fled in the night, returning to Maltep to live as a witch and outcast among her people.

"We cannot change how things were," Savashbahar said. "Only how things can be. Come, let us return."

When they entered the audience chamber, they discovered plans had been made without them.

"Enverpasha brings up a novel idea," one of the chiefs said. "One we cannot ignore."

Enverpasha shrugged, a smug smile on his face as if it took no effort to think of novel ideas. "I have no need to fight with my own kind when so much threat exists for our people. I'm a bigger man than that. So I propose a challenge for you, Savashbahar. Together, we will go into the heartlands of the Jahnavar tribe, to the city of Ruh-Shadet with only a handful of men. Yes, I am willing to leave my bigger army to not woo their battle-minded hearts. There we will speak our causes to the last tribe to remain unspoken for. Whoever they join will not only earn the support of the Jahnavar, but the Balikesir as well."

"This is his novel idea we cannot ignore?" Bulmak asked. "We would let the blood drinkers decide our fates with theirs?"

"We have little problem seeing the righteousness in Enverpasha's cause," the chief replied. "Still, he wants to prove that it is not the size of the army, but the needs of all nasrankind that will justify our swords. Is it not better that Savashbahar have an opportunity to sway us in a manner that few of us feel she can with words? Will she not show us her cause is worthwhile with action?"

"You need not talk as if I am not in the room," Savashbahar said. She looked at Enverpasha and thought about how easy it would be to pull a hex from her belt and dissolve him into the pile of sludge he was. "I accept his challenge. We make way to Ruh-Shadet."

NEXT TO THE GOD OF Power, another aian sat on a log rooted in place by thick tendrils of kelp. He wore a turquoise robe and both his gills and eyes moved in sync with one another. His smile seemed honest and genuine.

"So, you're Cephrin," he said. "Verily, it is a pleasure to meet you."

Jason was a bit taken aback by these two dudes, one of them the Corrupter, sitting pretty much in the lake. While they were fairly close to the shore, it wasn't close enough to keep their feet from being wholly submerged in water. Between the two of them sat a table with rounded black and white stones on it. It was all weird, strange enough to be unnerving. Jason decided to play it straight, in a sense, and roll with the tide of bizarre.

"Pleasure to meet you too. And you are?"

The stranger rose. "I am sorry. I assume most of our people know me at a glance. It's hubris I don't need. I am Baligoz, the Watcher, Diviner of Thought, the Sustenance of the Hungry Soul."

Jason knew the name instantly. Baligoz was the god of the Fifth House. Jason looked at the two gods, confusion so thick he could feel the gears in his brain grinding to a halt. He kept silent, not knowing what to say, still trying to parse just what the holy hell this all meant.

Onus looked at him with dead eyes and a disappointed frown. "Really, Cephrin, your lack of awareness in your own culture is appalling. Our epithets are earned. Baligoz here is the Watcher. Of all my brothers and sisters, he is the only one truly non-partisan."

Jason pointed at the fish god. "You mean, you don't care? That you're playing a game with Onus? Or that the High Fane wants to see me slow roasted over a fire?"

Baligoz rubbed his chin thoughtfully. "I wouldn't quite say the words 'don't care' describe my disposition. After all, I did have a mind to meet you. You're heralded as a promise of a new age, after all. And I definitely care about the game; Onus is quite the adversary at ballist."

His answer was definitely nothing like how Yol's would've been. Baligoz was markedly different. He moved only to take his seat, where he pondered over the game board before moving a white stone. Onus returned his attention to the game, moved a black stone, then looked at Jason while holding up three fingers.

"Three times you've called on me," Onus said. "It's getting easier isn't, wielding power? It feels rightfully yours, does it not?"

Jason didn't want to answer his questions. He asked one of his own. "What's it matter how it feels?"

"Because it is how I feel. Power is your right. It is everyone's right. And I know you feel this way as well. As I have spoken, your wants and desires will align perfectly with mine."

Baligoz shook his head. "I caution you on the desire for power, Cephrin. Power is a cannibal; it only grows by eating the power of others."

"Mantras and metaphors won't save your life, Cephrin," Onus said. "Power will. War comes."

"It does, unfortunately," Baligoz said with a heavy sigh. "I have seen enough war through the length and breadth of my undying." He moved a white stone across the board and looked at Jason. "How do you feel about the war, god-to-be?"

"Which one?" Jason asked. "I hear the Temple of Houses and the Hiero-phane are about to go at it. Then the nasran's either want a piece of the tem-ple or the tower, depending on who you talk to."

Baligoz looked at Jason with sympathetic eyes. "Why do you believe that these conflicts are not all one in the same?"

Onus frowned at the game board, moving a black piece with a rough shove. "You noticed the city of Laetmus on the distant shore," he said. "They are aians, mostly of Baligoz's house," he said, then he held a hand up to shield the side of his mouth facing Baligoz, as if he was speaking conspiratorially, "with a few of mine sprinkled in. They fish and farm the lake, trading freely with the nasrans in Bafakoy. The two towns have coexisted peacefully for two centuries. And they both have prospered because of it. How long do you think this union will last?"

Jason shrugged. "I don't see why it wouldn't last indefinitely."

"Spoken with optimism," Baligoz said, moving one of his white stone game pieces. "There is potential in that."

"The potential for ignorance," Onus said, moving a black stone in front of the recently moved white stone. "It can't last indefinitely because all things are defined," Onus said. "Power defines this system. When one side has more power than the other, the powerless are swept away."

"You need not listen to our fellow god, Chosen One," Baligoz said. "One who hungers for power sees a meal in all things. You need only look at my house for a different example. Some of my followers will pick up arms with the temple. Others will seek respite from the violence in the Free States. Oth-ers still will make a pact with Onus for the gains he promises. They are no more followers of me than you are. The people of my house follow their own hearts and minds, wherever this may lead them." He moved a white stone.

Onus answered the move with one of his own. "How is that a different example? Your house ways have no bearing on the fate of these two cities."

Baligoz smiled. "Yes, and also wonderfully no. You see the only choice is power while I see the power of choice, in all things." He moved another stone and stood up. "A good game."

Onus looked at the board and flicked one of his black stones into the wa-ter as if it disgusted him. "Yes, a good game."

CHAPTER 32
The Touch of Real Magic

Rich sweated as he tried to focus his spellcraft. As much as he wanted to blame the relentless heat of the day, he knew trying to control the spell was really the culprit causing the sweat to trickle. He let out a sigh and the energy building in his hands fizzled and died.

"Not so slice-of-pie easy after twenty is it?" Vylar asked his mouth turned up into a wry smile.

"No," Rich admitted with a frown. He was now Brown of the 23rd Kind, and he was starting to realize how tough the journey back to gray would be. Not only would he have to learn the thirty-six degrees of brown, but once he graduated, he'd have to pick his primary color and learn another thirty-six degrees of even harder spells. Then he would have to learn the thirty-six degrees of all the other schools of magic before he'd wear gray. It didn't seem humanly possible.

"No need to sound so ruined by it," Vylar said gruffly. "It takes months for most mages to get to twenty-four. Destruction is a hard thing to control. We're not talking about destroying your spell parameters or augments. You're removing physical matter that existed well before you showed up."

The sun beat down over the valley, a hot fact that Vylar seemingly ignored. He faced the endless field of brown grasses, his hands outstretched toward a bowl shaped pit of dirt amidst the grass. Rich turned behind them to peek in on Mel.

She sat in the house, the only shade around, with the door open, the only way to let the stifling heat out, but as far as Rich could tell she was a million miles away from noticing the temperature. She had requested from Vylar all the books, maps, histories, drawings and diagrams he could find on the Hierophane and the surrounding city of Ardenspar. Now she sat before a table littered with documents, doing the next best thing to browsing Wikipedia that could be had in this world. A bead of sweat trickled down her temple and she didn't affect to notice as she poured over the parchments.

"Pay attention now," Vylar said, bringing Rich's attention back to the field and the concave bowl of dirt. "Focus is the most important part of destruction. You have to know what you're destroying; you've got to see it. While you're seeing what's there, you also have to see it gone. Then you have to see the rest of the world without it. All this must constantly stay in focus, as you attenuate the spell."

Vylar spoke the spell for the nth time. Even though Rich had long memorized the words, he listened intently as Vylar went through the augments describing length and depth and texture. At the end of the spell, Vylar clenched both fists and the dirt imploded with a groaning whoosh of air, sending up a spray of dust particles. When the dust settled, the bowl was a bit deeper, a little wider, the dirt magically destroyed.

"Any questions?" Vylar asked.

"I got it," Rich answered.

"Good. Because I'm going to leave you to it." Before Rich fully understood what he was saying, Vylar had a portal open.

"You're leaving?"

"I've got odds and ends to take care of, plus some ins and outs. Besides, it's furnace hot here. I think I'll head to cooler climates today. You'll be fine." He took a step towards the portal then stopped.

"Don't forget, if you just can't climb to the 24th, there's no harm in revisiting all the spells you didn't cast getting to twenty-three."

"Huh?" Rich asked confused.

"Are you dumb, Bendy Sleeves? You've only been casting one spell per tier, the spell that would promote you," Vylar said, pointing up. "You've forgotten about all the spells that don't take you up, but take you out." He spread his arms wide for emphasis. "Each rank has several spells in the tier. They won't get you higher up, but they will increase your knowledge and mastery of the level you're in. Maybe that's what you need. You get it now?"

Rich nodded. Vylar had a solid point. Doing something different when he hit a wall might provide both relief and insight.

"Are you nodding?" Vylar asked. "Because I'm blind you know."

"Oh, sorry. Yes, I get your point."

"I knew you would. I leave you to it." With that, Vylar stepped into the portal.

Mel made her way out into the field. She looked at the still active portal with a hint of envy on her face.

"If I wasn't inclined to believe the other side led to acid caves or polar bears, I'd hop that portal."

"Sucks pretty bad here, huh?" Rich asked.

"It's not the place," Mel said, panning her head around to look at the brown grass valley. "I actually don't mind the peace and quiet. It's the heat. And the dusty dryness. I'll be all smiles once it cools down to real autumn temperatures."

"I would've thought you were too busy in the books to notice the heat," Rich said, "which is ironic for me to say, right?"

"That's just my war face," she said flashing a bright smile. "Mission focus. When I remembered Mike's story about the secret smuggling caravan tunnels under Ardenspar, it got me thinking of castles and secret passageways, Prohibition and speakeasies back home. I figure there's gotta be a secret entrance into the Hierophane, just need enough intel to know where to look."

Rich nodded as Vylar's portal winked out of existence. He knew where to find the Rift Pendulum's instruction manual. If they could find a secret entrance into the Hierophane, it seemed like an easier escape plan than a full on war between nasrans and mages.

"Besides," Mel said. "I take breaks, like now for instance, and that's when I really feel the heat. But I like to watch the magic. It's nice to see you doing it without a look of utter fear on your face."

Mel made a face of mock abject horror, with eyes bugged out and mouth open and askew as if she was about to let forth a blood curdling scream.

"I don't look like that," Rich said.

"You're right," Mel said. "I forgot to cast a spell." She made the same look, only this time she started moving her lips back and forth furiously. "...humina humina, pollo loco, penny lane, oochy-wally..." she intoned.

"Real funny," Rich said with a grin. It was impossible to be mad at Mel. He was thankful for her company these days as he tried to climb the ranks of brown. She didn't look at him like Jason had, with judgment, telling him his choice to strip away the gray robes was a total waste. She had made the loss of power manageable, the time in this uninhabited place less lonely.

"So what's next in your spell book?" Mel asked. "Trying to dig more holes like Vylar?"

Rich looked at the dirt pit, the surrounding tall grass, felt the heat of the midday sun pounding like a hammer and realized plainly he did not have the focus for it. He was tired of trying to climb to twenty-four.

"I'm going to play around with some spells of my rank," Rich said. "Grow out instead of up, as Vylar put it." He rustled through his library pocket and brought out his spellbook.

"Here's to hoping there's something in there funner than playing in dirt," Mel said as Rich leafed through pages.

Rich looked through the front pages of his book, what he called the generic section, looking at mid level brown spells. As excited as he was to climb higher and access more pages of the book, he had to admit there were certain things he didn't know he could do at this level and below. He stopped at the right spell—hands down perfect—a creation spell exactly on his level.

He put the spellbook back into his pocket, focused on the words, spoke them carefully and clapped his hands together at the end of the spell. His clap sounded as loud as a thunderclap. High up in the sky, a small, dark cloud burst forth out of nothing. It was tiny, an odd thing out of place in an otherwise vast and cloudless sky. But it was directly overhead, right between them and a blazing noon sun. A cooling shadow fell over Rich and Mel. She giggled with delight. They stood underneath a quaint, perfect circle of dark cloud, an oasis in the midst of clear skies in all directions.

Then the rain came down, a magical and torrential downpour.

Rich saw Mel close her eyes and tilt her face up to heaven as the rain poured over them. Her hair, now wet and slick, framed her face and hung down her back. He saw her lips part, just enough to let the water in. And in seeing all this, he realized this was the real magic. The joy in that smile, her beautiful reaction to what he had caused, it went so far beyond formulas copied into a book.

He reached for her instinctively, answering the compulsion to hold real magic in his hands.

THROUGH THE COOL OF the rain, Mel felt the warmth of Rich's hand on her face, his fingertips gently brushing the wet strands of her hair back.

She looked down from the sky, to Rich. Her eyes looked into his, searching for meaning. Such a short time ago, Mel had wondered why Rich could see the girl she had become but somehow still did not see the girl. Now the look on Rich's face left no doubt how he saw her.

"Why now?" she asked.

"Why now?" he repeated with a nod of consideration as he gazed at her. "The reason I'm working so hard to be a better mage is because of you. I see things in my cost dreams I don't like. I need to be stronger for you. And while I was thinking about that it dawned on me how right you've been. All of this we're in is deadly and dangerous and it's a small miracle we're still in one piece. No guarantees we're going home to the bodies we remember and it's definitely not happening today. Today we're who we are, in bodies we may as well come to terms with because they're impossible to run from. You said you didn't want to die without knowing what this thing is and you're right. I don't want to not know either.

"So why now?" he repeated, "because it took all that time for me to realize how dumb I've been. This was the time it took for me to finally catch up to you."

"Listen," she said, "you don't have—"

His lips met hers, cutting her off before she could finish. She kissed him back. The tingling warmth from his lips and tongue radiated in waves throughout her body, a body growing ever warmer under the cooling drops of the magic rain.

When they broke kiss, she took off her blue cloak. The black catsuit followed while Rich took off his robe. He knelt before her cloak on one knee, allowing Mel to see the well defined muscles in his shoulders as he spoke a spell. Suddenly her cloak grew in volume, the material expanding and thickening until it was the size of a queen-sized mattress pad. He looked up, smiled and held out his hand in invitation.

She smiled back. "Why, Rich, did you have that spell memorized for such an occasion? Is that why you're grinning like the devil?" she asked as she took his hand.

"I'm smiling because you're extremely naked and completely beautiful. It's making me misuse adverbs. And a magician never tells his secrets."

He guided her gently down to her cloak turned cot. The rain overhead had lessened and was sprinkling the couple with fine, delicate drops. Just a few feet away from their cot, the sun continued in its unabated assault on the dry grasses. Underneath the shade of the small cloud, Rich kissed the water off her breasts and stomach. His kisses and touch sent electricity rippling through her body. She caressed his hair, gently pulled his face away from her navel so their eyes could meet.

"Now," she whispered.

He moved up, until his weight on top of her gave welcome pressure, until his lips met hers. She felt him, a stiff, solid presence pushing, parting her. She yielded to the push and it moved deeper. Slow at first, back and forth, and everywhere it touched, absolute joy blossomed out in delicious waves. She moved to meet the presence, to help it get deeper. Faster. She could feel his need, his eagerness in the pushes. It mirrored her own. Faster. She breathed his air. Nothing in the world existed in this moment save the push, the pleasure, the pained and unrelenting need to keep going, driving, building, building, building, until...

"Oh!" she exclaimed as all her nerve endings bloomed open, as if her body had saved all those waves of pleasure into a capacitor and discharged in this moment. She shuddered under the burden and Rich, still deep in his own painful need, spurred from her reaction, drove even faster. She felt him swell and push painfully as he let out his own hoarse cry of release.

He collapsed beside her, panting with exhaustion. The two of them were quiet for long moments, just breathing, just trying to recover. He looked at her with a lopsided grin.

"So how was it for you?" he asked.

She smiled back. "You know how you're almost about to level up and you turn in a huge quest and once you say okay your whole body erupts in an explosion of sparks and there's a tiny sonic boom and you're thinking 'finally' and you let out a sigh?" she asked, "it's a lot like that."

Rich laughed his naked butt off, nodded the whole while.

Suddenly a portal swirled into existence in the dry field beside them. Vylar walked through. Confusion etched his features and he took a tentative sniff of the air. He looked down to where the couple were.

"Bendy Sleeves! When I suggested you practice other magic, I didn't think you'd pull out the ol' magic wand."

CHAPTER 33
The Turn

Mike didn't like sleeping with one eye open, much less traveling for days on end looking sideways at the new guys for signs of treachery. The group of eight, which was really two groups of four, made their way through thick forest foliage and even thicker fog. It was slow going, trying to find solid footing while working your way uphill on uneven, muddy terrain. Having to look, through mist covered goggles, at the fools next to him for a knife made the going even slower. But damned if he wasn't gonna look.

The scarred up warrior, Suikast, looked mean beyond reason, the type of dude that would cook his son's pet dog just to see the kid cry so he could tell him to man up and take a bite of Fido. The Hexenarii called Gozbahji looked jaded, like people had become as disposable as the hexes that jangled from his belt. Enverpasha was just a pompous ass, something Mike really hated, especially when the pompous ass was in a position of command authority like Enverpasha was. And the last dude, a worker bee they all called Fetcher, pulled the cart in which Enverpasha sat comfortably with their supplies, hauling it through all the mud and slick leaves while getting yelled out from time to time for not providing a smooth ride. Even though Mike believed Fetcher capable of treacherous moves—after all, if you're willing to pull a grown ass man through this muck you're probably willing to stab a woman and her friends in the kidneys—with Fetcher, Mike mostly felt damn sorry for.

Unlike the times he traveled with Savvy and her army of tribes, Mike kept his lightning gloves on and diskbow cranked taut. The tension was thick enough to butter bread with. It mixed with the smell of desiccated plants, the forest's way of telling them death was all around them.

The Jahnavar highlands had no downhills. They made their way up one hill, gripping tree trunks and grasping exposed roots with muddied hands to help their traction, only to be greeted by another hill when they got to the top. What angry god was mad at the Jahnavar to do this?

"Savashbahar, your foreigners don't look up to the task," Enverpasha said as he bounced around slightly in the cart. "I will totally understand if you let them return to the comforts of Bafakoy."

"Real talk, I'd be a lot more comfortable with the task if you and me switched seats," Mike said.

"Here is your first lesson in leadership, megrym," Enverpasha said. "A leader must be seen, always seen, in a position of prominence. What good comes of him toiling alongside his people?"

"You mean outside of increased productivity, leading by example and improved morale?" Mike asked. "Couldn't tell ya."

"I will tell you," Enverpasha said, talking as if Mike hadn't answered his question sarcastically and was waiting for enlightenment. "You will find mutiny. Your people will look at you and say 'he works as we do. Why can we not lead as he leads?' They will think themselves just as good as you and they will seek to replace you."

Mike was about to comment on how stupid that was, when somewhere beyond the trees that disappeared into the fog, a howl sounded, long and piercing. More howls joined the one, none of them sounding quite animal. Enverpasha smiled.

"The Jahnavar, they welcome us. The end of this hard road comes soon, yes?"

RICH HAD A PROBLEM with destruction in more ways than one. He couldn't let go of his bond with Rew. Yes, she hated him. Yes, there was Mel now. Despite this, thoughts of her still lingered, refusing to go.

He leafed through the Song of Ardor Swain, the book Rew had given him, the one they had read together in his room in the High Fane. If nothing else, he was sorry, sorry for not telling her the truth, of trying to take the coward's way out. He couldn't bring her father back nor did he regret casting the spell that killed him and saved his friends' lives. But he was sorry that he had brought that pain into her heart, and this was something he had never really been able to tell her.

Perhaps she would take his scry. This time he wouldn't try to get her to see his side or defend himself from her accusations. He would tell her he was sorry for the pain he had caused her. Then he could close the book.

He put the Song of Ardor Swain back in his library pocket, calmed his breathing, and sent out a request to scry. Nothing but silence answered back. Then the room opened up and a wave of fear coursed through Rich.

Rew sat on the floor of a room just like the one he had shared with Delv. Her robe was dirty, her hair disheveled with several braids hanging listlessly. She looked at Rich with anger in her eyes.

"So, you've heard, then? Have you come to laugh at me? To tell me how wrong I was while you parade your freedom? Go ahead, I am waiting."

Rich took a step forward, and the scry on her side seemed to jump roughly. "Rew, what's happened?!"

"I've only slightly cracked this witchlock. I cannot keep the scry long and there's not the time enough to explain the things you see plainly. Tell me instead why you've chosen to scry with me. Is it to see me in chains instead of you, twisted revenge for what I said when we last scried?"

"I want to know how this happened! I want to know how to get you out of there."

"This is my punishment, for protecting you of all things," she said with hollow laughter that seemed to make her side of the scry shiver. "If your robes are truly brown, I don't see there being much you can—"

Abruptly, the scry died.

SAVASHBAHAR HEARD THE howling of the Jahnavar warriors and an involuntary shiver coursed down her spine. They were savage fighters, known among the other tribes as the blood drinkers. It should feel like good news to her heart. They were finally near the city of Ruh-Shadet to argue their cases. So why did it feel so wrong?

Enverpasha's smugness unnerved her more than the approaching howls. He looked at her with gleeful eyes. Wouldn't a man like him be looking out toward the dense fog, eager to smile and greet and pander to the tribe he had come all this way to impress?

"Feel free to go ahead of us, Enverpasha," she said. "I would like a moment to explain to my companions a few things about Jahnavar customs."

"After all this way together?" Enverpasha asked putting a hand on his chest and looking extremely offended by the proposition of being first seen and heard. "That is no way for the leader of our peoples to act."

His smile grew at his own words.

"I do not want my preparations to get in your way, just as I'm sure there are things you would like to do to prepare."

"For once, you are right, Savashbahar." He reached behind his neck and took down the chain holding the signet rings of the tribes he commanded. He placed another ring onto the chain and tied the necklace back into place. Savashbahar plainly saw the signet ring of the Jahnavar glinting back at her.

Enverpasha had already been to Ruh-Shadet and had gotten the Jahnavar's support. So why had he made this plan to bring them all this way?

The howls of the approaching blood drinkers answered the question. This is where Enverpasha planned to kill them all.

MEL WENT FROM THINKING Rich was the most awesome person ever to swearing he was the dumbest man on the planet in two seconds flat.

"What do you mean, you have to go to the Hierophane?! Are you stupid?"

"Rew needs me," he said pacing back in forth in front of the house. "I've got to help her, Mel."

"Help her? She had us locked up!"

"That doesn't matter now. She needs my help."

"You're talking like she needs five dollars or a ride to the store! Rich, the woman is imprisoned underneath the same place Mike swears he needs an army to get into. That's more than needing help. Besides, she's queen mage who got locked up by other mages on mage business. It's not your concern. Let it play itself out."

"If you're not going to help, at least tell Vylar where I'm heading." With that, Rich took a step past Mel.

Mel moved in front of him, barring his way. "No."

Rich looked at Mel. "What do you mean, no?"

"I mean you're a brown robe. And I'm seriously, seriously pissed off. Do not try me. You will not like it. I absolutely refuse to let you go off and kill yourself saving that broad. No."

"Are you jealous, Mel?" he asked. "Is that why you're trying to stop me?"

"Does that matter?" Mel countered. "You can call keeping my friend away from his suicidal uber-macho, gotta-save-the-damsel tendencies jealousy if you want to, if that helps you sleep better. Either way, I'm not going to let you go marching headfirst into a place we barely got away from."

Rich chewed his lip for a moment, glaring at Mel as if she was a wicked stepmother. Then he let go. His face relaxed and he sighed, long and deep.

"You're right, you're right," he said. "It's just hard to kind of sit back, you know? Do nothing. We're supposed to be pendulum heroes, right?"

"We can't save everybody," Mel said soothingly. "We couldn't even help ourselves when it came to getting out of this world."

Rich dug his spellbook out of his robes. "I'm going to go inside and study," he said. "I'll be out in a minute with some new crappy brown spells to try."

Mel smiled. "OK."

Rich went in and closed the door. Mel breathed out a bated breath of relief. She looked out over the golden fields, letting their peaceful calm soothe and relax her. Rich was safe, and she didn't have to resort to beating him up to keep him that way.

He also wasn't coming out. Was he still mad at her? Mel knocked on the door. "Rich?" she called. No answer. It didn't feel right. She flung the door open and was greeted by the harsh blue and white light of an open portal. Rich was nowhere to be seen.

Apparently, portals were on his list of crappy can-do brown spells. Mel looked with dread at the portal. She had no illusions where this one led.

What else was she going to do? She jumped in after Rich.

CHAPTER 34
End of the Hard Road

Mel looked around the Hierophane gardens for some sign of Rich. She was in the garden overlooking the same veranda they had ate breakfast in the day they were captured. She saw nothing telling in the flowers and trees, and hoped Rich wasn't dead someplace. Because once she found him, she was going to kill him.

She pulled the straps of her pack tight and ran off toward the Underthral. Deciding on a strategy of "inconspicuous as possible", she ran without her sword drawn. Just a warrior girl out for a jog, nothing to see here.

En route to the prison, she ran upon one brown robe unconscious in the grass with another one standing over him. Upon hearing Mel's approaching footsteps, he turned and his eyes grew wide in alarm. Instead of asking for help for his fallen comrade, he sent his sleeves barreling toward her.

Deftly, Mel side-stepped the sleeves and tugged them hard as she kept running. She figured her strength against that of the magic wouldn't be enough to pull the mage off his feet; she just wanted him off balance for a second. It was all she needed. She closed the gap and rapped her fist twice in succession into his solar plexus, followed up with a chop into his throat, and finished by grabbing a handful of the mage's face, lifting him off his feet and slamming his head into the ground.

Mel kept running, not bothering to see if the mage was knocked out. She knew, she was all Zhufira, and electricity seemed to spark from every nerve ending. More than electricity, unquenchable anger drove her on.

Thankfully, no one was around to hinder her as she ran toward the Underthral. It was a good thing not even the mages wanted to be anywhere near the prison, because she was pretty sure the Hierophane had their equivalent of an APB out on all of them. The brown robe she had just put down seemed to verify that. Within minutes, the single story dome of the Underthral came into view, its distinctive outcroppings shooting out from the dome every which way.

Mel noticed two brown robes running toward the Underthral. In the distance, she saw Rich kneeling before the prison's entrance. He had finished the spell that made the prison open, and now these two robes were onto him. Leave it to Rich to remember that stupid opening spell.

She gained ground on the brown robes. Mel leapt in the air and came down into the first robe's back with her knees. She held on fast, clutching ample amounts of brown robe with her hands. He fell with a yelp as she drove him into the ground. Mel tucked into a roll and threw the brown robe into the other mage as he turned to see what was going on. Mel was on them before they could recover, striking fast and hard to keep them down.

She continued on into the Underthral. After traversing the stairs she saw Rich in the courtyard below, beside a cart filled with hay, battling it out with the brown robe guarding the way deeper. The inmates cheered as Rich and the brown robe traded blows in a flurry of sleeves. Goddammit, they didn't have time for this stupid slapfight. Mel didn't even negotiate the distance; she dived off the railing and landed on top of the mage guard. She stood up holding the necklace that would take them deeper.

"Thanks, Mel," Rich said breathing heavy.

"Shuttup," Mel said slamming the necklace onto the desk. "Let's just get this over with," she said as the door to the Castworks dissolved.

SAVASHBAHAR WAS FORCED to react to Enverpasha's murder attempt before she could react to his betrayal. Donning the signet ring was Enverpasha's cue to attack and his men wasted no time following his unspoken command.

Gozbahji pulled a hex, named it fire and threw it at Savashbahar's party.

"Ambush!" Mike yelled as the hex blossomed into a fireball and came down at them.

"Wait? What? Oh, shit!" Jason cried.

No time. Savashbahar dropped to a knee, pulling a hex along the way. "Wall!" she cried, sticking it into the mud.

A wall of mud shot up into the air. The fireball hit it a second later, superheating the mud while sending the wall down on top of them. Runt ran up against the oncoming mud, pushing it aside with his giant forearms in a sizzle of half-weagr skin.

Gozbahji wasn't done. He pulled a hex for each hand. "Steel" he named one, "Armor" he named the other. He stuck them both together and tossed them on the warrior Suikast.

Suikast charged at them, his sword poised to strike. From the hex stuck on him, gleaming metal radiated out, spreading all over his body like a second skin until he was fully covered in steel.

Meanwhile, Gozbahji was pulling another hex.

They couldn't stay on the defensive. Savashbahar sprang to meet the steel covered Suikast. She pulled a hex. His sword came down. "Weagr!" she named the hex and punched at Suikast with blinding speed.

Her fist met his chest with a resounding clong before his blade could strike home. The force of the blow sent him careening towards Gozbahji and Enverpasha's cart. Gozbahji side-stepped Suikast as he blasted past. Enverpasha dived out of the cart as Suikast barreled into it.

Gozbahji took the hex he was holding and named it "Thicken." Then he crushed it in his hand and threw the crumbled bits in the air. The fog around the treacherous nasrans became a dense cloud and started to reach for them as well.

Savashbahar had never hexed with fog, and she knew better to try such a thing in the thick of battle without training and guidance. No good could come from fighting the Hexenarii in the encroaching cloud, where he was comfortable. No good could come of fighting in general. The whole purpose Savashbahar had come here had been nullified.

The Jahnavar warriors howled again. They were close. Any moment, they would be visible.

"Quickly," Savashbahar said. "Downhill."

Mike, Runt and Jason wasted no time sliding down the hill. Savashbahar grabbed the nearest tree. She pulled a hex and named it "Snap" and pushed it into the tree. The tree broke at its trunk where she had placed the hex, falling toward the rolling fog. She took to the slope after that, to catch up with her comrades.

"Where do you run to, war chief of the Maltep?" Enverpasha called out from the fog. "Now you fear my paltry parade?"

Savashbahar slid down the hill with her comrades. They pushed past ferns and trees in their haste to get distance. Savashbahar noticed movement on the right. A Jahnavar warrior rose up from the brush. He was easily identifiable in wolf fur and stylized wolf mask. The mask kept a fixed smile, a grim rictus made more sinister by the Jahnavar's use of real wolf teeth. Howling madly, the warrior threw his spear.

Savashbahar fell down on her back to avoid the spear. Before she had time to answer back with a hex, Mike had discharged his diskbow, putting a disk through the mask and dropping the warrior.

Runt came to haul her up. Two more Jahnavar warriors emerged from the brush. Just as fast Jason let loose two arrows that felled them.

"C'mon," Jason said as Savashbahar got back on her feet. "Downhill's supposed to be faster than up."

As in answer, howls echoed up to them from downhill. A chorus of howls joined those. They were cries for blood, and they came from all around them.

RICH LED THE WAY THROUGH the Castworks even though he was next to useless at this level of magic. He would still probably be sleeve fighting with the other brown robe if Mel hadn't come along. As much as it pained him to admit, he missed his command of magic as a gray robe.

Together, Rich and Mel ran through the dark, sloping causeway ramp of the Castworks, making their way toward the bottom. Rich remembered a red robe guarding the way to Broken Alley, and futilely tried to plan how he was going to subdue a mage of higher caliber when all he could really do in a fight was bend his sleeves.

Sure enough, when they reached the bottom they found sitting behind the stone desk a red robe, the same man Brigitte had called Kerr. Next to the man Rich knew he couldn't take in a duel stood a brown robe, a guy Rich wasn't sure if he could take. The brown robe saw them and lashed his sleeves out.

Before Rich could respond, Mel surged ahead in a sprint. She jumped on one sleeve, hopped to the other, ran down the length of the sleeve and cold-cocked the mage in the face, sending him sprawling. She quickly turned to face the red mage.

Kerr didn't try to fight. He held up a hand and looked at Rich.

"Rather than duel, I would much prefer to continue recovering from the last time you and your friends came here," he said, rubbing his gut as if it was sore. "I have seen your face advertised when it comes to charges of treason and the Lady Majora. I assume this is why you're back now, to aid a friend?"

Rich nodded.

Kerr took the necklace off and placed it on the slab in front of him. The way to Broken Alley dissolved.

"I have known Rew Majora for a long time," Kerr said. "If you've known a woman for ages and only good things come from her, you lot can't be all that bad."

"Thank you," Rich said.

"Go," Kerr said nodded toward the doorway. "Give her my regards."

Rich headed into Broken Alley, followed by Mel. Gone was the all white, antiseptic aesthetic, replaced by burned walls and flickering lights. Rich made his way carefully through the passageway, checking every aperture for signs of Rew. They passed nook after nook of sleeping, tortured mages until—

"Rew!" Rich cried. She looked up at him, eyes wide with shock behind locks of braided hair. Mel drew her sword and stabbed up into the lights, causing a graying of walls and shower of black sparks as the magic barrier came down. Rich rushed over to Rew, taking the witchlock hovering over her and crushing it.

It seemed the whole Underthral groaned with the resultant shock wave. Rich knelt down, hugging Rew, helping her rise in his embrace so she could find her legs to stand.

"Why did you come?" Rew asked into his shoulder.

"Why the hell would I not?" he answered stroking her hair.

"Ahem!" Mel yelled, not bothering to disguise it with a cough. "We fucking leaving already?"

Before anyone could answer the question, the blue and white light of a portal opened up in the hallway next to Rew's room.

"I didn't do that," Rich said. "And I know Rew doesn't have the strength yet."

"Go, go, go!" Mel shouted. Rich hurried as much as he could, half dragging Rew as he carried her into the hallway, trying to make distance between themselves and the new portal. Mel walked backwards, sword drawn, never taking her eyes off the swirling vortex.

They had only gone a handful of steps when a black robe emerged from the portal. Brigitte smiled. She shook her head as if she couldn't believe she was seeing this.

"Honestly, the bigger part of me thought this trap was useless, that no one with a couple of brain cells to rub together would be stupid enough to come back here. You must be really committed to living your life like you're some dumbass gamer hero. Fine. Let's see if I can make you cough up some quarters."

Mel charged at Brigitte but the destruction mage was faster. Brigitte spoke a spell too fast for Rich's ears to pick up the words. A torrent of wind rushed from her sleeves, sending Mel off her feet to crash into Rich and Rew. They all hit hard against the wall.

Brigitte turned her hand into gleaming steel and then thrust the hand into the floor. Her hand emerged with a burst pipe, spewing water. "*Buuz zen-jiler*," she said.

The spewing water reached out towards them with a life all its own. The water gripped around their legs, arms and throats, solid in its cold substance. It got colder still, colder, until thick tendrils of blue ice bound them in place.

Back in the recess of the hallway, Brigitte held the ice tendrils like leashes in her clenched fist. "First, the gamer hero," Brigitte said, tugging at one of the lines. The icy block around Rich's neck began to swell.

He couldn't breathe as the ice constricted. His face was turning hot. No words escaped his lips, not even a pathetic call to bend his sleeves. His vision tunneled.

Out of nowhere, droplets of fire rained down on the ice, melting it back to water. Rich felt a violent tug, and he along with Mel and Rew were pulled out of the hallway. They skidded to a stop in the antechamber of Broken Alley in front of Kerr.

"I will delay Brigitte," Kerr said. "Go quickly."

He headed into the flickering lights of Broken Alley. Moments later, Brigitte turned the distant corner and the flickering lights fell into darkness followed by sparks of lightning and fire and ice. A hand shaking Rich brought his attention back to this room.

Mel looked at him. "Can you portal us?" she asked.

He nodded.

"This way, to the Fouls," she said, helping him and Rew up and leading them to a giant door. Mel lifted the iron beam sitting across the door and pulled the door open to reveal a giant sewer pipe. She ushered them inside and nodded for him to cast the spell.

He spoke the words and the blue and white light swirled into existence, promising them salvation. Rich led Rew in. A moment later they emerged inside Vylar's humble house. Rich turned around to give Mel a giant hug.

He saw only the swirling light of the portal. Mel hadn't come through.

MIKE TOOK A POSITION near Savvy as she led the way. Jason followed right after, his eagle eyes severely diminished in the fog but still effective for early warning. Runt was in the rear, protecting their asses as they tried to find some way out of this mess.

This was the worst battlefield scenario possible. There was nowhere to really go when all sides were surrounded. Savvy made the best of it, running downhill and eastward, trying to maximize speed with the slope of the hill to keep the ring of enemies from closing in.

But no matter what she did, they would eventually close in. The noose was tightening.

Five warriors came at them in four different directions. Jason killed one with an arrow. One warrior thrust his spear at Runt, who caught the spear with his Z-blade. Once the Z-blade and spear had been raised in the air, Runt disassembled the bottom blade and cut into the warrior then reassembled the Z-blade again as the warrior fell. The remaining three came at Mike.

He clapped his hands together and released a burst of lightning that surged through them all.

Even Mike with his poor eyesight could see more warriors bearing down on them. Savvy stopped in her tracks near a big tree leaning on the slope. She pulled a hex.

"Snap!" she cried and smacked the base of the tree. The tree fell on two of the encroaching warriors.

Savvy pulled another hex. "Push," she said and put this one on the recently felled tree as well. It began to roll downhill with the ease of a snowball.

"Follow the tree," she said. They all took to the path it was clearing. The tree couldn't protect their flank or rear, but it gave them forward progress without confrontation.

There was a trade off. While they didn't have to worry about warriors in the front, they also couldn't see what lay beyond the tree. They were flying blind, with only a foot of visibility as the tree rolled down.

Suddenly the tree dropped out of view in front of them, exposing empty air and a chasm. The sheer face of the hill on the opposite side of the gap was too far away to jump. Jahnavar warriors were coming toward them from both sides. Behind them, an entire army seemed to bear down on them.

They didn't have time to stop running towards the chasm. There was no way to discern how far down it went.

"Jump and pray!" Mike yelled. Savvy took the plunge, then Mike. He looked down to see a hard drop, made only slightly easier by the tree that had just fallen.

Mike landed hard on the tree trunk and rolled off it, followed by Jason and Runt. They were in a ravine with steep walls where two hills met. There was no easy way to climb out. A small alcove had formed between the two hills. Savvy stood under it, beckoning them to come to her.

Under the alcove, Mike only had a view of the opposite side of the ravine. The face of the hill was almost sheer. There was no else for them to go.

Above them, the howls of the Jahnavar went up in unison.

MEL KNEW SHE WOULDN'T be able to take the portal when Rich was casting it. Looking behind them all, she saw Brigitte making strides towards them. There was no way the portal was going to close in time before Brigitte could hop through as well.

Mel walked back out of the Fouls as Rich and Hierophant Majora went through. Brigitte walked up and stopped a few feet from Mel.

"As much as I wouldn't mind your death, it's the mages I'm after," Brigitte said. "And I don't want to risk the portal closing because I'm busying messing around with you. You know you can't beat me. I'm a destruction mage and you're a bitch in a cat suit. So how about you step away from the portal and I'll call you and me even. You don't have to die for them."

Mel nodded. Brigitte was right. Unlike novice brown robes, she was extremely powerful with her magic, a destruction mage of the highest order. Fighting her was suicide. Mel did the only thing her heart would allow her, she turned and kicked the giant door leading to the portal closed. The iron bar fell across the door as if providing emphasis for her decision.

"Stupid broad," Brigitte said. "*Su elimlerina gael,*" she intoned and water came flying out of the dark passageway of Broken Alley to rest in both her hands in the form of giant spheres. Brigitte whipped her hands at Mel and the water in either hand stretched out into a dozen barbed ice whips.

Mel ducked and dodged, but she couldn't evade them all. Places along her arms, legs, and sides where the whips found her they dug into her clothes and pierced her skin with a sharp bite. Brigitte pulled and the whips came back, tearing out flesh before they reverted back into water in Brigitte's palms.

Pain flashed into red hot anger, and a Melvin that was pure Zhufira charged at the destruction mage with her sword out. The water whipped out as ice again. This time, Mel ducked some tendrils, cut others and jumped past the remaining whips, an angry yell roaring from her throat as she bore down on Brigitte.

Mel jumped at the mage her sword coming down to cleave Brigitte in two. The mage held up a globe of water that met Mel before she could connect.

"*Katilash!*" the mage cried and the water turned to ice, freezing around Mel's sword-clenching fist and arm up to the elbow. Brigitte spoke another word that hurtled the ice ball into the cavernous dark of the distant ceiling as if it had gotten smacked with an oversized bat.

Mel shot fast in the air. The floor disappeared and Brigitte with it. But Brigitte's voice came up to Mel from the depths as a single word, a spell. "*Patlama!*" The ice ball exploded into a million, sharp pieces. Mel closed her eyes as the driving hail of it pummeled her entire front half. Her eyes stayed closed, and she was left with a sense of raw burning everywhere the ice had pierced, a sense of falling faster to an unseen ground, a sense of imminent death.

Her stomach lurched with nausea as she landed on her shoulder; she cried out hoarsely as she felt a ripping, unnatural movement. The pain of having the shoulder knocked out of socket force her eyes open. She lied on the ramp leading up to the Heart. The ramp curved around and down to where Brigitte stood, smiling up at Mel as she tossed a sphere of water playfully in her hand.

"*Not here. Not to this bitch,*" Mel thought. She gripped the sword that had fallen next to her with her left hand, the only one good to her now, and used it as a cane to struggle her way back to her feet. Her right arm hung useless and limp at her side. She turned and ran up the ramp, towards the Heart.

"Where are you going?" Brigitte called after her. "You wanted this, remember?"

She ran as fast as she could, feeling the utter futility of her flight in every step. A hard, crunching sound followed behind Mel. She turned as she ran and saw a giant wall of ice sliding up the ramp. Wicked icicles protruded from the wall. Powered by magic, it moved faster than she could, gaining ground fast. At three times her height, there was no question the giant wall would impale Mel unless she leapt off the ramp, where Brigitte and possibly a broken leg awaited her.

In the distance, she saw the doorway to the Heart. Mel's legs pumped as fast as she could move them. She could hear the ice crunching, getting louder as it got closer and closer.

The groaning roar of it was almost on top of her.

The doorway was still so far away.

She closed her eyes and ran for all she was worth, diving for the doorway. Her body crossed the threshold, into the Heart.

Behind her, she heard a shattering. A second later she was blown across the courtyard of the Heart by the force of the ice exploding. Again, she got a blast of searing pain as the ice hit her.

She sailed over the cart of hay and careened head first into a glass column of illusionary magefire. A fierce eruption of light followed the breaking of the glass. As Mel hit the ground face first, darkness settled in the courtyard, casting this quadrant of the prison into darkness.

Mel struggled to get up but her useless shoulder protested. A surge of rage flashed at her body's refusal to cooperate. Zhufira took over, and she raised herself to her knees, braced the arm against a floor littered with glass and ice shards and rammed herself into the shoulder, popping it back into place.

Pain and exhaustion consumed her, depleted her, and she collapsed back to the ground. Weakly, she looked over to the door leading down to the Castworks. Thankfully, it was closed. She noticed the desk that normally held the necklace key was empty of anything save ice chunks. The necklace must have been blown off in the explosion, which had caused the door to reappear.

She thought she would have some time to gather herself, to gather some strength. Suddenly a boom echoed through the courtyard and the door to the Castworks crept open an inch. Another boom sounded, and the door creaked open another inch.

If she wanted to escape, there wasn't much time. She took off her pack, which was pulling at her awkwardly. I giant icicle was stuck in the pack, pushed deep into it by the explosion, and only whatever hard thing had been packed in there had kept Mel from being impaled already.

Another boom moved the door. Mel tried to scramble to her feet and found herself falling back to the floor as her footing painfully gave out from her. She looked at the back of her leg and saw an icicle driven through her calf.

Mel wasn't going anywhere, at least not quickly. Another boom moved the door. She stared at the floor, the pieces of glass and ice glimmering in the low light. There was no doubt; she was going to die in here. Unbidden, tears came to her eyes. "All I ever wanted to do was go home," she whispered, pleading to any god who would listen.

Another boom moved the door. Somewhere in the back of Mel's mind a voice spoke to her, the voice that had belonged to Mel ever since she came to this world.

You done crying now?

She was. It wouldn't get her home. What she wanted was her right and she'd be damned if she'd let anyone stop her. She wasn't going to lie down and die. Mel grit her teeth and reached for her pack.

Another boom came. And another. Mel worked furiously in the dark. Fighting exhaustion, she clenching her jaw at the pain caused by her hurried movements. She prayed she had the strength to see it through.

SAVASHBAHAR HEARD A voice above the brays and howls of the Jah-navar, which silenced them immediately. Enverpasha was laughing.

"I laugh because my quarry is trapped," Enverpasha called down to them. "It is exactly as I planned it. It is the way things must be, war chief of the Mal-tep."

Savashbahar looked to her friends. They were all huddled under the al-cove, safe from any spears but that would change once Enverpasha decided to rush the nook. This was the end.

"You may think you are my quarry, Savashbahar, but you are not," Enverpasha called down. "It was never about having an army. It was about having all armies, to be the closest thing to the *Buyukata* our people have known since the lost tribe abandoned us. You can help make this happen, Savashbahar. The question is do you want to help with breath still in you, or without?"

In the front of the recess, a fishing line came into view. It dangled further and further down. A hook hung from the end of it. It came to rest in front of Savashbahar.

"Have I your word, Enverpasha?" she called up.

"Without my quarry, you are merely a woman," he called down. "You and your foreign friends will not come to harm."

There was nothing to be gained from protest. Enverpasha had won. She pulled off the chain holding the signet rings of the four tribes she had been pledged and placed it on the hook.

The line ascended out of her view, lost forever. Moments later cheers resounded from the warriors above. Enverpasha called down.

"You have chosen well and wisely, woman. Once you find a way out of your predicament, I invite you to dine at my table. I will be seated in the halls of the Temple of Houses, in the heart of the Enduring City, our beloved Nasreddin."

Another round of cheers resounded, loud and raucous. Those cheers slowly faded out of earshot as the warriors left. They took with them the support of all the tribes, even Savashbahar's native Maltep, and with it her hope of avenging her son. Her knees gave out and she sank into the mud of the alcove.

SOON ENOUGH THE DOOR boomed a final time and fell like a domino. Brigitte stepped over the door, a smile on her face that was hard to see for the dim light.

The mage cast a spell and fire blossomed in her palm. Under its light, she saw the dark shape of the warrior girl lying prone next to the broken column.

"Was it worth it?" Brigitte asked, throwing the fireball at Mel.

The fire careened in the air, illuminated the space around it as it passed. A moment before it hit the body, Brigitte noticed hay protruded out of the openings of the cat suit instead of a head, arms and legs.

The next moment Brigitte gasped as her insides spiked with fire. She looked down to see the warrior girl's sword protruding through her chest, glinting red with her blood. Brigitte craned her neck to see the warrior girl standing behind her, a fierce gleam in her eyes.

Bruised and battered, the warrior girl gave Brigitte a beleaguered victory smile. "You can't beat me. You're a destruction mage and I'm a bitch in a steel bikini."

Brigitte's eyes flickered down to see it was true. It was the last thing she saw.

EPILOGUE

Druze stood over the body of his dead lieutenant in the weighty dim of the Underthral, searching for an indication of how she fell. It stacked on top of the laundry list of questions he had with no one to answer them. Did his daughter kill Brigitte in her escape? How did Rew get out from under the witchlock? Was it Kerr's doing?

Netherfire erupted in his hands, illuminating his face and this portion of the dungeon commons in cobalt blue and dancing shadows. He scanned the area carefully, eyes panning through shards of glass, blood, scattered hay. Near the upturned cart, a dead lizard lay, a couple of its diminutive limbs bent back awkwardly.

He paused at the lizard. A sheen coated the animal, a surreal, barely-there shimmer. Even under the wan light and the blue tint of netherfire, Druze had seen that effect too many times in his five hundred years to not instantly recognize it.

"Show your form or I hurl the netherfire," Druze spoke calm and even to the dead lizard.

After a long moment, the shimmer bubbled away, leaving a scar-faced blue robe. The man's left leg and arm were clearly broken, bent in awkward unusable angles. He lay propped up on his right side, looking back at Druze with a rather calm demeanor despite what must have been a pained state of existence.

"Vereyn," Druze spoke the man's last name. "Brigitte reported you dead."

"Imagine," Delv Vereyn began, "if she was in a condition to see the irony, well, it would no longer be ironic."

"Explain this broken state in which I find you."

Druze walked over and listened as the man recalled Brigitte mangling him in their duel and his escape through the glamor of blue magic mind trickery. He had subsequently managed to crawl to a forlorn corner of the commons, assumed his lizard guise and began casting whisper magic at the convict populace. First, he whispered the lizard was bait, best left unmolested, to bring a bigger, fresher animal. Then the lizard became a good luck charm, even luckier if you gave an offering of food and water.

Druze assessed the prone mage with a raised eyebrow. "So you've been down here this whole time, almost three weeks since that duel, surviving off a fraction of these prisoners' meager rations?"

"Well, I was in the process of turning them into a convict lizard cult," Delv said, "at which point I would have revealed my true godly self to a competent worshipper, if such a thing exists among imbeciles, and demand they fix and set my broken bones. Once I had a working body, true escape from the Underthral would've been rather perfunctory I suspect. And it was proceeding clockwork until this," he finished by nodding his head at Brigitte's body.

Druze looked back at his fallen lieutenant. "You witnessed this. Use your glamor, Verayn. Show me what happened."

A shimmer bubbled up and a picture formed before Druze. He saw the warrior girl run Brigitte through while she was busy burning a decoy. Moments after Brigitte fell, the warrior girl collapsed beside her.

The scene stayed still for several minutes until the sounds of rushed footsteps echoed in the darkness.

"Mel! Mel!" cried the boy robe, a voice Druze had no trouble discerning. Rich appeared in the scene a moment later, Rew at his side. They both rushed to Mel.

Rich scooped Mel up, cradling her in both arms.

"I got you," he crooned. "It's ok."

Mel looked up at him weakly. "Yaaayy," she murmured, "saved you."

Rich nodded. "Yeah, you did."

"In the... least. Suitable... armor. Ever," she struggled to say with a wan smile before passing out.

The scene ended with Rew opening a portal and the three of them leaving Druze with a busted prison and a dead aide. At least he could fix one of those problems now. He looked at Delv.

"Would you like to be my chief lieutenant?"

Delv raised a skeptical eyebrow. "Strange. Your tower locked me away in the lowest part of its dungeon, and admittedly not without reason. Now you want me to help you helm it. Why?"

"Easy answer, Vereyn," Druze told him. "The best servants don't die."

ALSO BY JAMES BEAMON

MELVIN MORROW HAS BECOME A WARRIOR MAIDEN.

He's a teenage boy not used to being ogled or the real world consequences of wearing a steel bikini. But the real world has shifted... him, his friends Jason and Rich, and his big brother Mike are stuck in a place where danger doesn't lurk because it prefers to boldly stride out in the open.

Mages import game players like Melvin via the Rift Pendulum. The reason: the work's suicidal and pendulum heroes are insanely powerful. Usually. Melvin and his friends can be, too, if they're in the right emotional state to trigger into character. Melvin's a one-man, uh, one warrior maiden army when he's angry but anger's hard to find with all that mortal danger striding around everywhere.

The road back home is at the end of a suicidal quest. Melvin better find something to rage about... because being genre-savvy only gets you so far.

$10.49
ISBN 978-1-7323862-0-4
51049>
9 781732 386204

PENDULUM HEROES JAMES BEAMON

back cover of Pendulum Heroes print edition, artwork by Micaela Dawn

Don't miss out!

Visit the website below and you can sign up to receive emails whenever James Beamon publishes a new book. There's no charge and no obligation.

https://books2read.com/r/B-A-CEHG-PYVY

BOOKS 2 READ

Connecting independent readers to independent writers.

About the Author

James Beamon is a science fiction and fantasy author whose short stories have appeared in places such as Fantasy & Science Fiction Magazine, Apex, Lightspeed and Orson Scott Card's Intergalactic Medicine Show. He spent twelve years in the Air Force, deployed to Iraq and Afghanistan, and is in possession of the perfect buffalo wings recipe that he learned from carnies. He currently lives in Virginia with his wife, son and attack cat. He's serious about the attack cat... do not point at it.

Read more at fictigristle.wordpress.com.

www.ingramcontent.com/pod-product-compliance
Lightning Source LLC
Chambersburg PA
CBHW020411260626
47156CB00007B/2334